He could still t
his lips.

he temptation to take her back into his arms was
amn near overwhelming.

Cody looked down into her dazed, upturned face.
His breathing had yet to return to normal. "If
ou're waiting for me to say I'm sorry, you've got
long wait ahead of you," he warned.

atherine moved her head from side to side—
owly so as not to fall over. "I don't want you to
y you're sorry," she whispered.

Good," he finally declared. He pulled his Stetson
wn farther until the brim all but obscured his
ebrows and hid his eyes. "'Cause I don't know
ny the hell I just did that, but I know I'm not
rry that I did," he emphasized.

d then, just like that, Cody turned on his heel
d went back to his vehicle.

Dear Reader,

Welcome back to Thunder Canyon, Montana, and the fine citizens of that town who make life there so very interesting. Last time, I got to write about Calista Clifton, one of eight brothers and sisters (perhaps you see a pattern here?). This time around, my book centers on Catherine Clifton's story. Catherine is the oldest girl and has always been the caretaker in the family (my lord, can I relate to *that*), sublimating her own needs and dreams in order to care for everyone else. Well, now just this one time, it's her turn to get something. Jasper Fowler's neglected antiques store had closed its doors and was up for grabs. Summoning her courage, Catherine took the plunge, buying it with the intention of turning it into not just a place where forgotten antiques were kept to gather dust, but a shop where vintage clothing and intriguing one-of-a-kind items were sold. Catherine was looking for customers. She certainly wasn't looking for a man to win her heart, but she got both in Cody Overton, a genuine cowboy who was still grieving for his late wife eight years after he'd lost her.

This is a story about two lonely, independent and self-sufficient people who found each other and accidentally wound up filling the void in the other's life. I hope you like it.

As always, I thank you for reading my book, and from the bottom of my heart I wish you someone to love who loves you back.

Marie Ferrarella

REAL VINTAGE MAVERICK

BY

MARIE FERRARELLA

First published in Great Britain 2012
by Mills & Boon, an imprint of Harlequin (UK) Limited,
Eton House, 18-24 Paradise Road, Richmond, Surrey TW9 1SR

Special thanks and acknowledgement to Marie Ferrarella for her contribution to the MONTANA MAVERICKS: BACK IN THE SADDLE series.

ISBN: 978 0 263 89480 6
ebook ISBN: 978 1 408 97156 7

23-1112

Harlequin (UK) policy is to use papers that are natural, renewable and recyclable products and made from wood grown in sustainable forests. The logging and manufacturing processes conform to the legal environmental regulations of the country of origin.

Printed and bound in Spain
by Blackprint CPI, Barcelona

Marie Ferrarella, this *USA TODAY* bestselling and RITA® Award-winning author has written more than two hundred books for Mills & Boon, some under the name Marie Nicole. Her romances are beloved by fans worldwide. Visit her website, www.marieferrarella.com.

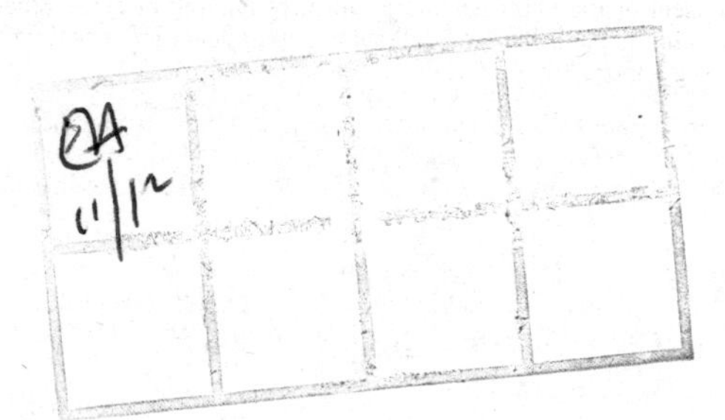

To
Stella Bagwell,
who is strong enough
to actually live the life
I can only write about

Prologue

The sound of her laughter filled his head as well as his heart, echoing all through him. Generating within him, as it always did, a feeling of tremendous joy and well-being.

It was one of those absolutely perfect Montana mornings that begged to be pressed between the pages of his memory. Cody Overton tried to absorb it as much as possible, instinctively knowing that it was important he do so.

Very important.

He and Renee were at the state fair—Renee always loved the state fair—and, as always, the love of his life had coaxed him onto one of the gaily-painted horses on the weathered carousel while she had mounted the one right next to it.

"Tame stuff," Cody had pretended to grumble before they got on—as if he ever could have denied Renee anything. "At least let's ride the Ferris wheel instead."

But Renee paid no attention to his protest. His wife absolutely *loved* riding the carousel; she always had, even when they'd been in elementary school together. He'd teased her that he was surprised she hadn't insisted on their taking their wedding vows sitting astride two of the horses on the carousel.

Renee had laughed and said that they would have had to wait for the state fair to come through and she hadn't wanted to delay becoming Mrs. Cody Overton a moment longer than she had to.

She had always had a sense of urgency about living life to the fullest. It never made any sense to him.

Until, sadly, it did.

"Maybe, if we close our eyes and wish real hard, the carousel'll go faster. C'mon, Cody, give it a try. Close your eyes and wish," she'd entreated, wrapping her hands around the horse's pole before her. She was like a ray of sunshine. "Don't you believe in wishes?"

Not anymore.

The words seemed to silently resonant in his head even as the carousel began to speed up, spinning faster and faster. Just as she'd wished it would.

And as the speed increased, so did the sound of her laughter, until that was all there was, just her laughter overpowering everything else.

And all the while, they were spinning ever faster and faster.

Cody kept trying to see her, to fix his eyes only on his beautiful Renee, but suddenly, he couldn't find her, couldn't see her.

Couldn't see anything at all except a sea of smeared color bleeding into itself.

She was gone.

Twenty-five years old and she was gone.

His soul realized it before his mind did.

He began calling out her name, but nothing came out of his mouth except for an anguished, guttural cry.

With a start, Cody bolted upright in his bed. As always, when this dream came to him, he was covered in sweat and shaking.

The crisp September weather had slipped into the bedroom, thanks to a window he'd forgotten to close, but he was still sweating.

Still shaking.

Still praying it really wasn't just a dream. That Renee was still alive and with him.

Nurturing a hope that was completely foreign to his very practical, pessimistic outlook, Cody slowly looked to his left, to the spot beside him that had once belonged to Renee.

Aching so badly to see her that it physically hurt. But he didn't see her. She wasn't there, as he knew she wouldn't be.

She hadn't been there for eight years.

Hadn't been *anywhere* for eight years because she'd been dead for eight years. Another statistic to the ravages of the insatiable cancer monster.

His heart had been dead just as long.

At times, Cody was surprised that it was still beating, still keeping the shell that surrounded it alive and moving.

A man with nothing to live for shouldn't be required to live, Cody thought darkly.

He tossed off the covers and got out of bed despite the darkness that still enveloped the room. He knew it was useless to try to go back to sleep. Sleep was gone for the remainder of the night. If he was lucky, a glimmer of it might return by that evening.

Most likely not.

Slipping on the discarded jeans he picked up from the floor, Cody padded across the bare floor to the window and looked out.

There was nothing to see, just a vastness that spread out before him.

His ranch.

Their ranch.

"Why did you leave me?" he demanded in angry frustration, not for the first time. "Why did you have to go?"

He wasn't being reasonable, but he didn't much feel like being reasonable. It wasn't fair that he had been left behind, to face each day without Renee after she had filled so much of his life before then. He couldn't remember a time when he hadn't known her, hadn't been aware of her. The very first memory he had was of her.

Eight years and he still wasn't used to it. Hadn't made his peace with it. Eight years and a part of him still expected to see her walk through the door, or see her standing over the stove, lamenting that she'd burned dinner—again.

He'd never minded those burnt offerings—that was what he'd teasingly called them, her burnt offerings—and he would have been willing to eat nothing else for the rest of his life if only he could see her one more time. Hold her one more time…

He supposed, in a way, that was what the dreams were about. Seeing her one more time. Because they were so very vivid that, just for a moment, Renee was alive again. Alive and the cornerstone of his world.

He wished he could sleep forever, but that wasn't going to happen.

Cody dragged his hand through his hair and sighed. He might as well get dressed and get started with his day, even if it was still the middle of the night. The ranch wasn't going to run itself.

"I miss you, Renee."

His whisper echoed about the empty bedroom just as it did about his empty soul.

Chapter One

It happened too quickly for him to even think about it.

One minute, in a moment of exasperated desperation—because he hadn't yet bought a gift for Caroline's birthday—Cody found himself walking into the refurbished antique store that had, up until a few months ago, been called The Tattered Saddle.

The next minute, he was hurrying across the room and managed—just in time—to catch the young woman who was tumbling off a ladder.

Before he knew it, his arms were filled with the soft curves of the same young woman.

She smelled of lavender and vanilla, nudging forth a sliver of a memory he couldn't quite catch hold of.

That was the way Cody remembered it when he later looked back on the way his life had taken a dramatic turn toward the better that fateful morning.

When he'd initially walked by the store's show window, Cody had automatically looked in. The shop appeared to be in a state of semi-chaos, but it still looked a great deal more promising than when that crazy old coot Jasper Fowler ran it.

Cody vaguely recalled hearing that the man hadn't really been interested in making any sort of a go of the shop. The whole place had actually just been a front for a money-laundering enterprise. At any rate, the antique shop had been shut down and boarded up in January, relegated to collecting even more dust than it had displayed when its doors had been open to the public.

What had caught his eye was the notice Under new ownership in the window and the store's name—The Tattered Saddle—had been crossed out. But at the moment, there was no new name to take its place. He had wondered if that was an oversight or a ploy to draw curious customers into the shop.

Well, if it was under new ownership, maybe that meant that there was new old merchandise to choose from. And that, in turn, might enable him to find something for his sister here. As he recalled, Caroline was into old things. Things that other people thought of as junk and wanted to discard, his sister saw potential and promise in.

At least it was worth a shot, Cody told himself. He had tried the doorknob and found that it gave under his hand. Turning it, he had walked in.

Glancing around, his eyes were instantly drawn to the tall, willowy figure on the other side of the room. She was wearing a long, denim-colored skirt and her shirt was more or less the same color. The young woman was precariously perched on the top step of a ladder that appeared to be none too steady.

What actually caught his attention was not that she looked like an accident waiting to happen as she stretched her taut frame out, trying to reach something that was on a higher shelf, but that with her long, straight brown hair hanging loose about her back and shoulders, for just an instant, she reminded him of Renee.

A feeling of déjà vu seized him and for a moment, his breath caught in his throat.

Balancing herself on tiptoes, Catherine Clifton, the former Tattered Saddle's determined new owner, automatically turned around when she heard the little bell over the front door ring. She hadn't anticipated any customers coming in until the store's grand reopening. That wasn't for a couple more days at the very least. Most likely a couple of weeks. And only if she could come up with a new name for the place.

"We're not open for business yet," Catherine called out.

The next thing out of her mouth was an involuntary shriek because she'd lost her footing on the ladder and both she and the ladder were heading for a collision with the wooden floor.

The ladder landed with a clatter.

Catherine, fortunately, did not.

She was saved from what could have been a very bruising fate by the very person she'd just politely banished from the premises.

Landing in the cowboy's strong, capable arms knocked the air out of her and, along with it, anything else she might have said at that moment.

Which was just as well because she would have hated coming across like some blithering idiot. But right now, not a single coherent thought completed itself in her head. It was filled with just scattered words and a myriad of sensations.

Hot sensations.

Everything had faded into the background and Catherine was instantly and acutely aware of the man whose arms she'd landed in. The broad-shouldered, green-eyed, sandy-haired cowboy held her as if she weighed no more than a small child. The muscles on his bare arms didn't even appear to be straining.

A tingling sensation danced through Catherine's entire body, which was stubbornly heating up despite all of her attempts to bank the sensation—and her reaction to the man—down.

Her valiant efforts to the contrary, for just a moment, it felt as if time had stood still, freezing this moment as it simultaneously bathed her in a heretofore never experienced, all but debilitating, feeling of desire. For two cents proper, using the excuse that this rugged-looking cowboy had saved her, she would have kissed him. With feeling.

Catherine could absolutely visualize herself kissing him.

The fact that he was a complete stranger was neither here nor there as far as she was concerned. Desire, she discovered at that moment, didn't have to make sense. It could thrive very well without even so much as a lick of sense to it.

And for no particular reason at all, it occurred to her that this man looked like the real deal. A cowboy. A real vintage cowboy.

Was he? Or had she managed to bump her head without knowing it and was just hallucinating?

Their eyes met and held for a timeless instance. Only the pounding of Catherine's heart finally managed to sufficiently rouse her.

"Thank you," she finally whispered.

Doing his best to focus and gather his exceedingly scattered wits about him, Cody heard himself asking, "For what?"

Catherine let out a long, shaky breath before answering. "For catching me."

"Oh." Of course that was what she meant. What did he think she meant? Cody nodded his head. "Yeah. Right."

The words emerged one at a time, each containing a sealed thought. Thoughts he couldn't begin to convey, or even understand.

Cody cleared his throat, then realized that he was still holding the woman in his arms. He should have already released her.

Feeling awkward—he hadn't spontaneously reacted to a woman in this manner since his wife had died—he set her down. "Sorry about that."

"Don't be," she told him. "I'm not." *I'm not sorry at all.* "If you hadn't caught me just then, I might have broken something—either some of the merchandise or, worse, one of my bones."

The fact that if he hadn't come in just now, her attention wouldn't have been thrown off and she very well could have remained perched on the ladder was a point Catherine had no desire to bring up. Thinking of him as her hero was far more pleasant.

Rather than comment, the tall cowboy merely nodded his head in acknowledgment. At the same time, he began to back away.

"Didn't mean to trespass," he murmured by way of an apology. He reached behind him for the doorknob, ready to make his getaway.

"You're not trespassing," Catherine was quick to protest. She didn't have the heart to chase out someone who could actually *buy* something in the store. "It's just that I haven't exactly gotten the store ready for customers yet. But you can stay if you like."

If he didn't know better, he would have sworn that her tone was almost urging him to stay. And she had shifted her body so that she was now standing between him and the front door.

Cody glanced around the store, still mulling over her initial protest. "Looks okay to me," he told her. "Actually, it looks a mite better than it used to look when that old guy owned it."

Catherine was eager to bring out the shop's better features and play them up so that she could attract actual customers rather than just the pitying or dismissive glances that the store had been garnering before she'd bought it. After the former owner had kidnapped Rose Traub, the people in Thunder Canyon had deliberately shunned the store. And from what she'd heard, before then the clientele was almost as ancient as some of the antiques that were housed here. She wanted to change that as well. She wanted all age-groups to have a reason to drop by and browse.

Fowler wasn't in the picture anymore, having been sent to prison, and the shop was something that she wanted to take on as a project, something that belonged to her exclusively. After a lifetime of being the go-to person, the main caregiver in a family of eight and always putting everyone else's needs ahead her own, it occurred to Catherine that time—and life—was slipping by her. She needed to make her own way before she woke up one morning to discover that she was no longer young, no longer able to grab her slice of the pie that life had to offer.

Since this sexy-looking cowboy seemed familiar with the way the store had been before she'd taken over, Catherine made a natural assumption and asked, "Did you come in here often when Mr. Fowler owned it?"

"No," he told her honestly. Antiques had never held any interest for him. And they still didn't, except that he knew his sister liked them. "But I walked by the store whenever I was in town and I'd look in."

Mild curiosity was responsible for that. He might not look it, but Cody had made a point of always taking in all of his surroundings. It kept him from being caught off guard—the way he had when Renee had become ill.

"Oh," Catherine murmured. All right, the place had held no real attraction for him, at least it hadn't before. But he'd walked in this morning. Something had obviously changed. "Well, what made you come in today?"

She glanced over her shoulder to see if there was anything unusual out on display that might have caught the cowboy's eye. But nothing stood out for her.

Cody wasn't sure what this gregarious woman was fishing for, but he could only tell her the truth. "I'm looking for a present for my sister. Her birthday's coming up and I need to get something into the mail soon if it's going to get there in time."

Okay, she wasn't making herself clear, Catherine thought. Desperate to hone in on a reliable "X-Factor," she tried again.

"Why here?" she pressed. "Why didn't you just go

to the mall? There're lots of stores there." And heaven knew a far more eclectic collection of things for someone to choose from.

The expression that fleetingly passed over the cowboy's tanned face told her exactly what he thought of malls.

But when he finally spoke, he employed a measured, thoughtful cadence. "I haven't put much thought into it," he readily admitted. "I guess I came here because I wanted to give Caroline something that's genuine, that isn't mass-produced. Something that isn't in every store from New York City to Los Angeles," Cody explained.

He looked around the shop again, but not before discovering that it took a bit of effort to tear his eyes away from the shop's new owner. Close up, the talkative young woman didn't really look like Renee, but there was an essence, a spark, an unnamable *something* about her that did remind him of his late wife. So much so that even as he told himself that he really should be leaving, he found himself continuing to linger on the premises.

"The stuff in this store is…" His voice trailed off for a moment as he searched for the right word. It took a little doing. For the most part, Cody Overton was a man given to doing, not talking.

Catherine cocked her head, waiting for him to finish his sentence. When he didn't, she supplied a word for him. "Old?"

"Real," he finally said, feeling the word more aptly described what he was looking for. "And yeah, old," he agreed after a beat. "But there's nothing wrong with old as long as it's not falling apart," he was quick to clarify.

Catherine smiled. She liked his philosophy. In a way, it embodied her own.

And then, just like that, an idea came to her.

Her eyes brightened as she looked up at the cowboy that fate had sent her way. This could be one of those happy accidents people were always talking about, she thought.

But first, she needed to backtrack a little. "I'm sorry, I completely forgot my manners. My name's Catherine Clifton," she told him, putting her hand out. "I'm the new owner," she added needlessly.

Cody looked down at her hand for a moment, as if he was rather uncertain whether to take it or not. He wasn't a man who went out of his way to meet people. Even an extremely attractive woman. He kept to himself for the most part.

But again, there was something about this woman that pulled at him. That nudged him. After a beat, he slipped his hand over hers.

"Cody Overton." He felt it only right to tell her his name since she had given him hers.

He watched in mute fascination as the smile began in her eyes, then feathered down to her lips. "Pleased to meet you, Cody Overton," she said. "You're my very first customer."

"Haven't bought anything yet," he felt obligated to point out.

The man was obviously a stickler for the truth, she couldn't help thinking. She liked that. Moreover, she could really use someone like that, someone who would tell her the truth no matter what.

She paused a moment, wondering how the man would react to what she was about to propose.

Nothing ventured, nothing gained, right?

Catherine felt good about this. The sparkle in her deep, chocolate-colored eyes grew as she dove in. "Cody, how old are you?" she wanted to know.

The question caught him completely off guard. The last time he recalled being asked his age like that, he'd been a teenager, picking up a six-pack of beer for his buddy and himself. At the time, he'd figured that his deep voice and his height would make questioning unnecessary. He'd assumed wrong.

He fixed the young woman with a look, wondering what she was up to. "If you're planning on asking customers their age, once word about that gets out, I don't think you're going to have too many of the ladies coming in." And everyone knew that it was women, not men, who liked this old furniture and knickknacks.

"I don't care how old *they* are," Catherine protested. "I mean, I do, but I don't—" She stopped abruptly, realizing that she was getting tongue-tied again. Taking a breath, she backtracked. "I'm trying to appeal to a certain dynamic—a certain age-group," she corrected herself, not wanting this rugged cowboy to think she was trying to talk over his head. But what she'd just said didn't sound quite right, either. "Let me start over," she requested. Taking a deep breath, she paused for a second before plunging in again. "What I want to do is attract a certain age-group—younger than the people who used to come into the store—so I thought if I could maybe pick your brain once in a while, find out what you think of some of the merchandise, it might help me improve sales once I open."

If possible, the woman was making even less sense to him than before.

Hell, if she was trying to find out what would attract guys like him, all she had to do was look in the mirror, Cody couldn't help thinking. Because, confusing though she seemed to be every time she opened her mouth, this new shop owner was a damn sight easy on the eyes. If she stood in the doorway— or near her show window—that would definitely be enough to bring men in on the pretext of shopping.

But, curious to see if there was something more to what she was suggesting, Cody asked, "Why would you want to pick my brain?" His taste was plain and, if it were up to him, he wouldn't have set foot in here in the first place.

In answering his question, Catherine didn't go with the obvious: that there was something compellingly fascinating about this vintage cowboy who had strolled into her shop just in time to keep her from breaking something vital. Instead, she gave him something they could both live with.

"Because what you like is what would appeal to other people in your age bracket."

He'd never thought of himself as being like everyone else. Not that he saw himself as unique, just...different. The gadgets out there that held such fascination for men—if he was to believe the occasional commercial he saw—held no interest for him. He was a man of the earth, a plain, simple man who'd never felt the need to be part of the crowd or to join anything at all for that matter.

With a shrug, he finally got around to answering the initial question she'd put to him. "I'm thirty-five."

That was about where she would have put him, Catherine thought, feeling triumphant.

"Perfect," she declared out loud, stopping short of clapping her hands together. "You're exactly what I'm looking for. Business-wise," she quickly qualified in case he got the wrong impression. She didn't want him thinking she was staking him out for some reason. The last thing she wanted was to chase this cowboy away.

Cody looked at the exuberant woman for a long moment. He sincerely doubted that he was the type that *any* woman was looking for, at least not anymore. There was a time when he would have been. A time when he'd been eager to plunge into life, to be the best husband, the best father he could possibly be. A time when he greeted each day with hope, thinking of all that lay ahead of him and Renee.

But all that had changed once Renee had died. Whatever he'd had to offer in terms of a normal relationship had died and had been buried along with his wife.

He was tempted to tell her she was wrong in selecting him, but he could see that there was just no putting this woman off. She had a fire lit under her, and if he wasn't careful, that fire could burn them both.

Still, he supposed he had nothing to lose by going along with her in this. She'd undoubtedly find his answers boring, but until she did, he could view this as a distraction. God knew he was always looking for something to distract him. Something to block his dark thoughts so that he didn't have to dwell on just how empty his existence had become and continued to be.

Eight years and nothing had changed. He was still just going through the motions of living, placing one foot in front of the other.

"I don't know about perfect," he finally said to Catherine with a self-deprecating laugh that sounded as if it had come rumbling straight out of his chest, bypassing his throat, “but if I can help—” he shrugged “—sure.”

If possible, her eyes brightened even more. It made him think of the way a satisfying, steaming cup of hot coffee tasted on a cold winter’s day.

“Really?” Catherine pressed, this time actually clapping her hands together as if he was some magical genie who had just bestowed the gift of three wishes on her.

Cody shrugged again in response to her question. “Why not?” he said even as a part of him whispered a warning that he had just taken his first step on a very narrow ledge. A step that could result in his tumbling down into an uncharted abyss at a moment’s notice.

All things considered, he supposed that there could be worse things.

Chapter Two

"So exactly how is this going to work?" Cody asked her after a beat. As a rule, he wasn't a curious man, but in this case, he had to admit that this woman had managed to arouse what little curiosity he did possess. "Are you going to be showing me pictures of the stuff you're thinking of selling at the store, or what?" Before she could answer the question, Cody felt it only fair to inform her of something. "Think you should know right from the start that I'm really not too keen on broken-down old furniture."

As far as he was concerned, furniture didn't have to be fancy, but it had to be functional—and not look as if it belonged in some garbage heap.

Catherine laughed. "That's good, because neither am I."

She was still feeling her way around as to the kind of focus she wanted to bring to the shop. Right now, she was pretty much making it up as she went along.

Catherine wondered if admitting that to this down-to-earth cowboy would be a mistake. Would it make him think less of her? Or would he just dismiss her present indecision as a "woman thing"? An inconsequential whim on her part? She realized that it would bother her if he did.

His expression registered mild surprise. Cody looked around at the showroom. Everything here was way older than he was. If it wasn't for the fact that Caroline had a weakness for this kind of thing, he would have just called it all "junk" and dismissed the whole place out of hand.

If this woman was really being on the level with him and felt the same way he did, that brought up another question. "Then what are you doing with this store?"

"Changing its image," Catherine answered without hesitation.

How was she going to do that with the things she had to work with? "To what?" he wanted to know.

"To a shop that sells vintage items, whether it's clothing, books, furnishings, whatever." It was a slight matter of semantics she supposed, but there was still a difference.

One she was apparently going to have to explain because Cody moved back his Stetson with his thumb and squinted at the merchandise in the immediate area. "Just what's the difference between something being an 'antique' and being classified as 'vintage'?"

That was easy enough, Catherine thought.

"Price mostly," she answered with a grin that he had to admit—if only to himself—he found rather engaging.

Cody rolled her words over in his head, then nodded. He was willing to accept that. But there was something else.

"Still haven't answered my first question," he pointed out. When she raised an eyebrow, silently asking to be reminded, he said, "What do you want with me?"

I could think of ten things right off the bat, Catherine thought in reply. But out loud she simply said, "I intend to use you for market research."

Cody laughed shortly. "Only market I know is the one I go to buy my supply of eggs, milk and bread."

That was *not* the kind of market she meant. "Think bigger," Catherine coaxed.

"Okay," he said gamely. "How about if I throw in a chicken, too?"

Obviously this wasn't going to be as simple as she'd hoped. "I'm talking about the general buying market out there," she explained. "You're just the age bracket I'm trying to attract."

Cody's eyes met hers. "You ask me, you keep on smiling like that and you'll attract more than your share of men my age—and older."

The remark pleased her, amused her and embarrassed her all at the same time. Not only that, but she could feel her cheeks growing hot. From the way he looked at her, she knew it wasn't just an internal thing or her imagination. Her cheeks were turning pink. She had an uneasy feeling that her new "researcher" could see the color creeping up into them.

Great, now he probably thought of her as some naive, innocent little girl playing at being a store owner.

"I'm not looking for attention," she told him with feeling. "What I'm looking for are paying customers who are interested in buying what they see."

The way he looked at her told Catherine that she was only making matters worse by talking. But she wanted him to take her seriously, to understand that all she was after at the moment was a business arrangement and a little input from him.

She cleared her throat. "There has to be something that you want—to buy," she tacked on when she realized that she was still sinking into the grave she had verbally dug for herself. She tried one more time, taking it from the top. "When you walked in here, what were you hoping to find?"

"Like I said, I was looking for something for my sister." As usual, he had put getting something for her off, telling himself he had plenty of time until he suddenly didn't.

"Such as?" she coaxed, trying to get him to give her something to work with.

The broad shoulders rose and fell again as Cody shrugged carelessly. "I figured I'd know it when I saw it."

She could accept that. Shoppers didn't always have a clear picture of what they were looking for. "Then look around," Catherine urged, gesturing around the store. "See if anything appeals to you."

She'd been the former Tattered Saddle's legal owner—using her life savings as a down payment—for almost a month now. During that entire time, she'd spent her days clearing away cobwebs, cleaning up and trying to put what she had gotten—the items in the store were included in the price whether she liked them or not—in some sort of manageable order.

To be honest, there was a lot here that she was tempted just to toss out, but she decided that she should seriously consider calling in an expert to appraise everything before she began throwing things out wholesale. However, experts cost money. Someone like Cody Overton did not and it was to the Cody Overtons that she intended to sell.

See if anything appeals to you.

Cody looked at her for a long moment as her words echoed in his head. And then the corners of his mouth curved—just a little. Had this been years ago, he thought, he would have been tempted to say that what appealed to him was her.

But that was a remark for a young man to make, not a man whose soul felt ancient—as ancient as some of the things in this little shop of hers, if not more so.

"Okay," he finally said, moving toward a newly cleaned shelf that displayed a few miscellaneous, mismatched items.

At the very end of the shelf was a small, cream-colored, fringed coin purse. Looking closer, Cody could see that it had been carefully cleaned up so that there wasn't even a speck of dirt or telltale grime on it. In addition, it had been lovingly polished with some sort of leather cleaner. He could tell by the trace of scent on it.

The coin purse felt soft to the touch.

Caroline had always liked things with fringes on them, he recalled. She'd had a vest with fringes on it that their mother had given her when she was a little girl. The vest was a little large for her, but Caroline didn't care. She wore it with everything until it completely fell apart.

There was no price tag visible on the purse, or on any of the other items on the shelf for that matter. Catherine must have just gotten started arranging the things, he reasoned.

Turning around, he held up the coin purse for Catherine to see. "How much you want for this?"

Catherine smiled, secretly relieved that he hadn't chosen one of the more expensive items. "Consider it a gift."

That was exactly what he considered it to be. A gift. The gift he was going to give his sister. "That's what I plan to do with it," he confirmed. Then he repeated, "How much is it?"

Rather than continue standing some distance away, Catherine crossed over to him. Maybe he'd understand her better if she was closer, she thought.

"No, I mean consider it my gift to you in exchange for your services. I can't really afford to pay you yet, but you can have whatever you want in the shop in trade for your help."

Cody was surprised. He hadn't assumed that this woman was going to pay him anything at all. After all, if he understood what she had proposed earlier, this enthusiastic woman was just going to be asking his opinion about things. Didn't seem right asking for money for giving his opinion.

It wasn't as if he was anybody special.

He felt a little guilty about accepting the purse, but then he had a hunch that she was determined to give him something for his services.

"Thanks. This'll do just fine," he told her. "My sister'll like it."

Pleased to have gotten that out of the way—she hated feeling indebted for anything—Catherine put her hand out for the purse. When he looked at her quizzically, she explained, "I'll wrap it up for you."

He was about to tell her there was no need, but then he decided against it. It seemed to make this woman happy to go through the motions of playing shopkeeper and, besides, he was really bad when it came to wrapping gifts.

So he surrendered the purse to her and watched as Catherine placed his sister's gift into a box that just barely accommodated the purse. The fringes spilled out over the side. She carefully folded them into the box until they all but covered up the purse.

"This'll make a nice gift," she told him. Catherine glanced up at him, thinking he might like to hear the story that went with the purse. "It's actually over forty years old. The original owner had it with her when she went to Woodstock."

Reaching beneath the counter, she pulled out a roll of wrapping paper she'd just placed there last night. With what appeared to be a trained eye, she cut exactly the right length of paper for the box.

Completely switching topics, she asked Cody, "Younger or older?"

That had come utterly out of the blue, catching him by surprise. He had no idea what she as asking him. "Excuse me?"

She glanced up at him just for a moment as she clarified her question. "Is your sister younger or older than you?"

"Oh." Why did she want to know that? It had nothing to do with wrapping the gift. "Younger."

Catherine nodded as she took in the information.

The questions didn't stop there. Why didn't that surprise him? "Are you two close?"

"I guess." But that wasn't exactly the real truth, so Cody amended his statement. "We were, once. But then she got married and her husband made her move away—to another state." Caroline's husband had done it to control his sister, Cody was sure of it. The man wanted to isolate and control her so that he could be the center of Caroline's world.

Catherine immediately picked up on his tone. It spoke volumes even if the actual man didn't. "You don't like him much, do you?"

Cody shrugged off the observation, then was surprised to hear himself saying, "Not much to like." He stopped abruptly and looked at this woman who seemed to coax things out of him so effortlessly. "What's with all these questions?" He wanted to know. "This part of your marketing thing?"

Catherine smiled as she put the finishing touches on the box by tying a big red bow on it. "This is part of my getting to know you 'thing,'" she corrected. Then, so he didn't feel as if she was dragging information out of him without giving some up herself, Catherine said, "There's eight of us in my family. I guess I'm just curious about how other people get along with their siblings." She raised her eyes to his, a look of apology in them. "Sorry if I sounded as if I was prying."

Because he couldn't think of anything else to do, Cody shrugged to show her that he hadn't taken any offense at the questions. "Guess there's no harm in asking questions," he allowed. And then he rolled over in his head what she'd told him. "Eight of you, huh?"

"Eight of us," she confirmed.

"They all like you?" If they were, it must have been one hell of a noisy household.

She wasn't exactly sure what Cody was asking her. "You mean are they all girls? No, I've got brothers *and* sisters."

But he shook his head. "No, I meant are they all *like* you," Cody repeated, then, because she was still looking at him quizzically, he clarified, "You know, all enthusiastic and excited, coming on like a house afire."

She'd never thought of herself as particularly enthusiastic, or excitable for that matter. Certainly not in the terms that he'd just mentioned. Shaking her head, she told him, "I'm actually the shy, retiring one in the family."

He laughed at that. It was a deep, all-encompassing sound that made Catherine smile rather than cause her to get her back up.

"Sure you are," he said, adding, "good one" under his breath as he commented on her sense of humor. After a moment, the smile on his lips faded just a little as he looked at her more closely. "Oh, you're serious." Cody took a minute to reassess his opinion. "You all must have been one hell of a handful for your parents to deal with."

"Actually, I was the one who did a lot of the 'dealing with,'" she corrected. "I'm the second-oldest in the family." He probably didn't even want to know that, she guessed.

She was talking too much, Catherine thought. She had a tendency not to know when to stop talking. That was probably one of the reasons she'd decided to buy Fowler's old store. Customers meant that there would be people for her to talk with, even if they left the shop without buying anything.

She liked the idea of meeting new people. Of getting to know things about them.

Catherine looked down at the box she'd just finished wrapping, remembering what Cody had said about the purse's final destination.

"If you're mailing this, I can see if I can find another box to put it in for you," she offered.

She was certainly going out of her way here, Cody thought, especially since he hadn't paid for the purse. On top of that, until a few minutes ago, the overenergized woman hadn't known him from Adam. That made her a pretty rare individual in his book.

"Are you always this accommodating?" he wanted to know.

She couldn't gauge by his expression whether he thought that was a good thing or a bad thing. Either way, she still felt the same about it.

"Nothing wrong with being friendly," she said, flashing a wide smile at him. "Or helpful."

"Didn't say there was," he pointed out. "Just not used to it, that's all."

Fair enough, Catherine thought. She pushed the gaily wrapped gift a little closer toward him on the counter. "So, about that bigger box, do you want it?" she wanted to know.

He was planning on mailing the gift once he left the shop. He supposed that having Catherine provide a box to ship the gift in would be exceedingly helpful in moving things along.

"Sure, I could use it," he allowed. Then he mumbled, "Thanks."

Her smile was triumphant. "You're welcome." And then she couldn't help adding, "There, that wasn't so hard now, was it?" she asked. Because she saw the furrow that had formed across his forehead that indicated to her that he was trying to understand what she was referring to, Catherine clued him in. "Saying thank you," she explained. "That wasn't so hard, right?"

Rather than answer her question, or say *anything* in response, Catherine saw that Cody was looking down at her left hand. Was he checking her out or about to say something flippant about her single status?

In either case, she decided to beat him to the punch. "No, I'm not married."

Cody nodded as if he had expected nothing else. "That explains it."

This time it was her turn to be confused. "Explains what?"

"Explains why you're showering me with all these questions," Cody told her. Then, because she apparently didn't understand what he was telling her, he elaborated, "You don't have anyone to talk to."

She felt a little sorry for the man. He obviously hadn't had the kind of upbringing and family life that she'd experienced. And, to some extent, was still experiencing.

"Oh, I've got people to talk to," she assured him. "Lots of people."

"Then what's with all the questions?" he wanted to know.

"I'm just a naturally curious person," Catherine explained.

Was Cody trying to tell her something? He didn't strike her as a man who worried about being perceived as subtle. If there *was* something that bothered him, she had a feeling he'd tell her.

Maybe not, a little voice in her head whispered. She'd better clear things up now, if that was the case.

"If that's going to be a problem…"

She let her voice trail off so that he could put his own interpretation to what she was driving at.

"No, no problem," he told her. "But it's going to take some getting used to if you're going to be 'picking my brain.'" He used her words to describe their working arrangement.

"You can always tell me to back off," Catherine pointed out.

He was mildly surprised at what she's just said. "And if I do, you'll listen?"

Her eyes seemed to sparkle as they laughed at him. Cody found himself captivated. It took him a moment to retreat from the reaction.

"We'll see" was all she could honestly tell him.

But it *was* an honest reaction and a man couldn't ask for more than that, Cody thought. Honesty was a rare commodity.

"There you go," she pronounced, placing the package wrapped up for shipping on the counter before him. "All ready to be mailed out."

Cody nodded his head in approval as he regarded the box.

"Thanks." He picked it up, then paused for a moment. "I guess I'll be seeing you."

"I certainly hope so." And then she bit her lower lip. Did that sound more enthusiastic than she meant it to? Catherine looked at his face for some sign that she'd made him wary, or worse, and her prime target was going to change his mind and back away.

"How's an hour in the morning every other day sound? Or whenever you can spare the time?" she quickly added.

"Whenever I can spare the time," he echoed, touching two fingers to the brim of his black Stetson just before he walked out of the shop.

Catherine watched him walk down the street through the bay window she'd cleaned that morning. She had a very good feeling about this alliance she'd just struck up.

She smiled, well pleased. Getting back to work, she started humming to herself.

Chapter Three

The need to replenish some supplies in his walk-in pantry brought Cody back into Thunder Canyon a scant two days later.

At least, that was the excuse he gave himself and the two hands he had working for him on his ranch.

The younger of the two ranch hands—Kurt—knowing how much his reclusive boss disliked having to go into town, offered to run the errand for him.

To the surprise of both men, Cody declined, saying something to the effect that he wasn't exactly sure just what he wanted to get. It was a comment that for the most part seemed completely out of character for Cody, a man who *always* knew exactly what he did or didn't want at any given moment.

But the ranch hands knew better than to question their boss, so they merely nodded and got back to cleaning out the horse stalls.

Driving in, Cody took the long way around, passing by the former Tattered Saddle to see how it—and its new owner—was coming along.

The first thing that he noticed was that there was a new sign leaning against the wall just to the right of the front door. From its precarious position, he figured it was obviously waiting to be mounted.

Making a spur-of-the-moment decision, Cody parked his truck close by. Then he got out and crossed to the store to get a better look at the sign as if it was the most natural thing in the world for him to do. The fact that he ordinarily didn't possess a drop of curiosity about *anything* didn't even occur to him or make him wonder at his own behavior.

So, she'd finally settled on a new name, he thought, looking at the freshly painted sign. Real Vintage Cowboy. It was all in tall capitals and printed in eye-catching silver paint.

Cody rolled the name over in his head a couple of times, then nodded to himself. If nothing else, it was a definite improvement over the store's previous name. He'd never quite understood why anyone would want a "tattered" saddle anyway.

Telling himself it was time to get a move on, Cody wound up remaining just where he was. He glanced up and looked through the bay window into the showroom rather than moving back to his truck.

Inside, Catherine was cleaning up a storm, just as she had been doing for the last two days. Although her sisters had initially offered to pitch in and help, she'd stubbornly turned them down. This was something that she was determined to manage on her own.

This way, whatever happened, success or failure, it would be hers alone.

But there were times—such as now when every bone in her body seemed to be protesting that it had been worked too hard—that she felt that perhaps she'd been a wee bit too hasty in summarily turning down her sisters' offer that way.

So when she saw Cody looking in, her heart all but leaped up in celebration. The cavalry had been sighted. Now all that was needed was to pull it in.

Wiping her hands on the back of the jeans she'd decided were more fitting to the work she was doing than the long flowing skirts that she favored, Catherine hurried to the door and quickly pulled it open.

"Hi!" she greeted him with no small measure of enthusiasm, beaming at Cody. "C'mon in," she urged with feeling.

Not waiting for him to make up his mind or to—heaven forbid—turn her invitation down, Catherine grabbed hold of his wrist with both hands and pulled him into the shop. She quickly shut the door behind him in case he was having second thoughts about their arrangement and wanted to leave.

Turning toward the shop behind her, she waved her free hand about. "It's beginning to shape up, don't you think?"

Cody looked around. To be completely honest, he was rather vague about exactly what the place had looked like two days ago, but he could see that she had painted the walls a rather soothing light blue. He assumed that she had done it because he saw a few light blue splotches of paint on her jeans.

Cody slowly nodded his approval, mainly for her benefit. His mother had taught him not to hurt people's feelings if he could possibly avoid doing it, and Catherine seemed rather eager to hear a positive reaction. That being the case, it cost him nothing to give it.

"Looks good from where I'm standing," he told her. Glancing down, he could see that she'd buffed the wooden floors as well. Had she been at this nonstop these last two days?

Well, at least the woman wasn't afraid of getting her hands dirty, he mused.

Taking a quick look around, he saw the back of the sign through the window. He brightened because at least there was something he could actually comment on. "Saw the sign outside. Is that the new name you picked out for the store?"

"You mean Real Vintage Cowboy?" she asked to make sure he wasn't referring to anything else.

When he nodded, Cody saw a strange, unfathomable smile curving her mouth. It piqued his dormant curiosity to some extent.

It piqued a little more when she told him, "Well, you're actually responsible for that."

The furrow above his nose deepened as he sought to understand what Catherine had just said. He was certain he hadn't suggested a name like that to her. He hadn't suggested any name at all that he could remember. She had to have him confused with someone else.

"Me?" Cody said incredulously, staring at her. "I don't understand. How?"

Again, he found the way the corners of her mouth curved intriguing—and completely captivating. "That was what I thought you looked like. A vintage cowboy. The more I thought about it, the more I began to think that it sounded like a good name for the store. So you inspired the name," she concluded brightly. "I guess you could say you're my muse."

"What the hell is a muse?" Cody wanted to know. He thought of himself as a plain man, given to speaking plainly. This sounded like some kind of double-talk to him.

She took no offense at his tone, although she would have thought that he'd be flattered. But then, there was no second-guessing men. Growing up with her bothers had taught her that.

"A muse is something or someone who inspires another person creatively," she told him.

He was having a hard time making the connection. He looked around the store and shook his head. It didn't make any sense to him.

"And I make you think of dusty old junk that people want to get rid of?" Cody asked her, not sure whether to be amused by this or offended.

Given his tone of voice, Catherine was instantly worried that he *was* taking offense and she didn't want him to. She'd meant it as a compliment.

"Not junk," she protested with feeling. "What I'm selling in the shop are rescued artifacts that once figured very prominently in people's lives."

To underscore her point, Catherine motioned toward the shelves directly behind her. Shelves she had so painstakingly arranged. The shelves were filled with newly cleaned merchandise, shown off to their best possible advantage. It was a potpourri of objects in all sorts of bright colors.

Currently, the sun was playing off the surface of several of the pieces, highlighting the metal and making them gleam like mysterious talismans.

"Everything you see here is vintage chic," she told him proudly.

He inclined his head, taking a closer look, then raised one shoulder in a half shrug. "If you say so," he murmured. Ever practical, he turned his attention to something that he was better equipped to understand. "Who are you getting to put your sign up?"

Catherine turned around to look through the window in the general direction he'd nodded in and said, "I hadn't thought about 'getting' someone. I figured that I'd just do it myself—"

That was what he was afraid of.

Cody looked at her up and down slowly, taking full measure of her. His expression when he finished clearly said that he had found her wanting.

He snorted rather than say anything outright. His point driven home, he then asked, "You got that ladder handy?" referring to the one she'd fallen off of at their first meeting.

Did he think she was a complete helpless idiot? she wondered. How else did he think she was going to get up to the roof to hang the sign?

"Yes, it's in the back." The words were hardly out of her mouth when she saw Cody start to walk to the back room. The man was just taking over, she thought. She liked him, liked his company, but that couldn't be allowed to happen.

"Where are you going?" she wanted to know.

"To get your ladder and hang that sign up for you," Cody threw over his shoulder as he disappeared into the back room.

She didn't want him to feel obligated to do anything except give her a little input on what he thought of certain things. That was their deal.

Hurrying after Cody, Catherine stopped short of the back room doorway because he was already coming out. He had the ladder mounted like a giant shield over one muscular shoulder while he carried a hammer he'd spotted and pressed into service in the other.

Pivoting a hundred and eighty degrees on her heel, Catherine followed him back through the showroom. Was he just displaying his machismo? Or was he feeling obligated for some reason?

"You don't have to do this," she protested with feeling as she continued to follow him.

He paused fleetingly to give her a quick, appraising look. Catherine could have sworn she felt a flash of heat pass through her.

That had to stop, she silently upbraided herself. She had no time to react to Cody in those terms. She had a business to launch.

"Yeah, I do," he answered with finality. "I'm better at hanging up a sign than I am at setting broken bones."

She was right behind him, step for step. "Contrary to what you might think, I'm not some helpless woman who's all thumbs," she informed him. "And I'm not a klutz. I've got great balance and I'm very handy."

"Good for you," he fired back. "Where I come from, men don't stand around watching women do this kind of work," he told her with feeling. He was thinking specifically of Caroline's husband. Rory Connors would have liked nothing better than to never have to move another muscle in his body for as long as he lived if he didn't want to.

That no-good SOB had his baby sister doing all the heavy work—and she wasn't up to half of it. He was certain that was why Caroline had lost the baby she was carrying before it had even gotten through its first trimester. He recalled with anger that his brother-in-law had expressed no remorse over the loss that had all but completely devastated Caroline.

On the contrary, Connors had actually been relieved, saying that there was no room for "brats" in his life right now.

Or ever, Cody suspected. The man was far too egotistical and self-centered to share Caroline with even a baby.

Cody slowly became aware that Catherine was laughing. When he looked at her quizzically, waiting for an explanation, the woman was quick to let him in on the joke.

"Um, this might not have occurred to you but you and I come from the exact same place," she pointed out.

He frowned as he steadied the ladder, picked up the sign and then began to climb up. She was right. "Yeah, well, then you should know that I wasn't about to have you climbing up to the top, tottering on the ladder while you tried to hang this sign up. I was quick enough to catch you last time. I might not be this time."

"I wasn't going to *try* to hang it up," she corrected with just a slight edge to her voice. She liked him and she knew he meant well, but she didn't like being thought of as inept. "I was *going* to hang it up. There's not exactly a need for an engineering degree when it comes to hanging up a sign," Catherine pointed out. "And I figure I've filled my quota of falling off ladders. That was my first time and my *only* time," she emphasized.

Cody looked down at her in silence for a long moment. For a brief second, she thought that he was just going to let go of the sign, climb down off the ladder and walk away.

But then, uttering an unintelligible noise—at least she couldn't make any sense of it—Cody turned his attention to what had brought him up here in the first place. With an amazingly accurate eye, he hung the sign exactly in the middle, directly over the doorway. He did it without bothering to measure first, without resorting to any sort of gauges and without asking her for any visual guidance from her vantage point.

The man had a fantastic eye, she thought. It was obvious that he was a natural. One of those incredibly gifted souls who could build an entire building using a bent spoon, a wad of chewing gum and a set of popsicle sticks. He was creative without even knowing that he was. She was more convinced than ever that she had chosen the right man as her inspiration. He obviously came with fringe benefits—and muscles, she noted.

Her stomach seemed to tighten of its own accord.

Catherine stepped back, admiring the sign. "That's absolutely perfect," she pronounced as he came back down the ladder.

He didn't bother looking up at his handiwork. Instead, he merely said, "I know."

That sort of statement reeked of conceit, and yet, she realized, the man wasn't conceited, nor did he actually sound that way. Instead, what he sounded was self-assured. He was a man who knew his limitations—if he actually possessed any—and he was obviously fairly comfortable in his own skin.

That, she knew, wasn't often the case. Most people were usually hounded by insecurities, whether large or small.

"Must be nice," Catherine couldn't help commenting to him.

Again Cody raised a quizzical eyebrow as he looked at her, waiting for some sort of explanation or further elaboration.

"What is?" he finally asked when she didn't elaborate further.

Her eyes met his. She consciously banked down the shiver that rose within her. "Being so confident."

"Not a matter of confidence," Cody told her. "Just a matter of knowing what I can and can't do."

She thought that was one and the same, but it was obviously different to him.

Be that as it may, she had no intention of getting into a discussion with Cody over this. She didn't want this cowboy—who really did come across like the genuine article to her—to think she was trying to challenge him or trip him up. He seemed just perfect the way he was and she was fairly certain it would help business along for her if she could tap into this man's likes and preferences. There had to be a lot more like him around here, right? And she wanted her merchandise to appeal to people with his sensibilities and preferences.

Cody took the ladder and returned it to the back room, pausing next to her just for a moment to ask, "Got anything else you need hung up?"

Catherine smiled as she shook her head. "Not at the moment," she replied.

In response, he nodded his head and continued on his way. He replaced the ladder where he had found it, along with the hammer.

"I would, however, like to get your input on a few things," she said, raising her voice so that it followed him into the back room.

He didn't answer until he came out again. "Well, I'm here, might as well use me. Ask away," he told her.

Might as well use me. Now there was a straight line if ever there was one, she couldn't help thinking as she bit her tongue to keep quiet.

Instead, she beckoned Cody over to the counter where she had her laptop up and running. She'd set it up the minute she'd come in this morning, thinking to get a little online shopping done whenever she felt like taking a break. She had all the sites bookmarked.

"I've been looking through some eBay auctions of things I thought would be perfect for the shop," she told Cody.

"So get them," he advised.

"I'd like a second opinion," she told him honestly. And that second opinion was where he came in. That was the deal.

"Why?" he wanted to know. "Don't you trust your own judgment?"

"Yes I do," she said. "But it's always good to have reinforcement."

He considered her words. The woman wasn't headstrong, but she wasn't wishy-washy, either. He found himself nodding in silent approval of this woman he'd just barely met.

Catherine Clifton was a good blend of various personalities, he thought. She was definitely different from most of the women he had interacted with since Renee's passing. It wasn't that he was in the market for another wife—one heartache in his lifetime was more than enough for him—but hell, at his age he wasn't looking to up and join a monastery, either.

Only problem was, most of the women around here fell into two groups. The first group was mainly concerned with trivial things—things like what outfit or hairstyle looked best on them. Mindless things. And then there was that other group. The women who made no secret of the fact that they felt he was "broken" and they knew just how to "fix" him.

He wasn't about to let that group get their hands on him, not by a hell of a long shot, he thought. He wasn't "broken," at least, not in a way that any of them could even begin to heal, and he wasn't lonely, either. At least, not lonely enough to take up with any of those women for more than a couple of days or so. After that, he just lost patience with them, preferring his own company or the company of his horses to being subjected to endless, mindless chatter that somehow always managed to work the phrase "How do I look?" into the conversation.

Any conversation.

Looking at Catherine now, he couldn't help wondering if ultimately she was going to fall into one of those two categories. He was probably wrong, but he had a hunch that she wasn't.

A larger part of him felt that it really didn't matter either way.

But just the smallest part of him hoped that he was right.

Chapter Four

"You planning on selling used clothes in the store, too?" Cody wanted to know when she showed him some of the things she'd acquired.

While the main focus of the shop was going to remain on vintage pieces of furniture, Catherine thought that bringing in a few items of clothing might actually draw in more potential customers and provide her clientele an eclectic selection to choose from. She intended to display the clothing in the same section of the shop that Cody had found the fringed coin purse he'd sent to his sister.

"They're not used," Catherine corrected, employing a euphemism. "They're pre-owned."

Cody snorted. "Fancy words," he said, dismissing the term she'd substituted with a wave of his hand. Whatever she called them, if someone had worn them before, the clothes were still used.

To his surprise, Catherine didn't argue. "Yes, they are, and they're meant to convey a different image," she told him. To show him what she meant, she opened up a large cardboard box. Inside were the various articles of clothing that she had managed to collect so far. "Everything in here has been cleaned, pressed and, in some cases, mended," she allowed. "But they're not rags," she quickly specified, guessing what was going through Cody's mind. She raised her eyes to his face. "Every item in here has a story. Every castoff has potential."

Cody realized that she was looking at him and not at anything in particular that she had inside the box. For a second, he was going to ask her if she was trying to tell him something, then decided he was probably reading far too much into her tone.

Glancing at the contents of the box, he saw a brightly beaded shirt and a multicolored scarf that would have looked more at home around her neck lying right on top of the pile of clothing.

He fingered the scarf for a second. *Soft,* he thought. Just like her skin.

Now how the hell would he have known that? A little unnerved, he let the scarf drop back into the box.

"So this is going to be like a thrift shop?" he asked, trying to get a handle on what her actual intent was.

A thrift shop tended to suggest rock-bottom prices, and she was going for an image that was a little more exclusive than that.

"No, it's not going to be *that* inexpensive," she explained with a smile. "I'm thinking more along the lines that one man's 'junk' can turn out to be another man's treasure."

Cody rummaged a little deeper into the box, then

laughed shortly. There was nothing exactly impressive to be found in there.

A hint of amusement was evident in his eyes when he looked at her. "Kind of stretching the word 'treasure' a mite, aren't you?"

She didn't quite see it that way. "It's like that saying about beauty being in the eyes of the beholder," Catherine pointed out. "You never know what might appeal to a person." And then she smiled broadly at him. "Which is what I have you for."

Cody looked at the woman he'd struck a bargain with. Maybe he needed to rethink this arrangement a bit. Since she *had* given him that purse for Caroline in exchange for his so-called services, he felt obligated to give her *something* in return. But at the moment, that wasn't as easy as it might have sounded to an outsider. The truth of it was, he really had very few "likes" himself. For him it had always been more of a case of just "making do."

Cody felt it was only right to try to explain that to her. "I'm a simple man, Catherine," he told her. "If you're waiting for me to get excited about something, you've got a long wait ahead of you."

There was that shiver again, Catherine thought as it shimmied up and down her spine. That wonderful/strange sensation that insisted on undulating along her back as if she was anticipating something.

Something from him.

Pressing her lips together, Catherine did her best to block the feeling. To ignore it and just focus on the business at hand.

Still, she couldn't help saying, "I'm sure it'll be worth waiting for when it finally happens."

Damn, but there was something about this woman, Cody caught himself thinking, the thought flashing across his mind completely out of the blue. Something that stirred up his insides like one of those food processors he'd seen demonstrated once. All without any warning.

And when she tilted her head just like that—as if that could help her understand something—the sun wound up getting caught in her hair and he could see reddish streaks lacing through it.

Warming his blood.

Warming him.

And, yeah, by God, tempting him, he silently admitted.

Maybe he should just kiss her and get it over with, Cody thought, doing his best to be pragmatic. That way, maybe his thoughts would finally stop going where they didn't belong and he could get back to focusing on "paying up his debt" to her. He didn't like being beholden to anyone, even someone as pretty as Catherine.

For just the tiniest split second, he debated acting on the thought. Debated kissing her purely for practical reasons.

He even leaned into her a little. And once he did, he started to go through the rest of the motions. His eyes held her prisoner just as much as hers managed to hold him in the same cell.

His lips were almost touching hers—

And then the bell over the doorway went off, splintering the moment. Breaking the mood.

Announcing the presence of another person entering their private space.

Acute discomfort, laced through with a prickly dose

of guilt, had Cody taking a step back away from his intended target before he looked in the direction of the offending doorway.

"I thought you said you were closed," he said to Catherine, his tone dark.

It almost sounded like an accusation, Catherine thought, even as she tried to figure out exactly what had just happened here—and what hadn't happened.

"I am," she finally answered, the words emerging from her lips in slow, confused motion.

"But she's not closed to family," the person walking into the shop cheerfully declared. The smile in the young woman's voice was only rivaled by the one on her face. "Are you, Cate?"

A wave of disappointment washed over Catherine, although she wasn't altogether certain why or what it was that she was disappointed about. It took her a moment to catch her breath.

Belatedly, she looked toward the source of the cheery voice and identified the young woman for Cody. "C.C."

"Well, at least you still recognize me." Her youngest sister laughed. "That's hopeful." She looked pleased with the observation. Stepping forward as she took the muffler off from around her neck, C.C. put her hand out to her sister's friend. "Hi, I'm the cheerful sister." She cocked her head the exact same way that Catherine did. "And you are?" She waited for the man to identify himself.

"Just leaving," Cody replied gruffly, a feeling of uncustomary awkwardness invading him. It was a strange feeling and he couldn't say that he much cared for it.

"Well, Mister 'Just Leaving,'" C.C. said, tongue in cheek as she made her request, "please don't do it on my account. I just dropped by to see how things were going and to ask my big sister if she needed a hand for a few hours." Her grin grew to almost huge proportions as her eyes swept over the man she'd seen standing almost intimately close to her sister. "You obviously don't," she concluded, turning toward Catherine. There was blanket approval in C.C.'s eyes—as well as admiration and perhaps just the tiniest touch of envy. "You seem to be doing just fine." Her eyes all but danced as she turned toward the door again. "I'll just leave you two alone and—"

"No, stay," Cody said. It was very close to sounding like an order. "I was just going."

The grin—or was that a smirk, Cody wondered—remained as Catherine's younger sister seemed to take careful measure of him.

"You didn't look as if you were just going when I came in," she told him. "From where I was standing, you looked like you'd just arrived."

If that was a riddle, he had no time to untangle it. He missed the very annoyed look that Catherine shot at her sister. Glancing at C.C., he mumbled something that sounded like "nice meeting you" without any conviction whatsoever and then addressed Catherine. "I'll be seeing you," he told her with a nod of his head.

A few strides toward the door and then he was gone.

"I sure hope so," C.C. murmured under her breath as the door closed again. The tiny bell needlessly announced his departure. Turning on her heel to look at her sister, C.C. declared with no small enthusiasm, "If you're stocking those in the store, I'll take twelve."

"C.C.—" There was a warning note in Catherine's voice.

"Okay, okay," C.C. relented. "I'm being greedy. I'll take ten." Seeing her older sister's frown deepen, she stopped teasing. Kind of. "Who *was* that masked man?" she wanted to know. "He was absolutely, blood-pumpingly gorgeous."

There was no point in telling C.C. that what she'd just said made no sense. There were times when her youngest sister lived on a planet all her own.

So instead, Catherine simply said, "That was Cody Overton."

There was a great deal more to this man than just a name, C.C. thought. Her sister might not be aware of the sparks of electricity she'd just seen flying between them, but she definitely was. It's a wonder neither one of them had any of their skin singed.

"And?" C.C. wanted to know.

Catherine looked at the younger girl, completely confused. "And what?"

C.C. looked at her closely, as if she was attempting to delve into her sister's mind. With absolutely no luck at the moment. So she asked, "And have you been holding out on us?"

"Holding out?" Catherine repeated, at this point very thoroughly confused. There was no "holding out." Her life and what she did was an open book. A *boring* one, granted, but an open one nonetheless. She had no idea what C.C. was talking about.

C.C. gravitated toward the box of clothes that Catherine had just opened. Her attention was instantly captivated by the top two items, each of which she took out and held up for closer examination. She definitely liked what she saw.

"You know, like a secret lover," C.C. elaborated absently. Holding the beaded shirt against herself, C.C. smoothed it down into place. She tried to imagine what it would look like coupled with her favorite pair of jeans. It would definitely turn heads, she concluded. Holding the shirt up, she asked Catherine, "Hey, you give discounts to relatives?"

Pressing the blouse against her upper torso, C.C. went in search of a mirror or some sort of shiny surface to give her an idea what she looked like in the shirt.

"Only if I don't disown them," Catherine fired back. And then she softened just a little. "Seriously, what are you doing here?"

"'Seriously,' I came to help out for a few hours," C.C. told her again. And then a touch of remorse entered her voice. "I didn't mean to break something up."

"You didn't," Catherine quickly assured her.

C.C. laughed, shaking her head. Was her sister in denial—or just trying to pretend nothing was going on for her benefit?

"You obviously weren't paying attention," she chided, then tossed in an accusation for good measure. "You've been holding out on me." Rather than be annoyed, C.C. was delighted with this turn of events. "Have you known him long?"

Catherine was completely speechless at the way her youngest sister could jump to conclusions without any sort of real input at all. She made it sound as if there was something going on—and there wasn't.

"A couple of hours," she finally told her sister, hoping that was the end of it.

But this was C.C. and the "end" was a long way away, Catherine thought with a mental groan.

"Looked like he knew you a lot better than that,"

C.C. commented, putting the shirt on the counter before going on to explore the rest of the box's contents.

Catherine deliberately took the faded, flared jeans out of C.C.'s hands. She didn't want her sister "buying" the entire contents of the box. Knowing C.C., what she'd get was a series of IOUs that C.C. would conveniently forget about and that she herself would have no intentions of collecting on. Family was family through thick and thin and sales receipts.

"How is it you don't get a nose bleed from jumping to conclusions like that?" Catherine asked her matter-of-factly.

Rather than answer, C.C. cocked her head as she eyed Catherine again. She had no intentions of having her sister distract her. Something was up—and she had a pretty good idea what that something was all about.

"Methinks the lady doth protest too much," C.C. declared in a pseudo-cultured voice.

"What the 'lady' is desperately trying to do is keep from strangling her youngest sister to death," Catherine countered between clenched teeth.

She loved everyone in her family more than words could possibly begin to describe, but there were times when they—collectively and individually—got to be just too much for her. That was when she'd engineer a mini-getaway—sometimes all she needed was a few hours alone. But this time, she had a feeling she might need just to "disappear" for more than an hour—or five.

Despite the threat—obviously an empty one, C.C. thought—she didn't back off. For one, she was having far too good a time with this. For another, she knew that Catherine didn't even yell, so murder seemed as if it would be a little out of her comfort zone.

"Am I getting too close?" C.C. asked her.

"To your own demise?" Catherine shot back, then added a confirmation. "Yes."

For a second, C.C. did back off, but only to study her subject. "You know, I don't think I've ever seen you like this before." For C.C. there was only one conclusion to be drawn. "You must really like this guy."

Catherine's slender shoulders rose and then fell again in a dismissive shrug. "He's just a cowboy—"

"Yeah, I know." C.C.'s voice was almost dreamy as she talked. "I really thought he'd mount his horse and go riding off into the sunset. *Where* have you been keeping him all this time?" she wanted to know, refusing to believe that Catherine had just stumbled across this man a matter of hours ago, the way she'd alluded.

Catherine sighed. Her sister was a hopeless romantic and ever since Calista had announced plans for her upcoming wedding, C.C. had gone off on some impossible tangent, seeing potential grooms behind every tree and rock. She was surprised that the girl hadn't eloped with someone by now.

Surprised and grateful, Catherine added silently before tackling C.C.'s overly fertile imagination one last time.

"Once and for all, C.C., I haven't been 'keeping' Cody anywhere. He walked in here three days ago, looking to buy a birthday present for his sister. When he spotted a fringed coin purse, I decided to make him a trade—I'd let him have the coin purse for free in exchange for his opinion on a few items I was going to be carrying in the shop." She could see by the expression on her sister's face that C.C. just wasn't buying into this. Damn, but that girl could be stubborn. "I thought

I'd try to appeal to his demographic," Catherine tacked on, feeling almost helpless.

"So what you're saying is that you're planning on only selling to hopelessly sexy cowboys with killer eyes?" There were dimples winking in and out of the corners of her mouth as she made no effort to keep the amused grin off her lips.

For now Catherine threw in the towel. "Why don't you see if Calista needs help with her wedding plans?" she suggested forcefully.

"I'd rather stay here and torture you," C.C. told her with a straight face. But when she saw the exasperated look that entered Catherine's chocolate eyes, she held up her hands in protest. "Okay, okay, I'll cease and desist, I promise." And then a serious look flitted across her face as she said, "But I am sorry."

Okay, what was *this* about? "About what?" she asked aloud.

Wasn't Catherine paying *any* attention? "That I walked in at the wrong time. From where I was standing, it looked as if your so-called 'Mr. Demographic' was just about to kiss you—and would have if I hadn't picked just then to come barging in."

If she were being honest, Catherine would have had to admit that she'd been pretty certain that he *was* going to kiss her just then. But then, maybe this had all worked out for the best anyway.

"That's just your imagination," Catherine insisted, wanting the book to be closed.

Rather than continue the argument, C.C. merely shrugged. "Okay, if you say so, Cate. But I *was* serious when I said that I came here to help you out in the store for a little bit. I don't have to be anywhere for a few hours and I thought you might want some help sorting all this stuff. Unless, of course, you want to save it for Mr. Strong, Silent Type," C.C. amended.

Instead of answering, Catherine went into the back room. When she emerged again, she was armed with a large feather duster. The moment she was close to C.C., she placed the feather duster into her sister's hand.

"Here, if you really want to be useful, start dusting from the back to the front," she instructed. "I don't think this place has had a once-over since before Jasper Fowler got arrested."

"That's an awful lot of dust," C.C. commented.

"I know," Catherine agreed sympathetically. "So I guess you'd better get started if you want to finish before next Easter."

C.C. saluted her with the feather duster. "Your word is my command, Cate." She grinned as she looked around. "This really is pretty exciting," she agreed. "When are you opening for business again?" she asked as she started dusting.

Catherine thought of her target date. It was breathing down her neck. How did it get to be so late in the month? "Too soon," she murmured.

"Well, if you don't think you'll be ready in time, you could always ask Mr. Delicious Cowboy to come riding to your rescue."

"Just dust," Catherine ordered, pointing to an area that was completely obscured by dust.

Her sister laughed and saluted with the hilt of the duster. "Yes'm."

Catherine nodded her head and smiled at C.C.'s "obedient" response. She had to admit, she liked the sound of that. Especially after all these years.

"You're finally catching on, C.C.," she told her sister.

"I could say the same thing about you," she heard C.C. murmur under her breath.

About to make another comment, Catherine decided to hold her piece instead. A great deal more would get done in the store in the long run if she just pretended not to have heard C.C.'s last reply.

Chapter Five

That had been a very close call, Cody told himself as he drove his truck over to the General Store. He'd nearly forgotten to pick up the things that had supposedly brought him into Thunder Canyon in the first place. He could just picture what Hank and Kurt would say about that.

The ranch hands wouldn't say anything to him directly, but there'd be winks and nods and knowing nudges. He could damn well do without that.

But that wasn't what he actually regarded as his "close call."

If that blonde girl hadn't come into Catherine's store just when she did, he probably would have wound up kissing Catherine.

Not a good idea.

Not that he hadn't kissed anyone in the last eight years. He had. He'd done a lot more than just kissed those other women, too, but he had an uneasy feeling that while the other women he'd been with were just a way for him to satisfy the physical need he occasionally experienced, kissing the enthusiastic store owner would lead him down a whole different path.

Not one he was planning to take. Ever.

Anyone could see that Catherine Clifton wasn't like the others.

There was a purpose to her, one that did *not* include fixing or changing him. She was the first woman he'd come across in a long time who didn't strike him as being just one-dimensional. There was substance to her. He found he could carry on a conversation with her without having his mind drift off somewhere in the middle because he was bored.

No, Cody thought as he absently made his way through the General Store's aisles, looking for the items he'd said he was bringing back, the woman definitely wasn't boring.

Far from it.

He was attracted to her and therein lay his problem. He didn't want to be attracted to her, didn't want to be attracted to anyone. A strong enough attraction could lead to caring and that could lead to disaster. He knew that firsthand.

Caring was asking to have his heart ripped out of his chest and barbecued on a bed of hot coals when he least expected it.

Loving someone left you vulnerable to all sorts of things.

Been there, done that, Cody thought with finality, deliberately shutting the door on the very idea that he could *ever* allow himself to go down that particular path again.

The thought abruptly had him coming to a mental skidding halt.

What the hell was going on here? How had he gone from *almost* kissing Catherine to having his heart extracted without benefit of an anesthetic?

That whole analogy was way too dramatic for him. Rolling it over in his head now, it seemed more like something one of the women he'd gone out with after Renee's passing might have said.

He wasn't being himself.

Maybe he *should* have kissed her, Cody decided, rethinking the situation. Just to show himself that he could take it or leave it—and her—whenever he felt like it.

Just to prove to himself that the feisty shop owner had no power over him.

"Will there be anything else, Cody?" the older man behind the checkout counter asked him politely. All his groceries were tabulated and neatly stacked to the side, waiting to be packed up.

Cody blinked, coming out of his self-imposed mental fog as he suddenly realized that he'd come to a dead stop at the checkout counter and hadn't moved, even after he'd paid his bill.

The man he'd handed the cash to had to think that he was a little bit crazy just to remain standing there as if he was trying to imitate a statue.

"No, thanks." He forced what passed for a smile to his lips for the clerk's benefit. "That's everything," he said to him.

The man looked at him thoughtfully and with just

the smallest measure of concern. "Everything all right, Cody?" he inquired.

"Everything's fine, Jake," Cody replied immediately. His tone left no opening for any sort of further exchange. He wasn't one to discuss *anything* that was going on in his private life.

Taking the grocery bags off the counter, he hefted them outside to his truck and secured them in the back.

Without a backward glance—at the store clerk or at Real Vintage Cowboy—the shop was located down the street—Cody climbed into the cab of his truck, pointed it in the direction of his ranch and drove off.

Driving past Catherine's shop, there was a part of him that actually toyed with the idea of walking right back in and getting that damn kiss out of the way.

Another part of him—the part that wound up winning—thought it might be a better idea if he slept on his impulse first.

Then, if he still felt that he needed to get this whole thing out in the open and out of his system, he could always come back another day and do whatever he felt he had to do.

But right now, he decided, it was better for all concerned if he just kept driving and ignored any and all impulses—sharp or otherwise—that telegraphed themselves through him.

Cody frowned.

Deeply.

He'd never cared for complications, and this definitely felt like one hell of a complication in the making.

With effort, he forced his thoughts to focus on what needed to be attended to next on the ranch. After all, his ranch was the really important thing.

He had horses to train and ranch hands to pay, Cody reminded himself. Beyond that, nothing else mattered.

Or, at least, it wasn't supposed to.

It was just by accident that Cody was in the house two mornings later to hear the phone ring. Most days, he'd already be out, either helping to clean the stables or in the corral, working with and training the quarter horses.

For the most part, he looked upon a phone as strictly a convenience for him in case he had to call a vet for one of his horses. Otherwise, he looked upon it as just another decoration hanging next to the calendar on the kitchen wall.

He didn't really like being on the receiving end of a phone call.

There was a reason for that.

The ringing phone brought back bad memories. It reminded him of the time someone from the hospital had called to tell him that there'd been an accident and that his parents wouldn't be coming home.

Ever.

He'd been eighteen at the time, an adult by legal standards. But it had hit him hard, right in his gut, stripping him of his years and making him feel like some helpless kid again.

Suddenly, just like that, he found himself orphaned. Orphaned and yet catapulted into the scary position of being head of the household. And if that hadn't been intimidating enough, he also became—just like that—Caroline's legal guardian since his sister was four years younger than he was and, at the time, still a minor.

Cody had always been his own person, but suddenly,

without warning, he'd been thrown headlong into the deep end of the pool. It was up to him to make all the decisions. Decisions about his parents' funeral arrangements, about whether to sell the ranch or try to make a go of it. Most frightening of all, he had to make decisions involving his sister's welfare. Quick decisions. If he hadn't been willing to become her legal guardian, Caroline would have become a ward of the court for the next four years of her life.

As far as he was concerned, that part really required no debating at all. There was no way on earth that he would have allowed his sister to be swallowed up by the system.

One isolated early morning phone call and his entire life had changed. Cody had aged at least ten years in the small space of time between when he picked up the receiver and when he hung it up again.

Maybe Caroline would have been better off if he *had* agreed to let the court take her and place her in a foster home, he thought now. At least then she wouldn't have met that loser of a husband of hers and Rory wouldn't be controlling her the way he did.

All this shot through Cody's mind as he stared at the ringing phone on his kitchen wall. He debated just letting the phone go on ringing until whoever was on the other end hung up, but ultimately that was the coward's way out. He'd never been a coward.

With a sigh, Cody picked up the receiver and said, "Hello?"

"Cody?"

The high, female voice on the other end was timid. Despite the fact that he was hardly ever on the phone and that he hadn't heard from her in more than a year, he recognized the voice immediately.

"Hi, Caroline." He glanced at the calendar next to the phone to verify the date before saying, "Happy Birthday."

"Thank you," she responded warmly. "Your present came in the mail yesterday. I just called to tell you that I really love it."

"You weren't supposed to open it until today," he told her.

Caroline laughed softly and just for a moment, she sounded the way she used to, before reality had sliced through her life.

"I couldn't wait."

"Well, that hasn't changed any," Cody noted.

He recalled that when Caroline had been a little girl, his sister couldn't wait to open her gifts. No matter how meager they might have been, she was always excited, always appreciative, acting as if she'd received spectacular treasures instead of the mundane, practical gifts that she found under the tree each year, Cody remembered.

"I'm sure you have better use for your money than to spend it on me," Caroline was saying. "A card would have been more than enough." She paused for a moment, then added in a soft, almost shy whisper, "Thank you for remembering."

Cody didn't know how to respond to that. Moreover, he couldn't shake the feeling that something was off, was wrong. He knew he couldn't pry. That would only lead to an exchange of words that would make him lose his temper, and he didn't want to get into an argument with his sister today, not on her birthday.

His sister was a lot more loyal than that scum, otherwise known as her husband, deserved, Cody thought darkly.

He really wished there was a way to convince her to leave the no-account, wasted piece of flesh. But there wasn't.

"Why shouldn't I remember?" he finally asked. "You're my sister and it's not like I've twelve others to keep track of."

He'd often thought, because there was just the two of them after their parents were killed, that when he'd gotten married, Caroline had followed suit not long afterward because she was very vulnerable and Rory had used that to his advantage. He was attentive and sweet to her just long enough to get her to marry him.

He felt responsible for his sister's unhappiness even though both he and Renee had invited Caroline to come live with them. Caroline had turned them down, saying that newlyweds needed to be alone.

Only the look in her eyes had told him how truly lonely his sister actually felt. He shouldn't have listened to her. He should have *insisted* that she come live with them. But he'd been selfish. He'd wanted to be alone with Renee.

And Caroline was the one who wound up paying the price for that.

Rory had taken advantage of her loneliness. That alone would earn the man his place in hell. And the sooner the better.

"It was very sweet of you," Caroline told him. He could have sworn Caroline sounded as if she was about to say something more, but then her tone suddenly changed. A nervous uneasiness all but vibrated in her throat. "I've got to go. Thank you," she said again, the words rushing out of her mouth.

The hell with tiptoeing around because it was her birthday. Something was definitely not right here.

"Caroline, what's wrong?" he asked. But there was no answer. He strained to hear something, a telltale sound. But there was nothing. "Caroline?" Cody called, more loudly this time.

His sister had hung up. But just before the connection had gone dead, Cody could have sworn he had heard a male voice yelling Caroline's name in the background.

Cody scowled.

Caroline jumped every time her husband so much as snapped his fingers. Was she just being skittish or was there more behind her behavior than that?

Did that loser abuse her?

Cody clenched his fists at his sides in frustrated, impotent anger. There wasn't anything he could do. Caroline wouldn't listen to reason. Wouldn't listen to him when he'd all but begged her to leave that miserable excuse for a human being.

The last time he had gotten between Caroline and her husband, Rory had taken her and moved to another state. Cody had an uneasy feeling that if he turned up on his sister's doorstep, this time Rory would make sure that they completely disappeared without leaving so much as a forwarding address. Rory wouldn't put up with any interference. The man acted like a malevolent dictator who was exceedingly possessive of his tiny kingdom. Everything had to go through him.

Trying to convince Caroline to leave her husband wasn't going to work. She had to come to that conclusion on her own for it to actually take root and happen. He was powerless to do anything except pray that somebody would mistake Rory for a bear and shoot him.

He would have gladly volunteered to be the one.

But knowing he was powerless to do anything and living with it were two very different things. There were times when he was convinced that he could easily kill Rory with his bare hands. The man brought out the very worst in him.

Restless, Cody found himself pacing around the kitchen after he'd hung up. As the feeling kept building rather than dissipating, Cody decided that maybe a trip into town might help calm him down.

For some strange reason, Catherine and that ridiculously named shop of hers—what the hell was a Real Vintage Cowboy, anyway?—had a calming, almost peaceful effect on him.

When she wasn't stirring him up, he added with a bemused smile on his face.

Making his decision, Cody took his car keys off the peg where he kept them when he was home and went to get his truck.

The smile Catherine flashed at him when he walked into her showroom an hour later told him that he'd made the right decision.

The fact that it ignited a fire in his gut was beside the point.

What he needed right now was a little distraction. Fortunately, that was *exactly* what happened each time he came into the store. He got distracted.

And maybe a little lost in those chocolate eyes of hers, he added silently.

"I was hoping you'd come in today," Catherine told him, quickly crossing over to Cody.

She didn't strike him as someone who just stood around, wishing for something to happen. The woman was a doer.

"Why didn't you call me?" he wanted to know. After all, it wasn't as if he hadn't given her his number.

The answer Caroline gave surprised him. "Because I didn't feel I had the right to disturb you if you were busy working. After all, your ranch does have to come first."

A person who didn't think that the world revolved exclusively around them, he thought. If someone would have asked him, he would have said that he thought that was an attribute that only his late wife and his sister possessed. For the most part, he found people to be more and more self-centered.

He looked at Catherine for a long moment, debating whether or not to tell her that he came into town because he wanted to see her.

His underlying need for caution had him saying instead, "I needed a break for a while."

She nodded, not questioning his reasons for coming, just happy that he had.

"I'll try not to overwork you," she promised with a wink, then grew serious. "But I did want to ask your opinion on a few things that I found online." Tugging a little on his arm, she drew him over to the counter where she had set up her laptop. Turning the laptop so that it faced him, she said, "Take a look at this."

But rather than looking at the screen, Cody glanced around the shop first.

She'd done a lot of work on it since he'd been here two days ago. Didn't the woman ever sleep? Or did she have a legion of helpers when he wasn't around?

"How do you manage to do it all?" he wanted to know, allowing a note of admiration to slip through.

Catherine wasn't sure she was following him. "Excuse me?"

"The shop's a lot cleaner and neater than the last time I saw it," he elaborated. "And you've obviously had time to go looking on the internet—"

There were a lot more items in the shop now than there had been the last time he'd been here. Unless she had a warehouse somewhere close by, this had all been bought and shipped in the last couple of days.

Looking on the internet. Catherine smiled at his terminology. "It's called browsing," she supplied helpfully.

"It's called being superhuman," he countered. Just cleaning the place up like this would have required a great deal of her time. Yet she didn't look wilted. "Do you sleep at all?"

Catherine laughed. "Every day and a half I hang upside down in the closet for a quick nap."

He looked at her for a long, long moment, then declared, "You are one very strange lady, Catherine Clifton. You know that?"

Her grin widened. "I just know what I want, that's all," she replied, then tugged on his arm again, this time a little more insistently. "Now come and look at these things and tell me what you think."

What I think is that I have a tiger by the tail, he said silently.

"Might as well," he said out loud, sounding not nearly as reluctant as he might have just a few days ago. "Since I'm here," he tacked on.

"Since you're here," Catherine echoed warmly, her eyes crinkling as her smile deepened.

He did his best not to notice, but his best wasn't quite good enough.

The warmth she generated inside of him could have toasted marshmallows if the need arose.

Chapter Six

Cody sighed.

He and Catherine had been going over various estate sale sites on her laptop for a while now and next to nothing had stirred his interest. Certainly nothing he would have gone out of his way to own.

While he did like having an excuse to be around this vibrant woman whose very presence sucked the solemnity out of his existence, he had to be honest with her. She was wasting her time having him do this.

"You know," he began, turning away from the laptop. "I really think you should get someone else to help you with this."

Catherine raised her eyes from the laptop screen and looked at him for a long moment. She tried to gauge what his thoughts were, but she could have saved herself the trouble. The man had an expression that totally defied penetration.

Having nothing to lose, she took a stab at his reasons for saying what he just had. "You don't want to do this anymore?"

"It's not a matter of not wanting to do it," he corrected. Because, if he were being honest with her, he rather enjoyed these little impromptu sessions. He wouldn't have come into town so often in the last week if he didn't. He liked her company and, despite their different way of viewing things, they were comfortable with one another.

But that wasn't the point behind all this, was it?

"Then what?" she prodded.

She wasn't accustomed to dealing with someone who had to have words coaxed out of him. In her family, silence was something that only occurred if everyone happened to be asleep at the same time.

Otherwise, the air was filled with the hum of voices constantly crisscrossing one another. Sometimes several at the same time.

Her father had once referred to the boisterous exchange of words and opinions as a cacophony. She thought that was really an excellent word for it. There certainly was no denying that they were a noisy bunch of people.

Cody was the exact opposite. He had made silence into an art form. The man kept his peace inordinately long, sometimes not even speaking when he was spoken to. He didn't even make any noise when he entered a room. If she hadn't had a bell mounted against the front door, she would have never even heard him walking into the shop that first day.

"I just don't think I'm doing you any good," Cody confessed. She was trying to attract business and appeal to a certain age and income bracket. But while he fit the two requirements, he just was *not* into the kind of things that everyone else was. "I'm not your average guy," he pointed out.

Amen to that, Catherine thought, suppressing the smile that rose to her lips.

"So if you're trying to find things that appeal to most people," he concluded, "I'm not your man."

Ah, if only—

The thought caught her up short, coming out of the blue and utterly surprising her. It caused her to take a second—or was that a tenth?—look at this weatherworn cowboy who'd accidentally strolled into her shop.

There was no getting away from the fact that there was a certain undercurrent between them, a chemistry that she'd felt from the first moment she saw Cody and they began talking.

Or rather, *she* began talking. For the most part, Cody was just the recipient of her words, she silently amended, amused.

"When I bought the shop, I also wound up buying all the pieces that were still in it," she told him, gesturing in a vague pattern around the area. "The antiques that Fowler hadn't sold and probably had no intentions of selling."

Calista, who'd worked there part-time while waiting for her position at the mayor's office to go full-time, had told her as much. At the time, her sister had expressed confusion as to why the man would go to the trouble of owning and operating the store without any real interest in making a profit from the place.

That was before they found out that his focus had been elsewhere all along.

"So it's not like I have nothing to sell once I officially reopen the shop's doors," she concluded. There was no point in getting rid of the inventory. She'd do better just holding on to it until she could find interested buyers and collectors. Time and patience were on her side. She wasn't in this to score a fast profit. She was in for the long haul.

The long haul. That had a rather nice ring to it, she mused.

"Okay, then I don't understand," Cody confessed, confused. "If you're planning on keeping this stuff and trying to sell it, just what exactly is it you want me for?"

Catherine pressed her lips together, struggling to keep both her grin and the accompanying words that his question generated under wraps. There was a raw magnetism about the man that appealed to her on a whole different plane than any she'd ever encountered.

But Cody wasn't the type of man you said things like that to. She instinctively knew that he liked things simple. Even if they weren't.

Pausing to take a breath first, she made her case as best she could.

"I thought you could give me a more unique perspective and help me pick out things that the average person might have overlooked."

Cody chewed on that for a second, thinking it over. And then he shook his head as he hooked his thumbs through the belt loops of his jeans. "Still think you've got the wrong person."

She didn't feel that way.

"Do you care about other people's opinions about you?" she asked point-blank. When he didn't answer her immediately, she assured him, "This isn't a trick question. I'm not trying to trap you. Matter of fact, I'm trying to free you."

"No, I don't care what other people think of me," he responded.

And as for setting him free, it was going to take more than just a few innocent, glib words to do that, Cody couldn't help thinking. His soul had been entangled and trapped, basically hidden from the light of day, for the last eight years. Ever since Renee had died, leaving him alone on this isolated piece of rock, leaving him to deal with the emptiness as best as he could.

The man who didn't care what other people thought of him, *that* was the man she wanted on her team.

"I want the 'inner you' to respond to the merchandise I point out," she explained to Cody.

"And if I don't 'respond' to what you point out?" he wanted to know.

She shrugged. "Then I don't buy it. It's not like I don't have anything to sell," she reminded him with a laugh.

These last few days she'd worked hard to make the furnishings she'd found presentable. She'd painstakingly rearranged everything to show them off to their best advantage.

It still wasn't clear to Cody. Exactly what was his function at the shop? "Maybe I'm being thick here, but I don't get what you want with me if you're planning on trying to sell all this other stuff."

"Those are antiques that might appeal to the average person who fancies himself or herself to be a collector. But I'm also looking for a few unique things that would appeal to the discerning buyer."

And *those* people usually had more disposable cash

to spend than the average person, Catherine added silently. She wasn't about to say it out loud because she knew that Cody didn't quite fall into that category.

Cody looked at her uncertainly now. "And you think that I'd know what they'd want..."

His voice trailed off as he tried to make sense of what she'd just said. He really did want to follow her. Moreover, he didn't want to think of her as being like those empty-headed women who were only defined by what their husbands did. He knew in his gut that she wasn't like that.

"I think you'd know what *you* want," Catherine told him with emphasis.

"And that makes me your unique, discerning buyer?" he questioned.

The very corners of her mouth seemed to reach up to her eyes as she smiled. "Yes."

The idea of his being "unique" had Cody shaking his head in disbelief. That was the last word he would have *ever* applied to himself.

"Like I said, Catherine Clifton, you are a strange, strange lady."

"No, I'm a good businesswoman. I just want to make sure I have a good variety available for the customers. Fowler just had dusty pieces he didn't bother taking care of. The store was his 'cover,' but it's going to be *my* business."

"And you really think that you can make a go of it?" Cody wanted to know, watching her face as she answered.

Rather than give him a confident "Yes," Catherine addressed his question honestly. "I don't know, but I sure as hell am going to try."

He liked that.

Cody found himself admiring her. Catherine Clifton had drive. And that word his father liked to use when describing his mother. His father would say that she had "spunk." At the time, the word hadn't meant anything to him one way or another, but Cody understood now exactly what his father had meant and understood, too, the appeal behind it.

Taking a deep breath, Cody decided that he was ready for another round of online browsing. He nodded toward the laptop.

"Why don't you show me some more of the things you're considering buying," he suggested.

Rather than leave the laptop on the counter where it was, Catherine decided to move it over to a quaint table for two she'd acquired on her own. When she'd bought it, she'd thought that the table looked as if it would have been more at home in an old-fashioned ice cream parlor. She'd found it all but buried beneath a stack of papers and tarp at an estate sale she'd attended.

After cleaning and restoring the set, she'd brought the table and its matching two chairs into the showroom. She intended to use it as one of the themes within the shop.

"Let's get back to it, then," Catherine said with enthusiasm. She gestured for him to sit in the chair opposite hers.

"You're the boss," he allowed.

As if anyone could ever *be Cody Overton's boss,* Catherine thought, amused. She knew better.

The late afternoon sun had slanted its rays across the shop's polished wooden floor, then withdrawn again, tiptoeing away as nightfall began to slip in.

Catherine leaned back in her chair, slowly straightening her spine. It ached a little in protest. They'd been at this for several hours now without a break, she realized.

All in all, it had been a pretty productive afternoon. Out of the scores of things she'd wound up showing him, Cody had actually selected a few. She considered the session a huge success.

"I guess that's enough for one day," she told him, stretching and rotating her shoulders. Trying to undo the kinks.

She seemed completely unaware of the fact that she was thrusting her chest out, closer to him, as she stretched. Cody tried not to notice, but it was impossible not to.

He couldn't make himself look anywhere else.

The room felt decidedly warmer to him than it had just a few minutes ago.

Taking his cue from her that it was time to leave, Cody rose to his feet and picked up his hat from the counter where he'd left it.

"I guess that I'll be heading out then." But even as he said it—even though he'd been there for the better part of the day—he found himself reluctant to just walk away and leave her.

Just then, the little carved bird within the old-fashioned cuckoo clock on the wall began to announce the hour as only a cuckoo clock could.

How did it get to be so late? Catherine couldn't help wondering. It felt as if she'd just sat down and, somehow, five hours had managed to pass by.

She felt a pinch in her stomach.

They hadn't eaten anything in *hours,* she thought. It

was a short leap from her realization to an idea. "Tell you what, why don't I buy you dinner?" she suggested impulsively.

Being impulsive was new to her and she rather liked it. She'd always been the steady, reliable one. The rock her parents and everyone else relied on. She liked the new her.

She noticed the slight frown that creased Cody's mouth. "What?"

He didn't want to say anything—but it wasn't something that he felt comfortable with, so maybe saying something was for the best.

"The way I was raised," he began slowly, "a man usually asks a woman out for the first date, not the other way around."

Catherine's eyes widened. Was that what he thought this was? A date?

Well, is it? she asked herself. She decided it was safest to think of this as a nondate date.

Besides, labels were restricting and she wanted to keep what they had between them comfortable and easy. She definitely didn't want to do something that he felt was treading on his toes.

"This isn't a date," she told him. "It's just my way of saying 'thank you' for your effort. Call it professional courtesy," she suggested.

That made it sound too stiff, too mundane. *You're a man who doesn't know what he wants,* Cody's mind taunted. "So it's *not* a date." Cody eyed her as he got his facts straight.

If that's what made him happy, so be it, she told herself. "Not a date," she assured him.

"My mistake," Cody murmured, clearly embarrassed. "Sorry."

Now she was the one who was slightly confused. "There's nothing to be sorry about."

"I feel stupid," he admitted in a singular moment of honesty.

"No reason for that, either," she assured him quickly and with feeling. The dimples, like C.C.'s, in the corner of her mouth winked in and out. The man was adorable. "To be honest, I'm flattered. I didn't think you thought of me that way—as a potential date," she tacked on by way of an explanation.

The awkward moment only grew more so. Just what did she think of him?

"I'm thirty-five, I'm not dead," Cody pointed out, then thought that maybe he would have been better off if he'd just let the matter drop without being defensive about things. After all, he really didn't want her to think he was trying to get something going between them.

Although, he had to admit, whatever there was between them seemed to be taking on a life of its own without any encouragement from him.

Or, apparently, from her.

Even so, the smile on her lips seemed to burrow right into his gut, grazing his chest as well.

"Nice to know," she commented.

He had no idea what to make of her response or, for that matter, of the way this whole afternoon had made him feel.

There was no denying that she was having some kind of effect on him. That alone surprised him. He would have bet any amount of money that he *was* dead inside. That, as with a scorched earth policy, nothing inside of him could possibly ever flourish.

But when he was around Catherine, he felt definite stirrings. He felt a quickening of his gut that he just couldn't—or maybe wouldn't—pin down.

It was easier, he told himself, just to drop the whole thing.

Easier said than done.

As with the scent of new blossoms in the spring, he found that thoughts of Catherine insisted on lingering in his mind, popping up to tease him when he was least prepared.

The last time he had felt even remotely this way was when he and Ren—

He blocked the rest of the thought. This was neither the time nor the place. He'd deal with it later, he told himself.

"So," Catherine said, making the single word sound like an announcement, "where would you like to go to eat, Cody?"

He didn't eat out much, certainly not as much as the average man—unless sitting by an open campfire could be called eating out. Consequently, he didn't know the names of many restaurants in town.

"The Hitching Post still closed?" he asked her. The last he'd heard, it had shut down for repairs, but he couldn't remember exactly when that was. If something didn't affect his basic way of life and the ranch, he usually didn't pay attention to it.

She nodded. "I'm afraid so. How about DJ's Rib Shack?" she suggested. "The food there is really good. I think you might like it. And DJ might be willing to give us a break on the price of dinner." She was only partially teasing.

As far as he knew, there was only one reason for that. "You know DJ?" he asked as he followed Catherine out of the shop.

It was such a fact of life for her that she'd forgotten other people might not know.

"Sure."

Catherine paused to engage the lock on the front door. She left it unlocked during the day, but somehow, since there was merchandise in the shop, she felt that leaving the door unlocked was like issuing a challenge to the universe. She wasn't quite brave enough to risk that sort of thing. Not when everything she owned was tied up in the shop.

"The Cliftons and the Traubs are old family friends," she told Cody, then looked at him as she slipped the keys into her pocket. "Why?" The way he's asked made her think that there was a connection between the two men. "You know DJ, too?"

"Just in passing," he answered. And it had been years since he'd last seen the younger man. "I went to high school with Dax, his older brother."

The moment he said that, he suddenly remembered that Dax had gotten engaged to Allaire around the exact same time that he had gotten engaged to Renee.

But talking about it would only wind up opening up the wounds again and maybe it was time to finally try to let them start to heal.

There was something he wasn't saying, Catherine thought as she walked with Cody toward his truck. She could feel it.

Catherine was tempted to prod him a little. But she

knew she really shouldn't. Whatever he was holding back, if he wanted her to know, he'd tell her. She had to be satisfied with that.

It wasn't easy.

Rolling the matter over in her mind, Catherine stopped just short of the truck and turned toward Cody. "Would you rather not go to the Rib Shack?" she asked. "We could go somewhere else or maybe pick up something at the General Store and I could whip up dinner for us in the shop." She'd done it a couple of times for herself when she'd stayed late. "There's a hot plate in the storage room and I could—"

He knew where she was going with this and she didn't need to make the offer, although the fact that she did in deference to what she thought were his feelings impressed him.

Still, he shook his head, dismissing her offer. "You worked enough today," he told her. "DJ's Rib Shack'll do just fine."

"They make better ribs than I do," she admitted.

"I doubt it."

He was probably just being polite, Catherine thought. Even so, the words warmed her heart.

Chapter Seven

DJ's Rib Shack was a popular restaurant, part of a chain of barbecue restaurants founded by DJ Traub. This particular one was located on the ground floor of the Thunder Canyon Resort and, because of its location, it saw more than its share of foot traffic. Business was always brisk at the Rib Shack but somehow, in Catherine's experience, there always seemed to be enough seating available so that she could get a table anytime she dropped by.

The atmosphere was boisterous and loud and patrons found that they had to sit close to one another when speaking. Otherwise, parts of their conversations were swallowed up by the noise. As for ambiance, it had the feel of simpler times about it. The walls were covered with old sepia-toned photographs of ranches and cowboys from eras gone by.

As Cody followed Catherine through the maze of

tables, while an animated hostess led the way to their table, he could only think to himself that this was definitely *not* a place to bring a date for the first time. Brightly lit and friendly, there was absolutely nothing romantic about the setting. This was a place where friends came to talk about a game that was played down to the wire and good old boys came to chew the fat and talk about their glory days.

Embarrassment over his earlier misunderstanding took another bite out of him, but Cody kept his thoughts stoically under wraps.

The table the hostess brought them to was practically in the center of the main room.

"You have a clear view of everything," the woman enthused. Cody merely nodded.

Waiting for Catherine to take her seat first, Cody slid in opposite her. The hostess presented them each with a menu before she withdrew.

Catherine didn't bother opening hers as she looked around and took in the atmosphere. She seemed to brighten visibly right in front of him, as if the accompanying noise recharged her somehow.

"It's busy tonight," Cody commented.

That was nothing new. "It's like this every night, or so I hear," she told him. When Cody made no reply, Catherine looked at him, curious. "This isn't your first time here, is it?"

Cody shrugged carelessly. Removing his Stetson, he placed the hat on the side of the table where a third diner might have sat. "I don't eat out," he told her.

She expected him to tag on the word *much.* When he didn't, not wanting him to feel awkward, she said, "I hardly do, either. But I really like to." She grinned.

"Best part of eating out is that there're no dishes or pots and pans to wash afterwards."

"You could cut down on the number by making everything in one pan and then just eating out of it," he said matter-of-factly.

Was that how he took his meals? That sounded so lonely. Catherine suddenly realized that her mouth had dropped open. She quickly closed it. Recovering, she told him, "I'd say that you need to eat out more than I do."

What he needed, he couldn't help thinking, was a way to talk his sister into leaving that good-for-nothing, controlling husband of hers so she could go back to being the happy young woman he remembered.

"Don't know if *need*'s the right word, but I'll admit that the change of pace is kinda nice," he said, looking directly at Catherine.

What was nicer, he thought, was having someone to talk to while he ate. He hadn't realized that he'd missed that as much as he did until just now.

A waitress came to take their orders. That they were having barbecue ribs was a foregone conclusion. It was just a matter of how much and what they wanted to drink that had to be settled on.

"Catherine, it *is* you. I haven't seen you around for a bit."

The pleased greeting came from someone just behind him. Cody shifted in his chair in time to see DJ Traub lean over the table and warmly take Catherine's hands in his.

"How's everyone at home?" DJ asked. "All well, I hope. What are you all doing with yourselves?"

Catherine slanted a quick glance at Cody to see if

this interruption bothered him. But he didn't seem to mind the intrusion, which pleased her.

"Everyone's well," she told DJ, slowly reclaiming her hands. "Calista's getting married and I'm about to reopen the old Tattered Saddle under a new name with new old merchandise. Why don't you and your wife come by to the grand opening next Friday?" she invited him.

She'd talked her brother into putting up flyers around town, but the personal touch never hurt. The more word spread about the reopening, the better her chances were of getting more customers to come to the shop.

"We'll be sure to do that," DJ promised. "I'm sure that Allaire will find something she likes, she always does." He grinned at her. "She can be your first customer."

"I'm afraid that Cody's already beaten her to that," Catherine said with a laugh, gesturing at Cody.

When she said the name, DJ glanced toward the man sitting at the table for the first time. Recognition suddenly flashed in his eyes.

"Cody?" he repeated. He asked uncertainly, "Cody Overton?"

"Yeah, that's me," Cody replied without any sort of fanfare.

DJ made up for it for both of them. Grasping Cody's hand, he pumped it up and down enthusiastically several times.

"How the hell are you?" he cried with genuine pleasure. "I haven't seen you since—well, forever, I guess." Not content to just let it go at that, DJ did his best to try to pinpoint the time. "High school, wasn't it?"

Cody nodded. "That's about right." Debating with himself for a minute or so, he asked the question that was on his mind. "Did I hear you say something about bringing Allaire?"

Ordinarily, he didn't pry into other people's lives, but since DJ's brother Dax had gotten engaged to Allaire at the same time that he had slipped an engagement ring on Renee's finger, it made him wonder how the other couple was faring. Had DJ taken to escorting his older brother's wife around?

Nodding, DJ said, "Yes, you did. Allaire's my wife." The surprised look in Cody's eyes was impossible to miss. Explanations were apparently in order. "I guess you didn't hear. Dax and Allaire divorced. Dax got married again and he's really happy this time, so things worked out for the best for everyone," he assured his newest patron. His words echoed back at him just as he remembered hearing the news about Cody's wife's untimely death. "I never had a chance to tell you how really sorry I was to hear about Renee," he said solemnly to Cody.

"Thanks," Cody replied crisply. He really didn't want to get into that now. Not here. Actually, not anywhere. Especially not around the woman sitting opposite him at the table. He closed the topic by saying, "She would have been happy for you. She always thought you had a thing for Allaire."

DJ laughed softly, not bothering to deny what had been an open secret to everyone but his older brother. "I always said Renee was a class act." He placed a hand on Cody's shoulder. "Well, I've got to get back to mingling," he told them. "Really great seeing you again,

Cody. Order anything you like," he told them, beginning to back away. "Dinner's on me."

"Oh, no, that's all right," Catherine began to protest.

Already moving on to another table, DJ paused for just a moment longer. "One thing you're going to be learning, Catie, is that nobody argues with the owner. That's one of the perks of *being* the owner," he told her with a wink.

The next moment he was gone, absorbed by the din and the crowd.

"Well, I guess that means I still owe you a dinner out," Catherine said, leaning forward so that Cody could hear her.

"You don't owe me anything," Cody told her briskly. "You gave me that coin purse to send to Caroline, remember?"

The smile on her lips told him that she remembered, all right. "How did that work out, anyway?" Catherine asked. "Did your sister receive her gift in time?"

He remembered the call that morning and struggled to block the anger that accompanied the memory. "Yeah, it got there, all right."

He didn't sound very happy about it. Not that she expected him to do handsprings; she knew better than that. But she had seen him several notches happier on a couple of occasions.

"Something wrong with it?" she asked, wondering if the gift had met with an accident while en route or if his sister ultimately hadn't liked the purse.

"No, nothing was wrong with it." Why was she asking? He was fairly certain that he hadn't given anything away with his expression. "As a matter of fact, Caroline called this morning to thank me for it, so I guess

I should pass that thanks on to you since you were the one who insisted I take it."

"Okay, there's nothing wrong with *it,* but there *is* something wrong," Catherine insisted. "I can see it in your eyes."

No, she couldn't, he thought in protest. He always kept a tight rein on his emotions. "Just the lighting," he finally said with a shrug.

Catherine looked at him pointedly. "You know, if someone had asked me, I would have bet money that you didn't lie. I guess I would have lost that bet, huh?" There was a look of disappointment on her face.

Cody opened his mouth to protest, to insist that he wasn't lying, but the words never rose to his lips. Instead, he sighed in resignation.

He supposed there was no point in denying it any longer. "It's just that I wish she'd wake up."

He was going to have to elaborate on that one. "Come again?"

Instead, Cody just repeated what he'd just said. "I wish she'd wake up."

"About what?" she coaxed.

For an unguarded moment, anger flashed in his green eyes. "About that damned worthless piece of garbage she's married to."

Watching him intently, Catherine came to her own conclusions. For Cody to say that with such feeling... Only one of two things could have prompted those words from him.

She took a guess. "Does he abuse her?"

He laughed shortly. It was the sound of complete frustration. "She won't tell me—"

"But you suspect it." The waitress returned to refill their glasses. Catherine paused, waiting for the woman to leave again before she continued. "Why?" she pressed the second the waitress turned away. Was Cody just being overprotective or was there something concrete he was basing all this on?

"Why?" he echoed almost in contempt, but his ire was directed at the man who wasn't there. "Because every time I talk to her, Caroline sounds like she's afraid of her own shadow. She keeps her voice low, like she's afraid he'll overhear her. It's not that she's saying anything bad, I just get the feeling she's not supposed to talk to *anyone.* And she goes along with that," he lamented angrily.

Taking a breath, he continued, "She never used to be like that. She was a fighter who didn't take anything from anyone. At least—" he scrubbed his hand over his face "—she used to be like that. It's as if the bum just sucked out her soul and left this quaking shell in its wake." There was bitterness in his voice. "She called today to thank me for remembering her. She was hardly on the phone for two minutes when I heard him bellowing for her. I could almost *hear* her jump. She said she had to go and then hung up before I could say anything else to her."

That did sound like someone who was being at least mentally abused, if not physically as well.

"Well, if she were my sister and I really thought she was being abused by her husband, I'd drive up to wherever she was and *make* her come back with me until I could sort everything out—and meanwhile have the bastard arrested for domestic abuse."

The answer, coming from her, surprised him. He

studied Catherine's face for a long moment, his eyes searching hers.

She meant what she'd just said, Cody realized. She might look like she'd be easygoing, a person who just floated along with things, but she really did have more than her share of spunk—just the way he'd initially thought.

He liked that.

Liked the fact that she'd also just displayed that she had a very strong sense of family. "And that's what you'd do if it was your sister?" he asked.

She nodded with enthusiasm, then said, "Hell, I'd do it if it was *your* sister." Which brought her to another question. "You want me to go see her, talk to her for you?"

There was just no end to the surprises with this woman. And with each discovery, he found himself liking her more and more.

"You'd really do that?" he pressed.

There was no hesitation—or any bravado for that matter. Just a simple conviction. "Sure, if you think I could help. People should always be willing to help other people in trouble," she told him simply. "So," she said after a moment's pause, "do you want me to go see her, talk to her?"

"No," he said. Not that he wasn't grateful, but this was his battle to fight, not hers. "Besides, you've got a grand opening to get ready for," he reminded her. "I'll give Caroline a little longer to come around and start acting more like her old self." And then he shrugged. "Who knows, maybe I'm just overreacting. I never did like that guy," he freely admitted. And then he lowered his voice so that he was almost talking to himself. Catherine leaned in even closer. "And to be honest, I do feel a little responsible for her being with him."

There was only one interpretation as far as she could see. "You set them up when you didn't like the guy?" Catherine asked.

But even as she put the question to him, she couldn't imagine him doing anything like that.

"No, nothing like that," he said quickly. "It's just that I think she married Rory because she didn't want to be alone." He saw by the question in her eyes that he had some backtracking to do.

"Our parents were killed in a hit-and-run accident when I was eighteen. After I got married, my sister suddenly found herself all alone in a house that had once held four people. She felt abandoned, and when Rory asked her to marry him, I guess she just jumped at it, because she needed someone of her own. She thought Rory was that someone," he concluded with a deep, disgruntled sigh.

Cody usually just kept everything under wraps and part of him was really surprised that he was unloading this way to another human being. But there was just something about *this* particular human being that seemed to draw the words out of him.

"I should have insisted she come live with us. Renee thought it would be a good idea. I went along with it, but I have to admit I was a little relieved when Caroline turned the offer down. I was being selfish." When he looked up at her, Catherine could see the guilt in his eyes. "I wanted to be alone with Renee. I felt like we were still on our honeymoon and I really wanted that feeling to last."

She'd *known* there was a softer side to this man.

The fact that he could agonize over something he felt he could have done differently—rather than just shrug it off—proved it.

"You weren't being selfish," she insisted, putting her hand on top of his, unconsciously forming an unspoken bond. "You were just being a newlywed. There's nothing wrong with that." She found it touching and sensitive, but she had a feeling that if she said anything to that effect, it would only irritate him, so for the time being, she kept that part to herself.

Instead, she painted a slightly broader stroke. "The fact that you even *offered* to take your sister in shows that your heart was in the right place."

A lot of good that did Caroline now, Cody thought darkly as guilt scratched away at him. He could tell just by her tone and the things that Catherine was saying that the young woman was really trying hard to absolve him of that.

He did his best to pay her back by attempting to lighten the mood. "Are you always this Pollyannaish?" he asked her.

"Always," she told him. "I find that it helps get me through the day—and I've got a feeling that my positive attitude is going to come in real handy once I open Real Vintage Cowboy for business."

Catherine was well aware that she had a big, uphill battle before her. Most new businesses failed before the end of their first year.

She didn't intend to.

"The what?" he asked, realizing that his mind had drifted off for a second even though his eyes had been all but nailed down on one view.

Catherine.

He caught himself looking at her as if he hadn't seen her before. Was it just him or was she actually getting prettier as they sat here?

"The store," she reminded him tactfully. "Real Vintage Cowboy," she repeated. "That's the name I gave it, remember?"

"I do now," he admitted. His wince was exaggerated as he went on to ask her, "You sure you want to go with that name?"

She didn't understand why he didn't like it and she certainly wasn't about to be dissuaded from using it. She really liked the name she'd come up with. And he had been her inspiration.

"Yes, I'm sure I want to 'go with that name.' I named the store after this really grumpy cowboy I recently met," she told him, tongue in cheek. "And besides, I think it's very appropriate. They both seem to represent something that's a little old, a little new, a little reliable, a little unpredictable." Catherine was looking at him pointedly as she went over the various diametrically opposing traits she'd witnessed him display.

"You get all that out of a single name, huh?" he marveled with an echo of a laugh punctuating his question.

Catherine nodded. "Yup. Pretty good, don't you think?"

"Haven't given it that much thought," he lied. "I just think it's a mouthful, that's all."

She leaned her head on her upturned palm and asked, "Okay, I'll bite. What would *you* call it?"

He thought for a second, then said, "The Place."

She waited for more. There wasn't any. "'The Place'? That's it?" she asked, stunned.

He didn't see the problem. "Yeah. I figure that's enough."

Catherine shook her head. "Good thing it's my store and not yours" She laughed softly. The look in her eyes reinforced the sound.

It took Cody more than a couple of seconds to rouse himself before he could go back to eating his dinner. Not that there was much room left in his stomach, not after it had all but tightened into a knot the way it had just now.

Chapter Eight

All through dinner, Catherine had been trying to find a way to broach the subject that DJ had inadvertently introduced when he'd stopped by earlier. But here she was, more than halfway finished with the meal and the question still sat there in her mind like an impenetrable fortress that had no visible point of access.

Finally, she decided that if she wanted to know anything, she was just going to have to leap into the center of it like a paratrooper jumping out of an airplane.

"Renee was your wife?"

She kept her tone mild, upbeat. Even so, she saw Cody's shoulders instantly become rigid. When he raised his head to look at her, she found that she was looking into the eyes of a man who had completely closed himself off again.

Well, you started this. Get on with it, Catherine silently ordered herself. *There's no turning back for you anymore.*

"Yes." The single word sounded heavy with emotion, as if he was telling her that if she continued down this path, it was at her own risk.

Catherine pushed onward. She pressed her lips together, summoning courage and hoping that her words didn't wind up reopening any wounds.

"DJ said he was sorry about what happened." Her throat almost felt as if it was raw as she quietly asked the key question that had been preying on her mind, "What did happen?"

His face was utterly expressionless as he answered, "Renee died."

Catherine's breath immediately evaporated from her lungs. She wasn't exactly sure what she'd expected Cody to say. Something along the lines, she realized, that the woman, unable to put up with his sullenness any longer, had left him.

This put an entirely new spin on the matter.

She could feel her heart quickening as it overflowed with sympathy. "Oh—"

He'd heard that sound before, that sharp intake of breath that occurred before the woman who'd uttered the single word suddenly launched into an emotion-dripping speech aimed at helping him heal—and at obtaining his undying gratitude and loyalty in the process.

Ain't gonna happen, he thought with a vengeance.

Served him right for thinking that Catherine was different from the others.

Cody cut her off before Catherine could say anything further. His eyes narrowed as he asked, "You're not going to turn into one of those women who feels sorry for 'the poor helpless widower,' are you?"

Catherine could almost hear the sneer in his voice. "Well, I *am* sorry for your loss and for the grief you've obviously gone through," she told him.

She saw that Cody had moved back his chair and realized that he was getting up to leave. She talked faster, hoping to get him to change his mind with her words. It was all she had since she had no intentions of attempting to hog-tie him or throw herself in his path, blocking his exit.

"But I hardly see you as a 'helpless' anything. You're obviously fending for yourself. You've got that ranch of yours where I hear that you're making a decent living training quarter horses."

Almost against his will, Cody lowered himself back down onto his chair, then moved it back until his legs were squarely under the table again. But he wasn't completely settled in.

Yet.

His eyes narrowed again as he studied her. "How do you know I train quarter horses?" he asked. "Or that I even have a ranch, much less that I'm making—how did you put it—a 'decent living' at it?"

"Word gets around," Catherine told him matter-of-factly.

Especially if you ask, she added silently. She'd had her older brother, Craig, find out a few basic things about Cody for her, which he did just to make sure that she was safe around "this character," as he referred to Cody.

But Cody didn't need to know that part—especially since, she had a feeling, it would probably make him withdraw into whatever shell he was in the habit of residing in. The Cody Craig had told her about wasn't generally regarded as a "social" creature.

Cody pinned her with a long, penetrating look. She met it head-on, her chin raised stubbornly. She was waiting for him to *say* something.

"People don't spend time talking about me." He all but growled out the words.

"You'd be surprised," she countered cheerfully. "This is a small town. Not a heck of a whole lot to talk about *except* the people who come and go here. And you," she elaborated, "are tall—*really* tall—and you might not be 'dark,' but you do have this brooding air about you. That makes you just perfect for speculation and gossip from some people's point of view."

He resented people poking into his life, invading his privacy, but he supposed she did have a point. There were times when it seemed like gossip was the main thing that was produced in Thunder Canyon.

"Then you knew about Renee," he assumed out loud. And if she had, it suddenly occurred to him, why was she asking questions?

"No, I didn't," she maintained. "I wouldn't have asked you if I did. I don't go around inflicting pain on people, and I can see now that this talking about your late wife causes you a great deal of pain. I'm sorry, I didn't mean to open any old wounds."

He didn't like being seen as vulnerable—even when he was.

Unconsciously squaring his shoulders, he lowered his eyes to his meal, but he addressed the question Catherine had asked earlier and answered it more fully. "Renee came down with cancer. Fought it like a champion, but in the end, the damn disease won." There was a defiant look in his eyes when he raised them to hers again. "Anything else you want to know?"

"Yes," she answered. Then, as he visibly braced himself to be ready for whatever unintentionally painful question came out of her mouth, Catherine—an extremely serious expression on her face—asked, "You going to eat those?" She pointed to the fries he seemed to have abandoned on his plate as he'd turned his attention to the ribs he'd ordered.

"Yes, I am," he informed her. And then the formal tone he'd adopted slipped away as he added, "But I'll share 'em with you."

Catherine grinned. "Can't ask for anything more than that."

There was a challenge in the look he gave her. "Sure you can. Women always do."

"Maybe you haven't known enough women," she suggested.

"Maybe," he conceded.

Cody had to admit that he liked the way she held her ground and wasn't cowed or scared off by his somber reaction. He especially liked that her eyes hadn't filled with overwhelming pity when she'd heard about Renee. Maybe she really wasn't one of those women who felt they had an absolute obligation to fix every man they deemed was broken.

That alone made Catherine Clifton pretty unique in his book.

"You're right," he told her after several beats had gone by.

She waited until several more beats had slipped away. When Cody didn't elaborate on his initial statement, she felt that this time she was within her rights to press him.

"Right about what?"

He nodded at the spareribs on his plate, or rather at just the bare ribs since that was all that was left. "This *is* good. *Was* good," he amended.

"Never heard of anyone walking out of here dissatisfied," she told him, obviously pleased that he had decided to be straightforward with her and rescind his initial skepticism. There were men, she knew, who would rather go to their grave than to tell a woman that she was right and they were wrong.

She wasn't exactly sure why it pleased her so much that Cody didn't fall into that category, but it did.

"I guess DJ's doing well for himself," Cody commented after a bit.

She couldn't tell if Cody was envious of the younger man or not, then decided that the man she was getting to know wasn't the sort to harbor emotions such as jealousy or even envy. He seemed to be above that kind of petty behavior.

"He doesn't have any complaints," she answered. "But I think he counts himself luckier that he has Allaire in his life."

The moment she said it, Catherine immediately clamped her lips together. Because she knew that nothing meant as much to DJ as his wife, what she'd just said had come out without any hesitation. But once her words echoed back to her, Catherine realized that it had to seem to him that she was rubbing salt into his wounds.

"I'm sorry," she apologized haltingly, not sure how

to phrase this or even if she should just keep quiet altogether. "I shouldn't have said that."

"Why not?" Cody wanted to know. "It's true, isn't it?"

That wasn't the point. The point was that she'd accidentally seemed callous. "Yes, but—"

"If it's true, then there is no 'but.' What, you're afraid that what you just said will set off a fresh wave of pain in my gut?" he wanted to know. The laugh that emerged from his lips was harsh, without a single trace of humor in it. "I don't need to have to hear someone saying something for that to happen. The pain's there all the time, but I'm doing my damndest to finally make my peace with it."

"Well, I wasn't exactly helping the process—" she began before becoming bogged down in her apology. She wasn't really sure where to go from here.

He looked at her for another very long moment. So long that it seemed almost endless to her, but she didn't flinch, didn't look away. And then he finally spoke. "Oh, I don't know. Maybe you were. You certainly thought you were, bringing me out here."

She wasn't trying to be underhanded, she thought defensively. "I brought you out here just to say thank you," she reminded him.

"For that, all you had to do was just move your lips, not drive all the way over here." Then, because it did sound to him as if he was complaining, Cody amended his statement by saying, "But, to be fair, this did turn out to be a much nicer experience than I thought it was going to be."

Was that actually a compliment? Catherine looked

at the source of her inspiration uncertainly. "Just what was it that you were expecting?"

He lifted one shoulder in a vague half shrug. "Mediocre food at best and awkwardness."

Catherine couldn't help laughing. "Well, you certainly are honest."

He appeared surprised by the assessment and by the fact that his being that way would have caught this deceptively easygoing woman off guard. He was beginning to realize that she was pretty damn sharp.

"No point in being anything else," he told her matter-of-factly. Finished, he wiped his lips with his napkin then looked down thoughtfully at his plate. "You know, maybe I will have seconds."

Although he saw it quite by accident as he was looking around for their waitress, Cody caught the pleased look in Catherine's eyes. Caught it and found himself responding to it in ways he would have *sworn* on a stack of Bibles were all behind him.

Part of him thought he'd made a mistake when he'd changed his mind about leaving earlier. The part that was warming up, though, felt he would have made the mistake if he *had* picked up and left.

Right now, it was a toss-up which part was actually right.

The rest of the evening turned out to be even more fun than he'd thought possible. And it all had to do with something he'd told himself he no longer felt up to doing: socializing.

Several people he hadn't even given a thought to in the last eight years stopped by their table to greet him, exchange a few words and express their pleasure at seeing him "out and about again," something that had last occurred just before Renee had been diagnosed with cancer.

While he had never been one to crave company and had been more than content when it had been just Renee and him tucked away on his ranch, Cody'd found that interacting with some of their neighbors and Renee's friends had amounted to a fairly pleasant experience whenever it occurred.

In large measure, he'd done it for Renee because he knew that it pleased her to mingle like this. The same way it pleased her to help others whenever she could. It was just the kind of woman she was.

Selfless.

Being here with Catherine now brought all that back to him. But rather than overwhelm him with waves of unbearable sorrow, it seemed to pull him toward the present and away from the past.

And ever so slowly, it was beginning to make him feel that maybe, just maybe, there actually was a future for him after all.

Maybe it was a stretch to admit this, but if he was being honest—with himself if with no one else—he'd have to say that he was really enjoying this effervescent woman's company.

He was even enjoying listening to her share her plans for the shop with him. In a way, it was like listening to a child anticipating a visit from that iconic jolly old elf, Santa Claus.

Though Cody was fairly certain that this woman probably *wasn't* really as innocent as she seemed, Catherine did display an innocent, almost childlike exuberance when she talked about making a success of the shop she'd bought. He realized that she was really committed to that.

He caught himself thinking that he could listen to her talk about the shop for hours.

Which was, more or less, what he wound up doing.

As if suddenly becoming aware that she'd had gone on and on, dragging Cody into all her plans and hopes, Catherine's narrative came to an abrupt halt as she cried, "I've talked your ears off."

After they'd finally left the restaurant, Cody and she had driven back to the shop and then had gone on a long, leisurely stroll—to "walk off the calories."

At least that was the way that Catherine had put it, but he had a hunch that if those calories were actually falling away, they were doing so in what felt like complete slow motion.

The lengthy stroll came to an end right before the shop. It was where she'd decided to crash tonight in order to get an early start in the morning. When Catherine had bought the boarded-up store, she'd realized that there were two inhabitable floors directly above the ground floor. She'd decided to retain the second floor for herself, creating an office and a place to crash when she needed to. The third floor she wound up renting out to a woman who was working at the Gallatin Room as a part-time waitress/bartender.

In response to her protest that she'd talked his ears off, Cody quietly made a solemn show of touching first one ear, then the other.

"Nope," he deadpanned. "You didn't talk them off. Looks like they're both still there."

Her eyes widened as if she'd just been privy to a huge revelation. And in a way, she was.

"You've got a sense of humor," she cried in delighted surprise, then smiled. "That's a really good thing to know for future reference."

He didn't see why, but he had a feeling that asking might get him even more deeply embroiled in a scenario he didn't understand. Instead, he merely shrugged carelessly. "Didn't know that my having or not having a sense of humor was a point of concern."

"It's just better to have one than not have one," Catherine told him. She really couldn't relate to someone who didn't have a sense of humor. "Well, I'm really glad you let me drag you out," she said, putting out her hand to him.

Saying that was her way of letting Cody maintain his solemn facade. In her heart she knew that if Cody hadn't wanted to come along, not even dynamite would have compelled him to go out to DJ's.

Her smile widened as she fixed it on Cody. "I had a great time."

He inclined his head, covering her slender hand with his own. "Yeah, it wasn't bad," he conceded.

Emulating a heroine in a melodrama, Catherine placed the back of her free hand to her forehead, like a woman subject to "vapors."

"Please, such heady praise. I'm not sure I can handle it." And then the sound of her laughter—light and melodic—filled the still night air like silver bells. "Don't forget, I'm counting on you being there at the grand opening next week," she said, wanting to remind him before he left.

"I'll be there," Cody promised.

Okay, this was the part, he told himself, where he slipped his hand from hers and walked off to his truck.

The only problem was, his hand wasn't slipping from hers. He was still holding it, still looking down into her mesmerizing, upturned brown eyes.

Still feeling all sorts of things going on in the pit of his stomach. Things that had nothing to do with the meal he'd just had and everything to do with the woman he'd had it with.

Before he knew it, rather than releasing her hand and turning away to walk to his vehicle, Cody found that he'd pulled Catherine *to* him.

When he finally let go of her hand, it was because he needed both of his to frame her face.

His heart was suddenly doing a fair imitation of a race car's engine. He felt it launch into triple time as he anticipated what he knew was coming next.

With his breath lodged in his throat, Cody felt like some damn teenager. Even so, he framed Catherine's face between his hands, inclined his head more than a little in order to reach her lips—and then he kissed her.

A second later, all hell suddenly broke loose, threatening the stability of the immediate world.

It certainly threatened his.

Chapter Nine

What the hell was he doing? Had he completely lost his mind?

Faintly whispered questions involving the condition of his sanity assaulted Cody from all sides as the kiss that had surprised him just as much as it did the woman who was on the receiving end of it deepened and grew in intensity.

Cody had no answers to those questions, nor could he spare the energy to formulate any. Every molecule in his body was entirely focused was on what was happening right at this moment.

The longer he kissed Catherine, the greater his *need* to kiss her became until Cody felt as if he was being pulled into some bottomless vortex where the only thing that truly mattered was this woman and the feeling generated between them.

Cody dropped his hands from her face and used

them to draw her closer to him. So close that it seemed as if they were melding into one another, two halves of a very unique whole.

He really wasn't sure where he left off and Catherine began.

It didn't matter.

Damn, but she made his blood rush and his head spin. Not only that, but he was fairly certain that there was very little air left in his lungs. That, too, didn't matter.

Nothing mattered but this moment, this feeling. This woman.

Caught completely off guard, there wasn't even half a second to spare for surprise to register. What *did* register was pleasure. Absolutely, profound, exquisite pleasure.

Catherine had had her suspicions that this loner of a cowboy could make her blood heat to almost boiling and now she knew that she'd been right.

But this wasn't the time for any triumphant feelings or even the time to think.

Because she couldn't.

Couldn't, she was fairly certain, even answer the simplest of questions because her brain had just short-circuited in the intense heat that had flashed through her like a raw current from a lightning bolt. All she really knew was that she was grateful Cody was holding her as closely as he was because she was sure that her entire body had taken on the composition of a liquid.

More specifically, the composition of molten lava.

Cody knew he had to step back and step back *now* because even five more seconds like this and the whole situation would be completely out of his hands and *way* out of control.

Even now, all he really wanted to do was take Catherine inside her store and make love to her until they were both light years beyond exhausted.

But there would be consequences if he did that. Consequences he wasn't sure he was ready to deal with.

So, with more effort than he'd thought would be necessary, more effort than he'd ever had to employ with anyone before, Cody forced himself to pull back.

Even after he did, his heart continued slamming against his rib cage like a newly incarcerated prisoner trying to break free of the iron bars he found looming before him.

Hell.

He could still taste Catherine on his lips. The temptation to take her back into his arms was damn near overwhelming.

Cody looked down into her dazed, upturned face. His breathing had yet to return to normal. "If you're waiting for me to say I'm sorry, you've got a long wait ahead of you," he warned.

Catherine moved her head from side to side—slowly so as not to fall over. "I don't want you to say you're sorry," she whispered.

He took in a deep breath, nodding his approval even though he was uncertain exactly what it was he was approving. Right now, confusion ruled and he wasn't even sure which direction was up and which was down.

Kissing her had turned his world on its ear.

"Good," he finally declared. He pulled his Stetson down farther until the brim all but obscured his eyebrows and hid his eyes. "'Cause I don't know why the hell I just did that, but I know I'm not sorry that I did," he emphasized.

And then, just like that, Cody turned on his heel and went back to his vehicle.

Catherine stood exactly where she was, watching the truck as it grew smaller and smaller before disappearing around the corner.

The crisp September air had a definite chill in it, whispering of winter's nearness. She didn't feel it. At this very moment, she was aware of being extremely hot to the point that had she been dressed in shorts and a tank top, she would have still been radiating heat from every pore in her body.

Catherine did her best to think, to review the events as they had transpired, and found that she was going to have to delay that until a later time. Her brain had temporarily ceased functioning and gave no indication that it was about to kick in again.

At least not for a while.

Hugging her shawl to her, Catherine went inside the shop, encased in the moment and a contentment she'd never experienced before.

Her mouth curved. It looked like her vintage cowboy was certainly full of surprises.

"Anything I can do to help?"

The deep voice rumbled into her consciousness, making her jump. Catherine looked in the direction of the voice—although there was really no need to. She knew who was asking the question because the sound of his voice had hardly left her head these last few days.

Cody had been on her mind and in her dreams ever

since that life-altering kiss in front of her shop the other evening.

She'd tried to busy herself with plans and bury herself in work that was all targeted for her grand opening. But even that wasn't enough to drown out his presence.

Catherine was beginning to doubt that anything was.

"Help?" Catherine repeated the word as if it was completely foreign to her.

"Yeah. To get ready for that grand opening, or reopening, you're holding for this store." He could see how much making the store a success seemed to mean to her and if that was what made her happy, then he wanted to ensure that the grand opening was going to be the success that she was hoping for. "Thought you might need an extra hand or two," he added as an afterthought.

Just then, the door to the rear storage area opened and three people came in, two young women and a man, all of them looking enough like one another—and Catherine—to make him realize that they had to be related.

Seeing all of them here made him feel slightly out of place, so he lifted a shoulder in a vague, dismissive shrug.

"Or not," he tossed in. "Looks to me like you've already got enough hands."

He was going to leave, Catherine realized in alarm. Without thinking, she grabbed hold of his arm, her survival instincts kicking in before she could stop herself with any logical thought process.

"Never enough hands," she told him, recovering. And then she smiled up at Cody. "I could use you for some of the heavy lifting." It was the first thing that came to her mind and she felt that it might appeal to the machismo in him.

Cody arched one very quizzical eyebrow as he looked at her. Almost everything around them in the shop looked as if it weighed at least a ton. He was strong, but he wasn't *that* strong.

"Just what is it that you want lifted?" he asked suspiciously.

"Moved actually," she amended, pointing to an armoire that she'd spent hours working on in order to return it to its original shine. "I thought that might look better against the far wall."

Cody regarded the heavy piece of furniture. "I don't know. I think it might get more attention out in the open right where it is. The customers can't help but see it when they walk in," he added for good measure.

"Okay." Catherine nodded, considering his argument. "I'm open to advice. If you think it'll be noticed faster this way," she allowed, "then we'll keep it right where it is." She flashed a grin at him, guessing what he was probably thinking. "Don't worry, I've got smaller things to move."

"Never doubted that you did," he quipped. "Just point them out and tell me where you want them."

"Where do you want us?" Craig asked. He glanced at his watch. C.C. and Cecilia had dragged him here to give Catherine moral support. "I don't have that much time to give."

"So you've said four or five times already," C.C. cracked.

"But who's counting," Cecilia, ever the peacemaker, chimed in. She made sure to suppress the grin that wanted to rise to her lips.

"I've got another batch of flyers," Catherine said, reaching underneath the counter.

After pulling them out she stacked the pile beside the old-fashioned cash register she'd dug up after an extensive search. She wanted to be able to ring up sales on something that was in keeping with the general motif of the shop.

"Of course you do," C.C. murmured, offering her older sister a tolerant smile.

Catherine divided the flyers into three equal batches, then handed a stack to each of her siblings. "Put them up wherever you see an empty space," she instructed.

Cecilia looked at the flyers she had in her arms. "You mean there's actually wall space left that doesn't have one of these things pasted on it?" She'd already been recruited to hang up flyers earlier in the week.

"Lots of places," Catherine assured her sister. Then, in case one of them wanted to challenge her statement, she added, "I checked."

"Well then, let's get to it, shall we?" Cecilia proposed to her younger sister and older brother, tongue in cheek. She paused to salute Catherine, then left the shop with C.C., ready to post flyers wherever she found an open spot.

Craig was a little slower in his follow-through. Instead, he carefully scrutinized the man his sister had asked him to look into.

The man had to represent her newest project, Craig decided. Once a caregiver, always a caregiver, he thought. And from what she'd had him find out about Cody Overton, the man was a project that would keep her busy for quite some time to come. He hadn't had the easiest life and it had made him distant and reclusive.

Catherine, he had a hunch, was going to try to change that.

"You're not giving a batch to your friend?" Craig asked, nodding at Cody.

"I've got other plans for him," Catherine told him, sparing Cody a quick, decisive glance.

I just bet you do, Craig thought.

But out loud he made no quip, saying instead, "Then I guess I'd better get going." He glanced in Cody's direction. He was still undecided whether he liked what he saw or not. As the oldest, he felt responsible for all his sisters.

"See you around," Craig said to his sister's project. With that, Craig, armed with an armload of fliers, made his way to the front door and left.

Cody took off his hat, laying it carefully on the counter, then rolled up his sleeves one at a time. "What did you have in mind?" he asked, nodding toward the furnishings.

Catherine pointed out a group of bookcases she'd picked up at an estate sale. She had painted them an antique white when the initial old color had defied restoration.

"I'd like those all brought over there." She pointed to a spot that could easily be viewed through the front window.

As Cody moved the bookcases one by one, she debated whether or not to say anything. But after a moment, she decided that her truthfulness was an asset in this case. She had a feeling Cody could spot a phony—even a well-intentioned phony—the proverbial mile away. "I wasn't sure if I'd see you here again."

Cody stopped moving the bookcase and looked at

her, surprised by her admission and that she'd thought it in the first place. After all, they weren't exactly sophomores in high school anymore.

At this point, he was beginning to doubt that he had ever been that young.

"You mean after I kissed you the other night?" he asked.

When he said it out loud like that, it sounded pretty foolish. But she'd started this, so she had no choice but to answer him.

"Well, yes," she admitted.

He couldn't read her expression. It had been a long time since he'd felt the need to try to second-guess what another person—a woman, specifically—was thinking. He'd gotten rusty at it and for once, Catherine's face was not completely animated.

Maybe he made her uncomfortable, Cody thought. "You want me to leave?"

No! But she knew she couldn't say that, at least, not with the kind of emphasis that had just echoed through her head. It might make him feel hemmed in or smothered. God, but men were so hard to read.

So instead, she forced herself to ask a question. "Do you want to?"

"It's not about me," he said pointedly. "It's about you. What *you* want. So, do you want me to go?" he asked again.

Her mother had always said that a lady never allows her true feelings for a man to show completely, especially not at the outset. Her mother said that it made a woman look too needy, too accessible, and she lost the air of mystery that was her main bargaining chip.

But all those rules, it seemed to Catherine, were for

games and she didn't think that something as important as a person's feelings should be treated as some sort of game.

So, drawing her courage to her—and desperately trying to still her nerves—Catherine answered Cody truthfully. "No, I don't. As a matter of fact, I was afraid that you wouldn't come back at all, not even for Real Vintage Cowboy's grand opening."

"Why would you think that?" he wanted to know. He was really trying to understand her reasoning. "Was the kiss really that bad?"

"No," she whispered, afraid that if she spoke any louder, her voice might quake and give her away. "It was that good."

Cody stared at her as he took the news in. He wanted to kiss her again. Nothing else had occupied his thoughts since he'd walked away and left her on the doorstep that night.

The pragmatic side of him had wanted to kiss her again to make certain that what he'd experienced wasn't just a fluke. The free-spirited side of him had wanted to kiss Catherine again just to kiss her again.

He smiled then. One of his rare, starting in the middle and radiating out to all corners smiles that instantly warmed her and went on to warm the room around her as well.

Instead of saying anything, Cody touched her chin with the tip of his finger and raised it just a little, tilting her head back.

And then he brushed his lips over hers.

At first lightly, then again, and again, each time with more intensity, more fervor than the last until the kiss from the other evening was revisited in its full intensity.

She was sinking again—and it was exhilarating, she couldn't help thinking, grasping on to Cody's arms to anchor herself as well as to give herself leverage. Leverage she needed in order to rise up on her toes and absorb even more of the kiss than she had the first time around.

Slowly, as Catherine found herself falling into the kiss completely, she moved her hands up until they were around Cody's neck. Her heart pounding, she held on for dear life.

"Is that some new way to move furniture that I don't know about?"

The deep voice splintered the moment.

Her heart pounding madly, Catherine pulled away from Cody to see that her brother had returned and was standing there looking at them.

Pushing both her embarrassment and her annoyance over Craig turning up like this aside, Catherine finally found her voice and said, "It's a new technique we're trying out."

Cody felt the corners of his mouth curving in amusement. Who knew the woman could be a feisty little hellcat to this degree?

He was finding more and more about her to like each time he was around her.

"How's that working out for you?" Craig deadpanned.

"Just fine, thanks for asking." Catherine redirected the line of questioning to focus on him, not on her or Cody. "What are you doing back so soon? You couldn't have distributed all those flyers already." She looked pointedly at the stack of posters he was holding in his hand.

"Sharp as a tack, this one," Craig commented to

Cody before answering her question. "I forgot my tape." He picked up a roll from the counter and deliberately held it up for her inspection as if it was exhibit A in a trial. "I'll be on my way now," he announced. "So you two can get back to trying out your new 'technique' again."

And with that, Craig left the shop for a second time, closing the door behind him.

Humor echoed in Cody's voice as he said, "Think I might get to like him," just before he pulled her back into his arms.

Catherine never got a chance to comment on his assessment of her brother. Cody's mouth had found hers again with no trouble at all.

The rest was a blur.

Chapter Ten

Without meaning to, Cody had upended her life to such a degree that it became increasingly difficult for her to focus on anything else except for the man who had inspired her shop's new name.

Still, she *did* have a lot of work left to do and the work was not about to do itself. There was a deadline breathing down her neck. The flyers were out and the grand opening of Real Vintage Cowboy was set for Friday at two, so the shop absolutely, positively had to be ready by then.

That meant that there was still an overwhelming amount of work get done.

She had endless checklists connected to that goal running through her head, and at times, Catherine felt as if she was going in four different directions all at the same time. Each time she started doing one thing, she thought of something else she needed to attend to, another estate sale she wanted to monitor on her laptop, another piece she thought could be improved upon, et cetera.

Consequently, she found herself doing six things at once, completing none because yet *another* thing demanded her attention.

Catherine began to feel as if she was wearing out from the inside out.

Cody put in as much time as he could spare away from his ranch and the quarter horses he was training. He was lucky in that the two ranch hands who worked for him had been with him since the beginning and knew the routine that was involved as well as he did.

For the first time since Renee's passing, he found himself actually wanting to leave the ranch rather than using any excuse to hide there. Things, he thought, were definitely changing for him.

And Catherine was the reason behind the change.

Watching her move quickly about the shop brought to mind the image of a propelled ball bearing that had been released in an old-fashioned pinball machine. He shook his head, growing exhausted by proxy.

"You might want to just finish one thing at a time," he finally suggested.

"I would if I could, but there's always something else I realize I've forgotten to do," Catherine told him as she raced by Cody on her way to the storage room.

When Cody suddenly blocked her path and took hold of her shoulders, she came to a skidding, abrupt halt. Confused, the look she shot at Cody was ripe with impatience.

Was he trying to make some kind of point?

Now?

"What?" she bit off, then flushed because she realized that she must have sounded like some kind of a shrew. "What?" she repeated, saying the word a little more softly. In both cases, however, her impatience all but vibrated through the word. She didn't have time for this. She still had eight hundred and ninety-seven things to do before Friday, or at least that was the way it felt to her.

"Slow down a little," he advised in the same tone he used to gentle an agitated horse.

Easy for him to say. His success or failure wasn't riding on how well the shop was initially received. She was up against the specter of the previous shop and its far-from-liked owner.

"I *can't,"* Catherine insisted, trying to shrug him off. To her surprise, he didn't remove his hands but kept them—and her—right where they were.

"Slow down," he repeated a bit more firmly. "Otherwise you'll wear yourself completely out before you officially open your doors to the paying public. Then all this work will be for nothing." His eyes held hers, all but hypnotizing her. "Breathe, Catherine, breathe," he instructed.

When she finally did as he instructed, taking a breath in then slowly exhaling it, she never took her eyes off him.

Cody knew defiance when he saw it.

The smallest hint of a smile curved his lips. "That's it, in and out. Good." He slipped his hands from her shoulders, but his eyes continued to hold her in place. "The shop doesn't have to be perfect, you know. *Nothing's* perfect," he underscored.

"I don't want it to be perfect," Catherine protested.

She gestured around the shop helplessly. "I just want it to be…"

"Perfect," he supplied knowingly. "People don't like perfect, Catherine," he told her. "It makes them feel even more imperfect than they already are."

Catherine looked at him for a long moment, clearly surprised. And amused. "I had no idea you were a philosopher, Cody," she said. Maybe she should have called the shop The Philosophical Cowboy, she mused.

Cody inclined his head, amused at her assessment. *You don't know the half of it, Cate.*

"Hell," he said out loud. "I'm a lot of things when I have to be."

Only after a beat had passed did she decide that Cody was just pulling her leg.

Or was he?

Now that she thought of it, a little homespun philosophy actually seemed to be right up his alley.

"How about if I just shoot for clean and presentable?" she suggested, waiting to see what he'd say.

Cody nodded, then qualified his response. "As long as you don't wear yourself out. Okay, I'm finished with this," he said, indicating the large, dapple gray horse that had once been attached to a carousel. Working on it had brought back memories, but none that stopped him in his tracks. He supposed that meant he was making progress. "What's next?" he asked gamely.

"Next," C.C. announced, walking into the shop with a bag that had a wonderful aroma emanating from it, "you stop what you're doing and eat your lunch." Nodding a greeting at Cody, C.C. held the bag she'd brought up to her sister. "You'll find a little of everything in there including a hot pastrami sandwich that tantalizingly announces itself way before you even open the bag and look inside," C.C. cheerfully continued, her sweeping glance taking in both her older sister and the cowboy who had become more or less a fixture in the shop for the last few days.

Catherine frowned. She really didn't have the time to stop and eat right now. "You make this hard to ignore, C.C.."

Her sister smiled broadly. "That, dear sister, is the whole point." She addressed her next words to Cody, issuing a command brightly. "If she doesn't stop to eat, sit on her."

"Will do," Cody promised.

Her errand of mercy over, C.C. left the shop, convinced that Cody would look out for her sister. Cody looked at Catherine expectantly. "You heard the lady."

She had no intention of being ordered around—or intimidated—by her younger sister. "That's not a lady, that's my sister. My *younger* sister," she emphasized as if that made her argument for her.

Cody shrugged. "Younger or older, doesn't matter. What does matter was that she was making sense." Opening the brown bag, he took out the aromatic sandwich and unwrapped the first third. "You need to eat to keep your strength up."

"My strength is just fine," she informed him crisply, determined to ignore both him and the sandwich he was brandishing as she turned her attention to yet another item she'd added to the shop's inventory. This was an extremely fancy saddle that was said to have once belonged to Teddy Roosevelt back in his Rough Rider days, years before he became the country's president.

Not to be put off, Cody warned her, "I'll feed you if I have to."

Armed with the partially unwrapped sandwich, he took a step forward, then another, forcing Catherine to take the same amount of steps backward. Before she knew it, Cody had backed her up against the wall and was using his long, lean body to bracket her in place.

Suddenly, she had no room to move. "Cody, what are you doing?" she protested.

"You must have been without food even longer than I thought if you can't figure it out." Then, in case she was unclear on his intent, he told her, "I'm feeding you for your own good."

She refused to be bullied by either her sister *or* him. "No, you're n—"

The rest of her protest went unsaid because she suddenly found herself confronted with the sandwich that C.C. had left with Cody. Not just confronted with it but her lips were now smack-dab up against it with no leeway to move to the left or to the right. Catherine had no choice but to take a bite or be faced with eventual death by sandwich.

Grudgingly, she chose life.

"There now, that wasn't so hard, now was it?" Cody asked, using the same tone he might have taken with a particularly stubborn five-year-old.

Holding up her hands in the universal sign of surrender, Catherine managed to get a temporary reprieve from her meal.

"Okay, okay," she cried. "I'll eat the sandwich. You can stop force-feeding me. You know, I didn't take you for the nurturing type," she said. There was a slight accusing note evident in her voice.

An enigmatic smile creased his lips. "Like I said, you'd be surprised. I'm not the one-dimensional cowboy you seem to think I am," Cody told her.

Although, in her defense, he added silently, he'd been coming across that way for a while now. Eight years to be exact. But all that was behind him. Right now, he felt as if he'd just woken up from a long, long sleep. Just like the fictional Rip Van Winkle. Woke up to a whole new world around him. Woke up with a desire to *explore* that new world.

"I never thought you were one-dimensional," she protested, then added, "just maybe not all that articulate. But if I insulted you, I'm sorry." That had never even crossed her mind. The last thing she wanted was to make him feel belittled by her.

Cody inclined his head. "Apology accepted," he said mildly. Then he pointed out, "You've stopped eating."

"Only for a second," she quickly countered. "I was taught never to talk with my mouth full."

There was a simple solution to that. "Then don't talk, eat. I'll work, you chew," he told her, assigning a new, albeit temporary division of labor. "That should work for you."

What worked for her, Catherine realized with a silent mental jolt, was Cody. Having him around made her blood rush a little faster, her heart beat a little harder. It energized her and, she had to admit, really scared her at the same time.

She'd told herself that it was this venture that scared her, that made her act as nervous as a cat on a hot tin roof, but she was beginning to realize that her nerves concerning opening the store were actually hiding the bigger, real cause for her internal unrest. She'd found herself in uncharted territory. What was unfolding between Cody and her was something she had never experienced before, especially not to this degree of intensity.

She wanted him.

Badly.

And that both excited her and frightened her to the very brink of near paralysis.

But this was no time to suddenly become immobile. There was much too much to do. She couldn't allow herself the luxury of wallowing in her feelings and thinking rather than doing.

"You're not chewing," Cody noted, his serious tone prodding her on. "I can always take over feeding you again."

Even that had her blood heating. Which in turn sent a pink hue to her face she neither wanted nor liked. Embarrassed, she snapped, "I'm eating, I'm eating."

Cody nodded his approval, managing to get under her skin yet again. "Atta girl," he said, turning his attention back to work.

She mumbled something unintelligible in response. He didn't ask her to repeat it. He had a feeling it was better that way all around.

She'd both dreaded and anticipated this moment. And now, here it was. The moment when she threw open her doors, officially declaring the shop, Real Vintage Cowboy, to be open for business.

The second she opened the doors, the people who had been waiting outside like groupies at a rock concert gate poured in.

Granted the first wave had only ten people in total, but the second those people crossed the threshold, they instantly transformed into ten customers, customers looking to buy something unique to take home with them.

Catherine had gone to great lengths to keep prices on the low side, allowing more people to be able to make purchases. Going this route, it would take her a while to finally turn a profit and get ahead, but if the prices started out being prohibitively high, then she would never be able to get the shop out of the red and finally into the black. And that, after all was said and done, was her ultimate goal.

In next to no time at all, it began to feel as if she was everywhere at once, talking to one group of people, directing another to the food that she'd been up all night preparing, exchanging more words with yet another cluster of friends, family and curious strangers.

Catherine knew she was running on pure adrenaline and at least for now, she was going strong. And each time she rung up a sale, she felt as if she was becoming a little stronger.

It was going very, very well.

Midway through the evening, Catherine forced herself to stand back and take the entire scene in. Her shop was crowded with well-wishers who were doing double duty as the shop's customers as well. She was pleased to note that she had sold more than a token number of items, including the armoire that she'd thought no one would be interested in buying.

At this point, she'd sold enough to make her believe that she had made the right decision when she'd bought the old antique store. Impressed with what he saw of her inventory, her cousin Grant, who managed the Thunder Canyon Resort, had promised to feature some of her merchandise in the hotel gift shop.

It was all starting to fall into place, Catherine thought, pleased and, more than that, greatly relieved.

It seemed that everyone she had ever known had made the effort and shown up at the shop's grand opening. They were now all milling about, examining everything from trendy knickknacks to the paintings she'd hung up on the wall to the original antique furniture that had, along with the shop, passed into her hands when she'd paid the asking price.

Someone, she'd noted with no small pleasure, had actually bought the old-fashioned sewing machine she'd pulled out of the storage room. She'd worked hard to polish the faded black metal until it all but gleamed seductively at one and all who passed by.

And now it had a new home. She felt rather proud of that. She hoped that the machine's new owner would treat it with patience and love. And remember that it worked strictly by man power. That meant pumping the foot pedal rhythmically in order to get the machine to sew. In effect it was almost a unilateral tap dance.

It turned out that the buyer's great-great-grandmother had been a seamstress in a factory from the age of fourteen until her eyesight failed her at seventy. The woman was long gone, but the man had bought the machine to remind him of his roots.

Each piece Catherine sold had a story to tell. But in this case, the story had belonged to the buyer, not the item that was sold.

She loved this, Catherine thought, looking around the showroom. Absolutely loved this.

"Hard to believe that this place never saw any foot

traffic when old Jasper Fowler owned it," she heard DJ Traub say to someone.

Both DJ and Dax had brought their wives to the opening. Dax's wife had already bought two items and gave no sign of stopping there.

"He wasn't trying to make a go of it, he was too busy laundering money for that no-good thief Arthur Swinton," Dax chimed in.

As far as Dax was concerned, he and his brother had an extra reason to despise the old man. "Hey, you remember when Swinton went around claiming that he'd kept company for a time with Mom?" DJ asked his brother.

"Remember?" Dax echoed. "Hell, I had to restrain myself from teaching that old liar a lesson whenever I saw him."

"He wasn't a liar," Forrest Traub interjected. "At least, not about keeping company with your mother."

The look in DJ's eyes hinted that if anyone except for his cousin had just said that, he would have found himself communing with the floor and sporting a black eye. "You've had too much punch, cousin."

"No, no, he's right," Braden, Forrest's brother, chimed in. "It's kind of foggy now," he admitted, "but I seem to remember that Swinton *did* go out with your mother and it was more than once. It was for a while."

The outrage, mingled with horror, that Dax experienced at the mere *thought* of his mother seeing a low-life like Arthur Swinton was all but overwhelming. For a second, it looked as if he was going to throttle his cousin. But his wife intervened by hooking her arm through his and pulling Dax over toward one of the paintings exhibited on the back wall while Allaire did the same with DJ, saying she wanted him to look at some unique bookends she was thinking of buying.

The two women managed effectively to bring an end to the heated discussion.

But not an end to the haunting possibility that there was some truth in the story that the ex-mayor had told after all.

Catherine breathed a sigh of relief. For a moment there, she'd thought that she was going to have to act as a referee and break up a fight between DJ, Dax and their Rust Creek cousins, Forrest and Braden. Although, she had to admit, she was sympathetic to DJ and his brother. True or not, she wouldn't have wanted stories about her mother dating Swinton to be making the rounds.

Turning away from the remaining Traubs, Catherine almost bumped right into Cody.

"Sorry," she murmured, taking a step back.

She'd had no idea that he'd been so close, although she should have sensed it, she told herself. Lately she had developed this sixth sense when it came to the cowboy. Whenever he was nearby, she could feel the hairs on the back of her neck standing up as if they were acting on an attraction all their own.

Rather than say anything in response, Cody wordlessly took her by the hand and led her toward the back of the shop. Puzzled, assuming he wanted to show her something, Catherine allowed herself to be led off.

But instead of showing her something inside the shop, he opened the back door and took her outside.

Stunned, Catherine tried to pull her hand away. When he kept on holding it, it just increased her confusion. "Cody, let go of my hand. I can't just walk out like this. I've still got a shop full of customers in there."

"Relax, they're not going anywhere," he assured her. "They're too busy talking, looking and scarfing up all that food you put out. Take a couple of minutes," he coaxed. "Beautiful though you are, nobody's going to miss you if you're gone for just a couple of minutes or so."

All she really heard was that he'd called her beautiful.

Chapter Eleven

It took Catherine a couple of minutes to finally find her tongue.

"You think I'm beautiful?" she asked. Each syllable echoed with disbelief.

She was serious, he realized.

Cody looked at her quizzically. There were several ornate mirrors hanging in her shop. Didn't she ever look into any of them?

"Well yeah, sure. Don't you?"

She'd always been the dependable one, the den mother who was always looking out for and making things easier for her siblings. She was the one who both her parents turned to whenever they'd needed a responsible person to handle something. No one had ever really commented on her looks. At various times and occasions, her sisters were complimented on their looks, but she was always the one with "the level head on her shoulders."

Shaking her head now, Catherine laughed dismissively. "Not even close."

"Then I'd go see about getting a pair of glasses first chance I got if I were you. Because you are," he told her in a matter-of-fact, no-nonsense voice that testified he was neither trying to flatter her nor gain her favor unfairly. A half smile played on his lips as he looked at her. "Pink's not exactly my favorite color," he told her, "but it works on you."

Where had that come from? She was wearing a royal blue dress, not a pink one. "Pink?" she questioned, looking down at her dress.

Touching her as lightly as possible, Cody ran his callused fingertips along one of her cheeks. "Pink," he repeated.

And then it came to her.

Oh, God, she was blushing again.

Embarrassed, Catherine turned back toward the door and murmured, "I really have to go back inside."

But, unwilling to release her so quickly, Cody didn't let go of her hand.

"And you will," he told her patiently. "I just want you to take a minute to appreciate what you've just accomplished."

She wasn't sure exactly what he was referring to. "And just what have I accomplished?" she asked him.

"You brought that old store full of flea-bitten stuff nobody wanted back from the dead, that's what you've accomplished. Not everyone could have pulled it off, made people look at this decrepit old place in a new light. Make them forget that it was once owned by that crazy old man Fowler," he emphasized.

She thought of the look on DJ's face when his cousin mentioned Fowler's partner in crime, the ex-mayor of their town, hinting that there actually *had* been something between their mother and Mayor Swinton.

"Not everyone is so ready to forget," she interjected.

"Most," he amended obligingly. "And from what I saw, you did some handy business tonight." He saw that she was shrugging this off as well. Didn't the woman know how to take a compliment? he wondered. Especially since she'd earned it? "All I'm saying is take a minute, savor it. Take a deep breath of this pure Montana air, look up at the stars," he pointed out, then said, "Take a minute just to *be*." Ever so slowly, he drew closer to her. Close enough to feel her breath along his skin. "You're rushing around so much, Cate, you're not taking the time to enjoy what's happening. None of it's worth it if you don't take the time to enjoy it," he told her quietly.

She was acutely aware of Cody's closeness. When had he put his arm around her shoulders? She didn't remember him doing that, yet there it was, lightly resting on her shoulders, drawing her into him just as much as the sound of his voice did.

"Okay," she allowed quietly, trying to still the erratic beat of her pulse, "I'm taking a breath, I'm looking up at the stars." She did each as she spoke, then, enveloped in an almost unbearable warmth, she looked up at him. "Now what?" she wanted to know, her question a barely audible whisper.

He was going to say, "Now do it again." But somehow, the words were shanghaied before they ever had a chance to emerge, evaporating into the night air as he found himself bending his head and brushing his lips against hers. Softly, lightly, and then again with just a little more intensity.

Even so, that same wondrous feeling exploded in his veins, that feeling that fairly shouted of his longing for her.

This wasn't the time or the place to act on any of his urges, and he had to pull back now, before his logic just burned away to a crisp in the ever-growing heat of his desire for this woman.

Catherine was surprised that she was still standing, given the fact that her knees had just melted away to nothing. When Cody drew back, she'd been leaning into him, her body speaking to his in a timeless language that needed no words. It took her another second or so to realize that her eyes were closed. Forcing them open, she sternly ordered herself to suck it up and pull herself together, but she knew she was still trembling when he looked at her.

"What are you afraid of, Catherine?" he asked, gently pushing her hair away from her face.

Catherine tossed her head and said with far more bravado than she was feeling, "That my customers will go away if they can't find someone to ring up their purchases."

Not knowing how much longer she could hold her ground—Cody seemed to have the ability to see right through her—Catherine quickly turned on her heel and all but ran back inside.

"No," Cody said to the empty evening air, "that's not it."

Cody remained where he was for a few minutes, allowing Catherine to have her space. When he finally did go back inside, he saw her in the midst of a crowd of her friends, laughing, flitting from one person to another, playing the role of the friendly neighborhood shop owner to the hilt.

The word "playing" stuck in his head for the remainder of the evening.

He decided to stay out of her way, merely observing her as she continued interacting with the people who had come to either be supportive of her or to satisfy their curiosity about the reincarnated shop.

For her part, Catherine made no effort to seek him out, no effort to even say anything at all to him. If he were assessing the situation honestly, he would have had to say that she was going out of her way in order to avoid him.

For the time being, he decided to let things remain that way. He'd obviously shaken her up and until they both understood why, it might be best for both of them if they stayed apart for a while. It wasn't in his nature to push.

But you did this time, didn't you? a voice inside his head taunted.

Maybe he *had* come on a little too strongly, Cody silently conceded, but that had come as a surprise to him as well. God knew he never expected to feel *anything* again, let alone the degree of attraction that he felt taking hold whenever he was anywhere around Catherine.

It was that first spur-of-the-moment kiss that had triggered it, he thought.

Ever since then, he'd found himself seeing the world differently. Seeing *her* differently. And his own part in his life had taken center stage again. He wasn't sleep-walking through life anymore, wasn't just standing on the sidelines the way he had these last eight years. And while he was still working through some residual guilt over being able to finally move on, it really *did* feel good to be alive again.

He just had to convince Catherine that she wanted the same thing he did: a relationship that, as it grew in intensity and scope, would eventually culminate in marriage.

Perhaps even sooner than later.

Life was good.

The amount of business she'd done that first day hadn't just been a fluke or flash in the pan. A week after the shop's grand opening and customers were still turning up, still buying. Not out of acts of kindness or blind support but because they *liked* what they saw.

She knew she owed that, at least in part, to Cody. In tapping into the cowboy's preferences, she'd managed to unearth the kind of things that held genuine appeal for the average citizen of Thunder Canyon. She'd never been so wildly busy or felt so happy and fulfilled, so empowered before.

Or so scared, either, she silently admitted in a rare moment of respite from the steady traffic of questing customers. Scared because the feelings she had whenever she thought of Cody—and she thought of Cody *all* the time—were so incredibly strong she felt that they could very easily overpower her.

Since that first day, he was never far from her thoughts.

Hell, he was in them *all* the time. While she was talking to customers, opening the shop up in the morning, closing the shop down at night, Cody's face would suddenly rise up in her mind without warning, his voice echoing in her head.

Making her lose her train of thought.

She had to work extra hard to keep her growing clientele from thinking she'd lost her mind.

Maybe she actually *had* lost her mind, Catherine thought. How else did she explain the overwhelmingly strong feelings she was having about a man she'd know for less than a month?

This wasn't the reaction of a woman viewed by one and all as "the level-headed one."

It just didn't make sense.

And yet, there it was, part of her every waking moment and part of her dreams as well.

Maybe if Cody continued to stay away, as he had these last few days, she had a chance—albeit a slim one—of getting over him, of actually getting back to the way her life had been before a racing pulse had become her normal state of existence.

Why *hadn't* she seen Cody these last few days? she wondered uneasily. Had he felt rebuffed that night at her grand opening when she'd hurried back inside, leaving him just standing there? Had she wounded his pride because she'd chosen the store over him?

And if she had wounded his pride, how did she undo that?

Catherine pressed her lips together. All she was doing was succeeding in making herself crazy, she silently admonished.

When she heard the tiny bell ring, announcing yet another customer, she was relieved by the diversion.

Pasting a wide smile on her lips, she turned around to greet whoever it was.

"Hello, welcome to the Real Vintage— You," she cried abruptly.

"The real vintage me?" Cody pretended to roll the words she'd just uttered over in his head, frowning as if he was trying to make sense of the greeting.

"Cowboy," she said, supplying the last part of the shop's name. "Cowboy," she repeated with emphasis through clenched teeth. He knew damn well what she'd meant to say, she thought, exasperated. "Where've you been?" she asked before she could think to stop herself.

The smile on his lips was equal parts mystery and satisfaction.

"Miss me?" he asked innocently.

Underneath it all he was relieved because until just this moment, it had all been a gamble for him. He'd been dealing with the very real possibility that she might not have missed him at all. But one look at her face told him that she apparently had. All was well with the universe.

"Yes. No," Catherine quickly amended, not wanting to appear too eager. But then she shrugged, knowing that to pretend that she hadn't missed him was tantamount to telling a lie.

So, in order to save face, Catherine compromised and settled on "Kind of." She waited a beat, then asked again, "So, where were you?"

"I had some catching up to do on the ranch." Which was true, although Hank and Kurt were more than capable of running the ranch and training the horses for a few days at a time. "Besides, I figured I'd let you get being exclusively a shop owner out of your system."

She raised her eyebrows. Now what was *that* supposed to mean? "Oh, you did, did you?"

"Yup." His grin was completely unassuming and incredibly boyish, despite his age. "Also figured that after five whole days of that, you might be ready for a break, so here I am. Consider me as your break."

Her eyes narrowed and she tried very hard to look indignant. After all, he couldn't just waltz in here after five days of hibernation and think he could just take over this way.

Oh, who was she kidding? This wasn't the time to mark her territory. She was just happy to see him. Exceedingly happy. "What did you have in mind?" she wanted to know.

That was when Cody held up the large wicker basket he'd brought in with him. "Guess."

She couldn't just jump into his arms after he'd deliberately stayed away. It would be setting some kind of precedent. Moreover, it would be giving him permission to take her for granted, letting him know that she'd always be waiting for him to make his appearance no matter how long he stayed away.

She was her own person, damn it. That meant that she couldn't have him thinking that he could just pop up after pulling a disappearing act and all would be summarily forgiven.

"Look," she began, doing her best to sound annoyed, "you might think you know me, that you can read me, but you don't and you can't."

"Is that so?" he asked, setting the basket down on the counter.

Summoning her bravado, Catherine raised her chin

as she tossed her head. Silken brown hair went flying over her shoulder. "Yes, that's so."

The words sounded angry. But inside, she was trembling, praying that she hadn't overplayed her hand.

Damn it, he had her so twisted up inside she didn't know what to feel, how to react.

What to want.

"Damn, but you are stirring me up like a pot of stew over a campfire flame when you do that," Cody told her.

She wasn't aware of doing anything out of the ordinary. "Do what?"

Catherine barely got the words out before her lips were rendered immobile. Or rather, recruited for another activity that did *not* involve talking.

She wanted to protest, to cling to her shredded indignation and tell Cody that he wasn't following the rules, wasn't behaving the way she thought he should.

But it was very, very hard to be indignant when her whole body felt as if it was on fire even as it was radiating insurmountable joy.

One kiss from this cowboy and her thought process was reduced to a pile of useless rubble.

What was worse was that she didn't care.

Giving herself permission to enjoy this one kiss, Catherine wrapped her arms around her rough-hewed cowboy's neck. In response, Cody swept her into his arms and her feet lost contact with the ground—just as the rest of her lost contact with the world around her and slipped effortlessly into the one he was creating just for the two of them.

You'd think, she tried in vain to reason, that she would be getting used to his kisses by now instead of lighting up like a Christmas tree inside each and every time his lips found hers.

It wasn't getting old; it was getting better. And better.

As she sighed in utter wonder and contentment, Cody gently set her back down. And then he stepped back, away from her. Taking a second to pull himself together, Cody took her hand and led her to the front door before she realized what was happening. With the picnic basket handle slung over his forearm, he flipped the open for business sign that hung in her window over so that it now proclaimed: Closed. Please come back tomorrow.

He was closing down her store. He couldn't do that, she thought in sudden agitation.

"But it's the middle of the day," Catherine protested. Wanting to sound angry, she realized that her voice sounded oddly compliant to her.

"Yeah, I know," Cody acknowledged. "Best time to have a picnic," he added with a wink.

Once outside, he waited for her to lock the door, then he took her over to where his truck was parked.

"Where are we going?" she asked uncertainly as she got into the passenger side.

"To my ranch," he answered, turning on the ignition. He backed out of the parking space slowly, then pressed down on the accelerator once he was in Drive. "There's someone I want you to meet."

She couldn't begin to imagine who he was referring to. Had his sister come for a visit?

"Who?" Catherine asked, unable to contain her curiosity.

"My horse."

"Your horse?" she echoed incredulously. "You want me to 'meet' your horse?" Was that some kind of code? Or a joke? Cody couldn't possibly be talking about an actual horse—could he?

"Uh-huh." He looked at her as they stopped at one of the few lights in Thunder Canyon. The bewildered look on her face made him laugh. "Honey, you can't begin to understand a 'real vintage cowboy' if you haven't met his horse."

His laugh, deep and rich, wrapped itself around her, instantly heating her blood. Catherine settled back in her seat. "Can't wait," she told him.

He knew she was being flippant, but she was coming along—in more ways than one—and that was all that really mattered to him.

Chapter Twelve

They'd been driving to his ranch for several minutes when he turned to Catherine and asked, "Can you ride?"

"In a car," she answered, her expression the personification of innocence.

"No, a horse," Cody corrected. "Have you ever ridden a horse before?"

He knew that just because this was Montana didn't automatically mean that everyone listed horseback riding as being among their skills. Some people were even afraid of horses.

It hadn't occurred to him until just now that Catherine might be in that group. Mentally crossing his fingers, he really hoped that wasn't the case.

"Does sitting on a pony and having my picture taken at the age of five count?" she asked him, obviously amused by his question.

He made a right at a large oak tree and kept driving. His ranch house was now visible in the distance. "That all depends," he allowed.

She wasn't exactly sure what Cody meant by that. "On what?"

Even if she'd never ridden a horse, as long as she was game to try, that was all that counted. "On whether the photo was taken at a full gallop or not."

"Not," she answered. "Neither the pony nor I were galloping at the time," she assured him. She added, "It was a very docile pony."

So posing for a picture atop the pony hadn't spooked her. That led him to a logical question. "If that was the case, why is it that you never went horseback riding after that?"

She lifted her slender shoulders in a careless shrug as she continued looking around and taking in the scenery. There was a sprawling ranch house in the distance that looked at if it could have accommodated three families, not just one lone man.

Didn't he get lonely rattling around that big old house by himself?

"Too busy with everything else to take the time I guess," she told him. "Is that your ranch house?" she finally asked, unable to bank down her curiosity any longer.

He nodded. "That's my ranch house," he acknowledged, sounding about as cheerful as she'd ever heard him. "Stables are to your left." He pointed them out to her.

Coming to a stop before the house, he parked and got out. Going around the vehicle, he came over to the passenger side. He held the door open for her. Once she was out, Cody leaned in to retrieve the picnic basket from the backseat.

"Almost forgot this." His laugh was self-mocking. Hooking his arm through hers, Cody ushered her toward the aforementioned stables. "I picked out a really gentle horse for you, just in case." He didn't want to give her a headstrong animal that insisted on getting its own way, not if she was unfamiliar with how to handle a horse. Besides, getting a spirited horse might give her an excuse not to ride with him. "Looks like I was right." His smile was encouraging, coaxing. "C'mon, let's go meet your horse."

An uncertainty nibbled away at her, an uncertainty that had nothing to do with the proposed riding session. Cody was moving fast, maybe too fast.

If something moved forward fast, it could also move on just as fast, she reasoned, leaving her behind in the dust. She wasn't sure if she wanted to risk that. Wasn't sure if being with Cody for only a little while was something she could accept.

"My horse?" she echoed quizzically.

"Well, your horse for the day," Cody qualified. "You can't go riding without a horse."

Okay, she'd play along, Catherine thought. "And why am I going riding?"

"Because the perfect place for a picnic is at the top of a bluff. The view you get there is guaranteed to take your breath away," he promised.

"Do I really want to be breathless on a picnic?"

It took him a moment to realize she was pulling his leg. He grinned. "You do this time."

Catherine nodded, accepting his answer. But she

still had another question for him. "And you can't get there by truck?"

"Nope."

Okay, he silently admitted, he was stretching the truth a bit. In reality they actually *could* access the bluff that way, but it was a mite tricky. One wrong move and they could find themselves sliding back down the incline. Getting there by horse was a lot safer and, as far as he was concerned, a lot more pleasurable.

Cody set the basket down right behind the stable door. The last thing he wanted was to have one of the horses come over to investigate the tempting aroma emanating from the basket. Most likely it would be knocked over on its side and scavenged, a casualty to the animal's curiosity.

Cody placed his hand on the small of Catherine's back and gently prodded her into the stable.

He brought her over to the first stall. "This is Buttercup," he told her, introducing her to a mare the color of light butterscotch. The horse had a small white star on its forehead that almost matched the color of her mane. "She's very gentle," he promised Catherine. Then, turning to the mare, he said, "Buttercup, this is Catherine. Go easy on her—she's new at this. Be sure not to spook her."

Catherine didn't know whether to be amused or worried. "You talk to your horses?"

He looked surprised that she would even ask. "Why not? They understand me about as well as people do. Sometimes better," he amended. "Pet her muzzle," he coaxed. Then he said to Catherine with a grin, "I'm talking to you, not the horse, in case that wasn't clear."

This time, she was amused. Hesitating at first, she

gently ran her hand along the horse's sleek muzzle. Buttercup remained perfectly still, as if she understood that she couldn't make any sudden moves.

Catherine smiled as she continued stroking the mare. "She's a beauty," Catherine enthused.

"Funny," Cody told her thoughtfully, "that's exactly what she was thinking about you."

Catherine looked at him sharply. "You can't know what a horse is thinking," she protested.

Cody's mouth curved, a completely unfathomable expression on his face. His tone gave nothing away, either. "You'd be surprised."

Hank walked into the stable in time to hear the last exchange between his boss and the attractive guest he'd brought.

"I wouldn't put nothin' past this man if I were you, ma'am," he warned amiably. "I've seen him tame and charm a horse that was behavin' as if he had the devil himself inside of him. Nobody could handle Wildfire but this here boss man," the man testified with a solemnity that rang with pride.

And then the tall, wiry man touched two fingers to the brim of his worn, weather-beaten hat as a sign of respect and said, "My name's Hank, ma'am, and I've been working for the boss man here for close to five years now—in case he didn't mention me," he added by way of an explanation for his talkativeness. The lines on his weathered face deepened as he smiled slyly and looked at Cody. "I can see why you've been going into town so much lately. She's a real looker."

Out of the corner of his eye, Cody could see color begin to creep up Catherine's cheek. Hank's comment had embarrassed her.

"Since you seem to have so much time on your hands, McCarthy, why don't you saddle Buttercup for the lady?" It was more of an order than a request.

Aware that he might have unintentionally crossed over a line, the ranch hand snapped to attention.

"Oh, yeah, sure thing, boss man." But despite his hurry to do as Cody instructed, Hank paused for one extra minute, smiling directly at Catherine. "Really nice meeting you, ma'am." And, after a quick tip of his hat, the ranch hand went to fetch a saddle for the mare.

"Don't pay any attention to Hank," Cody told her, feeling the need to explain the man's actions. "He's not used to having anyone come to the ranch."

She looked at Cody to see if he was teasing her. But his expression looked serious. "You don't have any visitors at all?"

He shook his head. There was a time when the ranch rang of laughter and the sound of company coming and going. But that had all ended when Renee left his life. Now it was only about getting the job done. For eight years, that had been his only focus.

Until now.

"Visitors get in the way of the work," he told her bluntly.

She couldn't imagine what being isolated on a ranch like that was like. As far back as she could remember, there were always people around her. Granted at times it was just the family, but when there are seven other siblings as well as two parents, "just" the family could amount to quite a crowd.

Apparently his life was the complete opposite of hers, Catherine thought. "Doesn't that get lonely?" she wanted to know.

He looked at her for a long moment. What was he looking for? she wondered. What did he see? "It didn't before."

The way he said it made her think that perhaps Cody had reassessed his lifestyle recently and found it to be lacking. Was it that the loneliness had finally penetrated so deeply that he had become dissatisfied with his lot and decided to see about changing it or was she just reading too much into his tone, turning it into what she *wanted* to hear? She honestly didn't know. All she knew was that she didn't want him to be lonely anymore. She wanted him to be happy.

Within the quarter hour, their horses saddled and ready, they were about to head toward the bluff. The picnic basket Cody had prepared was strapped down and anchored across his saddle horn. Mindful of disturbing it, Cody swung himself into his saddle, carefully avoiding jostling the basket.

As he took his reins into his hands, he glanced at Catherine and promised her, "Don't worry, we'll take it slow."

He was completely unprepared for the gleam he saw suddenly entering her eyes as she listened to what he had to say.

"Slow is for old people!" she declared with a laugh.

The next thing he knew, she kicked her heels into the mare's flanks and cried, "Let's go, Buttercup. Let's show him what you've got."

Before he could say a word or even register his total surprise, Catherine was galloping away, essentially leaving him and the stallion he was riding staring after her, dumbfounded.

He'd been played.

It took Cody less than a heartbeat to come to. The second he did, he pressed his heels into Wildfire's flanks, urging the horse to give chase. The horse obliged at lightning speed.

Cody caught up to Catherine quickly enough, despite the fact that Buttercup'd had a decent lead. Fast as she was, the mare was no match for his own mount, a horse he'd picked for speed as well as his willingness to be trained—once the stallion was finally tamed.

When the two horses were finally side by side, Cody leaned over his own mount and grabbed the reins out of Catherine's hands, pulling her mare—and her—to a dead stop.

The look in Cody's eyes was part surprise, part annoyance. "Why didn't you tell me you could ride like that?" he demanded.

It took her a couple of seconds to stop laughing and answer him. She hadn't meant to trick him, but when he given her an opening, she just couldn't resist playing the part of a helpless novice.

Catherine prefaced her explanation with an apology, hoping that would erase any hard feelings he might be nursing.

"I'm sorry. But you seemed so caught up in your role as the big, protective cowboy, I thought I'd let you enjoy it for a while." She tried to keep a straight face, but it was next to impossible. Laughter kept bubbling up in her throat. "You should have seen your face when I kicked Buttercup's flanks. You looked as if you thought I'd lost my mind."

"That's because I *did* think that," he admitted honestly. Either that or she had a death wish. He'd believed her when she'd initially alluded to not being able to ride at all.

Who knew she was setting him up?

Catherine laughed with pleasure again, then took a deep breath as she tried to get herself under control. It wasn't easy at first, but she finally managed. That was when she finally looked around at her surroundings.

Her breath caught in her throat. "You were right," she said almost humbled. "It *is* beautiful up here. And it definitely is the perfect place for a picnic." She flashed him a wide grin that, unbeknownst to her, came very close to unraveling him. "Thanks for making me come, Cody."

Inclining his head, Cody murmured, "You're welcome," just before he dismounted. Untying the picnic basket, he lifted the handle up over the saddle horn and took it down. "That wild ride couldn't have been good for what's inside," he surmised, lifting the lid to look into the basket.

Just as he'd suspected, everything looked as if it'd had an eggbeater applied to it.

Catherine had already slid off her horse. Holding on to Buttercup's reins, she crossed over to Cody. "I'm sure it's fine," she told him, her eyes smiling up into his.

Having her this close to him in a place that meant so much to him made Cody want to toss the basket aside and just sweep her into his arms. Hell, he could feast on her lips alone for hours.

The temptation was almost overwhelming. But despite the whimsical way she was behaving this afternoon, Cody had a strong gut feeling that if he acted on his impulse, the only thing he'd wind up doing was scaring her off.

There was no doubt in his mind that she was a complex character, this woman who had managed to take his heart out of the deep-freeze it had been residing in these last eight years.

So, with soul-crushing reluctance, Cody reined himself in. Setting the wicker basket down on the ground, he took out the tablecloth he'd packed. With a snap of his wrists, he tried to get the entire tablecloth to gently float down onto the grass in a straight fashion.

The wind had other ideas.

Catching the underside of the tablecloth, the wind wrecked havoc on any hopes of getting the tablecloth down evenly.

Catherine came to his aid, taking two of the corners and pulling the cloth taut.

Between them they spread the checkered tablecloth—how typical, she couldn't help thinking, doing her best not to allow him to see her amusement—out evenly on the grass. Cody quickly placed the basket on one end to anchor down the cloth and then proceeded to empty it out, putting everything he'd packed within Catherine's easy reach.

Within minutes, it was ready.

Catherine sat down cross-legged on the edge of the tablecloth, directly opposite her vintage cowboy. The appreciative look in her eyes was genuine.

"Looks like a feast fit for a king," she told him, then suddenly looked up at him. "Don't tell me you cook, too."

If he had to, he could survive, but there wasn't a hell of a lot of variety in what he could prepare.

"I can make simple things," he admitted freely. "But I didn't make this meal." He had no intentions of taking credit for something he didn't do, even though it might have been fun to see her reaction. "JC did."

"JC?" she repeated. He hadn't mentioned that name to her before. Maybe he wasn't as lonely on the ranch as she'd initially assumed.

"My cook," he clarified, then thought better of his explanation. "Well, he's not really mine. JC used to do the cooking for my mother and father when I first started going to school. When they died, he hung around, making meals for my sister and me even though I told him that I couldn't pay him. He told me not to worry about it, that he was keeping a running tally and I'd pay it off someday. He was only kidding, but I did. I paid him back and when I got the ranch back on its feet again, I officially hired him on."

"And you paid him back every penny you felt you owed him for those years, didn't you?" Cody really didn't have to answer. She knew that he had. She was beginning to know a great deal about this soft-spoken cowboy without actually behind told.

He shrugged as if he couldn't see doing it any other way. "Didn't seem right not to," he told her matter-of-factly.

Catherine could feel her smile spreading when she looked at him. Cody really was a very good man, she couldn't help thinking. Not everyone had as much integrity as he did.

"Someone else would have just chalked it up to having a Good Samaritan intervene. They'd see it as a favor, a good deed done by a man who felt sorry for two motherless orphans. That way, they'd completely forget about paying anything back. But you didn't." She brushed a quick kiss against his cheek, completely surprising him. "You're a very good person, Cody Overton."

The compliment warmed him, but at the same time, it made him uncomfortable. He didn't like being in the spotlight, even for a second. He'd never cared for any undue attention. The truth of the matter was Cody really preferred staying in the background.

Wanting her to focus on something else, Cody nodded at the food he'd spread out.

"Try the fried chicken," he coaxed. "It's JC's specialty. He'd be offended if I came back with any leftovers."

"Well, I wouldn't want to offend the man," she agreed, humor curving her mouth. She picked up a strip of chicken that had been fried to a golden crisp. Biting into it slowly, she was rewarded with an explosion of tantalizing tastes that immediately seduced her. "Wow, this really *is* good," she marveled, more than a little pleasantly surprised.

She'd been prepared to offer lip service about how delicious everything was because, after all, a lot of effort had been placed into this. But she didn't have to fake anything. It really *was* good.

Catherine made short work of the piece she'd been given. Closing her eyes, she savored the taste for a moment. Then, opening them again, she asked, "Does JC share recipes?"

Cody thought before he answered and came up with nothing. "I don't know. I never asked. But I've got a feeling that he would only surrender his recipes on his deathbed—and maybe not even then."

The sound of her delighted laughter seemed to slowly weave its way under his skin and burrow itself deep into his inner core, then it quickly fanned out to effectively take him prisoncr.

A willing prisoner.

Cody really wasn't aware of what he was eating. He was only aware of the way Catherine was enjoying herself—and JC's fried chicken.

Aware of that and also aware of the all-too-profound fiery ache he was experiencing in his gut as he watched Catherine squeeze all the enjoyment she could out of the moment.

Chapter Thirteen

"You missed a spot," Cody prompted.

Catherine had surprised him by more than doing justice to the fried chicken he'd packed for their picnic. Wiping her mouth after she'd finished what was her fifth piece of chicken, she'd left behind a tiny crumb at the right corner of her mouth.

Rather than act flustered that she wasn't picture-perfect, the way most of the women he'd gone out with would have reacted, Catherine laughed softly and said, "You're probably thinking that you can't take me anywhere, right?"

She brushed the napkin against her mouth again and somehow still managed to miss the offending crumb.

At a loss for a response, Cody mumbled, "No, I never thought—"

He didn't get a chance to stumble through to the end of his sentence because she asked, "Better?" as she tilted her face beguilingly up for his closer scrutiny.

"No." He nodded at the offending golden speck. "It's still there."

Rather than try again, Catherine surrendered her napkin to him. "Here, you do it. At least you can see what you're doing."

Taking the napkin from her, Cody gently took hold of her chin and with strokes that were even gentler, sent the small, crisp crumb into the grass and parts unknown. He held her chin a second longer, feeling the full impact of the very strong attraction that was radiating between them.

Cody dropped the napkin, leaned closer to Catherine and softly brushed his lips against hers.

There was an instant quickening of his pulse, not to mention his loins, but he didn't want to push anything, didn't want Catherine thinking that he was attempting to take advantage of her in this isolated spot.

Drawing back, Cody looked at her, desperately searching for something to say that wouldn't have him stuttering like some damn fool kid out on his first date—even though that was exactly how she made him feel. As if he was on the brink of something brand-new and exciting that he'd never experienced before.

Wildfire's whinny brought Cody's attention to his mount and, at the same time, to hers. She'd looked like poetry in motion, riding away from him earlier. It had made for a mesmerizing picture.

"Where did you learn to ride like that?" he wanted to know.

There was a fond look in her eyes as she answered, "My Dad put each of us on the back of a horse before we even learned how to walk. He insisted that we all learn how to sit on a horse as if we were part of the animal. He told us that knowing how to ride well could someday save our lives. When you're a kid, you believe everything your father says. I'm sure that watching us learn probably stopped my mother's heart more than once, but in the end, all of us were glad Dad was so adamant about making each of us learn."

Having all but been born in the saddle himself, Cody couldn't argue with that kind of reasoning, but he could definitely take exception with something else.

"You could have given me a heads-up, you know," he told her, "instead of making me look like some damn fool idiot."

Catherine shook her head at the very idea. "I doubt if *anything* could make you look like a 'damn fool idiot.'" The intimacy of the moment gave her the courage to ask something she would have normally pretended to ignore. "Why'd you stop kissing me, Cody?"

The wide shoulders rose and fell swiftly. The question surprised him. "I didn't want you to think I had an ulterior motive, bringing you here."

"So all you wanted to do was just eat?" she asked innocently.

"When you say it like that..." His voice trailed off as he tried to get a handle on whether or not she was serious or putting him on. Did she *want* him to do more than just eat and talk or was she testing him?

His limited experience with women left him at a complete loss for an answer.

"Yes?" Her voice was almost melodic as it coaxed him to continue.

When she looked at him like that, everything inside of him felt as if it had just been thrown into a churning whirlpool—and it was about to go over the side. "Oh, hell, woman, you're driving me crazy."

"Why, Cody?" she whispered, her eyes lowering to his mouth. "Why am I driving you crazy?"

She was less than a heartbeat away from him. He could feel her breath on his mouth when she spoke. His gut tightened.

Instead of saying anything, he showed her. Pulling Catherine into his arms, he kissed her again. Except that this time, there wasn't anything gentle, anything polite about the way his mouth covered hers. This time, there was an urgency to it. Kissing her came across like a matter of survival, that if he *didn't* kiss her just like this, he'd be completely depleted of everything that allowed him to draw breath.

But after a moment, his self-control reared its head again, warning him that a second longer like this and he would have gone over the edge, gone to a place from which there was no turning back, at least not for him.

So with his very last ounce of strength, even though everything within him was screaming for him not to stop, Cody pulled back again.

"*That's* why you're driving me crazy," he almost shouted, his frustration taking solace in unproductive anger.

Rather than scare her off or at least make her back away, creating a safe distance between them the way he'd hoped this display of temper would accomplish, Catherine whispered, "The feeling's mutual," saying the words so close to his lips that they almost seemed to come from him instead.

The words sealed his doom.

"Oh, damn," Cody groaned again, giving up the fight. Taking her and surrendering to her at the same time.

The next moment, Catherine was back in his arms again and his mouth was pressed against hers. Except this time, he knew he wasn't having his way with her. It was mutual. She was having her way with him as much as he with her.

And *that* triggered almost a frenzied response within him, a frenzy that at the same time dictated that he exercise extreme control over himself, otherwise these wild, strange feelings would all wind up crashing into one another, and who knew the consequences of that?

No matter what, Cody wanted some semblance of control over her, over himself so that his struggle, as it happened, wouldn't seem as if it had all been triggered by her. Because *that* would certainly remove the last shred of power from his hands.

But maintaining restraint wasn't easy, not when she moaned the way she was moaning. Not with the way she felt like liquid gold in his hands, hot, pliable and so very spellbinding and enticing.

Though he doubted if she would even understand if he told her, it was restraint that had his hands running along the curves of her body like this. He was employing restraint because he was touching her while leaving her clothes where they were. They served as barriers against his eager palms and questing fingers.

All in good time, a voice in his head whispered.

But before Cody could act on the insistent impulse that was throbbing in his brain, to his stunned surprise, Catherine began opening buttons. *Catherine* was the one removing layers of her clothing, pushing aside material so that he could touch her bare skin.

And when he did, it was his turn to groan. To groan and grow short of breath as the very air seem to heat up between them.

There was no path to satiation.

The more Cody touched her, the more he wanted to touch her.

And the more he wanted her.

His breath all but backed up in his throat when she slipped her hand underneath his shirt, her fingers splayed, then moving as she seemed intent on memorizing the very contours and hard ridges of his chest.

For the life of him, Cody couldn't have said which of them actually unbuttoned his shirt or pulled it from his shoulders and torso, tossing it aside in a bunched-up heap. Or, for that matter, which of them wound up disposing of the rest of Catherine's clothing.

It all occurred within an all-consuming haze, marked by sudden, hot arrows of passion that pierced right through him, reminding him what it meant to want a woman, to make love *to* a woman as well as *with* her.

Catherine became all things to him at once, a revelation, a homecoming and a humbling novelty all rolled up into one.

She had no idea what came over her.

She'd never in her life reacted this way before, never wanted what she wanted at this moment before. The power within Cody's kiss made her want to please him, to be desired by him.

Be possessed by him.

Her body had instantly heated when he'd touched his mouth to hers. Suddenly there were passions and desires erupting within her at an incredibly breathtaking pace. Catherine couldn't think clearly, didn't *want* to think at all, just experience all the wondrous sensations that were currently racing through her body, making it sing in a language she'd never known before.

Never known before, but wanted desperately to learn.

Being with Cody this way fueled an eagerness within her, an eagerness that made her almost rip off his clothes in her desire to touch and be touched. To press her naked skin against his equally bare torso.

It seemed to her that Cody instantly conquered every place his lips touched, branding her. Making her his for all time.

Her neck, her shoulders, her belly, the skin all but burned as his mouth passed over each and every area. She twisted and turned, her body eager to spread the sensation, to share it equally even as those sensations continued to explode all along her body.

When Cody came close to her throat, she seized her opportunity, took hold of his face between her hands and kissed him so hard she thought her soul would crack from the impact.

And still it wasn't enough.

She wanted more, craved more even though she had no idea where this rampaging need was coming from or how it was all going to end.

Heretofore she'd been almost docile and had little to no desire to enter this fiery wonderland she was racing through now.

But then, how could someone miss what they'd never known? The small handful of partners she'd had before had never even had the keys to the back door of this exquisite paradise.

Now, however, she knew that when this was gone, she would severely mourn the loss.

Moving by instincts she'd had no idea she possessed until just now, Catherine did her best to teasingly goad him on, silently entreating Cody not to hold back any longer.

Her body ached for him.

As did her soul.

For his part, Cody knew that he'd come close to self-destructing if he didn't take her now, this second. Rolling over so that she was beneath him, he watched Catherine's eyes as he positioned himself over her. Even in this amped-up state, he was watching her eyes for any telltale sign of fear, of hesitation. For some indication that she'd suddenly changed her mind and wanted him to stop before the ultimate act occurred.

But there were no signs, no silent entreaties.

The exact opposite was true.

His hands braced on either side of her, Cody slowly drove himself into her. Almost at the same time, he covered her mouth with his and pulled her close against him, his arms woven tightly around her, sealing the bargain completely.

Ever so slowly, he began to move, to rock. But right from the very start, the pace instantly increased.

And she matched him.

Echoed each movement, returned each thrust until, evenly matched, they found themselves racing higher and higher along that rarified incline. And then, joined, they leaped off the peak together.

Exhilaration seized Cody.

He was breathing so hard, he didn't know if he could ever successfully catch his breath again.

Ultimately, he decided that didn't matter. Because this one time, he'd been part of something that had been exquisitely perfect.

Gradually, he became aware that her short, staccato breaths were lengthening in breadth and scope, as were his own.

And after a few minutes, Cody found he had enough air in his lungs to enable him to form words. But, to play it safe, he took in a few more breaths before venturing to say something.

Catherine hadn't moved a muscle since they'd plunged off the cliff together—now an eternity ago. She remained tucked against him and he had his arm protectively around her.

Turning toward her now, Cody felt he had to make something crystal clear in case he hadn't before. "I want you to know I didn't plan on this."

He could feel the small, guileless smile as it formed on her lips. Watched it as it entered her eyes, all before she finally said, "I know."

Cody raised himself up on his elbow, wanting to get a better look at her face. The smile notwithstanding, she seemed serious, at least about this.

"You know?"

She nodded. Again her eyes crinkled into a smile. "I could *feel* you struggling with yourself."

He sank back down again, trying to make sense out of everything that had just happened and how he was supposed to deal with it. The goalposts ahead seemed clear to him, but he wasn't so sure how to put what he was feeling, what he wanted her to know, into words so that she knew as well.

He began with something he'd already said, wanting to build on it and go from there.

"I didn't want you to feel I was taking advantage of you." He got no further because he could feel her laughing softly. Was she laughing at him or something he'd said? "What's so funny?"

"Taking advantage of me?" she repeated, then reminded him of a very crucial fact in their coming together, "You didn't exactly have to tie my hands and feet to a tree, you know."

"No," he agreed, "but you might think that I seduced you."

Seduced her?

The fact that she didn't burst out laughing testified that she had developed *huge* restraint herself. Catherine congratulated herself.

And then she smiled to herself again. Cody was incredibly sweet. She'd had no idea he could be this thoughtful, this sensitive about her feelings and reactions. Who knew that beneath all that solemnity beat the heart of a kind man who intentionally put her needs ahead of his own?

"If anything, Cody, I seduced you," she told him with a very straight face. And then her grin popped up as she continued, "You did your best to resist. By the way, a girl could get a complex from that, you know."

"A complex?" he repeated quizzically.

"Sure. I started to wonder what was wrong with me if I had to all but rip your clothes off to get you to finally come around and make love with me."

"I came around way before you got started taking my clothes off," he informed her.

"Oh?" She grinned at him. "Really?"

He couldn't tell from her tone of voice if she was teasing him or actually surprised by what he'd just said. Or if she was saying that she didn't believe him.

All he could do was give her an honest reply. "Yes, 'really.'"

"And exactly what was it about me that made you come around?" she wanted to know, not sure if she believed what he was telling her or not. Cody seemed honest enough, but men were known to lie if it suited them.

"Everything," he answered without any hesitation.

"You know, for a taciturn cowboy," she marveled, "you really do have a way with words when you try." Her eyes began to shine as she added, "But I have to admit that I like the fact that you don't need words to get your point across."

It was his turn to feign innocence even though he knew exactly what she was referring to. "Oh?"

Catherine shifted so that she was looking down at him, her long brown hair moving teasingly along his bare chest.

"Yes, 'oh,'" she repeated, mimicking his tone.

Then, before any more dialogue could be exchanged, she moved seductively along his body, her bare torso singeing his.

And then she kissed him as hard as she could, with every fiber of her being.

And just like that, Cody found himself engaged in another exhilarating, mind-bending marathon—and loving it beyond words.

Chapter Fourteen

It was time, Cody decided.

He'd thought on it long and hard these last few days and made up his mind that it was time. Time to move on. Time to have a talk with Catherine about what was on his mind.

But he needed to take care of something else first.

Looking for just the right words that he wanted to use, he didn't notice Hank walking toward him as he hurried down the front steps. Didn't really notice him at all until Hank all but planted his tall, wiry body in front of him.

Hooking his thumbs through his belt loops, Hank asked with a wide, guileless grin, "Is it my imagination, boss, or is that a spring in your step I've been seeing these last few days?"

The look on the man's face was a cross between a smirk and something that looked like vicarious pleasure. Cody knew that if he allowed himself to get sucked into a conversation with his ranch hand, it would throw his schedule completely off. Hank, given half an opportunity, could talk the ears off a bronze statue. He was a damn hard worker, but he had a bad habit of never using five words if he could use fifty instead.

"Your imagination," Cody said crisply, deliberately moving around the man.

Rather than take the hint, Hank fell into step beside him, staying closer to him than a shadow. "No, no, I think that's a definite spring." Hank pretended to take a second, long look at his boss to convince himself. "Yup, that's what it is, all right. A spring." Hank was definitely smirking now. "It wouldn't have anything to do with that nice young woman you brought up to the ranch last week, now would it?" Before Cody had a chance to say "no," Hank boasted, "I've got a keen eye for these kinds of things."

"It's a shame you don't use that keen eye of yours to focus on getting your job done instead of trying to figure out someone else's business," Cody said. There wasn't even so much as a *hint* of a smile on his face or in his voice.

A lot of men would have backed off. But Hank had worked for him since he'd bought the ranch nearly five years ago and he didn't scare easily.

"I can do both," Hank volunteered, punctuating his statement with another wide grin.

"Ask me, it's about time," Kurt chimed in. The second, younger ranch hand seemed to come out of nowhere. "Hank and me were starting to worry that you weren't never gonna come around."

Stopping, Cody looked from one man to the other.

"Is my personal life all you can find to talk about?" he wanted to know.

"Ain't been all that much to talk about until just now," Hank answered. Thumbs still hooked into his belt loops, he rocked back on his heels. "I'd strike real fast if I were you, boss. That little lady isn't going to be single for long. Not with that face and figure."

"I'm with him," Kurt said, jerking a thumb in Hank's direction.

Cody frowned. He knew they meant well, but he wasn't about to start a precedent by condoning this kind of talk from men who were working for him.

"You two through gossipin' like two little old ladies?" he demanded, looking from one to the other, his expression unreadable. "'Cause if this is what you want to be doing, I can hire two hands to take your place faster than you can say 'mind your business.'"

Hank held his hands up in the universal sign for surrender. "We're just being happy for you, boss. No cause for you to go all ornery on us."

Kurt merely shook his head. "Ask me, I don't think he knows how to be happy without acting like a wounded bear," he said as if Cody wasn't standing within three feet of him.

Hank appeared to mull the assessment over. Both men began to walk away from Cody and toward the stable. "Well, that's a habit he's sure gonna have to change if he wants to go on keeping company with that pretty little shopkeeper. There's only so much scowling a woman like that would be willing to put up with before she just walks away," Hank estimated.

Kurt was quick to agree with him. "Ain't that the truth?"

"If you two are through dissecting my life," Cody called after them, raising his voice to be heard, "there's a little matter of cleaning out the stalls to attend to." Cody was doing his level best to sound annoyed, but at the moment, thinking about the life he pictured ahead of him, it was really becoming difficult to maintain a gruff exterior. Especially when everything felt as if it was all rosy inside of him.

Hank stopped just short of the stall entrance. "You gonna go see her?" he wanted to know.

Cody left that part unanswered. Instead, in case they had to come looking for him for some reason, he told the two ranch hands where he was going to be for the next half hour or so. "I'm going to the cemetery."

Kurt came out of the stable, a pitchfork for mucking out the stalls in his hands. He exchanged looks with Hank.

Hank was the one who spoke first. "Uh-oh, you have a setback, boss?" he asked sympathetically.

"Not that I'm aware of," was all Cody would volunteer. With that, he slid into his truck and drove off, leaving both of the ranch hands staring after him, trying to puzzle out just what was going on.

It was too good to be true and she knew it.

He was too good to be true.

These last few days she'd spent with Cody had been as close to perfect as humanly possible—and it had her worried.

Ever since Cody had whisked her away on that impromptu picnic, he'd been turning up at the shop, saying and doing things that absolutely made her heart sing. Cody Overton had turned out to be everything she had ever wanted in a man.

Which, she was convinced, meant that it was all too good to be true. This was more like a dream than reality and everyone knew you had to wake up from a dream sooner or later.

No dream went on indefinitely—did it?

Dreams didn't, but maybe a man did, she thought hopefully. Maybe what she was seeing was the real Cody—the one who was kind and considerate beneath that rough-hewed exterior.

But, more likely, the real Cody had been temporarily sublimated and this was just an aberration, someone who would fade away all too soon once he tired of being like this.

No two ways about it, Catherine realized that she was waiting for the other shoe to drop. And while she was doing this waiting, she kept looking at the clock on the opposite wall, waiting for Cody—any version of Cody—to come walking in.

Because right now he was late, she thought. Not that Cody actually clocked in, of course, but for the last five days, he'd been turning up bright and early and it was no longer early now—and growing less bright by the moment.

As a matter of fact, it was going on close to noon.

Chewing on her lower lip, Catherine glanced at the phone by the register and wondered if she should try to call Cody.

Would that seem too eager to him? Too needy? She didn't want to come across as some clingy female, but if by any chance there was something wrong, she wanted to know.

Cody would have called if he'd decided not to come, right?

The question echoed in her brain as a dozen reasons—both pro and con—assaulted her. She couldn't come up with anything definite on either side.

Unable to talk herself out of it and growing progressively shorter and shorter on patience, Catherine hurried over to the phone and picked up the receiver.

Just as she did, she heard the bell ring behind her. Swinging around to face the front of the store, she cried, "You're finally here," before she could think to stop herself.

The new chef at the Gallatin Room in the Thunder Canyon Resort, Shane Roarke, was surprised at the nature and tone of the greeting. His eyebrows drew together in obvious confusion.

"I guess I am," he murmured, not quite sure how to respond to the shop owner's strange greeting.

Embarrassed, Catherine flushed slightly. The man probably thought she was crazy.

"I'm sorry," she apologized. "I thought you were someone else."

"I'm sorry I'm not," he said with a smile. Putting his hand out, he introduced himself. "Hi, I'm Shane Roarke."

"Catherine Clifton," she responded, returning his handshake.

"I'm new in town and I just bought a place that doesn't have a stick of furniture in it. Someone at the Thunder Canyon Resort said that you've gotten some good, sturdy pieces for sale at decent prices so I thought I'd come in and look around."

Idiot! Catherine upbraided herself. She'd almost lost

a customer, letting thoughts of Cody crowd her head and push everything else out. This was her livelihood she was jeopardizing, and if she wasn't careful, she'd find herself losing everything. She was going to have to keep her mind on business and everything else was going to have to go on the back burner, including Cody.

Easier said than done and she knew it.

Out loud she said, "Please," as she made a sweeping gesture with her hand, taking in most of the shop. "Look all you want. I'm sure you'll find something here to your liking—and on the outside chance that you don't, let me know what you're looking for and I'll see if I can track it down for you at some estate sale."

In the last couple of months, she'd gotten rather good at that, finding small, out-of-the-way places that had both furniture and vintage clothing that seemed to be all but waiting for her to come and rescue them for her shop.

"Any piece in particular on your mind?" she wanted to know.

Shane shook his head. "To be honest, it's one of those things that I'll know it if I see it."

Catherine nodded. "I know just what you mean." And she did. An item had to appeal to her—to "speak" to her—before she made an offer to buy it. "So I'll get out of your way and let you start looking around," she concluded, giving her new potential customer her most accommodating, friendly smile.

Less than two minutes later, her heart leaped into her throat again when she heard the bell go off for a second time.

Swinging around to look, she found that it wasn't Cody walking into the shop this time around any more than it had been the last time. Instead of the tall cowboy, a very pregnant-looking Antonia Wright crossed the threshold, moving slowly.

Catherine's disappointment faded as she greeted one of her oldest friends. Despite being seven months along, the single mother-to-be was still going strong, running the only boardinghouse in Thunder Canyon and managing to do it all practically single-handedly.

Stubbornness, Catherine thought, was one of the key things that she and Antonia had in common.

"Antonia, what brings you here?" Catherine asked after she gave the woman a quick hug that required some artful bending on her part.

"Swollen feet," Antonia answered wearily. With one hand protectively on her protruding abdomen, she looked at Catherine. "Tell me, do I have two different shoes on?" she asked.

Amused, Catherine looked down, then shook her head. "No, they're both the same. Why?"

"Because the right one feels a lot tighter than it did just a couple of days ago. I thought maybe I made a mistake and put on two different shoes." Antonia sighed, her frown deepening. "Oh, God, I can't wait—"

"For the baby to be born?" Catherine asked. By the time the seventh month hit, she knew that some women felt as if they'd been pregnant forever and that they'd never have a waist again.

"Well, that, too," Antonia allowed with a vague nod of her head, "but what I was going to say was that I can't wait to see my feet again." Pausing, the blonde looked around at the items on display. "When I came to your grand opening, I saw this rocking chair that really caught my attention—it had carvings along the back headrest. Roses I think or maybe buttercups. Anyway, it looked perfect and I decided to get myself a present. Do you still have it?" she wanted to know.

The mention of buttercups had her thinking of Cody and the horse he's selected for her. And what came after their picnic.

This isn't focusing on work, she admonished herself silently.

Looking at Antonia, she pasted a smile on her lips and beckoned for the woman to follow her.

"It's right back here," she told Antonia, leading the way. She glanced over her shoulder to see if her friend was following her or had decided to forgo the twists and turns of the small, makeshift aisles and was waiting to have the rocking chair brought to her.

"I'm coming," Antonia reassured her, guessing what was on Catherine's mind. "I don't waddle as fast as I used to."

Antonia was forced to stop short or find herself running right into a tall, handsome stranger who possessed a smile that warmed the room, increasing its temperature by at least two degrees.

Why was it that all the good ones were either taken or choosing to pop up now, when she couldn't do anything about it?

The man nodded at her as their paths crossed. He looked vaguely familiar, and then she remembered where she'd seen him before. He was the new chef the Traubs had brought in to work at their resort.

The next moment, the handsome chef had disappeared behind another row of furnishings.

"So, are you thinking about actually buying this

rocking chair?" Catherine asked as she moved the hand-carved chair to a more accessible place.

Gripping the armrests for support, Antonia lowered herself onto the seat. She was trying it out to determine if the rocking chair was wide enough to comfortably accommodate her. Of late, she felt as if she'd spread out like an overfilled cupcake.

"No, I'm just going to sit here until I deliver," she quipped. She rocked a little and smiled. This would do fine. "Speaking of which—" she looked at her friend "—do you deliver or am I going to have to find a way to bring this to my house?"

Even if she didn't have any delivery system, Catherine wouldn't have left Antonia in a lurch. "Don't worry, I'll have one of my brothers deliver it," she promised.

"Excuse me," Shane interrupted politely, popping up again. "I was just wondering—"

Hoping for another sale, Catherine raised her eyes from her friend and turned her attention toward the good-looking bachelor. "Yes?"

"The previous owner, does he still come in once in a while?" Shane wanted to know.

Why would hc bc asking about Fowler? No one had liked the man even before he'd suddenly kidnapped one of their own in a desperate attempt to escape the law.

"You mean Jasper Fowler?" Catherine asked just to make sure he was actually asking about the man and not someone else. When Shane nodded, she said, "Lord no, I haven't seen him since before I bought the store."

Mercifully, everything had been handled through the bank and she hadn't had to endure any one-on-one dealings with the horrible little man.

Shane took in the answer, but he wasn't finished yet. What neither of the two women knew was that he was actually approaching the heart of his real question, circling it slowly so as not to give himself away until he was ready to.

"Is it true that Fowler was using the store as a front for some kind of an illegal business that actually involved the mayor as well?" Shane was doing his best to sound only mildly curious, the way a newcomer to a town might as he gathered information about his new town.

"Ex-mayor," Catherine corrected pointedly.

The present mayor of Thunder Canyon was a distant cousin of hers and completely upstanding, unlike the double-dealing Arthur Swinton, who'd landed in prison for his misdeeds, then managed to escape. The money he'd wound up skimming thanks to his position as mayor hadn't been found so far.

"But as far as your question goes, that was the general belief," she acknowledged. "However, if you're looking for details, I'm afraid that I don't have any." He'd aroused her curiosity. Most people who came in asked questions about the origins of the furniture and knickknacks, not about the location of the former owner and his supposed cohort. "Why do you ask?"

Shane raised his shoulders in a vague shrug. "No reason, really. I'm just trying to pick up a little background information on the town since I'm new around here."

He'd asked too many questions, Shane thought, frustrated and annoyed with the situation. God knew he didn't want to arouse anyone's suspicions until he was ready to make his move. He definitely didn't want his secret coming out before people thought well of him.

Flashing a smile at Catherine that was also directed at the woman in the rocking chair, he said, "Thanks for your help. I'm going to take a few measurements at home and then I'll be back," he promised.

Tipping his hat to both women, Shane left the shop.

"I certainly hope he'll be back," Catherine murmured loud enough for Antonia to hear. Turning toward her friend, Catherine couldn't help remarking on the obvious. "Now *that* was one good-looking man."

Antonia shrugged. "He wasn't bad," she agreed.

"Not bad? God but you have high standards." Then, looking at Antonia pointedly, she said, "I think he liked you."

Antonia rolled her eyes. "Oh, puh-lease. The man was probably thinking how relieved he was that I wasn't his problem. Trust me, *no* man notices someone in my condition, except in that light." She shifted slightly in the chair. "Speaking of men, how are things going with Cody?"

In her exuberance, she'd shared her thoughts about Cody with Antonia. In hindsight, that might not have been a good idea. Antonia was a little bitter when it came to the subject of men. "So far, so good. To be honest, almost too good," she confided.

Antonia looked at her, then shook her head. "Oh, I know that starry-eyed look. I saw it in my own mirror about seven months ago," she said, unconsciously placing her hand on her swollen belly. "My advice to you is stay grounded and don't let yourself get carried away. Most men, sad to say, don't live up to their own hype. Honey, I don't want to see you disappointed the way I was." She stopped herself from saying more. There was no point in complaining. What was done, she thought, was done. "Remember, you're the only one you can depend on."

There was more than a trace of bitterness in Antonia's voice, but then, Catherine supposed the woman was entitled to it. After all, the man she'd been in love with had suddenly found a reason to disappear, leaving her single and pregnant, neither condition was one that Antonia had foreseen for herself at this point in her life.

"I like it," Antonia declared, changing the subject and nodding at the rocking chair. Struggling, she began to get up in almost slow motion, using the armrests to push herself to her feet. "Ring it up." Antonia began to rummage through her purse for her wallet.

"I'll be happy to. It's a sturdy chair that'll last you a lifetime," Catherine said, slowing her pace as she accompanied her friend to the register.

"Good," Antonia replied, still looking through her purse. "So I can use it in my old age."

"Sounds like a plan," Catherine laughed.

The moment Antonia left the store, Catherine reached for the phone. After talking to her friend, she needed reinforcement. She needed to hear the sound of Cody's voice. It didn't matter what he actually said—as long as it wasn't to tell her that he'd decided not to see her anymore.

Antonia's state of mind had gotten to her, Catherine thought.

She let the phone ring ten times. When it rang for an eleventh time, she gave up and started to hang up. Just before the receiver met the cradle, she thought she heard a deep voice say, "Hello?"

Snatching the receiver back up to her ear, Catherine cried, "Cody?" then upbraided herself for not attempting to sound at least a little calmer. This was going to scare him away for sure.

"No, this is Hank."

Hank. Trying to associate the name with a face, she came up empty for a second, then remembered the ranch hand Cody had introduced her to last week. "Um, Hank, is Cody around? I'd like to speak to him."

"Sorry, ma'am, he's out."

Had Hank been told to say that or was Cody actually out? Crossing her fingers that it was the latter, Catherine did her best to sound upbeat as she asked, "Would you know where he is?"

"Well, last I heard, he said something about going to the cemetery."

"Thank you."

Catherine hung up and stared at the phone.

The cemetery.

That was where Cody went when he wanted to talk to his wife. He'd told her that the other day.

A sinking feeling began to take hold of her. He'd gone to "talk" to Renee. This didn't sound good.

Trying to tell herself that she was overreacting, Catherine nevertheless hurried to the front of the shop. She flipped the closed sign so that it was visible from the outside and then quickly left the store.

She had to find out what Cody was doing at the cemetery.

Chapter Fifteen

Approaching the cemetery, Catherine slowed her vehicle to a near crawl as she looked around for an inconspicuous place to park. Cemeteries were far from her favorite place to be, even in daylight.

As she looked around, she saw Cody's truck parked not too far from the entrance. So much for wondering if he'd actually come here.

Driving farther on, she finally found a space to leave her car that wasn't visible from where Cody had left his vehicle.

Oh, God, she'd gone from vintage/thrift shop owner to stalker, Catherine silently upbraided herself. There was no other explanation for why she'd just closed up shop and driven straight over here in the middle of the day.

And exactly what was she going to do once she located Cody in the cemetery? She had no claim on him.

They'd only been seeing one another—if that was what it could actually be called—for a little more than three weeks. Moreover, they'd only become intimate less than a week ago.

It was all so whirlwind fast with no commitments, no promises. Which meant that she and Cody were free to do whatever they wanted with whomever they chose.

Besides, coming here wasn't like Cody was sneaking around, cheating on her with another woman. After all, a man couldn't cheat on a girlfriend with his own wife, she thought ruefully.

His *late* wife, she reminded herself, searching for something to grasp on to.

She couldn't find it. Renee being dead didn't exactly matter, did it? Dead and gone, the woman could still come between them if Cody was still in love with her.

Because if he was, then most likely he'd feel guilty about what they'd been doing together these last few days. The way he'd talked about Renee that night at DJ's Rib Shack told her that to Cody, making love with her was somehow being unfaithful to Renee's memory.

Catherine could feel her anxiety growing.

Oh, God, she thought, resting her head on the steering wheel, what a mess this had turned out to be. Why couldn't things just be simple for a change?

She was in love with Cody—and at the same time, afraid of being in love with him. Afraid of being hurt by him. And he, well he was here at the cemetery, wasn't he? That could only mean that he felt he owed his loyalty to Renee.

Her brother Craig had told her that Cody had been extremely broken up when his wife died. In the months that followed, he'd turned into almost a hermit, only venturing out occasionally. Eventually, that changed a little bit, but not a great deal. None of the women he'd been seen with were ever repeaters—no one saw them in his company more than once. It was as if he was determined to keep moving, to keep ahead of anything that even hinted at becoming permanent.

But he'd seen *her* more than just once, Catherine reminded herself. She had obviously broken whatever rules he'd been adhering to.

Except that maybe now that didn't count anymore—because Cody hadn't shown up today. Hadn't come to her shop the way he had for the last few days. Instead, he'd gone to his wife's grave.

To ask for forgiveness?

A spark of hope entered her heart. Maybe she was wrong, Catherine fervently prayed as she finally got out of her car and walked toward the cemetery entrance. Maybe Cody was here visiting his parents' grave—or someone else's for that matter.

It didn't *have* to be Renee's grave that had brought him here.

Clinging to that and crossing her fingers, Catherine walked through the towering black iron gates and entered the cemetery proper.

Cody removed his Stetson as he took a couple of steps back from his wife's headstone. He'd just laid a large bouquet of carnations—her favorites—on her grave.

"I've got something I need to tell you, Renee," Cody said softly, then smiled ruefully. "But you probably figured that out because of the flowers. You always used to say you knew whenever I'd done something I didn't think you'd like because I brought you flowers." He fidgeted slightly. "Some things don't change, I guess." Cody ran his fingers along the brim of his black hat, searching for the right words so that this could come out coherently. "And then, other things do. And that's why I'm here," he confessed, addressing the headstone. "Because something's changed."

Pausing, he took a deep breath then pushed on. This was not easy for him.

"I know that you told me that you wanted me to move on once you weren't here anymore." It was one of the very last things Renee had said to him as her time grew short. As he remembered, emotion threatened to close his windpipe even after all this time.

"And when you said that, I told you that I couldn't. That it was going to be hard for me just living inside each day that you weren't part of anymore. And it was," he told his wife with feeling. "For a long, long time, it was. But I kept breathing and I kept working—and I kept missing you," he admitted.

He paused again, waiting for the tears that threatened to spill out to retreat. A man was supposed to be able to control his grief better than that, not let it control him.

"I *still* miss you," he told his wife in a low voice. "You need to know that, and to know that I'll always love you. You'll always have a piece of my heart, Renee, a big piece.

"But there's someone else who's come along…." And then he laughed at himself. "But I suspect you already know that. Hell," he reflected, "you know everything I'm about to say, don't you?" He smiled at the headstone, remembering Renee the way she used to be before the cancer left its mark on her. "I know you've been lookin' down, watching me so that means you've already seen her. Her name's Catherine Clifton—you know that, too," he realized the next moment, and a touch of irony echoed in his tone. "She makes me happy, Renee. I never thought that was going to be possible, but it is and she does. And I love her. Not like I loved you," he admitted. "You only fall in love for the first time once. So this is kind of different, but it's love all the same."

Cody cleared his throat, his discomfort surrounding him. But he needed to push on. He needed to say all this to Renee. He owed her that.

Or maybe this was just to close a chapter in his life so that he *could* move on.

"So what I'm doing here today, Renee, is asking for your approval. You see, I'm going to be asking Catherine an important question, one I don't know if she's going to say yes to—but I'm hoping." He saw that he was beginning to leave a mark on the brim of his hat and forced himself to stop fingering it. "But I didn't want to ask her before I told you and asked if it was all right with you.

"I'd be obliged if you could find a way to give me a sign, something that'll tell me you're all right with all this. Doesn't have to be anything big," he added quickly. "No bushes set on fire or stuff like that. As a matter of fact, I'd be relieved if you don't burn anything, but just find a way to give me a sign nonetheless."

He stood there for a moment, looking at the headstone. Waiting. Others might have called him a fool or scoffed at what he was doing, but Cody was completely confident that Renee would find a way to let him know if she approved.

Cody knew that he should just be going by what she'd told him on her deathbed, that she wanted him to move on with his life and not be alone, but that had been eight years ago. What he really needed was something more current. He wanted to be assured that it was still all right for him to marry someone else.

That he had her blessings.

Maybe he was asking for too much. Maybe he should just go and—

And then he heard it. A meadowlark. A western meadowlark, and it was singing. Renee had always loved hearing the bird's melodic tune. Whenever she'd hear it, she'd stop whatever she was doing or saying and just listen.

She used to say to him that it was a boy bird singing to his girl. He'd tease her, saying that there was no way for her to know that, but she'd remain adamant about it, certain she was right.

That was just the way she was.

Grinning as he recalled all this, Cody looked up at the sky, searching it for a sign of the meadowlark. And then he saw it. There was no mistaking the yellow throat and belly, the bold, black V at its throat. It was a meadowlark, all right.

The next moment, the bird had flown out of range, disappearing into the horizon.

But his message lingered in the air.

"Thank you, Renee," Cody whispered softly as he put his Stetson back on his head.

Catherine's heart sank as she stood in the shadow of a massive oak tree, out of sight as she observed Cody from a distance. She was too far away to hear what he was saying, but she saw the flowers and she could tell by the set of his shoulders that the tension that had been there when she'd first walked up was gone.

He'd probably confessed his transgressions with her to his wife and was asking for her forgiveness for what he'd done.

She watched his lips move. Everything about him spoke of an overwhelming sadness.

He was still in love with his wife.

Tears gathered in Catherine's eyes.

Served her right for being dumb enough to fall so hard and so quick, she chastised herself. That wasn't like her; she never reacted that fast. And because she had, she was now paying oh, so dearly for this break in her behavior.

Her heart breaking, Catherine turned and fled the cemetery. She didn't want to take a chance on Cody seeing her.

It was over.

She didn't remember finding her car or even driving back to the shop. The entire way there had been marred by tears. Tears that blurred her vision before sliding down her face.

In the grip of despair and exasperation, Catherine kept wiping the offending tears away, doing her best to stop crying.

But she couldn't.

Each tear just brought more in its wake until she felt as if she was drowning in tears. Maybe it would have been better if she had.

But she didn't drown, didn't die of heartbreak. Somehow she managed to find her way back to the shop.

Parking her vehicle behind the shop, she locked it and entered through the back door.

She turned on lights as she went through the shop. They didn't help. Nothing helped, but it would eventually. She just had to keep going until then.

Meanwhile, there was still a huge list of things for her to do and she was going to throw herself into doing them, pushing herself until she was too exhausted to think or feel, she swore silently.

Even so, for a moment, she debated leaving the closed sign just where it was. The next minute, she decided against it. She needed customers, and talking to them would get her mind off the fact that she no longer had a heart that functioned properly. It was broken into what felt like a million pieces.

Maybe more.

Flipping the sign in the window back to Open for Business, Catherine crossed back to the counter in the center of the room, retrieved her apron from the bottom shelf and slipped it over her clothing.

There was a huge amount of dusting waiting for her in the storage room. If she was lucky, she'd wind up buried under it, she thought, unable to escape the bitterness that was assaulting her from all sides, trying to get a tight hold on her.

Fighting it off no longer seemed worth it.

Nothing seemed worth it, she thought dully, feather duster in one hand, lack of energy, of enthusiasm, in the other.

This time, when the bell over the door sounded some twenty minutes later, she was hoping to see a customer coming into the shop. She was prepared to see just about anyone from the town—except for the one person who *was* coming in.

Damn, where was he when I wanted to see him? And why is he here now that I don't? Catherine silently demanded.

The next second, she could feel her stomach constricting until it felt as if it had turned itself inside out.

Had Cody come to tell her he wasn't going to be seeing her anymore?

Another man would have just allowed his actions to speak for him by avoiding all contact with her. Not exactly a difficult thing to do, seeing as how she spent most of her day at the shop.

Cody isn't like other men, remember? That's why you like him.

Liked him, she corrected with silent anger.

"Hi," Cody said, watching as Catherine moved around the counter, flitting around and not alighting anywhere. Just like those birds he'd seen driving over here. They seemed to be all over at one point, before retreating, flying off somewhere else.

"Hi," she echoed, her teeth all but clenched together, straining the word. "You came at a bad time, Cody," she informed him coolly, deliberately turning her back on him as she gathered together a stack of papers for absolutely no reason she could think of except that she needed to have something to do with her hands. "I'm really busy today."

"Good, I'll help," he offered, reaching for the stack in her hands.

She instantly pulled it back, out of his reach. "You can't," she snapped.

He didn't understand. Why was she looking so angry? And why was she acting as if she'd been bitten by a squadron of mosquitoes?

"Why?" he wanted to know, wondering what had gotten her back up like this.

"Because you can't, that's all," she insisted, doing her best to keep the heat out of her voice as well as the hurt. "This is something I have to do myself." She nodded at the papers and realized, to her dismay, that the top sheet was blank.

And that Cody had already noticed that.

"You have to decode invisible writing?" Cody guessed, amused.

The amusement faded immediately as she said, "I don't appreciate you making jokes at my expense."

Wondering what had gotten into her, Cody nonetheless backed off. "No disrespect intended," he told her. He studied her for a couple of moments in silence, then asked with concern, "You okay, Catherine?"

"Yes!" It was the first answer that came to her lips, fashioned out of complete denial. But lying had never been her thing, even if it kept things simpler right now. So, reconsidering, she didn't bother curbing her hostile tone as she snapped, "No, I'm not."

Now they were finally getting somewhere, Cody thought. "Tell me what's wrong," he encouraged.

You, you're what's wrong. You came on bigger than life and when I fell for you, you hurried back to your dead wife, the excuse you hide behind for not living your life to the fullest.

Catherine pressed her lips together, knowing she couldn't just blurt that out. Cody would think she was crazy—and maybe she was.

So instead, she said something vague that would get him to leave. "I need some time, Cody. And space," she added.

"Time and space," he repeated, as if to check that he had heard her correctly.

Or was he just making fun of her? she wondered, ready to take on a fight despite the weariness that was rapidly invading her.

"Yes." It was a struggle to keep from shouting at him. The man had taken her heart and played handball against a concrete wall with it.

He looked at her closely, trying to see beneath the layers that had suddenly popped up between them. Had he been mistaken before, thinking she was the one?

No, he didn't think so, he decided. But right now, he needed answers. "Why?" he finally asked.

Rather than give him an answer, she snapped and pleaded, "Stop asking that."

"I'm asking that because I want to understand," he told her simply.

She closed her eyes, searching for strength. Searching for the will to just keep continuing. "Just go, Cody. Please," she entreated him. "Just go," she repeated with more feeling.

Cody looked at her in silence for a long moment, considering his options. If he did what he wanted to—dragged her into his arms and kissed her until whatever it was that was wrong was right again—she could easily press charges against him.

He had no choice, he realized, but to walk away just as she wanted him to.

Maybe if he gave her this "time and space" she was

asking for, it would somehow help her clear her head and come around again. Or at least get her to the point where she could explain to him what the hell was going on with her.

Blowing out an exasperated breath, he looked at Catherine for another long, pregnant moment, then quietly said, "All right. I'll go. For now," he deliberately qualified so that she understood that this wasn't over between them.

Not by a long shot.

Without another word, he turned on his heel and walked toward the front door.

Catherine remained exactly where she was. Only her eyes moved, staring after him. She could feel her heart sinking further down with each step he tread that took him farther and farther away from her.

The very fact that Cody was going, that he listened to her rather than challenged what she was saying and then stubbornly remained here, told her that she'd been right all along.

Cody *had* gone to his wife to apologize for his "transgression," for having any sort of feelings for another woman rather than remaining faithful to her memory.

Because, if she'd been wrong in her assessment, Cody would have fought her request, fought to remain in the shop.

Moreover, he would have tried to get her to change her mind. He would have argued with her until he managed to get to the bottom of all this.

Because Cody Overton wasn't a quitter, he was the kind of man who hung in there to fight for what he wanted.

But he obviously no longer wanted her. He wanted to leavc.

And he *was* leaving.

She'd given him a way out and he'd taken it.

"Nice going," Catherine murmured sarcastically to herself.

The tears came back. But this time, she didn't bother trying to wipe them away. It didn't matter.

Nothing mattered. Because she'd lost something very precious.

No, you didn't. You never had it in the first place, a voice inside her head jeered.

The tears fell harder.

Faster.

Catherine slowly walked up to the front of the store and flipped the sign back around so that it proclaimed Closed for a second time that day.

As closed as she hoped her heart would be. Once it stopped aching this way.

Chapter Sixteen

Cody shivered involuntarily as a feeling of déjà vu swept over him.

He was back at the State Fair. Back riding the same noisy carousel with its brightly painted horses.

Except that he didn't see Renee.

Where was she?

The anxiety was new, too.

It ate away at him. He couldn't shake it. Couldn't rise above the feeling.

Something was wrong.

And then he heard it, heard the laughter. For a moment, he breathed a sigh of relief. But then he listened again. The laughter was different. It didn't belong to her.

Didn't belong to Renee.

The timbere was off, but it still filled him, filled his head, filled his heart.

There was a presence with him, but that, too, wasn't Renee.

That was when he knew. The presence he felt, the woman who was suddenly beside him, riding the carousel, was Catherine.

It was Catherine riding on the painted horse beside him. Catherine whose slender hands were wrapped around the pole that was inserted into the horse's saddle. Catherine who looked at him with love in her eyes and laughter on her lips.

Catherine.

Catherine's voice resonated in his chest and in his soul at the same time. She was saying something to him, but he couldn't make it out, couldn't hear the words. Her voice became a loud buzz, devolving into a disjointed hum that rang in his ears.

The anxiety rose up again, this time to engulf him, dark and foreboding. Because, just as Renee had all those other times, Catherine began to fade away right before his eyes.

When he reached for her, to try to somehow hang on to her, Catherine only faded faster.

And as he lunged forward, grasping the empty air, she disappeared altogether.

Heartsick, Cody tried to cry out her name, but his voice was stuck in his throat, becoming just as much of a prisoner as he was in this maddening time warp that insisted on continually replaying itself in his head.

"Help me, Cody. Free me."

He could *feel* Catherine pleading for him to save her rather than actually *hear* her.

And then there was silence. Nothing but deafening silence.

He was alone.

"Catherine!" he cried. His voice came echoing back to him as he stood looking down into the mouth of the abyss. "Catherine, where are you?"

Nothing but the sound of his own voice, vibrating with panic, came back to him.

And then the darkness closed over him as well. A sickening sense of finality washed over him.

It was over.

Cody bolted upright, sweating profusely and shaking so badly he thought he would never be able to stop.

It took him several minutes to get himself under control. This latest version of his nightmare had really spooked him.

Trying to think, to piece what he could together, he had no idea what to make of this new twist. He wasn't a man who believed in omens, but this was different. This had been so vivid, so real, as if something out there was trying to tell him something.

Was it some sixth sense, warning him that Catherine was in danger?

He honestly didn't know, but he was certain of one thing. He wasn't going to have any peace until he'd reassured himself that Catherine was safe and well.

His eyes bleary, Cody switched on the lamp on the nightstand next to his bed and picked up the clock he kept there. With effort, the numbers on the clock's face came into focus.

It was almost two in the morning.

Five more hours until dawn and even *that* was really too early for him to be knocking on someone's door.

Taking a deep breath, Cody tried to reason with himself.

That lasted for exactly three minutes and gained no ground. Frustrated, he kicked off the covers and got out of bed. Adrenaline began to surge through his veins as a sense of urgency reared its head and seized him.

He couldn't make heads or tails of it, but that didn't matter.

The only thing that mattered to him at this point was seeing with his own eyes that Catherine was all right. Because if she wasn't and he'd just remained here, immobile and of no earthly use to her, Catherine would never forgive him.

Hell, *he* wouldn't forgive himself, Cody thought in exasperated anger.

It took him less than five minutes to hurry into his clothes and run down the stairs.

Once on the ground floor, he hopped from one foot, then the other, pulling his boots on while on the run. Moving even faster, he nearly forgot to close the front door behind him as he dashed to his truck.

Doubling back, he slammed it hard. The door locked itself.

At the moment, all he had was tunnel vision. He had to see Catherine with his own eyes. Nothing else mattered right now except for Catherine.

Once behind the wheel, Cody drove like a maniac, swerving from side to side to avoid creatures that used the cover of night to forage for their food.

The only reason he didn't get into an accident with another vehicle was because, at this hour, there *were* no other vehicles on the road.

It occurred to Cody that he'd probably broken some kind of a speed record getting from his ranch to the

Clifton house, but that wasn't something he could readily ask anyone to substantiate.

He could feel his breath backing up in his throat as he drew closer to her family's house. It was just a dream, he told himself, just a dream. Catherine was fine. She *had* to be.

His hands felt like ice as he clutched the steering wheel.

Pulling up in front of the tall, imposing Victorian house, he nearly strangled on the seat belt he forgot to release. Doing so, he jumped from the vehicle, taking the steps leading to the porch two at a time.

His boots resounded on the wooden, wraparound porch. Forgoing the doorbell, he knocked—pounded actually—on the front door.

"Are you home?" he called out as he pounded the door again. "Catherine, if you're all right, answer the door!"

Three minutes into his rant, the front door flew open. But instead of Catherine, Cody found himself looking down at a white-haired, slightly bleary-eyed older man in a navy blue robe thrown over a pair of light blue pajamas.

The confused scowl on the round face told Cody exactly what Amos Clifton thought of being dragged out of bed at this ungodly hour.

"What the hell is wrong with you, boy?" Amos demanded in a deep, booming voice. "You have *any* idea what time it is?"

Equally agitated and frustrated, Cody answered, "Yes, sir, I do."

"Then why the hell are you banging on my door, yelling at the top of your lungs like some drunken banshee?" He eyed Cody, not sure what to make of any of this. "You deliberately *trying* to raise the dead?"

Cody took a deep breath, standing his ground. "No, sir, what I'm trying to do is find out if Catherine's all right."

Amos's expression indicated that he thought he was talking to a lunatic. "Last I looked, she was, but that was before all this yelling and screeching started. Now she's probably hiding from the madman standing on our veranda," he predicted. He shouted a question at him, "Just what is your problem, boy?"

To be heard, Cody raised his voice as well and shouted, "I'm in love with your daughter."

White eyebrows drew together in suspicion. "That would be Catherine?" Amos asked impatiently. "Be specific. I've got more than one daughter."

"Yes, sir. Catherine, sir," Cody confirmed. Shifting nervously, Cody realized that this was going to be his moment of truth. There was no turning back from this now—not that he wanted to. "I take it that you're her father?"

"Well, I'm sure as hell not her mother," Amos retorted, wondering if Cody was dangerous or just some lovesick cowboy.

Cody took in another deep breath, silently warning himself not to hyperventilate. "Sir, I want to ask for your blessings."

"Done. You've got it. My blessings," Amos parroted. "Now will you go home?"

Determined, Cody plowed on. "I want to marry your daughter. Catherine," he added in case the man had forgotten he'd specified that earlier.

In response to his proclamation, Cody heard a round

of squeals. The noise was coming from inside the house. More precisely, from the young women gathered at the top of the stairs inside the house. Drawn by the sound of raised voices, they'd remained to listen to this exchange between their father and Catherine's suitor.

Flabbergasted, Amos stuttered, "Well, I—" Before he could finish, he was being gently pushed aside as Catherine came to the front door.

"I'll handle this, Daddy," Catherine told him, then turned to look at Cody. Part of her thought she'd just imagined this last part of the exchange between her father and Cody. "Did I hear right? Are you seriously asking me to marry you?"

Cody was at a loss as to what she was actually thinking. Her somber expression gave nothing away. It definitely wasn't what he was hoping for in response to his proposal.

"Yes," he told her emphatically.

She wanted to believe him. More than anything in the world, she wanted to believe that Cody actually wanted to marry her.

But what she'd witnessed this afternoon told her otherwise and very nearly negated his proposal. "You're still in love with your wife, Cody," Catherine told him crisply.

"Wife?" Amos echoed from inside the house. "This lunatic is married?" he demanded, growing incensed.

Catherine held up her hand, wordlessly asking for her father's silence. Her father was so stunned, he did as his oldest daughter requested. He held his tongue.

"I saw you at the cemetery yesterday," she told Cody. "Saw you standing there for a long time, talking to her."

He had no idea how Catherine came to be there, but

that wasn't the point right now. Getting her to understand why he'd gone to the cemetery was.

"I was," he confirmed. Then, before she could tell him to leave, he said, "I was saying goodbye."

"Goodbye?" Catherine repeated uncertainly.

Moving closer, Cody took her hands in his. "Yes. I was telling her that I was going to ask you to marry me." He smiled, certain now that he was doing the right thing. He could feel it in his bones. "I love you," he told her with feeling. "Ever since you fell into my arms, I've been thinking about the future. *Our* future."

"What do you mean, she fell into your arms? Fell from where?" Amos wanted to know, still not completely convinced that he didn't have a crazy man standing on his doorstep.

"I'll explain it all later, Daddy," Catherine promised, never taking her eyes off Cody. "Go on," she coaxed.

Cody shook his head, annoyed with himself. This wasn't coming out the way he'd planned. The words were all jumbled up.

"Let me start over," he said to Catherine.

Before she could protest for him to just keep going, she saw Cody getting down on one knee. Her heart began to beat faster as, still kneeling, he took one of her hands in his.

"I promise you that as long as I draw breath, you'll never know a day without my love." He paused, wanting to get the words just right. "Catherine Clifton, will you do me the incredible honor of becoming my wife?"

Stifling a shriek of joy, Catherine fell to her knees so that she could be on the same level with Cody. She threw her arms around his neck and cried, "Yes, oh, yes."

There was a chorus of cheers behind her as her sisters all ran down the stairs to be part of this joyful moment. Even her father was now beaming at the way this scene had just played itself out.

But all that Catherine would learn later. Right now, she was completely focused on the man who was able to make the entire world fade away when he kissed her.

The world was held at bay for a long, long time.

It completely astounded Catherine how incredibly quickly a wedding—with all the trimmings, yet—could be pulled together when the members of her family all worked in concert the way they did for her.

The moment she said yes and agreed to be married as soon as possible, Catherine's family went into high gear. A wedding dress was purchased and subsequently altered to meet with her delighted approval, miraculously ready the night before the wedding. The menu for the perforce large reception was decided upon before the sun set on the momentous day that had begun with such loud pounding on the family front door.

Cody even agreed to wear a modified version of a tuxedo—anything to make Catherine happy *and* his wife.

A week later, accompanied by a huge flock of butterflies that were flapping wildly and breeding at an incredible speed within the confines of her abdomen, Catherine clutched a large bouquet of pink roses as she stood beside Cody on the steps of her back porch, her sisters and brothers comprising the wedding party and standing up, grinning, behind the nervous bride and the contented groom.

Catherine truly couldn't remember *ever* being happier, despite the dive-bombing butterflies in her stomach. Funny how things managed to arrange themselves sometimes. All she'd initially wanted to do was to carve out a little independence for herself by buying the shop and turning it into a success.

She'd gotten her independence and so much more.

Though she'd thought about it a lot, she'd never thought that she would actually wind up getting married. Never thought that she could ever be as wildly in love as she was right now at this very moment.

If she was dreaming, then she never wanted to wake up.

For a split second, Catherine mentally took a step back and looked around. Everyone she'd ever cared about and loved, her family and her friends, were all gathered together to celebrate her happiness.

Their happiness, she amended, slanting a glance at the man who was several words away from becoming her husband.

It just didn't get any better than this, Catherine thought.

"And do you, Cody Overton, take Catherine Clifton for your lawful wedded wife, to love and honor, through sickness and health, for richer or poor, for better or worse, as long as you both shall live?" the minister asked.

There wasn't even a microsecond of hesitation on Cody's part. He gave his answer immediately. "I do."

"And do you, Catherine Clifton, take Cody Overton for your lawful wedding husband, for richer or poorer, for better or worse, in sickness and health, as long as you both shall live?"

The minister barely had time to finish his sentence before Catherine loudly cried, "I do."

With the rings in place and the vows taken, the minister nodded, closing the worn book he'd used for guidance for the last couple of decades. "Then, by the power vested in me by the state of Montana, I now pronounce you husband and wife. All right, you may now ki—"

The minister laughed, aborting what he was about to say. There was no need to utter those final instructions. The newlywed couple had beaten him to it.

With a chuckle, he commented, "Well, you certainly took to that like ducks to water."

His observation was met with laughter from everyone except for the bride and groom. They were otherwise occupied and intended to be so for a while longer.

Epilogue

Twilight was slowly creeping in on dusky feet outside the small, quaint bed-and-breakfast where Cody and Catherine were honeymooning.

And were officially beginning their married life together.

While it was growing darker outside, inside the room where they were staying was an entirely different matter. Catherine was fairly certain that any moment, their bed was going to ignite from the sheer heat that they were generating as they came together time and again.

Almost spent and tottering on the brink of sheer exhaustion, Catherine curled up into her husband as they lay together, waiting for the pounding of their hearts to subside to a normal rhythm.

They had been at the inn for two days and nights now and had yet to venture outside.

Cody brushed his lips against her forehead, sending yet another wave of absolute contentment sweeping through her.

"Any regrets?" he murmured.

"Just one," she answered after a moment's consideration.

Cody raised himself up on his elbow and looked at the woman who lay cradled in his arm. Her answer surprised him. Whatever was wrong, he intended to fix it.

"Oh?"

Catherine nodded and ran her hand along his cheek, the small movement testifying to the overwhelming love she felt for him.

"I regret that I didn't find my 'real vintage cowboy' years earlier," she told him, doing her best to keep a straight face.

Cody's features softened as he grinned at her. "Well, I figure we can always try to make up for lost time now," he told her.

"There is that," she agreed, turning her body into his, the very movement extending a silent, open invitation to her brand-new husband.

Cody paused for a second, overwhelmed by the realization that he was one hell of a lucky man, finding his soul mate not just once, but twice in one lifetime. What were the odds?

"Just let me catch my breath," he requested, following it up with a very sensual wink.

"I can do that," she answered, her eyes sparkling as she nodded her head.

Cody's arm tightened around her, holding Catherine closer than a prayer. "Tell me, how would you feel about having a whole bushel of little real vintage cowboys and cowgirls?" he wanted to know.

"Wonderful," she answered with enthusiasm. "I'd feel wonderful." She shifted so that she could look at Cody's face and gauge whether or not he was serious. To her delight, he was. "How soon can we get started?" she asked eagerly.

He pretended to consider the question in earnest. "Well, you know, it's a might tricky business, getting these little folks to be just right. I'd say that we're going to need some practice. Actually, lots and lots of practice," he amended.

She nodded, as if taking what he was saying seriously. "Practice, right," she agreed, adding, "Then I'm your girl."

Damn lucky, he thought again. "You most certainly are that," he responded, then said it again for reinforcement, in case she hadn't heard him the first time. "You most certainly are."

The words were barely spoken before he threw himself into the project they had both just committed themselves to. He kissed his bride long and hard.

"Work" never promised to be more exhilarating than right at this moment.

* * * * *

“Are you afraid of the rumor mill?” Clay asked.

“Well, it has chewed me up and spit me out before,” she admitted.

What could be juicier than pregnant and unwed Antonia Wright out on a date *(Can you imagine? In her condition?)* with the sexy cowboy who was staying out at her ranch? *(What could he possibly see in her? And is he really sleeping in the boardinghouse—or in her bed?)*

“You don’t strike me as the type of woman who would let one punch take her down.”

“I’m also not the type of woman who would let a man goad—or seduce—me into going out with him,” she informed him.

“Are you saying no to my invitation?”

“No, I’m saying yes—but because I want to go, not because I was coerced or challenged.”

“I only care about the yes,” he said, and brushed his lips against hers.

And when he kissed her like that, Antonia couldn’t imagine saying no to anything…

Dear Reader,

The Maverick's Ready-Made Family isn't a traditional family. Clayton Traub is a single father, Antonia Wright is an expectant mother and neither is looking for any kind of romantic entanglement. But sometimes love has other ideas…

This story held particular appeal for me because I also come from an untraditional family that, in addition to my mother and father and sister, includes a stepfather, half-brother, stepmother, two stepbrothers and a stepsister, and numerous in-laws. Consequently, holidays in my family are rarely traditional—but they're always interesting.

I hope you'll find Clayton and Antonia's story just as interesting and that you enjoy this addition to the latest MONTANA MAVERICKS series.

Happy reading!

Brenda Harlen

THE MAVERICK'S READY-MADE FAMILY

BY

BRENDA HARLEN

First published in Great Britain 2012
by Mills & Boon, an imprint of Harlequin (UK) Limited,
Eton House, 18-24 Paradise Road, Richmond, Surrey TW9 1SR

Special thanks and acknowledgement to Brenda Harlen for her contribution to the Montana Mavericks: Back in the Saddle continuity.

ISBN: 978 0 263 89480 6
ebook ISBN: 978 1 408 97157 4

23-1112

Harlequin (UK) policy is to use papers that are natural, renewable and recyclable products and made from wood grown in sustainable forests. The logging and manufacturing processes conform to the legal environmental regulations of the country of origin.

Printed and bound in Spain
by Blackprint CPI, Barcelona

Brenda Harlen grew up in a small town, surrounded by books and imaginary friends. Although she always dreamed of being a writer, she chose to follow a more traditional career path first. After two years of practicing as an attorney (including an appearance in front of the Supreme Court of Canada), she gave up her "real" job to be a mom and to try her hand at writing books. Three years, five manuscripts and another baby later, she sold her first book—an RWA Golden Heart winner—to Mills & Boon.

Brenda lives in southern Ontario with her real-life husband/hero, two heroes-in-training and two neurotic dogs. She is still surrounded by books (too many books, according to her children) and imaginary friends, but she also enjoys communicating with real people. Readers can contact Brenda by e-mail at brendaharlen@yahoo.com or by snail mail c/o Harlequin Books, 233 Broadway, Suite 1001, New York, NY 10279, USA.

To all the authors of the Montana Mavericks series,
past and present, for creating a fabulous world
that readers want always to return to.

Prologue

"Arriving at destination on right."

Clayton Traub turned and followed the long gravel drive until he saw a sign above the doorway of a two-story building that read Wright's Way, confirming that the vehicle's navigation system had been correct. Not that he'd doubted the device's capabilities—not really. He just believed in covering all of his bases.

In the case of following his brother, Forrest, on a three-hundred-mile road trip from Rust Creek Falls to Thunder Canyon, Montana, there were a lot of bases. Especially considering that Forrest had been more than a little...distracted since his return from Iraq.

Clay parked his Dodge Ram Quad Cab and assessed the residence. The clapboard siding looked as if it had been recently painted, the windows shone in the late-afternoon sun, and there were pots of bronze-colored mums flanking the entranceway. The cursory perusal assured him that it didn't look like a bad place to spend a few weeks, and he didn't plan on staying any longer than that.

He headed up to the main house, following the instructions of a ranch hand who'd told him that Tony would take care of the registration and give him the key.

A housekeeper answered his knock at the door and directed him to an office. It wasn't until Clay peeked into the room that he realized "Tony" was actually "Toni."

Which shouldn't have been a big deal, except that along with the realization came an intense jolt of basic masculine appreciation.

His first glimpse was of her profile, as she was seated at a desk and working at the computer. Her nose was straight, her chin slightly pointed and long, dark hair tumbled over her shoulders. Slender, graceful fingers moved expertly over the keys and though those fingers never faltered, she must have sensed his presence in the doorway because she glanced over her shoulder and smiled. And his heart actually skipped a beat.

Toni Wright was very definitely female—and exquisite.

"Can I help you?"

It took a moment for her words to penetrate the fog that had suddenly enveloped his brain, and another moment for Clay to get his tongue unstuck from the roof of his mouth. It had been a long time since he'd had such a purely visceral reaction to the sight of a woman. A very long time.

"Clayton Traub," he finally said. "I'm checking in."

"Welcome to Wright's Way." Her tone was pleasant, her smile natural, but there was more than a hint of reserve in the depths of her green eyes. "Do you know how long you plan to stay?"

Focus, Traub. The reprimand was silent but stern. He was here because he needed a break and because his mother wanted him to keep an eye on his brother while Forrest was rehabbing in Thunder Canyon. The absolute last thing he needed was to let himself be distracted by a pretty face. On the other hand, this trip to Thunder Canyon suddenly promised to be a whole lot more interesting.

"A few weeks, at least," he finally responded to her question.

"The rent is paid weekly, in advance."

"That's not a problem," he assured her, unfazed by her all-business attitude.

She passed him a page with Rental Terms & Conditions noted across the top. "Please review this and sign at the bottom."

He scanned the document, nothing giving him any cause for concern—until he got to paragraph eight. He tapped a finger on the page, beside the relevant clause. "What exactly does it mean by 'no overnight visitors allowed'?"

"It means that only registered guests are allowed to stay overnight on the premises," she told him.

"That could be a problem."

She shrugged. "Then there's a motel in town, The Wander-On Inn, that might be more to your liking."

"That wouldn't please my cousin, Dax, who recommended your boarding house. He said he went to school with Hudson Wright. I'm assuming he's your brother?"

"And another brother, Jonah, was in D.J.'s grade," she told him.

"How many brothers do you have?"

"Three, but the number has no relevance to your issue with paragraph eight. Like the rest of the rules, it's intended to protect the comfort and safety of our boarders.

We can't be responsible for unregistered guests wandering the halls of the boarding house or—"

"He wouldn't be wandering far," Clay promised. "In fact, he's just started to crawl."

Her brow furrowed. "He?"

"My son," he explained.

The firm set of her mouth softened, the edges curved. "You have a little boy?"

"A baby," he clarified. "Five months old. His name's Bennett."

The last of her reserve melted away. When she smiled at him this time, the impact hit the center of his chest like a wrecking ball. Lord, this woman could be dangerous.

"A baby," she echoed softly. Then, with a note of obvious concern in her voice, "Where is he now?"

"He fell asleep in the truck, so my brother, Forrest, is keeping an eye on him."

"I'd love to meet him." She pushed her chair back from the desk. "Let me just grab your keys and…"

Whatever else she said was drowned out by the sudden screaming of alarms inside his head warning of imminent danger. Because when Toni Wright stood up, Clay saw that she wasn't just female and gorgeous—she was extremely pregnant!

Chapter One

Five weeks later

Damn pregnancy hormones!

It was becoming a familiar curse to Antonia Wright, because as thrilled as she was that she was going to be a mother, she was completely unprepared to deal with the increasingly frequent surges of hormones through her system. Surges that had been nonexistent through the first six months of her pregnancy, but had become more regular and insistent over the past few weeks. Since Clayton Traub had taken up residence at Wright's Way, in fact.

But Antonia refused to believe that the link between his presence and her hormones was anything more than a coincidence. Most of the books she'd read had warned that sexual desire was likely to decrease in the last trimester, but Antonia was finding just the opposite to be true. Of course, nothing that she'd experienced since learning that she was going to have a baby had been what she expected. At least not since the initial excitement of having her pregnancy confirmed was usurped by the panic of realizing she was going to be a single mother.

Maybe having a baby without a father anywhere in the vicinity wasn't an ideal situation, but she was making the best of it. And she was genuinely excited about the opportunities and challenges that motherhood would entail, but she hadn't expected the hormones.

Because that was the only explanation she could come up with for the way her pulse raced every time she saw Clay in the dining room. And the way her knees got all weak and wobbly if he passed close to her. And the way her skin felt all hot and tingly whenever he even looked at her.

But she'd learned her lesson after Gene hightailed it out of town. She had no intention of ever following her heart again, and she *definitely* would never get involved with a boarder again.

Which only proved that her physiological reaction to Clayton Traub had less to do with her heart than her hormones. She didn't even know the guy, really, so it was ridiculous to think that she might have any kind of emotional attachment to him. But she was definitely attracted. The warm and achy feeling deep inside all of her womanly places confirmed that fact. Or maybe she was just severely sexually deprived.

It had been exactly seven months, one week and four days since she'd had sex. In the first six and a half of those months, she hadn't missed the physical intimacy. She hadn't even thought about it really, because she'd been too busy trying to come to terms with her pregnancy and anticipate the demands of impending motherhood.

But ever since Clay Traub had shown up at the Wright

Ranch, she'd found herself thinking about how very long it had been since she'd been held or kissed or touched. How very long it had been since she'd been wanted.

Not that any man in his right mind would want her now, with a belly that was rounder than her breasts. And so big that it was sometimes hard for Antonia to believe that she still had another seven weeks to go before she delivered her baby. As eagerly as she was counting down to the day that she would hold her child in her arms, her trepidation was growing along with her excitement.

What did she know about taking care of a baby? Not very much. And she was terrified that she was going to screw up. If only she could talk to her own mother—but that option had been taken away from her more than two years earlier when Lucinda had succumbed to a massive stroke. Nothing had been the same since her death—not Antonia's father, not her brothers, not even the ranch.

Or maybe it would be more accurate to say *especially* not the ranch. Devastated by the loss of his beloved wife, John Wright had started to neglect his responsibilities, which had resulted in the loss of some business and, consequently, trouble paying the bills. Antonia's brothers had taken over most of the day-to-day operations, and she had convinced them to turn the former bunkhouse into a boarding house to generate additional revenue. Most of the rental units had sat vacant for a while—certainly long enough to give her cause for concern—but once they'd taken in their first boarders and those boarders started chatting in town about the comfort of the accommodations and the quality of the meals, the rooms had begun to fill.

Now it was rare for any room to sit empty for more than a week or two, allowing Antonia to breathe a sigh of relief that she hadn't made a mistake with this venture. Especially considering that she'd given Peggy, the Wright's longtime housekeeper and cook, a raise to compensate for the additional meal prep that was required, and had recently hired Nora, a high school student who lived up the road, to help serve dinner.

Because now that she was in her third trimester, Antonia had finally acknowledged that she no longer had the energy to be on her feet sixteen hours a day. And when those days started at 5:00 a.m., as hers had this morning, she was usually feeling the first signs of fatigue before the breakfast crowd had gone.

"Good morning, Toni."

She recognized his voice immediately, and adrenaline rushed through her veins as her cheeks filled with color. There was just something about the way he said her name that actually made her knees weak.

"Good morning," she replied, deliberately focusing on the baby in his arms rather than looking into the warmth of Clayton Traub's dark brown eyes. "And how are you doing this morning, handsome?"

Bennett gave her a gummy smile and reached his arms out to her, and Antonia wanted nothing more than to scoop him up. Unfortunately, she had a full coffeepot in one hand and a trio of mugs in the other.

"Typical male," she mused. "Wanting yet one more thing from a woman who already has her hands full." But since she couldn't give Bennett a cuddle, she gave him a quick kiss on the forehead, then finally chanced a glance at his father. "I'll bring his breakfast as soon as you get him settled."

"No hurry," he assured her. "He had some oatmeal about an hour ago."

"We start serving breakfast here at six," she reminded him. She'd given him a dining schedule along with the rest of the paperwork when he'd checked in, and for the first several days, he had brought the baby to the dining room early. But then the time of their arrival had started getting later and later, until they were showing up near the end of the breakfast shift rather than the beginning.

"And at six, you usually have a pretty full house," Clay noted.

"A lot of the men need to get an early start because they have jobs in town or elsewhere that they have to get to." Which made her wonder how her handsome boarder was occupying his time in Thunder Canyon. Of course, as long as his checks didn't bounce, his employment—or lack thereof—wasn't any of her concern.

Not that she was completely in the dark about Clay. He might have been "one of the Rust Creek Falls' Traubs" but he was related to the Thunder Canyon Traubs, which meant that a fair amount of information about him was circulating around town. Including that he was one of six sons and had previously worked on the family ranch in Rust Creek Falls with four of his brothers. Only Forrest had opted for a different career, choosing to enlist in the military and fight for his country. He'd returned from the war in Iraq with an injured leg that was being treated by Dr. North at Thunder Canyon General Hospital. And PTSD, according to some whispers.

Since moving into the boarding house, both Clay and Forrest had been the subjects of as much admiration as speculation. The female population, in particular, seemed curious about these "real" cowboys who had come to town and were eager to get to know them better. Antonia didn't think either of the brothers had encouraged the attention, but she couldn't blame the women for their interest. Clayton and Forrest were both sinfully good-looking but, from day one, her heart had been firmly ensnared by Bennett.

"That's why we like to come later," Clay said, drawing her attention back to their conversation. "So Bennett can flirt with his favorite girl."

"You need to raise your standards," she told the little boy. Then, to his father, "And I really need to get this coffee into the dining room—where Forrest is already seated at your usual table."

"Of course." He stepped back so that she could move past him into the dining room.

As she did, she was conscious of his gaze following her. Or maybe she was just imagining it. Because why would Clay be watching her? Why would any man look twice at a woman whose belly entered a room ten seconds before the rest of her body did?

Okay, she knew she wasn't really as enormous as she felt, but having to sneak into her father's closet to find a shirt that would button over her baby bump made her feel huge and unattractive. Having a man pay any amount of attention to her was a boost to her battered ego—and when that man was as incredibly good-looking as Clayton Traub, well, she could probably be forgiven for letting her imagination run away.

Because even if he didn't have any kind of romantic interest—and again, she'd be more shocked if he did—she enjoyed the brief conversations they occasionally shared over breakfast or dinner. Even after five weeks, she wouldn't say she knew him well, but she did know him well enough to appreciate his straightforward manner and easygoing personality.

Mostly she appreciated that he didn't ask too many questions. Having been the subject of so many whispers and rumors since her pregnancy became public knowledge, she was happy to talk to someone who didn't want to know or seem to care about the father of her baby. And it warmed her heart immeasurably to witness the obvious affection between Clay and his son.

Obviously some men were able to embrace the joys and responsibilities of fatherhood. Unfortunately for Antonia, the father of her baby wasn't one of them.

There had been more than a hint of fall in the air when Clay made his way to the main house for breakfast, reminding him that he'd already been in Thunder Canyon for longer than the few weeks he'd originally planned to stay. As he settled Bennett into the high chair that Toni had set at one end of the long table, it occurred to him that maybe it was time to go back to Rust Creek Falls and the family ranch. But he wasn't ready to leave Thunder Canyon, not just yet.

He felt more than a little guilty that he'd bailed on his father and his responsibilities at the ranch—even if he'd done so with his mother's blessing. Of course, Bob Traub was more than capable of handling things on his own. Hell, he'd been managing the whole spread since long before any of his sons had even been born, and he'd be the first to take issue with anyone who suggested that he wasn't still capable of doing so.

He certainly hadn't tried to prevent Clay from leaving. In fact, he'd agreed that it was a good idea for him to get away from Rust Creek Falls for a while. But when he'd encouraged his son to head west, Clay suspected that he meant a little farther west than Thunder Canyon—no doubt hoping that he would track down Delia in California and convince her to marry him so that their son would have a proper family.

Bob and Ellie Traub had raised their sons with traditional values and a strict moral code of behavior, and Clay believed in accepting responsibility for his actions.

But he did *not* believe that marrying Delia was the answer, and he wanted something better for his son than a woman who clearly wasn't interested in being a mother.

But until he figured out what that was, he was enjoying his time in Thunder Canyon. He liked the town and he had no complaints at all about the accommodations at Wright's Way. The only real problem, from his perspective, was the inexplicable attraction he felt whenever he was around his landlady.

His *very pregnant* landlady, as he continually had to remind himself. Because any man could be forgiven for thinking lustful thoughts about an attractive woman—and Toni was no doubt an extremely attractive woman—but she was also an expectant mother, and contemplating any such ideas about a mother-to-be just seemed wrong.

Of course, that knowledge and even his own internal reprimands didn't stop the thoughts from forming in his mind. And seeing Toni at the family-style breakfast she prepared for the boarders every morning somehow only further fanned the flames of his desire. A realization that, as he settled into the chair beside his son and across from his brother, continued to baffle him.

He'd always appreciated the company of women and, in the past, he'd enjoyed countless casual dates and numerous carefree liaisons. But he wasn't that man anymore. He had a child to consider now—as would Toni in the very near future.

Clay had never imagined himself as a father. Not that he'd precluded the possibility from his future, he simply hadn't thought he was ready for the responsibility at this point in his life. Delia showing up on his doorstep with a baby had taken that choice out of his hands. And while he would fight tooth and nail to protect his child, the little boy was all the responsibility Clay could—or wanted to—handle at this point in his life. He certainly didn't want or need the complication of a personal relationship right now, and hooking up with a woman who had a baby of her own on the way would just be crazy.

No one had ever had cause to question Clay's sanity in the past, so why was he so drawn to this particular woman? Why now?

Toni set a plastic bowl on the tray of Bennett's high chair, and the little boy immediately reached into it, wrapping his fist around a handful of scrambled egg and then shoving his fist into his mouth.

She ruffled his hair and smiled. "You're a hungry little guy today, are you?"

Bennett's only response was to reach into the bowl with his other fist.

"He's got a healthy appetite," Clay told her.

"Growing boys need to eat," Antonia noted.

"So do grown men," Forrest pointed out.

Toni shifted her attention to the man seated on the other side of the table, her cheeks flushing as she took the empty platter from his hands.

"Coming right up," she promised.

Clay scowled at his brother. "Don't you think that was a little rude?"

"What was rude? Interrupting your flirting?" Forrest asked.

"I wasn't flirting."

His brother snorted.

"I wasn't," Clay insisted, though he wondered why he bothered. Because even if he had been flirting—which he wasn't—he didn't care what his brother thought. But he also didn't want Toni overhearing their conversation and thinking that he had a thing for her. Because he didn't.

"Wasn't it Shakespeare who said something about men who protested too much?" Forrest challenged.

Bennett banged his hands on his tray, giving Clay an excuse to turn his attention to the little boy and ignore his brother's comment.

"How's your breakfast?" he asked.

The baby responded by offering a fistful of scrambled egg.

Clay nudged the little boy's hand toward his mouth. "Bennett, eat."

And he did, happily.

Toni returned with a platter laden with scrambled eggs, crisp bacon, browned sausages and savory fried potatoes in one hand and a full coffeepot in the other. She set the platter on the table and filled Clay's and Forrest's mugs before making her way down the table, offering refills to the other boarders who were lingering at breakfast.

Forrest loaded up his plate, then immediately focused his attention on his meal. Clay scooped up a forkful of eggs, but found his gaze following Toni as she made her way back to the kitchen.

"Transference," Forrest said.

Clay looked up, startled by the abrupt pronouncement. "What?"

"Transference," his brother said again. "It's the redirection of emotions, usually in the context of a therapist-patient relationship but also occurring in other situations."

Clay wasn't sure he was following. Although he knew that one of the reasons Forrest had chosen to come to Thunder Canyon was to continue working in a therapy group with Annabel Cates and her dog, Smiley.

"Are you saying that you have feelings for your therapist?"

His brother snorted. "I'm talking about you, not me."

Now Clay was even more confused. "You think *I* have feelings for your therapist?"

"I think you're still feeling guilty about not being there for Delia when she was pregnant—"

"I didn't know she was pregnant," he interrupted to remind his brother.

"—and you want to make up for it by demonstrating an interest in the stages of pregnancy, resulting in your infatuation with our expectant landlady."

"I'm not infatuated with our landlady."

Forrest continued as if he hadn't spoken. "The fact that she doesn't have a husband just makes her a more obvious target of your attention."

"What's obvious to me is that you have too much time on your hands if these are the scenarios you're dreaming up."

"'That looks heavy, Toni,'" Forrest said, mimicking his brother. "'Let me get it for you.' 'I'm going into town, Toni. Do you need me to pick anything up?'"

Clay scowled at his sibling, although he was more annoyed because he realized that Forrest was right. "Is there something wrong with wanting to be helpful?"

"Not at all," Forrest denied. "So long as you're aware of the rationale behind your actions."

Clay thought he understood his rationale far better than his brother did, and it had absolutely nothing to do with Toni's pregnancy. Truthfully, every time he caught a glimpse of her rounded belly, his mind started, because when he looked at his gorgeous landlady, the absolute last thing on his mind was that she was a mother-to-be.

No, his feelings for Toni Wright had absolutely nothing to do with any latent parental instincts he might possess and everything to do with simple masculine appreciation. He was a man, she was a beautiful woman, and he wanted to get her naked.

"But what do I know?" Forrest said now, a teasing note in his voice. "I'm not a father. Maybe you want to double your diapers, double your fun."

Clay shook his head emphatically. "Bennett gives me more diaper changes than any man should have to handle."

As if in response to his name, the little boy looked up from the egg he was smearing on his tray and smiled, and Clay actually felt his heart squeeze inside his chest.

Maybe he hadn't thought too much about having children before Delia showed up at his door with Bennett, and maybe he'd denied—instinctively, and perhaps a little too vehemently—that he could be the baby's father, and maybe his offer to let Delia and the child stay with him had been made more grudgingly than willingly. But living with a woman and her child, even temporarily, had been a huge adjustment for Clay, especially considering that his relationship with Delia had been, by mutual agreement, a strictly no-strings arrangement.

But a child wasn't just a string. The possibility that he might actually be the boy's father had felt like a noose around his neck. A noose that grew tighter with every day that passed until he woke up one morning to the sound of a screaming baby and realized that Delia was gone. He'd almost accepted that he *might* be Bennett's father and had started to think about the practicalities of shared parenting, then suddenly, there was no one around to share any of the responsibilities.

Delia had the benefit of nine months to come to terms with the fact that she would have a baby—nine months to prepare for the arrival of her child and the realities of motherhood. But she'd shown up on his doorstep without any kind of warning and, not even giving him nine *days* to accept the fact that he was a father, ran off, abandoning the baby into his care. And with the realization that she was well and truly gone, the noose had pulled so taut that Clay could hardly breathe.

It was Bennett's frantic cries that had finally penetrated the chaotic thoughts swirling through his brain, that made him realize he didn't have the luxury of panicking or falling part because there was a tiny person who needed him. And with Delia well and truly gone, there was no doubt that Bennett needed him, so Clay stepped up to the plate.

The first time Bennett's tiny fist had curled around his finger, Clay had been lost. The wave of affection for the little boy had knocked him flat with all the subtlety of a freight train. And the first time that Bennett had smiled at him, just a few weeks later, Clay had vowed to his son that he would never let Delia take him away. By the time he got the report from the lab, he'd realized that the DNA results didn't even matter.

It was his mother who had encouraged him to open the envelope, anyway. Ellie Traub had accepted the baby more quickly and easily than he had done. In fact, from day one, she'd positively doted on the child, which was why she'd insisted he had to know what legal status he had with respect to the little boy. She was as thrilled as she was relieved to have scientific proof that Bennett was her grandson—and none too happy when Clay first told her of his plans to leave town with the baby.

Truth be told, Clay had vacillated for weeks before making the decision. As much as he wanted to get out of Rust Creek Falls for a while—and away from the nosy gossipers who liked to offer unsolicited suggestions to the new dad—he'd worried that he wouldn't be able to manage on his own with the baby. His mother had been an enormous help, offering not just her own tried-and-true baby care advice, but giving him hands-on assistance whenever he was feeling overwhelmed. Which, over the first few months, was quite frequently.

As if on cue, the phone he'd tucked into his jacket pocket began to vibrate. He checked the display and smiled as he connected the call.

"Hi, Mom."

"Where's your brother?"

He glanced across the table. "Why are you calling my cell if you're looking for Forrest?"

The brother in question shook his head and pushed away from the table, pointing to his watch and miming his intention to drive into town.

"Because he doesn't answer his phone," Ellie complained.

"Maybe he's driving," Clay suggested.

"Maybe," she allowed. "Or maybe he's ignoring my calls."

"Why would you think that?"

"Because he hasn't been very communicative since he got back from Iraq."

Watching his brother make a hasty escape from the dining room, he couldn't deny that was true. "He just needs some time, Mom."

"I've tried to be patient," Ellie said. "But I need to know that he's doing okay."

"He is," Clay assured her. "I promise."

"Well, I want to see for myself, and I need a grand-baby fix, so your dad and I are thinking about making a trip to Thunder Canyon this weekend."

"We'd love to see you."

"Good. I've already spoken to Allaire. She promised to

pull some strings to get the private dining room at D.J.'s Rib Shack for the whole family. Friday night at seven."

"That works for me," Clay told her.

"Make sure it works for your brother."

"I'll try," he said, unwilling to make any promises on Forrest's behalf.

"I guess I'll have to be satisfied with that," she allowed. "Now tell me how my grandson's doing."

Clay was happy to regale his mother with details about Bennett's growth and development and everything else he'd been doing over the past few weeks.

He didn't tell Ellie that the little boy seemed to have developed a major crush on their landlady at Wright's Way—because he was afraid that Bennett wasn't the only one.

Chapter Two

Antonia usually waited until most of the boarders had left before she started clearing the tables, and when she returned to the dining room today, she saw that aside from Clay and his son the room was completely empty. As she began to stack plates, she could tell that Clay was on the phone, and though she wasn't trying to listen in, she couldn't help overhearing bits and pieces of his conversation.

And then she heard him say, "I love you, too."

The words, spoken with easy affection, made her pause with a handful of cutlery in her fist. But before she could even begin to speculate about who might be on the other end of the line, he added, "Mom," and she let out a breath she hadn't even realized she was holding.

It wasn't any of her business, of course. And she really hadn't intended to eavesdrop. But when she glanced over as he disconnected the call, his gaze met hers and she knew that she'd been busted. Her cheeks filled with color.

He pushed his chair back as she picked up the stack of plates. "Let me get those for you."

"Thanks, but I've got it."

"They've got to be heavy."

She couldn't help but smile at that. "I've been working on this ranch since I was a kid. Before I got pregnant, I was mucking out stalls and training horses. I think I can handle a stack of plates."

"You've been carting plates and platters from the kitchen since 6:00 a.m.," he pointed out. "Why don't you sit down for a minute?"

"Because these dishes won't put themselves in the dishwasher."

Bennett banged his cup on his tray, then held it out to her.

"I think somebody wants more juice." Just a couple of weeks earlier, Clay had told her that he'd introduced the little boy to apple juice diluted with sterile water. Since then, Antonia had ensured she always had some on hand. "Can I get him a refill?"

"Sure," Clay agreed.

The baby smiled at her as she took his cup, and her heart melted.

"Coming right up," she promised.

While she was in the kitchen refilling Bennett's drink, Clay gathered up the rest of the dishes still on the table.

"Are you trying to get me fired?" she asked, when she returned with the juice.

"I don't think you'll lose your job because you let someone else carry a few plates into the kitchen," he chided.

He was right, of course, but that wasn't the point. The

point was that she was used to doing things for herself—she preferred doing things for herself. And she'd learned a long time ago that if she didn't depend on anyone else, she didn't have to worry about being disappointed.

Bennett took the cup and yawned.

"Are you ready for a nap already?" she asked.

His only response was to lift his arms up to her.

She hesitated, because every time she picked him up, she never wanted to let him go again. But Bennett was clearly tired of being strapped in his chair and, based on the sounds emanating from the kitchen, Clay was thoroughly occupied with the dishes and not planning to return to the dining room anytime soon.

With a sigh that was more resignation than reluctance, Antonia removed the tray from Bennett's chair, unfastened his belt and lifted him into her arms. He curled into her easily, his head dropping against her shoulder, his eyes already drifting shut.

She'd never thought it was possible to fall in love so quickly and completely, but since the doctor had confirmed the news of her pregnancy, Antonia had realized that none of the usual rules applied to babies. She didn't know if it was their innocence and vulnerability or her own maternal instincts, but she'd always had a weakness for children. From the moment she first suspected that she was pregnant, she'd been overwhelmed by emotion. And the first time Bennett had looked at her with his big blue eyes, she'd been hooked.

Now, with the slight weight of his body in her arms and the subtle scents of baby powder and shampoo teasing her nostrils, that hook snared her heart even more deeply.

She ventured into the kitchen and confirmed that Clay was loading up the dishwasher. Not with the skill or efficiency of someone who had a lot of experience, but he was getting the job done.

"Why don't you take Bennett back to your room for a nap and let me do that?" she suggested.

"He doesn't sleep for more than fifteen or twenty minutes after breakfast," Clay told her. "So if you could sit with him for a little bit while I finish up here, that would be great."

"Why don't *you* sit with him while *I* finish cleaning up?" Antonia countered.

"Because I'm almost done here," he pointed out.

His logic was indisputable and, with a sense of relief she refused to let him see, Antonia settled into one of the wooden ladder-back chairs beside the old kitchen table.

Bennett snuggled in, rubbing his cheek against her shirt, and Antonia's heart gave another squeeze.

She didn't know anything about the little boy's mother—who she was or where she was. She only knew that in the five weeks that had passed since Clayton Traub had showed up at Wright's Way with his son, she hadn't heard a single word about the woman who'd given birth to the darling little boy. And she had to admit, the lack of information made her curious.

Not any of your business, she mentally admonished herself.

Just like information about her baby's father was no one's business but her own.

"He's never taken to strangers," Clay noted. "But there's no doubt that he likes you."

And because it was too good an opening to resist, she ignored her own admonition to herself and said, "Maybe I remind him of his mother."

"Not likely," Clay said. "Considering that he hasn't seen her since he was two weeks old."

She looked up, startled by this revelation. "Why not?"

"She decided a baby was too much to handle and she left him with me and moved to California."

Antonia was stunned.

She couldn't imagine any mother choosing to walk away from her child. Her baby wasn't even born yet and she knew there was nothing she wouldn't do for him or her. But of course she didn't say any of that to Clay, she said only, "Why California?"

"To be a movie star."

"She was an actress?"

"A much better one than I ever suspected," he noted wryly.

She didn't have any trouble picking up on the undercurrents in that response. "It must have been difficult—to be on your own with a newborn."

"That's the understatement of the century," he admitted. "I hadn't planned on becoming a father at this point in my life and I knew absolutely nothing about babies. In fact, I'm not sure either Bennett or I would have made it through the first few weeks without my mom."

In many ways, Clay's story was similar to her own. She hadn't planned on becoming a mother at this point in her life, either, and while she wouldn't say she knew "absolutely nothing" about babies, her experience was limited. But unlike Bennett, her baby wouldn't have a grandmother to help them through the rough patches.

She shifted her gaze away, so Clay wouldn't see the tears in her eyes. "You're lucky to have her," she murmured.

"I'm sorry," he said. "I forgot that your mother passed away."

She nodded. "Two years ago."

"I bet you miss her."

"Now more than ever," Antonia admitted.

Lucinda Wright had been more than a parent. In a lot of ways, she'd been her best friend, and Antonia missed her gentle guidance and sage advice. Mostly she missed the way her mother always knew when she was worried about something, she missed the comforting weight of the arm she would put across her daughter's shoulders and the confidence in her voice when she promised that everything would work out for the best.

As her baby shifted in her belly, Antonia wanted desperately to believe her mother's promise, but right now she didn't have a clue what would be best for her baby.

Clay didn't see his brother again until later that night. Aside from the twice weekly group therapy sessions at the hospital, he wasn't sure what Forrest did to occupy all the hours in his day. Then again, some people probably wondered what Clay did to fill his days, but anyone who had ever been responsible for the full-time care of a baby wouldn't need to wonder. Bennett kept his daddy hopping 24/7.

He was in the common room on the main floor of the boarding house, watching a National League playoff game, when Forrest came in with a bowl of popcorn and a couple bottles of beer. Sometimes the room was so crowded it was impossible to find a chair, but most of the boarders started work early in the morning and, consequently, retired to their rooms early at night—particularly at the beginning of the week. So tonight, Clay had been alone with the ball game until his brother joined him.

He accepted the bottle Forrest handed to him and took a long swallow before setting it on the coffee table beside the baby monitor.

"Ben's asleep already?"

"It's almost ten o'clock," Clay pointed out.

Forrest looked disappointed.

Clay hadn't been thrilled when his brother enlisted, but he understood that Forrest wanted to serve his country and that it was his decision to make. But when he came home, it was apparent to everyone that the injury to his leg wasn't the deepest of his wounds.

And yet there had been rare moments when Clay caught glimpses of the easygoing brother he remembered. There had been a few more of those moments since they'd come to Thunder Canyon, illustrated by good-natured teasing and dry humor. But the clearest evidence was in his brother's interactions with Bennett. The little boy was the only one—at least so far—who had proven capable of breaching all of Forrest's defenses.

"There was a time when he didn't settle down until midnight," Forrest recalled.

"Then I wised up and stopped letting him nap after dinner."

"If you kept him up later at night, he wouldn't be awake so early in the morning."

Clay shrugged. "I'm used to starting the day early."

"Do you miss it?"

Forrest was asking about the work he'd done on the family ranch back in Rust Creek Falls, and Clay nodded. "I miss the physical labor, the satisfaction that comes from getting a job done, and I feel guilty as hell for leaving Dad, Dallas, Braden, Sutter and Collin with all the work."

"You didn't have to come to Thunder Canyon to babysit me," Forrest told him.

"I didn't come to babysit you," Clay told him. "I came because I couldn't stand being the center of attention every time I took Bennett into town. It was as if no one had ever known anyone who was a single father before."

"Try being the wounded war hero," Forrest told him. "People tiptoed around me as if my gimp leg was contagious—or maybe it's the rumors of my PTSD that freaked them out."

"Not everyone was freaked out," Clay reminded him. "In fact, Marla James only wanted to show her appreciation for the sacrifice you made for our country."

Forrest tipped his bottle to his lips, but Clay saw the color rise in his brother's cheeks.

"I still haven't decided whether I should thank you or kick your ass for deflecting her attention," he finally said.

Clay just grinned.

Marla James's crush on Forrest had been something of a legend in Rust Creek Falls. Her family had moved into town the summer before she started fifth grade, and on the first day of school, she'd set her sights on Forrest Traub and had never looked back. It didn't matter how many times he brushed her off or how many other girls he dated, she remained adamant that they would one day be together. When Forrest returned from Iraq, she decided that day had finally come.

She stopped by the Traub Ranch at least once a day to check on her injured hero. Forrest—wounded more deeply than the scars on his leg—wasn't even kind in his dismissal of her efforts, but Marla refused to be dissuaded. Not until Clay, with feigned embarrassment and reluctance, implied that his brother's injury had affected more than his leg and that he wasn't able to appreciate what she was offering.

Marla had cried genuine tears over that, but her lifelong love for Forrest clearly was not as strong as her sexual desires.

"You could always call Marla up and tell her you're all better now," Clay teased.

"If only that were true," Forrest said.

And Clay knew his brother's comment had nothing to do with the fabricated injury. Which was why Ellie was so worried about her son, and why Clay had to do everything he could to keep his promise to his mother.

"Bennett and I are going to take a drive to Billings for a farm auction in the morning to check out a tractor that's on the block. Did you want to come with us?"

Forrest just shook his head and munched on a handful of popcorn.

"Okay," Clay said easily. "How about dinner at D.J.'s Friday night?"

His brother looked up at that, his gaze narrowing. "Friday is three days from now," he noted. "Since when do you plan that far ahead?"

So much for thinking that he could slip anything past Forrest. But instead of answering the question directly, he only shrugged, as if his brother's response was of no concern to him. "If you've got a hot date and don't want to go, just say so."

Forrest lifted a brow. "Well, I've had so many hot dates recently I'd have to check my calendar to know for sure."

"You do that," Clay advised.

His brother mimed thumbing through a little black book. "I have Skinny Ginny penciled in, but I can reschedule. At least at D.J.'s, I'll get some meat on my ribs."

"I'm glad to see your sense of humor is still intact," Clay noted. "Even if it's deeply buried most days."

Forrest looked away. "Just 'cause I said I'd go out with you Friday night doesn't give you the right to turn this into some touchy-feely moment."

"I wouldn't dream of it," Clay assured him.

"Good." Forrest tipped the bottle to his lips and shifted his gaze back to the television.

* * *

D.J.'s Rib Shack in the Thunder Canyon Resort was usually busy, especially on a Friday night. While Antonia waited for her friend Catherine to arrive, she glanced around the restaurant with its sepia-toned pictures of cowboys and an extensive mural that depicted a visual history of the town. But more than the décor, it was the scent of D.J.'s famous sauce thick in the air that assured the customers packed into the benches and booths that they would enjoy genuine Western barbecue.

Antonia breathed in deeply, inhaling the rich aroma, and the baby kicked in approval—or maybe it was demand. If Antonia was hungry, it was a good bet that her baby was, too.

"I feel like Pavlov's dog," a familiar voice said from behind her. "I just walk through the door of this place, and my mouth starts to water."

Antonia laughed and hugged her friend. "I know what you mean."

The hostess led them to a booth against the back wall.

When the waitress came, they ordered right away, both familiar enough with the menu to know what they wanted. Fifteen minutes later, they were digging into plates laden with saucy ribs, fresh-cut fries and tart coleslaw. Antonia had considered ordering the daily vegetable option rather than fries, but the baby wanted fries and she'd learned not to ignore the baby's demands. If she indulged now, she wouldn't find herself raiding the fridge at three o'clock in the morning.

"I can't remember the last time I was here," Antonia admitted, popping a fry into her mouth. "Which proves that it's been way too long."

"I'm glad you finally hired someone else to serve dinner at the ranch," Catherine said. "We haven't had a girls' night out in far too long."

"You've been even busier than I have. As if getting Real Vintage Cowboy up and running wasn't enough, you had to go and fall in love with Cody Overton and get married."

Catherine grinned. "I guess I have been busy."

Antonia sat back, licking rib sauce off of her fingers, and assessed her friend. Tonight she was wearing a lacy white blouse over a long, flowing skirt with well-worn cowboy boots on her feet. Her long, dark hair hung loose over her shoulders and her chocolate-colored eyes glowed with a happiness that seemed to radiate from deep within her.

"But you look happy, Mrs. Overton. As if married life agrees with you."

"I am happy," Catherine agreed.

"And I'm glad that Cody turned out to be the real deal," Antonia said, and meant it.

She was genuinely thrilled that her friend had everything she'd always wanted—both professional success and personal happiness. But seeing the vibrant glow on Catherine's face, Antonia couldn't deny that she felt a twinge of something that might have been envy.

She had no cause for complaint. She was content with her life, grateful that things had started to turn around at the ranch so that their finances weren't stretched quite as tight as they'd been a few months earlier. But she was also conscious of the fact that, despite living with her father and her brothers and with a baby of her own on the way, she was alone.

"I just wish you could find someone like him," her friend said. "Someone genuinely wonderful and kind and smart and sexy."

"I don't think there is anyone else like Cody." But even as Antonia said the words, she realized that there was another man who at least came close. A man who doted on his son, who wasn't afraid to get his hands dirty in the kitchen, and who had an easy sense of humor and a quick smile. A man whose mere presence made every nerve-ending in her body stand up and take notice.

And then Clayton Traub walked into the restaurant with Bennett in his arms.

Not just Clay, she realized, but his brother, Forrest, too. But Antonia knew there could have been a parade of men, all of them tall and handsome, and it still would have been Clay who drew her attention.

"There's someone out there for you," Catherine insisted. And then, aware that her friend's attention had wandered, she turned her head to see the two men making their way to the private dining room in the back.

"Oh, my," she said in a reverent whisper. "Or maybe there's someone *in here* for you."

Antonia couldn't blame Catherine for her reaction. The first time she'd set eyes on Clayton Traub, she'd felt the exact same way. And neither time nor familiarity had done much to dim her reaction. But she had learned to ignore the physiological response—most of the time, anyway.

"I swear, the testosterone level in here just shot through the roof." Catherine turned back to her friend. "So tell me—which one of those very sexy cowboys caught your eye?"

Antonia felt her cheeks flush. "Neither of them."

"Liar."

"I do know them," she finally admitted. "Clay and Forrest Traub. They've been staying at Wright's Way."

"Now I know why you haven't been coming into town

very often. The scenery is obviously much better at the ranch than I remembered."

"They are nice to look at," Antonia acknowledged.

"Nice?" her friend scoffed. "Those are real vintage cowboys."

"How do you know?"

"You can tell by the way they carry themselves—the strength, the confidence, the swagger." She fanned her cheeks. "Those men have it in spades. And there's just something about a man with a baby in his arms that somehow enhances his masculinity."

"Newlywed," Antonia reminded her friend.

"Newly *and* blissfully wed," Catherine agreed. "But the ring on my finger hasn't rendered me blind."

"Proven by the fact that you did notice the baby he was carrying."

Catherine winced. "His?"

Antonia nodded.

"Married?"

She shook her head.

"Then what's the problem?" her friend demanded. "He's a single dad, you're a soon-to-be single mom—"

"Yeah, and I can't imagine why he wouldn't be attracted to me." Antonia's dry tone was accompanied by a pointed glance at her round belly.

"Are you kidding? Do you ever look in the mirror? You're gorgeous, Antonia."

"And that's why you're my best friend," she told Catherine. "Because you can actually say things like that with a straight face."

Catherine sighed. "Okay, tell me about him."

"I don't know a lot," she admitted. "Just that he's from Rust Creek Falls, he came to Thunder Canyon in September and he has an adorable six-month-old son named Bennett."

"His brother's the one who started that dog therapy group for veterans, isn't he?"

"Along with Annabel Cates, soon-to-be Annabel North," Antonia clarified.

"Love has definitely been in the air in Thunder Canyon," Catherine mused. "And maybe, if you just took the time to breathe..."

"I've got a baby on the way that I already love more than I ever could have imagined," Antonia told her friend. "I don't want or need anything more than that."

"Don't you think it's important for a child to have a daddy?" Catherine asked.

"In a perfect world, of course," she agreed. "But right now, I'm more concerned about being the best mother that I can be than finding a father for my baby."

"You're going to be a wonderful mother," her friend assured her.

Antonia hoped she was right, but she had so many questions and doubts—and no one she could talk to the way she'd always been able to talk to her mother. Catherine was great, of course, but her friend didn't have any experience when it came to pregnancy or childbirth, so she couldn't know anything about the worries and insecurities that plagued Antonia.

A mother's worries never went away.

Ellie Traub could attest to that. Even when her boys were grown—as all of hers were—she never stopped worrying about them. She'd had moments with respect to each of her boys, although Clayton had always given her more cause for concern—at least until Forrest had shipped out to Iraq, but that was something she wouldn't let herself think about right now.

Right now, she was focused on Clayton and her plan to get him back to Rust Creek Falls. The fourth youngest of her six sons and just as handsome as his brothers, Clay had done well in school, excelled at sports and had been popular with the girls. Maybe too popular.

He was a hard worker, she'd give him that, and he'd happily toiled on the family ranch alongside his father and brothers. He'd also boasted a very active social life, dating a lot of women over the years, although not any one woman extensively or exclusively. Certainly he'd never brought anyone home to meet the family, and when he hit his twenty-ninth birthday, Ellie had begun to despair that he never would settle down.

She'd only voiced her concerns to him once, at which time he'd confirmed that he was enjoying life too much to think about getting married or starting a family. And then an ex-girlfriend had shown up with a baby in tow.

There were worse things, Ellie knew very well, than having a son who'd fathered a child out of wedlock. But she worried that Clay's refusal to marry the mother of his child was further proof that he wasn't ever going to grow up and take responsibility. On that point, he'd quickly and definitively proven her wrong.

She couldn't fault him for making his son his number one priority, but now that he'd proven to be so intently focused on his child, she did worry that he was ignoring other aspects of his life. A man needed a wife—and Bennett needed a mother—and she doubted that Clayton was going to find any prospects to fulfill either role while he was living as a recluse at some boarding house on the outskirts of town.

She had Bennett in her arms and was returning to the

back room that D.J. had reserved for their family gathering when she saw the little boy's eyes light up and his arms stretch out as if reaching for something. Curious, she turned to see what had caught his attention, and found the answer wasn't a "what" but a "who"—a very attractive female who.

"You've got an eye for the pretty ladies, just like your daddy, don't you?" she murmured.

But Ellie noticed that the pretty lady was looking right back at the baby and smiling. She gave a little wave. "Hi, Bennett."

Ellie moved closer to her table. "I guess you know my grandson."

The young woman nodded. "I'm Antonia Wright. Your sons and grandson are staying at my family's ranch. And this is my friend Catherine."

"It's a pleasure to meet both of you," Ellie said, instinctively noting that while Catherine's left hand displayed an exquisite diamond solitaire and matching wedding band, Antonia's hand was bare.

She found herself wondering why neither Clay nor Forrest had mentioned that there was a gorgeous, unattached woman living at the ranch where they were staying. A woman who had obviously bonded with Clay's infant son.

Actually, she was sure that Forrest was oblivious to both Antonia's beauty and her gender. She was equally sure that Clay was oblivious to neither. And she started to think that it might not be such a bad idea for Clay and Bennett to stay in Thunder Canyon a little while longer.

"Do you know what? I think I forgot my lipstick in the ladies' room," she said to Antonia. "Would you mind if I left Bennett with you for a sec while I go back to get it?"

"Of course not," the young woman agreed, rising from her seat to take Bennett into her arms.

It was then that Ellie realized the situation might be a little more complicated than she'd thought.

Because while Antonia Wright might not have a ring on her finger, she definitely had a baby in her belly.

Chapter Three

Clay hadn't objected to his mother's offer to take Bennett to the ladies' room to wash him up while they waited for their food to arrive. He knew how much Ellie missed her grandson and anytime she wanted to help out with the baby, he was willing to let her. But he did wonder, after more than ten minutes had passed, what was taking her so long. When the food was delivered before she'd returned, he slipped out of the private dining room to track her down and saw Ellie handing his little boy over to...Toni?

He hadn't expected to see her here tonight, and his pulse gave a quick little jolt. He could lament the instinctive response as much as he wanted, but he couldn't deny it. The bigger surprise came when he watched his mother walk away, leaving Bennett with their landlady.

Clay wasn't worried—he trusted Toni implicitly. But he knew her; his mother didn't. And he couldn't help but be a little suspicious about Ellie's willingness to relinquish her beloved grandson to a stranger.

In a few quick strides, Clay was standing beside Toni's table. Bennett smiled at him but didn't lift his head off of Antonia's shoulder. Not that Clay could blame his son for choosing a beautiful woman over his daddy and, in this case, Bennett had the attention of *two* beautiful women.

"Small world," he said to Toni, and smiled.

"I'm not sure about the world, but Thunder Canyon is," she replied.

"Even so, there isn't anyone anywhere who can top D.J.'s ribs," her dinner companion chimed in.

"Can't argue with that," he replied, then offered his hand. "Clayton Traub."

"Catherine Clif—I mean, Overton," she said, then grinned and wiggled the fingers on her left hand. "I'm still getting used to the new name."

"Congratulations," Clay said.

"Thanks. But that reminds me, I should be getting home to my hubby."

Toni narrowed her gaze at her friend. "I thought you said Cody wasn't going to be home from Billings until late."

"That's what I thought, but—" Catherine held up her phone "—he just sent me a text to say he was home."

Toni's gaze shifted to the instrument in her hand, as if she didn't believe her friend was being entirely truthful about the message. In fact, she looked as if she might have snatched the phone from her friend's hand to verify the claim, if not for the fact that her own hands were full of baby.

"It was nice meeting you," Catherine said to Clay. Then, to Toni, "I'll talk to *you* tomorrow."

And with a quick wave over her shoulder, she was gone.

Clay slid into the seat she'd vacated. "I think your friend just stuck you with the bill."

"It was my turn to pay, anyway," she told him.

"And somehow you got stuck with my child again, too."

She smiled at that. "Your mom had to pop back into the ladies' room."

His mother had barely let Bennett out of her sight since she'd arrived in Thunder Canyon, so Clay was still suspicious of Ellie's motivations.

"You met my mom?"

"Bennett introduced us," she said, which didn't really explain anything, but Clay let it go.

"Do you want to come and meet the rest of the family?"

Toni immediately shook her head; he laughed.

"I'm sorry. I didn't mean to seem so adamant. It just looks like you've got some kind of family reunion going on, and I wouldn't want to intrude."

"It wouldn't be an intrusion," he assured her.

"Thanks," she said. "But I should be getting back to the ranch. Morning—and the breakfast crowd—comes early."

"It's pancakes on Saturdays, isn't it?" he asked hopefully, rising to his feet again.

"It is," she agreed.

"Then we will be there." He reached for his son, sighed when he saw that the little guy had fallen asleep on her shoulder again. "If I can get him up in the morning. Unfortunately, a half hour nap at this time of day will keep him up till midnight."

"Sorry," Toni apologized as she shifted the baby to him. "I didn't know I was supposed to keep him awake."

"You weren't supposed to do anything," he assured her. "That was my mother's self-appointed task. But thank you again for stepping in."

She tapped a fingertip to Bennett's nose. "It was my pleasure."

As Clay watched her walk away, he couldn't help but think that every moment he spent with Toni Wright was very much *his* pleasure.

The house was dark and mostly quiet when Antonia returned home—the only light and sound being that which emanated from the television in the living room. Her brothers had headed to Bozeman for a bachelor party for a friend of Hudson's and wouldn't be back until Sunday, so it had to be her father who was home.

The Wright brothers worked hard during the week, and partied harder on the weekends. The Hitching Post used to be their favorite hangout and, in the past, they'd been known to drink beer and hustle pool there until all hours. Unfortunately, the establishment had gone out of business the previous spring after the owner passed away, forcing the locals to find other watering holes—at least temporarily. But shortly after The Hitching Post shut down, local boy Jason Traub bought the property and planned to reopen the renovated establishment later in October.

If that timetable held, Antonia's brothers—and a lot of other Thunder Canyon residents—would be very happy.

Moving farther into the living room, Antonia saw that her father had fallen asleep in front of the television with a bottle of whiskey and highball glass on the table beside him. She sighed softly. For as long as she could remember, John Wright had always liked a glass of whiskey in the evening, but he'd rarely indulged in more than one glass. All of that had changed when his beloved wife passed away. John had turned to the bottle with increasing frequency, seeking solace in its contents, refusing to accept that there wasn't enough alcohol in the world to drown his sorrow.

But over the past few months, Antonia had gotten the impression that his drinking had lessened somewhat. Apparently that had just been wishful thinking on her part.

Except that when she reached for his glass, intending to take it to the kitchen, she noticed that the whiskey bottle still looked full. On closer inspection, she saw that the seal around the cap hadn't even been cracked.

She lifted the empty glass, sniffed.

It was clean.

She set the glass down again. She didn't understand why he'd taken the bottle out if he wasn't drinking, but she didn't care. It was only the *not drinking* part that mattered.

With a combination of relief and genuine affection, she touched her lips gently to his forehead, intending to slip out of the room and up to her own bed. In the past, if he'd drunken himself into a stupor, his only response would have been a snort or a snore. Tonight, he shifted, his eyes flickered open. Eyes that were weary but clear.

"Antonia?"

"Sorry, Daddy. I didn't mean to wake you."

"I didn't mean to fall asleep," he told her. "Where are you comin' in from so late?"

She smiled. "It's not that late, and I was out for dinner with Catherine."

"You missed a good meal right here," he told her. "Peggy made roast pork tonight."

She'd known what was on the menu, of course, since she and Peggy planned the week's meals together every Sunday. And she wondered, not for the first time, if John Wright had any idea what she did around the ranch, how many responsibilities she'd taken on to make sure the bills got paid.

At one time, she'd thought he was proud of her. Since she got pregnant, she wasn't so sure. And all she said now was, "I'm glad you enjoyed the pork."

"You had a good meal? It's important to eat right—" he cleared his throat "—for you and the baby."

She thought again about her choice of fries rather than veggies but refused to feel guilty. Besides, she figured the glass of milk she'd had with her dinner helped balance out the indulgence.

"Lucinda craved the most unhealthy foods when she was pregnant," her father told her now. "Especially when she was expecting you."

Antonia's breath caught in her throat at his mention of her mother. In the two years since Lucinda had been gone, she could count on one hand the number of times that he'd spoken his deceased wife's name. The fact that he'd mentioned her now—maybe even in an effort to connect with his daughter?—was the most precious gift to Antonia.

"What kind of unhealthy foods?" she asked, mentally crossing her fingers that he would keep talking, that her question wouldn't cause him to shut down.

"French fries, potato chips, ice cream." He sent a pointed look in her direction, no doubt to let her know that he'd found her stash in the freezer.

"Ice cream is a dairy product," she said, just a little defensively.

He smiled. "Just wait until your child uses that same line of logic on you."

"I'll be ready."

"We're never as ready as we think we are," he told her.

A familiar sadness clouded his eyes, and she knew that he was thinking of his wife again, but this time, the memories weren't nearly as happy.

"Life is so much easier when you have someone to

share the ups and downs with," he said. "I just wish you had someone by your side."

"I don't need anyone to hold my hand."

"I know you don't," he agreed. "You've always been so strong and independent. But sometimes it's nice to know there's a hand there—just in case."

She understood that he was only trying to be helpful, but she didn't agree. Experience had taught her that the only person she could truly rely on was herself.

Clay and Bennett didn't come to the dining room for breakfast the next morning.

It wasn't a big deal, really. Breakfast and dinner were part of the package at Wright's Way, but there was no obligation on anyone to eat in the dining room or announce their intentions to do so. But Antonia was surprised by their absence because Clay had made a point of saying that he was looking forward to her pancakes.

Still, she didn't dwell on it while she finished cleaning up the kitchen. And when she sat at the table with a bowl of chocolate chip cookie dough ice cream, she certainly didn't expect he would show up in the doorway. But he did, just as she was popping a spoonful of the frozen decadence into her mouth.

He raised his eyebrows when he saw what she was eating, but didn't comment, gesturing instead to the half-full coffeepot. "Mind if I steal a cup?"

She swallowed quickly, then winced at the ice cream headache which burned across her forehead. "Help yourself."

He found a mug in the cupboard and filled it with French roast.

"Sugar's on the counter beside the pot, cream's in the fridge."

"Black is fine."

He settled across from her at the table, and her heart started beating double-time. *Damn hormones.*

"Sorry we missed your pancakes, but my parents insisted on taking Bennett and me to the Mountain Bluebell Bakery for breakfast this morning."

"There's no need to apologize," Antonia assured him. "If someone offered to take me there for breakfast, I'd go, too. Lizzie's pastries are to die for."

"Then I should take you sometime, if only to make sure you aren't eating ice cream for your morning meal."

"I had breakfast," she told him. "This is a snack." She scooped up another spoonful. "What did you have?"

"A breakfast sandwich—and then a sticky bun," he admitted. "And somehow Bennett ended up stickier than me."

She smiled at that. "Where is the little guy?"

"Still with my parents. My mom has been suffering from serious baby withdrawal since we came to Thunder Canyon, so she asked if she could keep him for the afternoon."

"Lucky you."

"Except that I'm so used to organizing my time around Bennett, I don't have the first clue what to do without him," he admitted.

"I'm sure you'll figure something out."

"Well, when we were at the bakery this morning, someone mentioned there's a movie theater in New Town."

She nodded. "New Town Cinema, behind the mall. There are some pretty good movies playing now, too."

"Anything you'd be interested in seeing?"

"Sure," she said, scraping the bottom of the bowl. "But I rarely find the time—"

"Toni," he interrupted.

She looked up.

"I'm asking you to go see a movie with me this afternoon."

"Oh." She honestly didn't know what else to say. It was as if her mind had gone completely blank.

Amusement glinted in his deep brown eyes. "Is that a yes or a no?"

"Um...yes?"

He reached for The Thunder Canyon Nugget that was on the table, found the Arts & Entertainment page of the newspaper and offered it to her. "Check the listings and let me know what you want to see."

Screen number one was showing a new romantic comedy that had been getting good reviews, but Antonia didn't want to send Clay the wrong message by immediately choosing that one. Unfortunately, the only other option was a horror movie that she had less than zero interest in seeing.

She wrinkled her nose. "I really hate slasher films."

"Then we'll see something else," he said agreeably.

"There's nothing with car chases or nuclear explosions," she warned.

"I'll chance it if you will. Are you in?"

There was just a hint of a challenge in his voice. Just enough to entice her to throw caution to the wind.

"I'm in."

There were a lot of things Clay could have done with a free afternoon. He could have saddled up one of the horses and gone for a ride, or he could have curled up in his bed and indulged in a long *uninterrupted* nap, and both of those options held a certain amount of appeal. But when he sat down and tried to figure out what he wanted to do, only one thing was clear—he wanted to see Toni.

Maybe the answer had surprised him, but he didn't let it worry him. He didn't think there was any need to overanalyze the impulse. He liked Toni. She was smart and funny; she had her own opinions and wasn't afraid to share them. She was also beautiful and sexy—so beautiful and sexy that he frequently forgot that she was seven months pregnant.

But he wasn't going to forget that anymore. He wasn't going to make the mistake of thinking that today was about anything more than two adults spending a few hours together because they both had time on their hands.

They chatted easily on the drive into New Town, moving from one topic of conversation to the next without any awkward silences between them. Clay thought it was interesting that he'd seen this woman every day for the past month and a half and they still hadn't run out of things to talk about.

Of course, a lot of their discussion centered on Bennett, with Clay sharing anecdotes of his son's adventures and Toni marveling over his talents. And throughout their conversation, neither one pressed for information that the other wasn't willing to confide. It was as if, by unspoken agreement, they each respected the other's established boundaries, for which he was extremely grateful.

Toni pulled out her wallet at the ticket window, but he shook his head. "I invited you to come, so this is my treat."

"Then I'll get the popcorn," she told him. "Right after I make a quick trip to the ladies' room."

He didn't know if her determination to pay her share was a way of proving her independence or intended to assert—loudly and clearly—that this was not a date. Just in case he might have any illusions to the contrary.

And he was just perverse enough to want to make an

issue of it, which he did by purchasing their snacks while he was waiting for her to return.

Toni scowled when she saw the armload of boxes and cups he carried. "I said I was going to get the popcorn."

"Go ahead," he said. "This is for me."

She stared at him for a minute, trying to figure out if he was serious. Then she shrugged and started toward the counter.

He stepped in front of her. "I was kidding."

"Oh."

He handed her a cup. "I figured you're probably trying to limit your caffeine intake so I got you an uncola."

"I am. Thanks."

"But I went for butter on the popcorn," he confessed. "Because it was actual butter and not that fake topping stuff you get in some of the chain movie theaters."

"Did you get extra napkins, too?"

"I did," he concurred. "And Milk Duds."

Her eyes actually lit up. "Milk Duds?"

Clay chuckled. "I guessed that you'd want some sweet to balance the salty."

"Good guess," she said.

They'd started toward the doors for screen number one when a female voice called out, "Antonia?"

The easy smile on Toni's face slipped, just a little, before she secured it back in place and turned to face the speaker.

"Hello, Vanessa."

"I almost didn't recognize you. Oh, my god, you look like you're about ready to burst."

Toni shrugged casually, unfazed by the insensitive remark. "Not quite. I've still got several weeks to go."

"Really? Wow. I couldn't imagine letting my body expand like that for a baby."

"No, I don't imagine you could," Toni replied.

It was a subtle zing, and Clay had to fight a smile as he watched the comment fly right over Vanessa's shallow head.

"So," the other woman said, her cool, blue gaze giving Clay a leisurely once-over, "who's your friend?"

"Clayton Traub," Toni said, making the introductions with obvious reluctance. "Clay, this is Vanessa Wallace, a…friend from high school."

Vanessa blinded him with a smile. "Hel-lo, Clay-ton."

"It's a pleasure to meet you," he said with cool politeness.

She inched a little closer. "Are you one of the Texas Traubs?"

"No, I'm from Rust Creek Falls," he told her.

"Have you been in Thunder Canyon very long?"

"Since September."

His terse responses did nothing to dim the wattage of her smile. "Well, there's not a heck of a lot to see in our little town, but if you want a tour guide, feel free to look me up."

He couldn't believe the nerve of the woman. Even if he and Toni weren't together, she couldn't know that, and yet she was hitting on him—with absolutely no hint of subtlety—right in front of Toni.

In an effort to extricate them all from the increasingly awkward situation, Clay said, "If you'll excuse us, Toni and I should find seats before the theater fills up."

Vanessa giggled as if he'd made an outrageously funny joke. "I don't think you need to worry about the theater filling up. But yes, you and *Toni* should go find your seats." Then she touched a hand to his arm. "But don't forget to call me about the tour. I'm in the book."

He didn't even bother to respond to that.

Toni was silent as they walked into the theater.

"I said something wrong, didn't I?"

She shook her head. "No, not really."

"Come on," he said. "I can't fix my mistakes if I don't know what they are."

She followed him up the stairs to the middle row in the stadium-style seating area.

"It's just that 'Toni' was something of a childhood nickname I'd hoped I'd outgrown," she reluctantly admitted.

He took a seat in the center and she settled beside him. "Your real name's Antonia?"

She nodded.

"But your brothers all call you Toni," he felt compelled to point out in his defense.

"Because they came up with it first. I was always trying to keep up with them, to do whatever they were doing. It was Ace, my oldest brother, who decided that if I wanted to be one of the boys so badly, I needed a boy's name. That's when I became Toni.

"But most of my friends knew me as Antonia. At least until I started high school."

He was almost afraid to ask. "What happened then?"

"I was something of a late bloomer," she admitted. "Tall and skinny, with a chest as flat as that of a ten-year-old boy, and when Jonah used my nickname at school, it spread through the halls like…well, I can't actually think of anything that spreads like derision in a high school."

He winced in sympathy.

"But it didn't last long," she continued. "By the beginning of my junior year, I'd caught up with most of the girls, and the boys started to notice. For the most part, I was Antonia again, but the way they said it and the way they looked at me—it was just a different kind of awkward."

"Kids can be cruel," he admitted. "And adolescent boys can be pretty brainless when confronted with breasts."

"Yeah, I figured that out pretty quickly."

"I like the name Toni," he told her. "It's sassy and unique, like you. But now that I think about it, Antonia suits you, too. It's feminine but also strong and distinguished."

"That's quite a detailed analysis, off-the-cuff."

"I'm not an adolescent anymore," he pointed out. "Which means that I can usually manage to put together a coherent sentence even in the company of a beautiful female."

"Well, I know you've never had any trouble making conversation with me."

Although that wasn't entirely true, he was grateful for this confirmation that she was oblivious to the effect she had on him. "But now when we make conversation, I will remember to address you as Antonia."

"It really isn't a big deal."

"It is, and I'm sorry I didn't realize it sooner."

She tilted her head to look up at him. "You really want to make it up to me?"

"Absolutely."

She held out her hand, palm up. "Give me the Milk Duds."

He laughed and did as she requested.

The dimming of the lights forestalled any further conversation, but as the curtains opened, Clay found himself thinking about Antonia rather than the coming attractions advertised on the screen. She'd given him a tiny glimpse into her life, but it wasn't enough.

He wanted to know everything about her. He wanted

to know about her friends (he knew that Catherine Overton was one; he was pretty sure Vanessa Wallace was not) and her family, how and when she started working with horses, and who taught her to make such fabulous trail mix cookies.

Mostly he wanted to know if her lips would taste as soft as they looked, and he wanted to know how she'd respond if he took her in his arms. Would she press herself against him—or pull away?

He didn't know—but he hoped he would have a chance to find out.

Chapter Four

It wasn't a date.

Even as Antonia sat beside Clay in the darkened theater, she knew it wasn't a date. It was just two people hanging out at an afternoon movie together because they both had time on their hands.

Actually, there were lots of other things Antonia should be doing back at the ranch, but when Clay had mentioned seeing a movie, she realized there wasn't anything she wanted to do more. Partly because it had been a long time since she'd been to the theater and she was looking forward to a couple of hours of escapism, and partly because she would be with Clay.

She enjoyed spending time with him, sharing conversation. And she appreciated that he didn't ask a lot of questions about her personal situation. In fact, he'd never even commented on the fact that she was an unmarried woman in the final stages of pregnancy.

Of course, the fact that he was a single dad himself might have something to do with his reticence to pry. And aside from the one comment he'd made about Bennett's mother walking out on both of them when the baby was only two weeks old, Antonia knew nothing about the woman who'd given birth to his child. Was she still in contact with Clay? Did she regret leaving her baby? Was she still in love with the father of her child?

Assuming, of course, that she had been in love with Clay at some point in time. Because while Antonia had never gone to bed with a man she didn't love, she knew that some women weren't as particular. And while she'd always believed that she could never be physically intimate with a man without first sharing some kind of an emotional connection, her purely visceral response to Clay suggested otherwise.

In any event, Clay's relationship with Bennett's mother really wasn't any of her business. Because as much as she enjoyed being with Clay, she had no inclination toward romance at this point in her life.

Okay, maybe the occasional romantic thought had snuck into her head in recent weeks. But who could blame her for that? After all, Clay was one very sexy cowboy with long, lean legs and breathtaking brown eyes, and she was a woman in her sexual prime with pregnancy hormones running rampant through her veins. Which was why, although she might indulge in a harmless fantasy every now and again, she had no illusions about this outing. Because she knew that there was no way a man like Clay would ever be interested in dating a woman nearing her eighth month of pregnancy.

Yes, she knew it wasn't a date, but as she reached into the tub of popcorn and her fingers brushed against his, she couldn't deny that her heart gave a little flutter and her blood pulsed in her veins.

Clay noticed that Antonia had saved the Milk Duds until the movie was almost over. She did try to share, but he'd gorged himself on popcorn and shook his head when she offered the box to him.

She seemed to savor the chocolate-covered caramels, popping one at a time into her mouth, then letting the chocolate melt on her tongue for a moment before she began to chew the sweet confection.

The lights came up as the credits rolled, and he saw Toni touch a hand to her belly as a little smile curved her lips, almost as if she was enjoying some kind of silent communication with her unborn child.

Because Delia had never bothered to tell him that she was pregnant, he'd missed out on every step of his baby's development. She'd tried to justify her lack of disclosure, claiming that he wouldn't have been pleased by the revelation of her pregnancy, and there was some truth in that. Because he hadn't been ready to be a father—at least, he hadn't thought he was ready.

But once he'd recovered from the shock and the panic, he'd stepped up. And if he'd had any time to plan or prepare for fatherhood, he felt confident that he would have done whatever needed to be done—doctor's appointments, prenatal classes, midnight runs to the grocery store to satisfy the expectant mother's cravings.

He wondered if Toni—*Antonia,* he mentally amended—had anyone to do those things for her. He didn't think so, because in all the time that he'd been staying at the ranch, he'd never seen her with anyone.

It was rumored around town that she'd wanted a baby so much that she'd gone to a clinic in Bozeman. But he had to think that, even if she had chosen to have this baby on her own, there were probably moments when she wished that she had someone with whom to share the joys and fears of impending parenthood.

She popped another Milk Dud in her mouth and rubbed her belly again. His gaze dropped, and he actually saw a ripple of movement.

She caught his eye and shrugged. "The baby likes Milk Duds."

"Is that—" He glanced at her belly again. "Is he—she—kicking?"

Toni—*Antonia*—nodded.

His hand instinctively moved toward her baby bump, hovering above it. "Can I—"

She took his hand and placed it on her belly. Within a few seconds, he felt a subtle but distinct little kick. "Oh. Wow." The baby kicked again, then twice more. "That is so…amazing."

She smiled at the wonder in his tone. "Bennett wasn't an active baby?"

"I have no idea," he admitted. "I didn't even know Delia was pregnant until she showed up with Bennett."

Her eyes widened. "You're kidding."

He shook his head.

"Then you weren't…in a relationship…with Bennett's mom?"

"It was an on-again, off-again relationship. Usually more off than on."

"Oh."

She didn't sound disapproving so much as disappointed, and though he wasn't sure why her opinion mattered to him, he hastened to explain. "Neither of us wanted anything more than that at the time."

"So Bennett was an accident?" she guessed.

"Unplanned," he clarified, his tone firm. "But not unwanted."

She smiled then. "No one who has seen you with your son could ever doubt how much you love him."

Her baby kicked again, reminding him that his hand was still on her belly. And making him suddenly aware of the intimacy of the contact.

He'd never before thought that pregnant women were particularly attractive, but there was something about Antonia's lush, ultra-feminine curves that appealed to him in a way no other woman ever had.

Her gaze lifted to his again, those beautiful green eyes wide—and just a little wary. He snatched his hand away, reached for what was left of his now lukewarm soda and sipped.

He felt somewhat reassured by Antonia's comment. He did love his little boy and he wanted Bennett to never have reason to doubt it. Because he worried that his son would always have questions about his relationship with his mother—if he ever did have a relationship with her.

At this point, Clay had little knowledge of Delia's plans. And his most recent communication from her—a postcard tucked in a pile of mail his mother had brought to him from Rust Creek Falls—had been scarce on details.

Clay~
Just wanted to let you know that I'm in Hollywood.
Please don't worry, I'm doing fine. More importantly,
I'm finally following my dream.
Delia

That was it—no mention at all of the baby she'd given birth to and then abandoned into his care.

Obviously she wanted what she wanted and she wasn't

going to let anyone get in her way—including her own child. And Clay couldn't help but feel guilty that he'd made a baby with such a self-centered woman. Not that he'd been careless—he knew that Delia was on the Pill, but neither of them had realized that the antibiotics she was taking for a bronchial infection would interfere with her birth control.

Now that he had Bennett, he wouldn't wish his child away for anything in the world. But he did wish that he'd been able to give his son a mother who was capable of loving and caring for him. A mother like Antonia.

Which was a dangerous thought. The kind of thought that came from sitting in a dark theater watching a sappy movie with a woman who smelled like springtime and whose smile had the power to light up an entire room. Because while happily-ever-after was a frequent ending in books and movies, he knew it was a much rarer occurrence in the real world.

He'd had the benefit of a pretty good example in his parents, but he wasn't naive enough to think that having positive role models was any kind of guarantee. In fact, two of his brothers only proved the contrary. Dallas, who had married his college sweetheart at the ripe old age of twenty-four, was miserable most of the time and, on the rare occasions that his wife graced the family with her presence, Laurel didn't look any happier. And Braden, who wasn't even married, didn't dare blink an eye without first getting permission from Diana, his girlfriend of two years.

Not that Clay was opposed to matrimony, it just wasn't something he'd ever wanted for himself. A long-term commitment for Clay was making a dinner reservation more than a week in advance. He'd certainly never been with any one woman long enough to think in terms of next year, never mind forever.

Of course, having Bennett had changed a lot of things—including his perspective on relationships. Not that he was looking to settle down with any one woman now, but he'd at least acknowledged that he had to alter his dating philosophy. He wasn't going to confuse his son by allowing a parade of women to move through his life, and since Bennett was his number one priority, he'd decided the easiest solution was to take a hiatus from dating.

And he hadn't missed any part of the social scene over the past several months—not the meaningless flirtations or the superficial seductions. But being here with Antonia now, he realized the one thing he had missed was the one thing he hadn't experienced with any other woman in a very long time: the camaraderie.

He honestly couldn't remember when he'd wanted to spend time with a woman simply because he enjoyed being with her and without any expectation of getting her naked. While he couldn't deny that he wanted to get Antonia naked, he'd accepted that it wasn't going to happen. He genuinely enjoyed being with her. And he knew that was just one more reason why he needed to be cautious—because the more time he spent with her, the more he realized that Antonia Wright was the type of woman a man could seriously fall for.

And Clay had no intention of falling.

Prompted by the advertisement on the screen, Clay and Antonia had both turned off the ringers on their phones for the movie. But Antonia was sure Clay didn't like to be inaccessible, especially when he was away from Bennett, so she wasn't surprised that he immediately checked his phone after they'd exited the theater. She was, however, concerned when he frowned at the display screen.

"I missed a call from my mother."

Since his mother was watching the baby, she understood his concern.

"I have to call her back," he said, already dialing the number.

"Of course," she agreed. And while he was waiting for the call to connect, she slipped into the ladies' room to give him some privacy—and to grant her bladder some relief from the combination of a large soda and a baby sitting on it.

When she returned, the furrow in his brow was gone, his worry obviously alleviated.

"She just wanted to let me know that I was invited to Dax and Shandie's for dinner tonight."

He sounded almost apologetic, and she thought she understood his dilemma. Since it was after four o'clock, he wouldn't have sufficient time to drive her back to the ranch before he was expected at his cousin's house.

"I can catch a cab back to the ranch," she told him.

He scowled. "You cannot."

"You don't think I'm capable?"

"Of course not. I just meant that I brought you here and I'm not going to abandon you to find your own way home."

"I don't mind," she insisted.

He sighed. "I should have told her that you were with me. But I didn't because I was afraid that information would have generated more questions than it answered."

"You don't have to explain," Antonia assured him.

She herself had left a note for her father, just saying that she'd gone into town to see a movie with a friend. She hadn't identified the friend because she didn't know how her father might react. Not that he was likely to disapprove—after all, there was nothing to disapprove of—but he was likely to have questions that she didn't want to answer.

"If I'd told her, she'd at least be prepared when we show up at Dax and Shandie's for dinner."

"I'm *not* going to your cousin's house for dinner."

The adamant tone had him lifting his brows. "Is there any particular reason why you're so opposed to meeting my family?"

"Of course not," she denied. "But I need to get home to help out with dinner there."

"Peggy cooks the evening meal, and Nora serves it."

"And I help in the kitchen," she said, though she knew Peggy was more than capable of handling everything on her own and probably wouldn't even notice if Antonia wasn't there.

"Don't you ever get a night off?"

"I took the afternoon off," she reminded him.

"Okay," he relented. "If you really need to get back, I'll take you."

Antonia nibbled her bottom lip. It wasn't necessary that she return to the ranch, especially if doing so would only throw a wrench into Clay's plans, but she didn't really want to go to his cousin's, either. Talk about awkward situations.

She had no doubt that she would be made to feel welcome or that everyone would make polite conversation at the table. In fact, Clay's mother had been more than gracious when she'd met her the previous evening at D.J.'s Rib Shack. But she'd also seen the way Bennett's grandmother's eyes had widened when she'd realized that Antonia was pregnant, and if she went with Clay to Dax and Shandie's, she knew they would all be wondering what

Clay was doing with his pregnant landlady. It would be easier for both of them if they didn't give anyone reason to ask that question.

"Maybe there's a third option," she suggested.

"That third option being?"

"I can hang out with Catherine while you have dinner with your family, and you can pick me up at her place when you're done."

"You'd rather impose on your newlywed friend and her husband than have dinner with my family?"

"Yes." She replied to his question without hesitation.

His lips curved, just a little. "Well, no one can accuse you of not being honest."

"I try," she said, and reassured herself that repressing her lustful feelings for this sexy cowboy was not dishonest—it was self-preservation.

"Okay," he agreed. "Give Catherine a call and make sure she's home."

She took her own cell out of her purse and dialed her friend's number. Catherine was more than happy to accept her offer of company because Cody had gone to help a friend fix a shed that had been damaged in a recent storm and she, after having spent the whole day doing inventory at the store, was ready to put her feet up and order pizza.

Antonia's stomach rumbled; the baby kicked. Apparently popcorn and Milk Duds weren't enough—her unborn child wanted pizza.

Five minutes later, Clay pulled his vehicle into Catherine's driveway. Antonia got out quickly, before her friend had a chance to come out of the house. But not quickly enough, because Clay didn't make any effort to pull away before he saw the door open, and Antonia silently cursed his gentlemanly manners.

"Was that your sexy cowboy boarder?" Catherine asked by way of greeting.

And so the interrogation begins, Antonia thought. But she tucked her tongue in her cheek and replied, "Nope. That was just Clay."

Her friend's lips curved. "I thought so."

She sighed. "It's *not* what you're thinking."

"I don't think you have any idea what I'm thinking."

"I know how your mind works," Antonia reminded her. "And right now, you're so in love that you want everyone else to be in love, too."

"Okay, there might be some truth in that," Catherine admitted. "But I saw you with Clay last night—and there was a definite zing between the two of you."

Antonia sighed again. She couldn't say there was no zing, because she very definitely felt zing whenever she was near Clayton Traub, but she knew that was just the effect of pregnancy hormones on her end and that there was no way that he felt anything of the sort.

"Reality check," she said to her friend. "He is a single dad with a six-month-old baby and I'm nearing the end of my seventh month of pregnancy."

"So how did you end up in town with him?" Catherine wanted to know.

And this, Antonia knew, was why Clay hadn't told his mother about their outing—because the answer to Catherine's question was only going to raise a lot more questions in her mind.

"Antonia?" her friend prompted.

"We went to see a movie," she admitted.

Catherine's lips curved in a slow, satisfied smile.

"It wasn't a date," Antonia told her.

"A sexy cowboy took you to a movie. How is that not a date?"

"Clay only invited me to go with him because he didn't want to sit in the movie theater alone."

Her smile faded. "Did he say that?"

"Of course not, but it was implied."

"Hmm." Her friend considered. "Did he buy the tickets?"

"Yes, but—"

"Did he buy the popcorn?"

"Yes," Antonia said again.

"Did your fingers collide as you both reached into the tub?"

More than once, and every time, Antonia's pulse had skipped then raced. But there was no way she was admitting that to her friend. Instead, she only said, "You're making way too big of a deal out of this."

But Catherine wasn't nearly finished with her interrogation. "What movie did you see?"

Antonia revealed the title of the film with reluctance.

Catherine's brows lifted up. "A chick flick?"

"The only other option was a slasher film, which would have given me nightmares for weeks."

"He willingly sat through a chick flick," Catherine noted, with both authority and smugness in her tone. "It was a date."

Chapter Five

When Clay saw his brother at breakfast the next morning, he got a generous helping of cold shoulder along with his western omelet. Bennett's mood wasn't much better. Obviously his son didn't remember that Peggy did the cooking and serving on Sunday mornings because Antonia went to church. Not that his son disliked Peggy, and the Wright's housekeeper absolutely doted on the baby, but whenever Bennett went to the main house, he expected to see Antonia, and he was none too happy that she wasn't there.

But it was Forrest's mood that was the bigger cause of concern for Clay. "Are you gonna be mad at me forever?" he asked his brother.

Forrest stabbed a strawberry with his fork. "I'm undecided."

"I didn't ask to be put in the middle of this."

But his brother didn't care. "I came to Thunder Canyon because I needed some space," he reminded him. "I thought you, of all people, would understand that."

"No one objects to you wanting space," Clay said. "But you can't cut yourself off from the family."

"No matter how hard I try," Forrest muttered.

"Why are you trying so hard?"

His brother remained silent, whether unable or unwilling to answer the question, Clay didn't know.

"You're right," Clay said. "We don't know what you went through in Iraq. No one who hasn't been there can possibly understand the things that you saw and did. But you have to understand what Mom and Dad went through, not knowing, and not even knowing if you would ever come home."

Forrest stared into his coffee cup for a long moment before he responded. "I thought I knew what I was signing up for," he said, shaking his head. "Turns out, I didn't have a clue."

Clay didn't know what to say that wouldn't sound trite. He certainly didn't know what his brother had gone through in Iraq, and while he could—and did—imagine the horrors he had seen, he knew that the reality was probably ten times worse.

"A friend of mine went to help a kid who fell off his bike. The boy couldn't have been more than seven years old, but when Reg bent over to check the scrape on his knee, the kid stuck a dagger in his gut."

"Jesus."

"That's just one example," his brother said. "No matter where you went, you didn't know what to expect, who to trust. In the end, it was easier to trust no one, because you could be ambushed from any direction."

Clay winced, because he sensed where his brother was going with this revelation. And because he did feel guilty that he'd coerced Forrest's attendance at D.J.'s for dinner without warning him that the whole family was going to be there.

"That's what Friday night felt like," Forrest told him. "An ambush."

He refrained from pointing out that no one's life had been in danger, because he knew his brother wasn't referring to the level of risk so much as the breach of trust. Instead, he only said, "I'm sure Mom thought of it more in terms of a family get together."

"I'm sure she did," his brother agreed. "But you didn't even let me prepare for that much."

"I'm sorry," Clay said now, because he was. "But I needed you to be there because *I* wouldn't have been able to handle the disappointment on Mom's face if she didn't see you and see for herself that you're doing okay."

"I wouldn't have bailed."

And because Clay knew it was true, he felt even guiltier for his deception. "Do I need to apologize again?"

"Maybe a few more times," Forrest said.

Then one side of his mouth turned up, just a little, but it was enough that Clay knew he was forgiven.

While Forrest and Clay were lingering over breakfast, Ellie dragged Bob to the Thunder Canyon Community Church. She enjoyed attending services on a regular basis and didn't think being out of town was any reason to miss a Sunday morning. Besides, she'd learned a long time ago that after-service coffee hour in the community room was a great opportunity to catch up on all the latest news—and she wanted to know more about her sons' landlady, who had also been in attendance at the morning service.

Ellie had just added a generous drop of cream to her coffee when she saw a group of older women approaching the table of sweets, chatting among themselves. Most of them she recognized from previous visits to town, and she was curious about whatever topic of conversation had them so engaged.

"I can't believe she still shows up here to church every week," Helen Vanderhorst was saying.

"Who?" Bev Haverly asked.

"Antonia Wright. It's absolutely sinful the way she parades around in her condition. And her father stands beside her, as if he actually condones what's she's done."

"What she's done?" Judy Raycroft's tone was bored. "She's hardly the first unwed mother in Thunder Canyon."

"But she went to a clinic in Bozeman for a doctor to impregnate her with some stranger's baby," Helen informed her.

Ellie didn't like to encourage busybodies—and she knew that Helen Vanderhorst was one of the busiest—but in this situation, her curiosity outweighed her aversion to gossip, and she inched a little closer.

"Why on earth would she do something like that?" Gertie Robbins wondered.

"She's always been too independent for her own good." Helen's tone was disapproving. "Eager to prove that she could do everything on her own—even having a baby."

"Or maybe the clinic in Bozeman story is just that," Caroline Turner said. "More likely, she got knocked up the old-fashioned way and doesn't want anyone to know it."

As Ellie knew had been the situation with two of Caroline's three daughters, but—in her effort to remain inconspicuous—she managed to refrain from pointing out that fact.

Bev shook her head. "Antonia was never the type to run wild. Her mama raised her right."

"Lucinda's been gone two years," Helen pointed out.

"And John's been pickled for about the same amount of time. That girl's pretty much been on her own since they lowered her mama's grave into the ground."

"Pretty much running the ranch on her own, too," Gertie said. "And doing a fine job of it."

"Hardly an appropriate occupation for a young woman," Caroline protested.

"She did what needed to be done," Judy chimed in again. "I don't see how anyone can find fault with that."

Ellie had to agree, and she was grateful that at least someone had spoken up in defense of a young woman who was obviously navigating a difficult path.

"I just think it's a shame," Bev continued, "that no one seems to believe in traditional family values anymore."

"If women didn't occasionally buck tradition, we'd all still be barefoot and pregnant," Judy, who had been one of the first female circuit court judges in this part of the state, argued.

"But too many women are pursuing their careers at the expense of their families," Helen insisted.

The women continued to argue, but Ellie had heard enough. She set down her half-full cup and moved away.

The dialogue had told her more about the speakers than anything else, and she realized that if she wanted to know something about Antonia, she was going to have to get to know Antonia.

In the past six months, Clay had focused so much of his energy on learning how to be a father that he'd suspected it would be a long while before he had the time or inclination for a personal relationship. Since coming to Thunder Canyon, he'd realized that he still had the inclination. The bigger surprise was his attraction to Antonia Wright, and his habit of making excuses to justify his visits to the main house to see her. Today, his excuse was Bennett.

She was drying her hands on a towel when she responded to his knock at the door. "Is it a bad time?"

Her gaze shifted from Clay to the baby in his arms, and her smile widened. "I always have time for this handsome guy."

Clay told himself there was no reason to feel slighted. After all, it wasn't as if he was in competition with his own son for her attention. Was he?

"He missed you at breakfast," Clay said, offering the reason for their impromptu visit.

"Did you?" she asked Bennett.

He responded by reaching his arms out to her.

"Do you mind?" she asked Clay, seeking permission to take the baby from him.

"Does it look as if I have any say in the matter?"

She was smiling as she took Bennett from his arms. In the transfer, the back of his hand brushed the side of her breast. They both froze.

Then he took a step back, quickly.

Her cheeks flushed with color. "Did you want a cup of coffee?"

"I think I'm coffeed out," he admitted.

"Soft drink? Beer?"

"No, thanks. We really just stopped by because Bennett was getting restless. I tried to put him down for his nap but he refused to settle, and I thought if we got out and walked around for a bit, he might fall asleep. Instead, he kept looking toward the house, as if he was wondering where you were, and now here we are."

"I'm glad," she said. Then, to Bennett, "Why won't you go to sleep for your daddy?"

The baby yawned, confirming that he was, in fact, overdue for his nap.

"Do you want me to rock him for a little bit?"

"I would be eternally grateful," he assured her.

She smiled as she led the way into the living room. "Eternally?"

"Well, at least until his nap time tomorrow."

She settled into a glossy cherry wood rocking chair. He didn't know much about furniture, but it looked like an antique—either carefully maintained or impeccably restored.

He took a minute to look around the rest of the room, noted the couch and chairs were a little worn but not shabby, and the tables were polished to a high gleam. There was something of a portrait gallery on the wall behind the couch, starting with old black-and-white photos on the outside at each end.

"Your grandparents?" he asked.

She nodded. "It's kind of a pictorial family tree moving from the outside toward the center. My dad's mom and dad are on this end, my mom's mom and dad are at the other."

And at the center was a portrait of Antonia with her three brothers and her parents.

"You look like your mom," he noted.

"Considering that my dad's six feet tall and has a moustache, I always figured that was a good thing."

He smiled and lowered himself onto the sofa. When he glanced over to check on Bennett, he saw that the little boy's head was on Antonia's shoulder and his eyes were closed.

"You have a knack with him," he mused.

"He was just tired."

"He was tired when I was carting him all over the property, too."

"And he would have fallen asleep eventually."

"Maybe," he allowed. "But my arms would have fallen asleep first."

"You need one of those backpack-style baby carriers."

"I already have a backpack-style diaper bag."

She laughed softly.

The sound, so unexpected and somehow sexy, stirred something in his belly. He really didn't understand what was happening here—why he was so attracted to a woman who was wrong for him in as many ways as he was wrong for her. But he knew he was at least partially to blame. Instead of making up excuses to spend time with her, he should be staying away. Far away.

"We should get out of your hair," he said, rising from the sofa. "You probably have a million things to do."

Of course, he didn't realize that Bennett was literally entangled in her hair and that he would have untangle his sleeping son's fist from Antonia's dark, silky locks before they could make their escape. But Bennett's fingers were closed tight, and Clay had to lean in a little closer to complete the task. Close enough that he could smell the tempting, peachy scent of her shampoo.

He clenched his jaw and refocused on his task.

"I do have other things I need to do," she agreed. "First on the agenda being to find part-time help while Jonah's laid up."

"What happened to Jonah?"

"He was in Bozeman on the weekend for a friend's bachelor party and let himself be goaded into riding a mechanical bull, which he promptly fell off of and broke his collarbone."

Clay finally succeeded in releasing Antonia's hair from Bennett's grip and lifted the baby into his arms.

"I think the most damage was done to his pride," she continued her explanation of her brother's injury. "But he's still out of commission for the foreseeable future."

"Maybe I could help out." He didn't want to sound too eager, but he really had missed working with his dad and his brothers. The Wright Ranch undoubtedly had its own routine, but he was confident he could figure things out and pick up some of the slack.

She glanced pointedly at the sleeping child now nestled against his shoulder. "Don't you have your hands full enough already?"

"More than full enough," he admitted. "And as much as I love spending time with Bennett, I can't be a stay-at-home dad forever. Not that I'm in any hurry to put him in day care, but I could probably make arrangements with one of my cousins to keep an eye on him if I was helping out here."

"Or, if you're serious about putting in some hours on the ranch, I could keep an eye on Bennett."

"Because your hands aren't full enough already," he teased.

She shrugged. "I have a playpen I can set up in the office. He could hang out there if I needed to get some work done. Otherwise, we could take walks, visit the horses in the stables, throw soft blocks around."

The final suggestion being one of Bennett's favorite hobbies of late.

"You really wouldn't mind?"

"It will be like on-the-job training for when I have my own baby," she assured him.

"When is that going to be?"

"Hopefully November twenty-second."

"A Thanksgiving baby," he noted.

"If the baby comes on time, I'll be extremely thankful," she said. "I'm getting tired of carting this belly around."

His gaze dropped automatically. While there was no doubt that Antonia was pregnant, she didn't look overweight or ungainly. In fact, the distinct roundness of her belly only seemed to enhance her femininity and attractiveness.

He remembered—all too vividly—when she'd taken his hand to let him feel her baby kick. He'd been surprised at how taut and firm her belly was, and how amazed he'd been that there was a tiny person inside there. And he'd suddenly experienced a whole new level of appreciation for the female species.

True, a woman couldn't make a baby on her own, but the man's role was quick and pleasurable. After that, it was all on the woman—for the next nine months, and usually well beyond that, she was solely responsible for meeting the baby's needs. And while he still couldn't understand Delia abandoning her infant, he couldn't deny that she'd done a great job taking care of herself and their baby throughout her pregnancy.

"Be thankful you're not an elephant," he said in response to Antonia's eagerness to be at the end of her pregnancy.

Her brows rose. "You mean, as opposed to just looking like one?"

He smiled at that. "You look beautiful."

Her gaze dropped; her cheeks filled with color.

Okay, maybe that wasn't an entirely appropriate comment for him to make. But it was true—she was a beautiful woman—and Clay didn't want her to think that she was any less attractive because of her pregnancy.

"But I was actually referring to the fact that the gestation period of elephants is twenty-two months, and that their babies usually weigh in around two hundred and fifty pounds when they are born."

She winced. "Should I ask how you know that?"

Now it was his turn to be embarrassed. "When Bennett went through his colicky phase and I was up with him all night, I watched a lot of the Discovery Channel."

"Okay, I'm glad I'm not really an elephant," she agreed. And then, more hesitantly, "How bad was the colic?"

"More exhausting than a cross-country cattle drive," he assured her. "Thankfully, though, the worst of it only lasted a few weeks."

"I can only imagine how difficult that must have been for you—on your own."

Her hand instinctively went to her belly again, and he knew she was thinking about the fact that she would be on her own, too—and wondering how she would manage if her baby was colicky. He didn't tell her that even the non-colicky phases were an enormous challenge, because what was the point? She would figure that out for herself soon enough anyway.

"Do you know if you're having a boy or a girl?" he asked instead.

Antonia shook her head. "I didn't want to know."

"Do you have names picked out for both?"

"I have a couple of possibilities in mind," she admitted.

"You're not willing to share?"

She shook her head again. "Not yet."

"Delia—Bennett's mom—wanted a daughter."

"Bennett's a strange name for a daughter," she teased. "I like it, but I don't think it would work as well for a girl."

He managed a smile. "She was so convinced she was carrying Sarah Jane that she never even considered a boy's name."

"Was the name Bennett your choice then?"

"I didn't even know about him until he was a week old," he reminded her.

"Oh." It was obvious that his revelation raised more questions than it answered, but she didn't press for any more of an explanation.

Over the past six weeks, he'd learned that Antonia wasn't the type of woman to pry for information. He'd commented to Forrest that it was a refreshing change to have a conversation with a woman who didn't need to know all the details of his past or want him to reveal all of his secrets.

Of course, Forrest had warned that a woman who respected a man's secrets probably had plenty of her own, and Clay found himself wondering now if there might be some truth to that. Or maybe he was just trying to justify his own curiosity about Antonia. But he thought that confiding some of those difficult truths to Antonia might encourage her to do the same.

"Bennett is Delia's surname. Since she didn't have a name for the baby, the nurse put 'Baby Bennett' on his hospital ID bracelet and Delia decided it was good enough."

Antonia was as shocked as she was appalled by his story, although she realized that she shouldn't have been so surprised. Any woman who could walk away from her own child—especially one as wonderful as Bennett—clearly hadn't formed any kind of attachment to that child. And it worried her, just a little, to think that she could ever feel so disconnected from her own child.

Was it possible that she might not bond with her baby? Antonia honestly couldn't imagine the possibility. She already felt as if there wasn't anything she wouldn't do for her son or daughter, but she'd heard stories about women suffering postpartum depression who didn't want to be anywhere near their babies, or women who had endured such excruciatingly painful labor they couldn't stand to look at the infants they'd delivered.

But this wasn't about her—it was about Bennett, and Clay's apparent unhappiness regarding the origin of his son's name. "I don't think how he got his name matters as much as the fact that he's a Traub," she said to Clay. "And it's obvious that his family adores him."

"You're right," he admitted. "And I am grateful that she at least put my surname on his birth certificate."

"The right name—R-I-G-H-T," she clarified, with a small smile, "can give a child a sense of belonging in a community. In Thunder Canyon, there are few names that carry as much weight as Traub, Cates or Clifton."

"That's just because there's so many of us."

"That might be part of it," she agreed.

"What surname will your baby have?" he asked.

She should have been prepared for the question. He was hardly the first person to ask about the father of her baby, although she did give him credit for being a little more subtle than most. "The Wright name," she said, and smiled again. "W-R-I-G-H-T."

"Does that mean the rumors in town are true?"

"There are so many rumors, I've lost track."

"The one about you wanting a baby so desperately you went to a clinic in Bozeman."

"I do want this baby desperately," she told him honestly.

"You didn't want your baby to have a traditional family?"

"If you're asking if I ever dreamed about falling in love and getting married, the answer is yes. But it didn't happen that way for me and, even without a husband, I wanted a baby."

"Aren't you kind of young to have given up on your dreams?"

"I'm thirty," she told him.

"As I said."

She shook her head. "I'm ready."

"I wasn't," he confided. "In fact, there are still days that I'm not."

"Well, you do a pretty good job of faking it."

He smiled. "Now maybe, but you should have seen me at the beginning."

"I think every new parent is scared at the beginning."

"Well, I didn't have any time to prepare," he admitted. "The last time I'd seen Delia, she'd basically said, 'It's been fun but I'm moving on to bigger and better things,' and then she was gone. Nine months later, without any word or warning, she shows up on my doorstep with a baby in her arms and I'm just supposed to believe he's mine? Especially after she'd assured me that she was on the Pill?"

"No form of birth control is one hundred percent effective," Antonia pointed out.

Still, at least he'd been aware and taking precautions. Antonia had been aware and careless. Sometimes Gene would use a condom, sometimes he wouldn't, and she hadn't worried too much because she'd been in love and hadn't thought that having a baby with the man she loved would be a bad thing. It had never occurred to her that she might end up having that baby on her own.

"Yeah, I learned that one the hard way," he admitted.

"But you didn't run for the hills," she noted.

"I thought about it. It was an instinctive, knee-jerk response and, thankfully, one that didn't root too deeply in my mind, but I did think about it."

"And now?" she prompted.

He looked down at the baby in his arms, and there was no denying the affection in his gaze. "Now I wouldn't give him up for anything in the world."

"That's how I feel about my baby," she told him. "And I refuse to feel guilty that the absence of a ring on my finger is scandalous to Mrs. Vanderhorst."

He seemed satisfied by her response, and when he left with Bennett, she exhaled a sigh of relief that he hadn't realized she never truly answered his question.

Chapter Six

Antonia might have had her reservations about Clay—or, more specifically, about her own uncontrollable response to his nearness—but she couldn't deny that she'd started to fall for his son the very first time she'd held him in her arms. And after only three days of taking care of Bennett, she was completely head-over-heels.

Her absolute favorite time of day was their quiet time after lunch, when she would sit with him, rocking him gently, until he fell asleep. He was asleep now, and she nuzzled his cheek, inhaling his familiar baby scent. She felt an ache in her chest—an actual, physical longing—to hold her own baby in her arms.

The first indication of her pregnancy had come in the form of a plus sign on one of those home test kits, and she'd been torn between excitement and terror. By the time her doctor had confirmed the diagnosis, she'd managed to push aside most of the terror and focus on the joy of impending motherhood. But the baby was still more of an abstract concept than a reality. It wasn't until she'd had an ultrasound and actually saw the image on the monitor that her baby became real. And when she'd felt the subtle quickening inside that was evidence of her baby's movements, the terror started to come back.

During that time, she'd thought about Gene a lot, and spent far too much time hoping that he would have a change of heart and return to Thunder Canyon. When that didn't happen, she tried to put him out of her mind. But when she felt her baby move, when the life inside of her was no longer just real but suddenly imminent, her conscience had started to nag at her.

She felt confident that Gene had made his feelings about their child clear when he'd high-tailed it out of town, but there was a tiny part inside of her that refused to give up without another try. So after weeks of vacillating, she finally called and asked if they could meet. He'd told her that he was in Kentucky. That in and of itself should have been a pretty big clue that he'd wanted to get as far away from Thunder Canyon as was possible. He'd moved on and she needed to do the same.

She'd fought to hold back the tears that filled her eyes. She didn't want him to know how much he'd hurt her, how much his rejection of their baby continued to hurt. But for the sake of their child, she forced herself to make the effort, to ask if he wanted her to let him know when their child was born.

"It was your decision to have the kid, not mine," he'd said tersely. "As far as I'm concerned, that makes the kid yours, not mine."

As disappointing as his attitude was, Antonia had realized that, ultimately, it was for the best. At least she wouldn't have to worry about Gene ever showing up to make a claim on his child. In fact, she'd be surprised if he ever ventured near the Montana border again.

Bennett exhaled a soft sigh, and Antonia touched her lips to the soft, baby fine auburn hair on the top of his head. It was a rare, peaceful moment in her day—until she heard the back door slam.

Ace stomped down the hall into the living room, mindless of both the noise he was making and the dirt he was tracking in with his boots.

"Shh!" Antonia had to hush loudly so that he could hear.

He stopped in the doorway, a scowl on his face as he looked at her snuggling with Clay's baby. "Don't you have enough to do around here without babysitting someone else's kid?"

"Probably," she agreed easily. "But since that kid's father is currently doing Jonah's job, it seemed like a fair trade. Besides, hanging out with Bennett is good practice for when my baby comes along."

At the mention of her baby, his scowl darkened. "You really want to have this baby on your own?"

"I *am* having this baby on my own," she reminded him.

"Besides, it's not as if she could change her mind now," Hudson, who had followed his brother into the room, pointed out logically.

"But she could tell us the identity of the baby's father," Ace said, in a tone that left Antonia in no doubt as to what would happen if she shared that information.

"Haven't you heard the story about the clinic in Bozeman?"

Hudson snorted; Ace just glared.

"Mrs. Haverly might believe that story," her eldest brother said. "But I don't."

As he'd made clear to her on more than one occasion.

But she didn't care what any of her brothers believed. What mattered was that Mrs. Haverly had taken the little bit of information she'd given her and run with it.

It had been early in her fifth month of pregnancy, when wearing bulky clothes was no longer enough to hide the slight roundness of her tummy—and when wearing bulky clothes would have raised eyebrows, anyway, because it was July. Antonia had seen the speculative looks, heard the faint whispers.

Of course, Bev Haverly didn't want to speculate—she wanted to know. And the older woman had cornered Antonia outside of church one Sunday morning and bluntly asked, "Is it true that you're going to have a baby?"

Antonia, who had loved her baby from the moment she suspected its existence, refused to be embarrassed or ashamed about her pregnancy. She met her gaze evenly and said, "Yes, it is."

"But you haven't even been dating anyone," the widow noted, confirming to Antonia that she and Gene had done an even better job of hiding their relationship than she'd expected.

"Thanks to new medical procedures, a woman no longer needs a husband or a boyfriend to have a baby," she said.

Mrs. Haverly still looked skeptical. "Really?"

She nodded again. "Oh, yes. There's a wonderful reproduction clinic in Bozeman that's helping a lot of women have babies."

It was a simple statement of fact. At no time did Antonia actually say that she had gone to the clinic, so she didn't feel too guilty about the fact that Bev Haverly had put her own spin on the statement and spread the news far and wide. Besides, Antonia would much prefer people thinking she was stubborn and determined enough to choose to have a baby on her own than to know that the father of her child had abandoned them both.

"What are you guys doing in here, anyway? I thought you were fixing fences today."

"Got most of it fixed, but we need to go into town to get some supplies before we can finish up."

"So why are you here instead of on your way into town?"

"'Cause we worked through lunch," Hudson said, a subtle plea in his tone.

"There's leftover roast beef in the fridge," she told them. "You can make yourselves a couple of sandwiches."

Ace frowned. "Isn't that your job?"

Her brows lifted. "Excuse me?"

"Well, you're in charge of the household," he reminded her. "And the kitchen is part of the house."

"And you're a Neanderthal," she said pleasantly. "Hard to imagine why some lucky girl hasn't snapped you up."

"Are you gonna make the sandwiches or not?" Ace growled.

"I can do it," Hudson, the peacemaker, offered. "They won't be as good as Antonia's sandwiches, but they should fill the hole."

Antonia rolled her eyes as she pushed herself out of the chair. "You, on the other hand, are a charmer—and far too slippery for any woman to catch hold of."

He just grinned at her.

She sighed. "I'll make the sandwiches."

"Good," Ace said, and stomped off to the kitchen.

But Hudson stayed behind, watching as she gently laid Bennett down in the playpen and covered him with a thin blanket.

"You're going to be a great mother," Hudson said.

It was the sincerity in his tone as much as the words that had tears stinging Antonia's eyes. "I hope so."

"But a baby really should have two parents."

"Hudson—"

He held up his hands. "None of my business, I know. I'm just saying."

"Well, keep your 'just saying' to yourself or you'll be making your own sandwiches."

He made a show of zipping his lips and turned toward the kitchen.

Bennett was teething, which meant that he was cranky and sleep-deprived and his father was the same.

Because Clay didn't want to risk the wrath of the other boarders if they were awakened by a screaming baby, he'd started taking Bennett for walks outside if he woke up in the night. Tonight when he was walking Bennett, he noticed that there were lights on in the stables.

After the baby was settled back down and left in the care of his uncle, Clay wandered down to the stables to see what was going on.

He didn't expect to see Antonia. She was dressed in a pair of faded jeans topped with a bulky knit sweater with the cuffs rolled back. With her hair tied back in a loose braid and her face bare of makeup, she looked as if she was fifteen years old rather than twice that age—which made the roundness of her belly even more disconcerting.

"It's two o'clock in the morning."

She gasped and turned toward him, a hand pressed to her chest. "You scared me half to death."

She didn't look as scared as she did exhausted, with her cheeks devoid of all color and shadows beneath those deep green eyes.

"What are you doing out here by yourself at this time of night?" he demanded.

She frowned at the tightly controlled anger in his tone but only said, "Daisy Mae didn't have much of an appetite tonight, so I figured she was getting ready to foal and I came down to check on her."

"At two in the morning?"

"Horses usually foal at night," she pointed out.

"I'm aware of that," he assured her. "I was wondering what compelled you to take a trip—on your own—to the stable at two in the morning."

"I actually came down around midnight."

"Oh, well, that's a much more reasonable hour for a young woman to be wandering around in the dark," he said dryly.

"I grew up on this ranch," she reminded him. "I know my way around."

"That's not the point."

"Then why don't you tell me what is the point?"

He wasn't entirely sure. He just knew that when he'd seen her there, looking so alone and vulnerable, he'd suddenly been aware that she *was* alone and vulnerable, and his protective instincts had risen to the fore. "It isn't safe for a young woman to be wandering anywhere on her own at that hour."

Her lips curved, just a little. "This is Thunder Canyon."

"And last year my cousin Rose was kidnapped in Thunder Canyon," he reminded her.

"Not to disregard what she went through, because I'm sure it was a terrifying ordeal, but Jasper Fowler is crazy. And Jasper Fowler is now in jail and there's no one wandering around the ranch who shouldn't be here—" her eyes sparkled with humor "—because no overnight guests are allowed."

"Do you really think paragraph eight is going to keep any vagrants or drifters off of your property if they decide they want to be here?"

"I really think you're making a big deal out of nothing," she said. "I came down because I knew Daisy Mae's time was getting close and I wanted to see how she was doing."

"And if she was having any trouble?" he challenged. "What were you going to do?" Because the thought of her stepping into the birthing stall with an agitated, laboring horse made him crazy.

She sent him a look, as if she knew what he was thinking. "I was going to call one of my brothers."

"Were you?"

"I'm not an idiot," she told him. "And I wouldn't put my baby at risk for anything."

"Then why don't you go back up to the house and get some rest?" he suggested.

"Because I don't want her to be alone."

He wondered if she was really worried about the mare, or if she was thinking about her own impending delivery. Did she have anyone who would be with her for the birth of her child? Or would she be alone? Even if she'd consciously made the decision to have a baby without a father, she had to know it wouldn't be easy on her own.

He sighed. "Then I guess I'm staying, too."

"That's really not necessary," she protested.

"I'm sure you're right, but I'm staying anyway." He nodded toward the office. "Got any coffee in there?"

"I can put some on."

"I'll do it."

He came back a few minutes later with a steaming mug in one hand and a chair in the other. He set up the chair and gestured to her, half expecting that she would protest. But obviously more than two hours on her feet was enough, because she sat.

"So what are you doing here at 2:00 a.m.?" she asked him.

"I think it's closer to three by now," he noted. "And I was up with Bennett—he's cutting teeth and not very happy about it."

Her brows lifted. "You're chastising me for being down here on my own and you left your son alone in your room?"

"No, I left Bennett with his uncle."

"Oh." She turned her attention back to the laboring mare.

"When was the vet last here?"

"A few days ago. He said everything looked good, but when I came down, Daisy Mae seemed really uncomfortable and uneasy."

"I'm sure they don't call it labor because it's a walk in the park," Clay noted dryly.

"I'm sure you're right, but this is her first..."

"And you're worried about her."

"I just thought I'd hang around for a while to keep an eye on her," she said, unwilling to admit that her concern had progressed to the stage of worry.

"Do you think she'll object if I go in to check on her?"

Antonia shook her head. "She won't object, and I'd be grateful. I thought about calling Ace to come down just for that purpose, but he wouldn't appreciate having his sleep interrupted for the sole purpose of reassuring me."

"Is she yours?" Clay asked.

She smiled. "I think of them all as mine, but Daisy Mae is special to me. She was rejected by her dam and we didn't have access to a nurse mare, so my mom stepped in.

She stayed with her around the clock for the first week, feeding her from a bottle every two hours.

"Daisy Mae survived because my mom made sure of it. And if anything happened to her now…"

He nodded. It was never easy to lose an animal, but he understood that Antonia's connection to Daisy Mae was stronger than most because she saw this mare as a last link to the mother she'd lost. And he was determined to do everything he could to protect that link.

Clay set down his now-empty coffee mug and stepped into the birthing stall. Daisy Mae's eyes flickered in his direction and she whinnied nervously, as if seeking reassurance.

"You're going to be okay, Daisy Mae," he said as he knelt beside her.

Antonia remembered the wonder in his eyes and the awe in his voice when he'd placed his hand on her belly and felt the subtle movements of the baby inside of her. Obviously he had more experience with laboring animals than pregnant humans, because he showed absolutely no hesitation now, his hands moving confidently as he spoke to the mare in a low, soothing tone.

As Antonia watched him, she found herself wondering what it would be like to have someone at her side throughout labor and childbirth, and wishing that she didn't have to face the experience on her own. She felt the sting of tears in her eyes, and quickly blinked them away.

If wishes were horses, she thought.

But she pushed the thought aside and refocused her thoughts on the laboring horse rather than futile fantasies.

"I think she's going to be just fine," Clay said, exiting the stall. "All we have to do is let nature take its course."

Which it started to do then, in earnest, when the horse's water broke.

"Here it goes," Antonia murmured.

Clay reached for her hand, squeezed it reassuringly.

She held on, grateful for the comfort of his touch and his presence. She hadn't wanted Daisy Mae to be alone, but she hadn't wanted to be alone, either. She'd lost track of the number of births she'd witnessed on the ranch over the years, but Daisy Mae was special, and it meant a lot to her that she had someone with whom to share the experience.

And while the mare might have been a novice at the whole birthing thing, she pulled through like a pro.

Antonia had checked her watch when the membranes ruptured, and immediately began counting the minutes. With every contraction, Daisy Mae seemed to groan, and Antonia winced sympathetically. It seemed as if she was laboring forever with no progress, and just when Antonia was beginning to seriously worry, the foal's front hooves appeared, then the nose, and within minutes after that, the rest of the baby appeared.

Daisy Mae remained where she was for a few minutes, catching her breath after the arduous process while her foal struggled free of the birth sac. Then the new mother climbed to her feet and the cord broke naturally.

"So far so good," Antonia whispered.

"She's got herself a beautiful little filly," Clay said.

"She is beautiful, isn't she?" But she continued to hold her breath, waiting and watching while the placenta was delivered and Daisy Mae cleaned up her baby. But it wasn't until the foal stood up on her spindly legs and began suckling from the mare's teats—and Daisy Mae let her—that Antonia fully exhaled a sigh of relief.

"They're going to be just fine," Clay said, his words echoing her thoughts.

She nodded and touched her lips to his cheek. "Thank you."

His gaze locked with hers, the depths of his dark eyes swirling with something that she refused to let herself think could be desire. But she couldn't deny the desire that was pumping through her own veins, and she cursed herself for giving in to the impulse—and for wanting so much more.

He lifted a hand to her cheek, his touch both warm and gentle, but then dropped it away again and took a step back. "You should go get some sleep."

She was exhausted. Now that the excitement was over, every drop of adrenaline had drained away and fatigue washed over her like a wave. Unfortunately, sleep wasn't an option right now. "It's almost time for me to get breakfast started."

"Put some boxes of cold cereal and a gallon of milk on the table," he suggested.

"Yeah, that would go over well," she said dryly.

Clay shook his head. "Have you always been this stubborn?"

"I have a job to do and people counting on me to do it."

"And who do you count on?"

She blinked, startled by the question. "What do you mean?"

"Have you ever let anyone do anything for you?" he said again. "Or have you always been so fiercely independent?"

"I hardly think independence is a character flaw," she countered.

"Prove it," he said. "Put someone else in charge of breakfast this morning."

"Peggy already does everything else, my father can't cook, Ace is too stubborn to even try, Hudson would make the effort but the results would not be pretty, and Jonah's arm is in a sling."

Unable to counter any of those arguments, he only shook his head. "Promise me you'll get some rest after breakfast."

"I promise I'll get some rest after breakfast." She started to turn away, then turned back to him. "Maybe I do like to stand on my own two feet, but I don't always like to stand alone, and I appreciate that you were there for me last night."

"I don't want your gratitude," he told her and took a step closer.

Her brain was fuzzy with lack of sleep and her head was spinning because that was the effect his nearness had on her. But there was something in his eyes, something dark and unfathomable that didn't just make her head spin but her body ache.

She swallowed. "What do you want?"

He reached out and tucked a strand of hair that had come loose from her braid behind her ear. His fingertip traced the outer shell, and all of the hormones flooding through her system went on high alert. Then his hand dropped away and his lips twisted in a wry smile.

"Never ask a question if you aren't prepared to hear the answer," he told her.

It sounded like good advice, but in that moment, Antonia couldn't even remember what the question had been. And it wasn't even that she wanted an answer, she just wanted.

But she recognized the futility of wanting what she couldn't have, and she turned away and headed back to the main house.

Chapter Seven

Antonia managed to drag herself through the rest of the day, and the three-hour nap that she stole after lunch went a long way toward restoring her equilibrium. Of course, she also made a few treks down to the stables just to confirm that Daisy Mae and her baby were still on track. And each time she stood looking at the mare and her foal, she couldn't help remembering the arduous process of Maisy Rae's birth—and the unexpected comfort of having Clay by her side.

She hadn't needed anyone to keep her company any more than Daisy Mae had needed help giving birth, but it had been nice to have him there. She remembered him asking if there was anyone she counted on. The truth was, she tried not to rely on anyone but herself. That way, there was little chance of being let down by someone else's actions—or inactions.

By Friday, she felt fully recovered from her all-nighter

in the stables and was looking forward to spending the day with Bennett.

She took him to the stables in the morning, to introduce him to the new foal, then around to the paddocks to visit some of the other horses. Antonia had been advised to curtail a lot of her usual activities, so she tried to compensate for the lack of physical labor with moderate exercise. She figured hiking over the fields with a sixteen-pound baby strapped to her back was pretty good exercise.

By the time they returned to the house for lunch, they were both hungry and tired. Bennett had some rice cereal, pureed peas and a little bit of applesauce. Antonia was desperately craving a bowl of chocolate cherry ice cream, but she forced herself to eat a turkey sandwich first.

When the baby finally went down for his nap, she decided she should pay some of the bills that had started to pile up again. At least this time they weren't unpaid because of a lack of funds but simply because she'd been having too much fun hanging out with Bennett to think about such mundane tasks.

She was at the computer, inputting numbers onto a spreadsheet, when there was a knock at the door. As rare as it was for anyone to stop by the office during the day, it was even rarer for anyone to knock before entering. But the real surprise came when she recognized the unexpected visitor.

"Mrs. Traub. Hello."

"Hello, Antonia." The older woman's smile was warm and friendly as her gaze shifted to the clutter spread across the desk. "Am I interrupting?"

"I'm happy to be interrupted," Antonia assured her. "Although I'm guessing that you came to see Bennett rather than me."

"Bennett is here?" The little boy's grandmother seemed startled by that fact.

Antonia faltered, wondering if there was any particular reason that Clay hadn't told his mother about their arrangement or if he just hadn't had a chance. But he certainly hadn't told her not to say anything and, in any event, she had no reason to lie to Ellie.

"My brother Jonah has been laid up with a broken collarbone, so I've been taking care of Bennett on Mondays, Wednesdays and Fridays while Clay helps out on the ranch."

Ellie smiled. "I'll bet Clay jumped at the chance. Not that taking care of a baby didn't keep him busy enough, but I suspected that he would miss the ranching. And I know he's felt torn about his decision to come to Thunder Canyon rather than stay at home to work—as if Bob doesn't have enough hands with four other sons."

Then she spotted the playpen in the corner, and moved toward it. "There he is," she murmured softly. "I can't believe it—it's been less than a week since I last saw him, and he looks as if he's grown so much."

"He's got two teeth now," Antonia told her.

Ellie sighed. "I hate not being there for every little milestone."

"We have one room available in the boarding house right now," she offered.

The older woman chuckled softly. "As tempting as that is, I don't think either of my sons would appreciate having me underfoot, so I'll just have to content myself with occasional visits."

"Do you want to wake him up?"

"Goodness no," Ellie said, firmly but quietly. "I had half a dozen children myself, and I learned early on to let sleeping babies lie."

Antonia smiled. "Did you want a cup of coffee then?"

"Do you have decaf?"

"Of course." She turned on the transmitter that was set up beside the playpen and picked up the receiver. The kitchen was only at the back of the house, close enough that she would probably hear the baby when he awoke, but the monitor made her feel a little more comfortable about being out of sight.

Antonia made a fresh pot, then poured a cup of coffee for each of herself and Bennett's grandmother and put out a plate of homemade cookies.

Ellie waited until Antonia had taken a seat at the table before she said, "You haven't asked why I made the trip from Rust Creek Falls just to see my grandson."

"I didn't realize that was the only reason for your trip, but even so, I'd imagine that missing Bennett is reason enough."

Ellie smiled. "And you'd be right. But there was also another reason for this trip. I wanted to see you."

"Me?" That revelation was an even bigger surprise than finding the woman at her door, and one that made her immediately wary.

"When I met you last week, I couldn't help but notice that Bennett seemed quite attached to you," his grandmother noted.

"He comes here for breakfast and dinner almost every day," Antonia explained. "So I'm a familiar face to him—and one that he associates with having his tummy filled."

Ellie smiled. "That might be part of it," she acknowledged. "But I don't think it's the biggest part."

Antonia didn't know what to say, so she picked up a trail mix cookie and nibbled on the edge of it.

"Has Clayton told you much about Bennett's mother?"

"No, not really."

It was her hesitation as much as her response that warned Ellie she would have to tread carefully. While she could—and did—respect the young woman for not wanting to indulge in gossip about her boarder, she needed to figure out if her instincts about Antonia were correct. If they were, Ellie could go back to Rust Creek Falls with at least one less worry.

"So you probably know as much as I did when she showed up at his door with the baby," Ellie confided. "I'd never even met her before that. Of course, Clay had rarely ever brought any of his girlfriends home—told me that meeting the parents sent the wrong message."

"Sounds like my brother Hudson. All charm, zero commitment."

"That's about right," Ellie agreed. "Or so I thought until Bennett came along."

"No one could ever question his commitment to his son," Antonia assured her.

"I would hope not." Ellie sipped her coffee, hesitant about revealing information that wasn't hers to reveal. On the other hand, she felt strongly that Antonia had a right to know the truth about Clay and Bennett's situation. "Did you know that he tried to file a missing persons report when Delia left?"

Antonia shook her head.

"He contacted a friend of his in the Rust Creek Falls Police Department, but the officer told Clay that just because he didn't know where Delia had gone didn't prove she was missing.

"So he hired a private investigator to find her. Despite the letter she left, he was certain something must have happened to her, because he didn't believe that any woman would willingly walk away from her baby."

"I have trouble imagining it myself," Antonia admitted.

Before Ellie could say anything else, a soft babbling sound came through the monitor, and she felt as if her heart actually swelled in her chest. "Bennett's awake."

Antonia nodded.

"Can I go get him?" she asked, already halfway out of her seat.

The younger woman nodded. "Of course."

By the time Ellie reached the playpen, she saw that Bennett wasn't just awake but had rolled over and had a soft plastic block in his hand.

"Well, look at you," she said.

And he looked up in response to her voice and gave her a droolly grin.

"And look at those two big teeth." She reached into the playpen and lifted him into her arms. "You're going to be ready to chomp on some of D.J.'s famous ribs pretty soon, aren't you?"

But for now, Bennett shoved the corner of the block in his mouth and chomped down on it.

Ellie continued to talk to the baby while she changed his diaper, having found the well-stocked bag conveniently stored beside the playpen. And when he was clean and dry, she carried him back down the hall. She saw Antonia at the stove, stirring a big pot of something on the stove. She heard, rather than saw, the back door open and then Clay walked into the kitchen as if he felt very much at home there.

She didn't fail to notice that Clay's eyes lit up when he saw Antonia, very much like Bennett's did. And when Antonia looked up and smiled at him, Ellie was fairly certain she could feel the crackle of electricity in the air.

It was obvious to her that Antonia was more to both Clay and Bennett than just someone who put meals on the table. It was equally obvious that none of them had yet realized it.

And while she didn't like to interfere in the lives of her grown children—at least not too much, she couldn't help thinking that both Clay and Antonia could use a little nudge in the right direction.

"Something smells good in here," Clay said.

"I made a pot of beef stew to combat the gray and dreary day."

"My stomach is already grumbling." He snatched an apple out of a bowl on the counter and bit into it. "Bennett still sleeping?"

"No, he—"

"Just woke up," Ellie interjected, carrying the baby into the room.

Clay lifted a brow as he finished chewing. "Do I dare ask what you're doing here?" Though his tone was wary, he dutifully crossed the room to kiss her cheek, then nuzzled the baby's.

"I didn't come to check up on your brother or you," she assured him.

"Then why did you come?" he asked, though not unkindly.

"Partly for a baby fix and partly to check out Jason and Joss's new place since we can't be there for the grand reopening tomorrow." *And partly to check out the new woman in your life,* though she was hardly going to admit *that* out loud.

"Dad's with you?"

"He dropped me off on his way into town to see Frank Cates about getting some new bookshelves built for the living room." She glanced at her watch. "But he should be back soon and then we'll be out of your hair."

"You're welcome to stay for dinner, if you like," Antonia said. "And if you don't mind sharing a table with a bunch of hungry cowboys."

"That's incredibly gracious of you," Ellie said, "especially considering that we showed up on your doorstep without any invitation or warning. But I have a better idea. Jason promised to let us sample some of the new menu items at The Hitching Post tonight, so why don't you both join us there?"

Her son had always been sharp, and she felt his gaze narrow on her now.

Antonia seemed more startled than suspicious. "Thanks," she said. "But someone has to serve dinner to the cowboys."

"Clay?" Ellie prompted.

"Since I'll get a firsthand look at the new menu tomorrow, I think I'll stick around here for beef stew tonight."

She didn't have to feign her disappointment, because his response meant that she wouldn't get to spend that extra time with her son and her grandson. But she did have to hold back her jubilation, because his decision confirmed that her instincts regarding her Clay and Antonia were on target.

Now if only *they* could figure that out.

Antonia was putting together a shopping list after breakfast Saturday morning when Clay came into the kitchen. He and Bennett had shown up for breakfast much earlier than usual that morning and hadn't lingered after the meal, so she was more than a little surprised by his return now, especially since he didn't have the baby in tow.

"Where's Bennett?"

"Down at the stables with Forrest."

She smiled. "He's a cowboy just like his daddy, isn't he?"

"He does like the horses," Clay agreed. "But I'm not quite ready to saddle up a pony for him yet."

"Don't blink," she warned. "Or he'll be saddling up his own before you know it."

"Yeah, that's what my brother Dallas keeps saying."

"He has kids?"

"Three sons—nine, seven and five."

"Wow, the Traub boys are soon going to take over the whole state of Montana."

"There's definitely no concern about the family tree withering," he agreed. "But I didn't come up here to talk about genealogy."

"Why did you come up here?"

"To ask you if you had any plans for tonight."

Her heart did a funny little skip, and she immediately chided herself for the reaction. After all, it wasn't as if the man was going to ask her out on a date.

"Nope, I'm free," she said casually. "What do you need?"

"Well, Forrest ran into Jason in town the other day and committed both of us to attending the grand reopening of The Hitching Post tonight."

She'd heard about the event, of course, even before Ellie had mentioned it the day before. It was all anybody was talking about in town, and since Jason Traub—Clay and Forrest's cousin—now owned the place, it made sense that they would want to be there.

"It sounds like it's going to be a really big to-do," Antonia acknowledged.

Clay nodded. "Forrest and I figured we would head into town around seven."

"And you want me to look after Bennett," she guessed.

He seemed startled by her assumption. "Actually, I was hoping you might want to come with us."

Now it was her turn to be surprised. "You're taking Bennett to the party?"

He chuckled. "No. I've already made arrangements for him to stay with some of his cousins under the care of a highly recommended local sitter."

Which led her to ask, "So why do you need me?"

"I don't need you," he clarified. "I just thought you might like to go—to get away from the ranch for a few hours."

"I would," she agreed. "I was just—" stunned, shocked, completely flabbergasted "—surprised...by the invitation."

"Then you'll come with us?" he asked hopefully.

She mentally reviewed the contents of her wardrobe, trying to determine if she had anything that might be appropriate for such an event, and realized that the answer was a resounding no. Not anything that would fit over her enormous belly, anyway. Which meant that she would have to make a trip into town and, fingers crossed, try to find something suitable in the limited maternity selection at Second Chances, the thrift store in town.

Since she had to go into town to talk to Malcolm at the Feed 'N' Seed about making some changes to the ranch's customary feed order, she had a ready-made excuse for the trip. Except her meeting with Malcolm wasn't until four o'clock, and by the time she got home again after that, she'd hardly have any time to get ready. But if she did her hair and makeup before she headed into town—

"Antonia?" Clay prompted.

She flushed, realizing he was still waiting for an answer to his invitation. "Would it be okay if I met you at The Hitching Post?"

"Oh. I thought, if we were going to the same place, we might as well go together."

"It's just that I have an appointment in town this afternoon, so it actually makes more sense for me to stay in town."

"All right," he agreed.

Antonia refused to think about his invitation through the rest of the morning. She had too much to do to let herself be distracted by something that wasn't even a date.

She made a double-batch of chili for dinner and left it simmering in the slow-cooker. She hopped into the shower quickly, then used a wide-barreled curling iron to put a few loose waves in her hair. By three o'clock, she was starting on her makeup and feeling undeniable flutters in her belly that she knew were not caused by the baby she carried there.

"Hey, Toni, I just wanted—"

Jonah stopped in the open doorway of her bedroom and stared at her as if he'd never seen her put on makeup before.

"What did you want?" she asked with deliberate politeness.

"I wanted to make sure you remembered you had to go to the Feed 'N' Seed."

"I'll be on my way shortly."

"Since when do you put on makeup to go into town?" Jonah demanded.

"Since when is my personal appearance any of your concern?" Antonia countered.

"Since you look like you're getting ready for a date."

"Is that so inconceivable?"

He scowled. "Do you have a date?"

She wasn't entirely sure what was the appropriate response to that question. When a man invited a woman to attend a social event with him, it was usually a date. But

Clay had asked if she wanted to go to the opening with both he and his brother, which definitely didn't sound like a date to her. She shook her head. "No, but I am going to the grand reopening of The Hitching Post."

"Who are you going with?"

She sighed. "I'm meeting Clay—"

"Sounds like a date to me," Jonah interrupted.

"—*and* Forrest," she finished.

"It doesn't look right."

She set down her mascara wand. "My makeup?"

If one of them hadn't been in a sling, he would no doubt have folded his arms over his chest in a familiar gesture of disapproval. Instead, he leaned his good shoulder against the doorjamb and glowered at her. "A pregnant woman going out with a man who isn't even the father of her baby."

"I'm attending a social event along with at least a hundred other residents of Thunder Canyon."

"I've seen the way he looks at you," Jonah said.

And though his words were spoken in an ominous tone, her heart gave a happy little flutter. Clay had flirted with her a little, and she'd flirted right back. They both knew it wasn't going to go anywhere. Of course not. He was adjusting to life as a father, she was soon going to be a mother, and neither one of them had the inclination to take things any further. But the man did make her heart pound, and her blood pulse, and her knees quiver.

"And I've seen you looking right back," her brother accused.

Since she couldn't deny that was true, she only said, "There's no harm in looking."

"You're pregnant."

She looked down at her belly, made her eyes widen. "Oh, my goodness. When did that happen?"

Jonah glowered some more. "People will talk."

Antonia sighed. "People have been talking for months."

"It doesn't bother you?"

"I can't control what anyone else thinks or says."

"You don't have to add fuel to the fire," he told her.

"Jonah, I haven't been out socially since—" She thought about the movie she'd attended with Clay the previous Saturday afternoon, then decided it would be smarter not to mention that outing to her brother. No doubt he would go off the deep end about that, too. "Well, it's been so long, I can't even remember since when."

"If you want to go out somewhere, I can take you."

She crossed the room to her closet, grabbed another one of the flannel shirts she'd borrowed from her father's wardrobe, and pulled it on over her T-shirt. "I'm going to The Hitching Post with Clay and Forrest tonight," she said with finality. "But since I have to go into town this afternoon, I'll be driving myself in my own vehicle so that I can leave the party whenever I want."

Her answer must have appeased him somewhat because Jonah finally just said, "Don't be out too late."

She picked up her purse, slung it over her shoulder. "Don't wait up."

Clay had never left his son with anyone outside of the family. Well, aside from Antonia, of course. It had been surprisingly easy for Clay to entrust Bennett to her care, because the little guy didn't just adore her but obviously felt comfortable with her, which had made Clay feel a lot more comfortable about the situation.

But he was having second (or was it seventh by now?) thoughts about his decision to leave his baby with Shandie's sitter. Maybe he should have asked Antonia to watch Bennett tonight. But when his cousin's wife had suggested that the little boy could stay at their place with her eight-year-old daughter, Kayla, and four-year-old son, Max, and the babysitter she'd been using since Max was a baby, it had seemed like a great idea—and the perfect opportunity to get Antonia away from the ranch for a few hours.

Because Clay knew that she didn't just work hard but almost incessantly at Wright's Way. Through conversation with her brothers, he'd been surprised to learn that—before she got pregnant—she'd been primarily responsible for the care and training of the horses that boarded at their stables. It was only after her doctor had recommended a shift to less strenuous activities that she'd turned her attention to the administrative and housekeeping duties.

And she'd tackled those new responsibilities, Ace admitted with grudging admiration, with as much initiative and enthusiasm as she'd done everything else. Which made Clay wonder if she'd show the same initiative and enthusiasm in the bedroom—an inappropriate thought for which he immediately chastised himself.

He'd just finished changing Bennett's diaper when a brisk knock on the door preceded his brother's entry.

"Do I have to wear a tie to this thing tonight?" Forrest wanted to know.

"It's called The Hitching Post not Le Grand Maison."

"I take it that's a no."

"I'm sure you could wear one if you want," Clay told him. "But I'm not."

"But you shaved," Forrest noted.

"Of course I shaved."

His brother sniffed the air. "And put on cologne."

"It's aftershave," Clay said pointedly. "Which I usually put on *after I shave*."

"You're wearing dress pants."

"They're khakis."

Forrest shrugged. "They're not denim."

"Well, I did think the occasion warranted something different than my usual attire."

"The occasion—or the company?" his brother teased.

"As if you'd appreciate my efforts," Clay responded, deliberately misinterpreting the question.

Forrest grinned as he bent over to pick up the block Bennett had thrown down. The little boy smiled his thanks—then threw it down again. "You really like her, don't you?"

"Of course I like her. I wouldn't have invited her to go with us tonight if I didn't enjoy spending time with her."

"That's another thing." His brother picked up the block again, but instead of giving it to Bennett, he amused the baby by tossing it back and forth from one hand to the other. "Why did you invite her to go with us? Are you trying to pretend this isn't a date?"

"It isn't a date."

Forrest just rolled his eyes. "You know, she might be just what you need."

"How so?"

"You're a single dad, she's almost a single mom."

Which were just two of the many reasons that he couldn't let himself think of tonight as a date. Yes, he liked her. Yes, he cared about her. But their respective lives were too complicated to think that there was any way they could mesh, even temporarily.

"If you two got married, Bennett would have a mom and her baby would have a dad."

Married? Clay felt as if he was choking. He reached up and opened the top button of his shirt. "I am *not* getting married."

"Not before a first date, anyway," Forrest teased.

"You know me, Forrest. I don't do commitment."

"I used to think that was true," his brother admitted. "But the last six months with Bennett have proven otherwise."

"That's different."

"Why?"

"Because he's my son."

"His mother walked away," Forrest reminded him. "You could have done the same."

"No way." His denial was immediate and vehement.

"Which only proves my point." His brother's smile was smug as he handed the block to Bennett again.

"It's still not a date," Clay insisted.

Bennett threw the block at his head.

Chapter Eight

After Antonia's stop at the feed store, she drove to Second Chances, located beside Real Vintage Cowboy in Old Town. If she'd had more time, she could have gone to one of the big shopping malls in Bozeman. But she didn't have more time, which meant that she had two options: the plus-size store at New Town Mall or the maternity section at Second Chances. She would have preferred to avoid Main Street and the inevitable interrogation that would follow if she ran into Catherine, but the necessity of shopping within her budget proved stronger than her cowardice.

She'd been a frequent visitor to Second Chances since her waistline had started expanding. She hadn't stocked up on a lot of stuff for her baby because she didn't need a lot. In the attic at home, she'd found boxes and boxes of baby clothes that had once belonged to her brothers or herself. Apparently her mother had kept everything, and

Antonia had unpacked, sorted, laundered and folded the various garments into neat little piles according to gender and season, ready for her baby to make his or her appearance.

As for maternity clothes, she'd tried not to splurge unnecessarily in that department, too. But when her breasts had started to spill out of her bras, she'd made a trip to a specialty shop in Billings, not wanting everyone she knew in Thunder Canyon to be privy to the details of her lingerie purchases. She'd bought a few new bras and had looked—with apparent dismay—at the wide stretchy lace band at the top of the maternity panties. The sales clerk had laughed at her expression and confided that bikini underwear were a perfectly acceptable alternative.

Antonia was wearing one of those new bras and a pair of matching bikinis now, because she liked the sensation of the soft fabrics against her skin. Of course, she hadn't worried about the color of her lingerie when she'd pulled on her maternity jeans and flannel shirt, but she realized now that the crimson-colored lace might further limit her options. Because Helen Vanderhorst would just die if she caught a glimpse of Antonia's red bra through a white top—but not before she'd shared the news with all of her friends from church.

The store was empty of other customers when Antonia arrived and the clerk, who was tagging new merchandise, smiled at her. "Welcome to Second Chances. Can I help you find anything in particular today?"

"Please," Antonia said, just a little desperately.

The other woman, whose name tag identified her as Bonnie, laughed. "Are you looking for something for a special occasion?"

"Something a little dressier than what I'm wearing now but not too formal."

"You're in luck. A young mother of six-month-old triplets came in yesterday and dropped off two boxes of maternity clothes."

Antonia swallowed. "Triplets?"

"Three gorgeous little girls."

"Three…girls," she echoed weakly.

"Do you know if you're having a boy or a girl?" Bonnie asked.

She shook her head. "No, but I do know there's only one baby."

The sales clerk laughed again. "Well, you can imagine why this mom was adamant that she wasn't having any more kids. But she had fabulous taste—and the styles are much more current than most of the stuff on our racks." She rifled through the offerings, pushing aside tops and skirts and dresses until she came to what she wanted, and pulled out a hanger. "Try this."

So Antonia did, and the fit of the burgundy chiffon dress was perfect—and almost flattering, even.

"It looks fabulous," Bonnie said.

Antonia wasn't sure about fabulous—after all, it didn't hide the fact that she was seven and a half months pregnant. But she did think it looked pretty good, because the side shirring allowed the fabric to drape over the curve of her belly without emphasizing it.

"What color are your shoes?"

"Shoes?" Antonia echoed, slapping a hand to her forehead.

Bonnie just smiled. "What size do you wear?"

"Eight."

She moved to a shelf stacked high with boxes against the back wall and pulled one free.

Antonia slipped the low-heeled pumps onto her feet.

"Perfect," Bonnie decided.

Antonia mentally calculated the cost of the dress and the shoes and nodded. She was within her budget, and that was perfect for her.

It was an undeniable fact that a man was usually drawn to a woman he found attractive, and Clay had dated a lot of very attractive women. Antonia wasn't cover model gorgeous, but she was beautiful in a more subtle and natural way. She didn't wear a lot of makeup, but she didn't need a lot to enhance her innate beauty. Her skin was flawless, her lips were exquisitely shaped, and her deep green eyes could sparkle with humor, glint with anger and dim with shadows.

And while Clay usually appreciated Antonia's natural look, when he saw her walking down the sidewalk toward him, he also appreciated that she'd put some extra effort into her appearance tonight. She'd added some curl to the hair that tumbled over her shoulders, some liner and shadow to emphasize the green of her eyes, some colored gloss to showcase those exquisite lips—and she was wearing a dress.

He'd never before seen her in a dress. Especially not anything like this one that dipped at the front to show a hint of shadowy cleavage and finished just above the knee to reveal a long length of slender, shapely leg.

"You might want to pick your jaw up off the sidewalk before we go into the party," Forrest suggested, in a tone pitched low enough that Antonia couldn't hear.

Clay followed his brother's advice, albeit with some difficulty.

"She's really got you hooked, hasn't she?"

"I'm not hooked," Clay denied automatically.

Forrest mimicked the sound of a fishing line being reeled in.

Clay—his attention riveted on Antonia—didn't bother to respond.

"Am I late?" she asked, when she finally joined them on the wide, wood-pillared porch outside the front doors of The Hitching Post. "Have you been waiting long?"

Forrest shot his elbow into his brother's ribs.

"Um, no. You're right on time," Clay managed.

Forrest managed to do better. "You look very nice this evening, Ms. Wright," he said, his tone only a little gruff.

Her cheeks colored. "Same goes, Mr. Traub." Her gaze shifted from Forrest to Clay. "And Mr. Traub. Thank you both for including me tonight."

"The company of a beautiful woman always makes an evening more enjoyable," Forrest said, and offered his arm to Antonia.

Usually a man of a surly attitude and few words, he was laying on the charm tonight. And Clay could only stare as Antonia tucked her hand in the crook of his brother's arm and let him lead her inside.

The event was already a huge success, with the residents of Thunder Canyon having shown up in full force to support Jason and Joss in their venture. Of course, Antonia was acquainted with more than a few people in attendance, and Clay sensed several speculative glances cast toward their trio. Or maybe the glances were focused solely on Antonia and Forrest, since Clay had entered a few steps behind, feeling like the proverbial fifth wheel.

When Antonia excused herself to visit the ladies' room, Clay cornered his brother. "What are you doing?"

"Trying to enjoy myself," Forrest said easily.

"With Antonia?"

"You said your invitation to her wasn't a date," Forrest reminded him.

"And you decided that made it okay for you to hit on her?"

His brother shrugged. "She's sexy, we're both single."

Clay's fingers curled into his palms, his jaw clenched.

Forrest smiled knowingly. "You really want to punch me right now, don't you?"

Clay did, but he was determined to show better impulse control than his cousin Jackson had done in the past, or the Traubs would forever be known as rabble-rousers in Thunder Canyon.

He deliberately relaxed his fists and tucked his hands into his pockets. "Are you trying to make me hit you?"

"I'm trying to make you admit that you have feelings for the woman."

"Don't toy with her, Forrest," he warned.

"She can handle herself," his brother said confidently.

Which wasn't the reassurance Clay had been seeking, but Antonia's return prevented him from pursuing the topic any further. At least for now.

"Can I get you something to drink, Antonia?" Forrest asked her.

"Anything non-alcoholic and non-caffeinated would be great."

"*I'll* get it," Clay said, glaring at his brother.

Antonia's gaze shifted between the brothers, as if she sensed the undercurrents between them.

Forrest just shrugged. "I'll have a beer—whatever they've got on tap."

And Clay realized that he'd fallen easily into his brother's trap. By insisting that he get her drink, he'd left Antonia alone with Forrest. Not that he really believed his brother was going to put the moves on her, but there were times that he honestly didn't know what Forrest was going to do anymore.

As he made his way to the bar to get a glass of ginger ale for Antonia, he crossed paths with D.J. and Dax. His cousins had been raised by their father in Thunder Canyon after the death of their mother, and both had grown up to achieve success in their chosen endeavors. D.J. was renowned for his chain of restaurants, of course, and Dax owned a motorcycle shop in Old Town.

When Clay stopped to speak with them, he had a strange feeling, almost like déjà vu. For a minute, their voices sounded far away, giving him a niggling sense of another conversation he'd overheard, as if from a long time ago. But he couldn't remember anything about the content of that conversation and he didn't know why it had crossed his mind now, so he pushed the uneasy feeling aside and continued toward the bar.

Returning with Antonia's beverage, he found that she had moved on with Forrest and was now standing close to another man, laughing at whatever he said. He felt an unexpected stab of something that, if he didn't know better, might have been jealousy. But he did know better, and when he recognized the other man as his cousin Jason, who was now happily married to Jocelyn—a transplant from California and former runaway bride—he felt even more ridiculous.

When Clay reached the group that also included Jason's beautiful wife, his cousin offered to give them a grand tour of the new place. Having grown up in Thunder Canyon, Antonia was familiar with the long and colorful history of the establishment, but since Clay and Forrest were not, Jason entertained them with anecdotes—some of which he admitted had likely been greatly exaggerated through repeated narration over the years.

As interesting as the stories were, the guests were most impressed by the planning and attention to detail that had gone into the renovations. It had been important to both Jason and Joss to ensure that The "new and improved" Hitching Post continued to respect its Montana history and maintain its Western style. Cates Construction, the company that had been hired to oversee the renovations, had done both.

"The bar and restaurant area on the main level have been completely overhauled," Jason explained, leading them toward the stairs. "And the upper level, formerly comprised of a collection of rooms available to rent, has been converted into a salon."

A salon that had a decidedly cozy and distinctly Western atmosphere with overstuffed leather chairs, hand-carved rockers and deer antlers mounted on the walls. In addition, there were cowhide rugs scattered over the glossy wood floors, tables for card games and quiet corners for intimate conversations.

Antonia's lips curved as she moved toward the large stone fireplace. "I wondered if Lily Divine would still be here."

Jason grinned. "There was no way we could even consider getting rid of her."

"Who?" Forrest wanted to know.

The Hitching Post's proud owner pointed to the antique portrait hung above the mantel. And while the painting might have been old, many would consider it risqué even by contemporary standards. Because in the portrait, the undeniably lovely Lily Divine was undeniably stark naked, with any illusion of modesty preserved only by a bit of gauzy fabric strategically draped across her feminine attributes.

"She was the original owner of The Hitching Post," Jason explained. "Although back in the 1890s it was a house of ill-repute known as the Shady Lady Saloon."

"It might become known as a house of ill-repute again," Clay teased. "With Jason Traub in charge."

His cousin chuckled. "While Joss is hoping to establish a reputation for The Hitching Post, I'm not sure that's quite what she has in mind."

And it was obvious by the affection in his voice that Jason would do anything he could to make his wife's hopes and dreams come true.

"You've done a fabulous job with the place," Antonia said to him.

"It's been a labor of love," Jason admitted. "But now that it's open for business, can I get you some drinks?"

The response was unanimous. "Absolutely."

"Okay then, find some empty seats and I'll have a couple of beers sent up. And another ginger ale for Antonia."

"Sounds like a plan," Forrest agreed, and led the way to a vacant seating area tucked in a corner.

The waitress who delivered the drinks was yet another classmate of Antonia's from Thunder Canyon High School. After passing around the beverages, Trina paused to chat for a minute, ostensibly to ask Antonia about Jonah's injury. But Antonia could tell from the speculative glances that Trina sent to both Clayton and Forrest in turn that the waitress was more interested in the Traub men than Antonia's brother—a fact that was proven when Trina looked directly at Clay and said, "I'll be back to check on you guys real soon."

Antonia told herself it was foolish to be offended by the other woman's blatant flirtation, but it was just like the situation with Vanessa at the movies all over again. And while it wasn't as if the woman was making a move on her date, because this wasn't a date, it still smarted to be treated as if she were invisible. Well, Trina was acting as if Antonia were invisible, while Vanessa had taken an entirely different tack—focusing on the fact that her pregnancy made Antonia impossible to miss.

"Do you know everyone in this town?" Forrest asked her when Trina had finally gone.

"Probably everyone who went to Thunder Canyon High School during the years that I was there," she admitted.

"Did you ever want to live anywhere else?"

He sounded genuinely interested in her response, and Antonia found herself wondering if he was thinking about making Thunder Canyon his permanent home. "Not until recently."

The Traub brothers seemed to instinctively know that she was referring to the gossip that had surrounded her pregnancy.

"It's hard, living in a small town where everyone knows your business," Clay said.

"But it can be comforting, too," she told them. "The lack of anonymity means that you're never truly alone."

"I like being anonymous," Forrest told them.

Antonia had to smile. "You think you're anonymous here? You're the injured war hero who's helping to set up the animal therapy group for veterans."

"I'm not a hero," Forrest denied. And then, because the conversation was obviously taking a path he didn't want to follow, he rose to his feet. "I think I see Russ Chilton over there and I wanted to talk to him about a horse."

"I didn't mean to make him uncomfortable," Antonia said.

"You didn't," Clay assured her.

But she was unconvinced. "I shouldn't have mentioned his injury."

"It's not the injury. It's just that he doesn't like to talk about his time in the service."

"Not even to you?"

"Not to anyone—a reality that weighs more heavily on my mother than anyone else. None of her boys ever had a problem that she couldn't fix—until now."

Out of the corner of his eye, he saw Forrest was deep in conversation with Russ Chilton. He wasn't convinced that they were talking horses and suspected that his brother had maneuvered the situation to give Clay some time alone with Antonia. Although to what purpose, he didn't know. Even if he was attracted to Antonia—and Forrest had obviously clued into the fact that he was—he had no intention of making a move on his pregnant landlady. No intention at all.

Of course, now that they were alone together, he couldn't stop thinking about the possible moves that he might make—if he was going to make a move. But of course he wasn't. And it was ridiculous to feel awkward just because they were alone together. Over the past several weeks, they'd spent a lot of time together, although usually with someone else around—Forrest or Bennett or one of Antonia's brothers or a ranch hand. Without anyone else near and no movie screen to focus their attention, neither of them seemed to know what to say or do.

Then another server circulated through the upper level—this one wasn't a former classmate of Antonia's but the younger brother of her mechanic—delivering trays of hot appetizers to the guests. The arrival of the food alleviated the tension, at least for the moment. Antonia loaded up her plate with garlic parmesan grilled shrimp and spicy Buffalo wings and nacho chips dripping with cheese and jalapenos, and then she loaded it up again.

"Eating for two," she said unapologetically.

Clay set his now-empty plate aside and picked up his beer. “The baby doesn’t mind spicy food?”

“The baby doesn’t seem to mind anything so long as I eat.”

“Any bizarre cravings?”

“Ice cream,” she admitted.

“That doesn’t seem so bizarre.”

“At almost any time of the day, even seven o’clock in the morning.”

“Okay, that’s a little unusual,” he allowed. “Did you want me to go down to the kitchen to see if Jason has any in the freezer?”

She smiled and set her plate aside. “Thanks, but I think I’m good for now.”

“Are you going to leave that single nacho chip on the plate?”

She eyed the chip. “You don’t want it?”

“I’m good.”

She reached for the chip, but as she lifted it toward her mouth, a jalapeno fell off and landed on his thigh. She dropped the chip again and snagged a napkin. “I’m so sorry,” she said, removing the errant pepper and dabbing at the leg of his khakis with the napkin.

The touch of her hand on his leg triggered an immediate reaction. His heart jolted, his blood heated and every muscle in his body tensed.

She must have felt the strain in the muscle of his thigh, because she snatched her hand away, and when her gaze lifted to his, he saw that her cheeks were pink. That brief touch, combined with her undeniable response, suggested to Clay that the attraction he’d been battling for the past several weeks might not be as one-sided as he’d believed. And when Antonia started to draw back, he caught her hand and pulled her closer instead.

Her eyes widened, and he heard her breath catch in her throat, but she didn't protest when he leaned in and touched his mouth to hers. In fact, she kissed him back, her soft, sweet lips responding willingly to his.

He released her hand, his fingertips trailing up her arm, over the curve of her shoulder to disappear in the tumble of curls that spilled down her back. Her hair was as soft and fragrant as he remembered, and his fingers sifted through the silken strands, tilting her head back so that he could deepen the kiss. He felt the shudder of breath between her lips as they parted and then her tongue met his, somehow tentative and eager at the same time.

She tasted of the nachos she'd eaten—salty and spicy—and of passion, and he wanted to gobble her right up. He'd watched her for weeks, and he'd wanted her for nearly as long, but he'd never imagined that this might actually happen. It was only a kiss, and yet, he sensed it could be a prelude to so much more.

He hadn't expected such a response, or so much passion. He hadn't expected anything because he hadn't planned to kiss her at all. But then she'd touched him, and the heat that shot through his veins had obliterated all thought and reason. He'd only been aware of how much he wanted her, and the way she was kissing him back, he was pretty sure the attraction was mutual.

It was as if they were the only two people in the room, each conscious only of the other, aware only of desire for the other. He was wondering if there was any chance of getting Antonia out of that sexy dress when he heard his brother's voice—a stark and startling reminder that he and Antonia were not alone.

"I'll have to ask Jason what the cook put in those nachos."

Antonia jolted as if she'd been shocked by a cattle prod,

not just pulling away from Clay but jumping to her feet when she heard Forrest speak.

She couldn't believe what she'd done. She'd actually been making out with Clay—and in a public place. Not just kissing him like there was no tomorrow, but wishing that those kisses could lead to a lot more.

She didn't want to look at Forrest. She didn't want to see the smug satisfaction on his face that she could hear in his voice. But she knew that she should be grateful not just for the interruption but that he'd been the one to interrupt. Because as embarrassed as she was right now, she was fairly confident that Clay's brother wasn't one of the gears churning in the well-oiled gossip mill of Thunder Canyon.

"I didn't mean to interrupt," Forrest continued. "And I'm happy to disappear again, I just thought you might need a reminder that there are no longer rooms to rent in this part of the establishment."

Her cheeks burned even hotter. "There's no need for you to go anywhere," she assured him, unable to even look at his brother, unwilling to let Clay see how completely shaken she'd been by the kiss they'd shared. "Because I need to be going."

"Why?" Clay demanded.

"I'm suddenly not feeling well," she told him, and reassured herself that it wasn't really a lie.

Because she wasn't feeling well—she was feeling hot and tingly and more aroused than she'd ever been before. And that was definitely *not* good for a woman in her condition with no possibility of alleviating the desperate, aching need that coursed through her veins.

"Then I'll take you back to the ranch," Clay said.

She shook her head. "I have my truck."

"But if you're not feeling well—"

"I'm well enough to drive myself home," she insisted.

"You do look a little flushed," Forrest noted.

There was a glint of amusement in his gaze and a note of teasing in his tone, and she could only imagine how entertaining it was for him to find his brother in a liplock with their hugely pregnant landlady.

And while she was still having trouble wrapping her head around the fact that Clay had kissed her, there was no denying that she'd kissed him back. Not just responding to the touch of his lips but practically throwing herself at him. She might as well wear a sign around her neck that read Desperately Horny Woman Craves a Man's Touch.

Okay, so she wasn't desperate enough to want *any* man's hands on her body, but her out-of-control hormones clearly wanted her to get naked with Clay and there was no way that was going to happen.

She forced herself to meet Forrest's gaze, conscious of the burning in her cheeks. "I just need some fresh air."

"Are you sure?" Clay was beside her now, looking and sounding genuinely concerned.

"I'm sure." She stepped away, before he could touch her and send fireworks rocketing through her system all over again. "But thank you both again for inviting me tonight."

"It was our pleasure," Forrest said, then winked. "Although I'm guessing it was Clayton's pleasure more than mine."

She couldn't look at Clay, but she did, out of the corner of her eye, catch a glimpse of the elbow he shot into his brother's ribs.

"Well, thank you," she said again, and fled before she died of embarrassment in Jason Traub's newly renovated salon.

Chapter Nine

Why had he kissed her?

Why had she kissed him back?

And why the hell had she run out on him just when things were getting interesting?

Clay wanted answers to these questions and more that swirled through his mind, and the only way to get those answers was to go after Antonia. He started to take a step forward, intending to do just that. But he suspected that his desire to follow her wasn't just about getting answers but also wanting to finish what they started, and it was the desperation of the wanting that forced him back into his seat.

He wasn't the type of man to chase after a woman, and there were too many reasons why he should *not* chase after Antonia. Instead, he settled into the soft leather and picked up his beer.

Forrest dropped into the chair beside him. "You truly are an idiot."

"So you've said on more than one occasion," Clay acknowledged.

"You're really just going to let her go?"

"Obviously she wanted to go."

"If you want her, and I don't think there's any doubt that you do," Forrest noted, "you should go after her."

"And then what?"

His brother's brows lifted. "Since you already have a kid, I figured you got the logistics and mechanics of sex."

"And if Antonia was anyone else, I'd already be out the door," Clay admitted.

"But you don't want anyone else."

Which was, unfortunately, all too true. Since the first minute he'd set eyes on her, he'd felt an attraction that was as inexplicable as it was undeniable. At first he'd thought it was a simple matter of his hormones waking up after nearly a year of self-imposed celibacy, but no other woman stirred his blood the way that Antonia did.

And he'd tried—he'd flirted with the pretty barista at The Daily Grind, he'd checked out the checkout girls at the Super Save Mart, and he'd even contemplated the offers of various happily married cousins to set him up with a sister or niece or friend. But no other woman tempted him the way that Antonia did, and the only thing that had prevented him from succumbing to that temptation before now was the fact that she was pregnant.

He'd assumed that, being in the latter stages of pregnancy, Antonia's sexual desires would have waned. The way she'd responded to his kiss had him reassessing that assumption. Still, it seemed necessary to remind his brother of that one salient fact: "She's pregnant, Forrest."

"At least you won't have to worry about knocking her up."

"Instead I would have to worry about Antonia expecting that a casual hook-up might lead to something more." He shook his head. "No, getting involved—however temporarily—with my pregnant landlady is more complication than either of us wants or needs right now."

His brother didn't disagree. He just looked at Clay long and hard for a minute, and then he shrugged. "Your call," he said easily.

It was his call, and he'd made it. He was *not* going to pursue Antonia. He was *not* going to think about the warm, lushness of her mouth, or the softness of her curves, or the way she trembled in his arms—

Dammit.

He set his half-full glass back on the table and pushed to his feet.

"Don't worry about me," Forrest said. "I can find my own way back to the ranch."

Clay took him at his word, because now that he'd made up his mind to go after Antonia, he wasn't going to let anything stand in his way. And if she was already in the house, he would bang on the door until she answered. However, the possibility that her father or one of her brothers might answer the summons presented a potential snag to that plan. He pressed his foot down on the accelerator, determined to catch up with Antonia rather than risk that scenario playing out.

Thankfully, the roads were clear—no doubt most of the residents of Thunder Canyon were at The Hitching Post—allowing him to ignore the posted speed limit. At least until he came up behind a blue pickup whose driver was cruising along at a conservative fifty-two miles per hour.

Clay cursed under his breath and started to pull out to

pass the vehicle, then realized that he didn't need to be in such a hurry after all because the driver of the truck in front of him was Antonia. He eased off a little and pulled into the driveway of the Wright Ranch immediately behind her.

When Antonia climbed out of the truck, his game plan flew out the window. She slammed her door and strode toward him, her hands on her hips. "Are you crazy?"

Since he wasn't entirely sure what had prompted the question—and because he wasn't sure that his sanity wasn't in doubt—he didn't respond.

"You raced up behind me like a bat out of hell."

"I was anxious to get back," he said now. "To make sure that you were okay."

"And how many ordinances did you violate as you sped through town?"

"It's not against the law to look out for a friend," he countered. "And why did you take off in such a hurry, anyway?"

Now it was Antonia's turn to fall silent, confirming his suspicion that her excuse for leaving the party was just that—an excuse.

He took a step closer, noted that the pulse in her throat fluttered. But she didn't step back and she didn't look away. She held his gaze, waiting, wondering, and Clay knew that the next move was up to him.

He lifted his hand to her cheek. "What were you running from?"

She didn't respond, but when he brushed his thumb over her bottom lip, it trembled.

"If you're not interested, tell me you're not interested," he said. "But you better say it fast, because I really want to kiss you again."

* * *

Antonia wished that she *wasn't* interested. But although lack of interest wasn't an issue, there were other issues. Too many issues to allow them to take the next step.

"It's really bad timing," she said instead.

"This definitely wasn't in my plans when I came to Thunder Canyon," he agreed.

"I mean—you have a baby. And I get that he's your priority, because I have a baby on the way. But until I have my baby, I have a huge belly—and I can't imagine that any man would be attracted to a woman in the last trimester of pregnancy. Unless he was her husband or the father of her baby, which, of course, you're not."

She knew she was babbling, and almost incoherently. But how was she supposed to make any sense when she couldn't even think straight around him? Not on a good day, and especially not after that mind-boggling, body-numbing kiss he'd laid on her at The Hitching Post.

"So I know you can't be attracted to me," she continued babbling. "And I can't figure out why you would kiss me, why you'd want to—"

Clay effectively halted her rambling by covering her mouth with his own.

The kiss was long and slow and deep, and it stoked the fire of a passion that had been burning since that first unexpected kiss at The Hitching Post—or maybe even before that.

It didn't make any sense to her, but Antonia was beyond caring. She just wanted to be kissed like he was kissing her, like no one else had ever kissed her before. And he did—his lips hot and persuasive and very, very talented. They teased, they toyed, they made her burn.

And when his hand slid from her hip to her breast, her

knees nearly buckled. When his thumb circled her already taut nipple, she did whimper.

Clay immediately snatched his hand away. "I hurt you—"

"No." She took his hand and placed it back on her breast. "It just feels…sooo good."

His thumb moved over her nipple again, and she sighed. He rolled the peak between his thumb and finger, and spears of heat shot to her core. Then his lips were on hers again, his tongue in her mouth, and she could taste the desperation of his passion and knew that it matched her own.

She didn't think she'd ever experienced a desire like this before, so fierce and needy and demanding. When he pressed her back against the door of her truck, she could feel his erection against her belly. Tangible proof that he did want her, maybe as much as she wanted him. His hands slid down her body, over her hips to the hem of her skirt, then underneath. His fingers traced up the backs of her thighs, and the heat of his touch was almost unbearable—and not nearly enough—making her whole body tremble.

She could feel the tightening in her belly, knew that she was on the verge of orgasm. They were both still fully clothed, but she was almost ready to explode. She reached down and pressed her hand to the front of his trousers, gently squeezing his hard length through the fabric, and he groaned. She reached for his zipper. They were both near the point of no return, and she didn't care.

But apparently Clay did, because suddenly he pulled away. "This is crazy," he managed, his breath coming in quick, shallow pants.

She was grateful for the door of the truck at her back, because she wasn't sure her trembling legs could support her. He was right—it was crazy. But acknowledging the insanity of the attraction between them did nothing to dim it, and it certainly did nothing to cool the heat still coursing through her veins.

"You started it," she said, aware that she sounded just a little peevish.

But she was hurt by his abrupt withdrawal and angry that she'd let herself succumb to his seduction—and furious that her body was still aching for the completion of joining with his.

She'd never known anything like this. She'd never wanted anyone with such desperation. Even with Gene, she'd never experienced such an intense hunger. Or such an overwhelming sense of rejection. Even when the father of her baby had walked out on her, she'd been more disappointed than hurt.

Maybe it was the pregnancy hormones that were responsible for her feeling so much, so deeply, because there's no way that she could have been foolish enough to fall in love with Clay after knowing him for only a few weeks. No possible way.

Besides, she wasn't thinking about happily-ever-after right now, she was only thinking about how much she wanted to be with him. "And you shouldn't have started if you had no intention of finishing," she continued.

"There's nothing I want more than to get naked with you and finish," he told her.

"So why do we both still have our clothes on?"

"Because we're on the driveway outside of your house where your father and brothers are sleeping." He glanced toward the dark windows on the upper level. "At least, I hope they're sleeping."

She dropped her gaze so Clay wouldn't see the tears that filled her eyes. Being rejected was bad enough; she wasn't going to let him see her cry. Instead, she said only, "Forgive me for not thinking about my father or my brothers while your tongue was in my mouth."

He rubbed the back of his knuckles over the line of her jaw. "I wasn't thinking about them, either," he said. "I was only thinking about stripping this sexy little dress from your sexier body—"

She pushed him away. "Don't."

"Don't what?" he sounded genuinely baffled.

"Don't lie to me. You took it further than you intended and now you want to back out. I get that. But I have no illusions about how I look and I don't need any clichéd lines to make me feel better."

"Apparently you don't have a clue about how you look," he told her.

"I'm almost eight months pregnant."

He took a step closer. "You're lush. Feminine. Gorgeous."

He sounded completely sincere, which only confused her further. "And that completely explains why you don't want me."

"I *do* want you," he insisted. "I don't want to hurt you or your baby."

She wondered if he was telling the truth, and decided there was only one way to find out. "My doctor assured me that there was no need to avoid sexual activity during pregnancy."

"Really?"

"Really," she said. Not that Antonia had paid much heed to what Louise was saying at a time when she'd still been feeling so betrayed by Gene's abandonment that she'd been certain she wouldn't ever want to have sex again—or at least not before her child had graduated from high school. "So if that's the only reason you backed off..."

"It's the only reason," he promised, and took her hand, linking their fingers together.

She looked down at their joined hands. "I was kind of hoping you would prove it by kissing me again."

"I'm going to kiss you again," he said, leading her toward the boarding house. "I'm going to take you to my room, lock the door, strip you naked and kiss every inch of your body."

The heat in his eyes and the promise in his words left her breathless so that the only response she managed was a soft "Oh."

"And then—" he slipped his key into the lock of the main door, released the deadbolt "—I'm going to do all kinds of other things to your gorgeous body. Things I've been fantasizing about doing with you for several weeks now."

"You've been fantasizing...about me?"

"You've haunted my sleep," he admitted. "Tortured me in my dreams."

"Really?" She'd been convinced that the desire she'd been battling was entirely one-sided, and she couldn't help but feel a little thrill of satisfaction in response to his words.

"Really." He led her up the stairs and down the hall, unlocked the door of his room and gestured her inside.

She was familiar with the layout, of course. Most of the rooms in the boarding house had a similar setup. A bed, a dresser and night table, a desk and chair. But Clay's room was a little more crowded than most, with a crib squeezed between desk and the bed.

It wasn't until Antonia saw the crib that she remembered Clay's son, and felt a twinge of guilt that the little boy had been completely absent from her mind until that moment. "When are you supposed to pick up Bennett?"

"Not until the morning." He slid his arms around her waist, drew her close—or at least as close as he could with her rounded belly between them. "Which means that we have all night."

She was already so incredibly aroused from Clay's kisses that Antonia figured she needed only about five more minutes before she'd be ready to explode.

"Or we would," he continued. "If my landlady didn't have some ridiculous rule against overnight guests."

She smiled at that. "I'll make sure she doesn't see me sneaking out of here in the morning."

Though he hadn't turned on any lights, the open curtains allowed the faint illumination of the crescent moon into the room.

Antonia let Clay set the pace—at least at the beginning, because she thought he was as anxious to get naked together as she was. And the first thing he did after locking the door was to whisk her dress up over her head and toss it aside. Then his hands explored and admired the red bra and matching bikinis that she was wearing beneath.

"Did you put this on for me?"

"I hate to disappoint you," she told him, "but I had no reason to suspect that you would see my underwear tonight."

He lightly traced the scalloped edge of her bra with his finger, making her shiver. "Are you telling me that you wear this every day?"

She swallowed, tried to maintain a casual tone when everything inside of her wanted to beg him to take her. Right here, right now.

"Not this particular set," she said. "But I do have a

weakness for silky fabrics. I like the way they feel against my skin."

He cupped her lace-covered breasts, squeezed gently. "So do I," he said reverently.

"Speaking of skin," she said, her fingers moving to the buttons that ran down the front of his shirt. "I want to get my hands on yours."

He shrugged out of the garment, happy to comply with her request. Now it was her turn to look and admire—and she definitely liked what she saw. But looking wasn't enough, and she laid her palms on his chest, stroking them over the smooth, taut skin. His muscles were gloriously sculpted and rock-hard, proving that he was every inch a real rough and rugged cowboy. And right now, every inch of this cowboy was hers.

She unfastened the button at the front of his pants and lowered the zipper. She'd wondered if he was a boxers or briefs guy, and smiled when she discovered that he was a boxer briefs guy. She inched her hand beneath the waistband and closed her fingers around him.

His groan sounded equal parts need and frustration, and he carefully removed her hand from his pants and steered her toward the bed. He eased her back onto the mattress, then unfastened the clasp of her bra and slowly peeled the fabric away from her skin. Then he hooked his thumbs in her panties and eased them down her legs.

"You are…so…incredibly…beautiful."

And in that moment, with Clay looking at her with intensity and sincerity, and touching her with gentleness and reverence, she felt incredibly beautiful. And incredibly aroused.

His hands slid down her body, and the baby kicked sharply in response to his touch. Antonia stilled, wondering if this reminder of the child she carried would dampen his desire. But Clay didn't miss a beat. His lips followed his hands, skimming down her torso, over the roundness of her belly, and lower.

"Clay."

He must have heard the impatience and frustration in her voice, because he rose up again and brushed his lips over hers.

"We have all night," he reminded her.

"I know," she agreed. "But I was kind of hoping 'all night' could start right now."

He chuckled softly. "Let's see if we can't release some of your tension."

Then he parted her thighs and lowered his head between them, and all of the breath whooshed out of her lungs. His tongue found the sensitive nub at her center, flicked over it—once, twice. Her hips lifted instinctively, her heels dug into the mattress, and her body completely shattered.

"Better?" he asked, just a hint of smugness in his tone.

"Yes," she could only sigh her response, then she shook her head. "No."

"More?"

Before she even had a chance to respond, his hands and his lips were on her again, stroking and teasing. She'd already had one mind-boggling, earth-shifting orgasm, but she still felt unfulfilled, as if something was missing. And she knew what that something was: Clay. She wanted him inside of her, filling the aching emptiness that throbbed between her thighs.

"I haven't, uh, had sex…in a while," she admitted. "So I'm not sure—logistically—how this is going to work."

"We'll figure it out," he promised her.

"Do you have…protection?" She felt her cheeks burn with embarrassment, not so much because she was asking the question but because she'd let things go as far as they had already without any consideration of the issue. Obviously she wasn't worried about birth control, but she wasn't going to take any chances with her health—and definitely not with her baby's.

"Damn." He scrubbed his hands over his face.

"You don't?"

"I don't know," he admitted. "It's not as if I thought this was going to happen. Believe me, if I'd had even an inkling that this was possible, I would have made a trip to the pharmacy."

Which was extremely flattering but not, in the moment, very helpful.

His brow furrowed, as if he thought hard enough he could conjure up a condom. And maybe he had, because he slid off the bed and disappeared into the adjoining bathroom. Less than a minute later he was back with two square packets in his hand and a look of profound relief in his eyes.

"Two?"

"I'll go to the pharmacy tomorrow."

She hadn't let herself think about tomorrow. She hadn't dared let herself hope for anything beyond this one night. But the casual reference to restocking his prophylactic supply gave her hope that this might be something more than a one-night stand.

"You think we'll use both of those tonight?" she asked him.

"I know we will." He nibbled on her earlobe. "Because I want you so desperately I'm not sure the first round is going to be very good for you. But the second, I promise, will make up for the first."

She knew she wouldn't be disappointed. How could she be when he'd already given her so much more than she'd expected? But she did want more—she wanted him inside her. So she pushed him back on the bed and straddled his hips with her knees.

Clay's brows lifted, but he didn't protest.

"Let's get started on that first round," she suggested.

She took one of the packages off of the bedside table, carefully tore the edge of the wrapper. Then she placed the condom on the tip of his erection and slowly—very slowly—rolled it down the length of him.

He groaned. "Are you trying to torture me?"

"Maybe. Just a little."

Actually, what she was really trying to do was to give him back at least some of the pleasure that he'd given to her. But she was, admittedly, more than a little self-conscious. She didn't have a lot of experience when it came to seduction or sex, and the last time she'd been intimate with a man, she hadn't been seven and a half months pregnant.

So instead of experience, she let her instincts guide her. She rose up, slid forward, so that her pelvis brushed over his erection. He groaned again, the sound both encouraging and emboldening her. She shifted again until she felt the tip of his erection at the juncture between her thighs, then took him inside of her, just a little. Then a little bit more.

Clay's hands were on her hips, his fingertips digging into her flesh. She could feel the tension in the taut muscles of his abdomen, see the strain in his clenched jaw, but he held himself in check, determined to let her set both the pace and the rhythm.

Then his hands began to roam, his palms gently tracing the roundness of her belly, then moving upward to cup her breasts. His thumbs traced circles around her nipples, slowly moving closer to the aching peaks.

She arched, the instinctive movement pulling him deeper inside. She gasped; he groaned. Then she started to move, her hips rocking slowly at first, then fast, faster. Until she pushed them both to the pinnacle of pleasure—and beyond.

Clay's body was still shuddering with the aftershocks of his climax when Antonia collapsed on top of him. Her hair spilled across his chest, and he lifted a hand to comb his fingers through the soft, fragrant curls. She sighed contentedly.

"You're okay?" It wasn't usually the first thought on his mind after mind-blowing sex, but he'd never had sex with a pregnant woman before.

She sighed again. "I don't think I've ever been better."

It sounded like a positive endorsement to him, and he couldn't help but smile. "Yeah?"

She lifted her head so that he could see she was smiling, too. "Yeah," she confirmed.

His arm tightened around her. "You were pretty darn spectacular."

"I think *we* were pretty spectacular."

"Spectacular enough that you want to try again?"

"Well, there is one more condom," she reminded him. "If you're up for it."

He shifted closer, confirming that he was very definitely up for it.

Clay didn't know what time it was when they finally fell asleep, he only knew that when she slipped out from under the covers, he wasn't nearly ready to let her.

"It's not even light yet," he complained.

"It will be soon," she said. "And I need to get back to the house before my dad wakes up."

He had no argument against that, but he did wish that she didn't have to go.

He'd had his share of lovers—some would say more than his share—but he'd never had a lover who was as open and honest about what she wanted as the woman who'd shared his bed last night. He'd admittedly had some reservations about physical intimacy with a woman in the final stages of pregnancy, but being with Antonia had alleviated them all.

She'd been warm and willing, playful and passionate, and when he'd buried himself in the welcoming heat of her body, he'd felt a sense of rightness and completeness that he'd never experienced before. If he'd thought that having sex with her once would take the edge off of his desire, he was mistaken. Because he wanted her again, and it was only the knowledge that he needed to make a trip to the pharmacy that prevented him from reaching for her now.

But damn if he didn't get hard just watching her wriggle into those sexy bikini panties. It was both painful torture and exquisite pleasure to watch her put on the clothes he'd peeled off of her the night before.

When she'd straightened the skirt of her dress and slipped her shoes onto her feet, she brushed a quick kiss on his lips. "I'll see you at breakfast."

"Actually, I'll probably just grab a coffee and a muffin from the Mountain Bluebell Bakery on my way to get Bennett."

"Okay."

"Unless you want me to come to the house," he offered.

"It doesn't matter to me one way or the other," she said.

He eyed her warily. "Really?"

"Really." She lowered herself onto the edge of the mattress. "I promise you, I don't have any illusions that last night was about anything more than sex, and I'm not looking for a relationship or any kind of commitment just because we had sex."

He scowled, not sure if he was more annoyed or relieved by her assurance. Maybe he wasn't ready for a capital *R* relationship, but he wanted to think that the intimacy they'd shared was about a little bit more than scratching an itch. "Are you saying that you're finished with me?"

"I'm saying that I don't expect anything more than what we shared last night—although I wouldn't be opposed to a repeat performance."

That appeased him, at least a little. "I'll be making a detour to State Street Drugs today."

"Do that." She started for the door.

"Antonia?"

She paused with her hand on the knob.

"Now that I've seen your lingerie, I'm going to be thinking about it every time I look at you."

It amazed him that, after all of the intimacies they'd shared through the night, a teasing remark could still make her cheeks fill with color. "I already told you, your chances of getting me naked again are pretty good."

Her tone was deliberately light, so he followed her cue. "One more thing."

"What's that?"

"Watch out for my landlady."

She was smiling when she walked out the door.

Chapter Ten

Antonia was still smiling when she walked into the kitchen half an hour later to get breakfast started. Though she was freshly showered, her body still tingled and ached, but it was a good kind of ache. The kind of ache that only came the morning after a night of intense love-making

Sex, she hastily corrected herself.

As wonderful as the previous night had been, and it had been wonderful, she wasn't going to make it into something that it wasn't. She wasn't going to delude herself into believing that she had deep feelings for Clay just to justify their physical intimacy. She was a thirty-year-old woman. She didn't need anyone's permission to have sex and she wasn't going to feel guilty because she'd enjoyed it. In fact, she was already planning to enjoy it again at the next possible opportunity.

The smile slipped when she saw Jonah already sitting at the kitchen table.

"You forgot to set up the coffeemaker last night," he grumbled.

"And yet you somehow managed to fill the pot with water and measure out the grounds all by yourself," she mused.

He scowled at her. "I have an appointment at the hospital this morning."

Which was obviously the reason for his uncharacteristically surly mood. It wasn't just the physical pain that bothered him but the possibility that he might have to have surgery. The doctors had told Jonah it was unlikely, but because the initial fracture was displaced, they had scheduled this follow-up to reassess the injury.

And while she understood the source of his worry and frustration, she wasn't going to let him take it out on her. "Dock my pay," she suggested in response to his comment.

His scowl deepened. "What's for breakfast?"

She was tempted to tell him that he could have whatever he could manage to make with one good arm. Instead she asked, "What do you want?"

"French toast?" he asked hopefully.

She refilled his mug of coffee before pulling a heavy frying pan out of the drawer beneath the oven.

"Thanks," he said grudgingly.

"You're welcome," she said pleasantly, determined not to let his bad attitude dampen her good mood.

"I heard you were at The Hitching Post yesterday," he said, watching her whisk the eggs.

She nodded.

"How's it look?"

"Really good." She dipped a slice of bread into the egg

mixture, then dropped it into the hot pan. "Jason Traub knew just what he wanted and Cates Construction did an excellent job fulfilling his vision."

"Hopefully the reopening will encourage others to invest in the downtown core."

"I think it will," she noted. "The Hitching Post has always drawn customers, so the local vendors should note an increase in business now."

"I also heard you saw Trina there."

"No problem with your ears these days," she muttered, wondering when and how her brother had talked to the waitress between last night and this morning.

"She said you left early, but I didn't hear you come in, so you obviously didn't come home early."

Antonia flipped the bread in the pan. "I met a cute cowboy at the bar and went home with him, and we spent the rest of the night having hot, sweaty sex."

Jonah snorted at the outrageousness of *that* idea. "Is that your way of telling me to mind my own business?"

"Sometimes I wonder if that's even possible."

"It's a big brother's job to look out for his baby sister, even if she's soon going to have a baby of her own."

"I can take care of myself," she told him.

"Yeah," he agreed. "You always were Little Miss Independent."

"I had to be if I was going to hold my own against the three of you."

"You never had any trouble holding your own," he admitted. "You never had any trouble with anything you wanted to do—which is why this whole baby thing doesn't make any sense."

"By 'this whole baby thing,' you mean my pregnancy?"

"There are any number of good, respectable men in

Thunder Canyon who would have been happy to marry you and father your children."

She wasn't sure she believed the "any number" part of his statement, but the rest of it suggested that Jonah had accepted the Bozeman clinic story as completely as Bev Haverly had done. He was right in that she'd dated some great guys in Thunder Canyon, but she'd never fallen in love with any of them. She wasn't sure why she'd fallen in love with Gene—whether it was proximity or timing or a combination of the two factors—but her experience with her former boarder had shown her the dangers of following her heart. When he left, she vowed that she would never fall in love again.

That was one of the reasons she'd been so wary about getting involved with Clay. But she was confident that this situation was completely different, that what she was feeling now was only lust not love. And as long as she kept her heart out of it, there was no reason she couldn't continue to enjoy an intimate relationship with him.

Over the next few days, Clay and Antonia developed something of a routine. Sunday night at dinner, Antonia casually mentioned that she would be going down to the stable to check on Daisy Mae and her foal later. So Clay worked it out that his path crossed with hers, and they went back to his room together.

He didn't expect that the heat between them could continue to burn as fiercely as it had in the beginning. It was inevitable, to his mind, that the passion would fade. Not just inevitable but, in many ways, desirable. Because it was always easier for both parties to accept the end of a relationship when the spark had gone.

Not that they were in a relationship. At least, not according to Antonia. They were simply two consenting adults hooking up for the purpose of shared physical pleasure.

Her description of the situation should have relieved him, but with each night that she spent in his bed, he found that a few stolen hours of darkness weren't enough. He wanted…well, he wasn't entirely sure how to complete that thought, except that he knew he wanted more.

And that was why, when he planned to take Bennett out of town on Thursday morning, he decided to invite Antonia to go with them.

"We're going to run to the mall in Bozeman." He mentioned his plans casually as he helped her clear the dining room table. "Bennett's outgrowing almost everything and there isn't much selection at the few stores in town."

"Oh, there's a fabulous store there called Toddlers & Tots. You should check it out."

Encouraged by her enthusiastic response, he asked, "Did you want to come with us?"

"I'd love to," she said, and sounded as if she meant it. "Unfortunately, I have a doctor's appointment this afternoon."

His gaze dropped automatically to her belly. "Why? What's wrong?"

She touched a hand to his arm. "Nothing's wrong. It's just my monthly check-up. Well, actually, it's now a biweekly check-up, but nothing to worry about."

"You're okay? You're sure?"

"Yes, I'm okay," she said patiently. "Yes. I'm sure."

Still, he couldn't help but wonder…and worry. Their lovemaking was incredibly passionate—maybe too passionate? "And the doctor will let you know if it's still okay…"

She smiled. "Yes, she'll let me know."

"Do you want me to go with you?"

He wasn't sure who was more startled by the question—Antonia or himself. Because accompanying a woman to the office of a baby doctor implied all kinds of things about a relationship that didn't apply to their non-relationship. So he wasn't at all surprised when Antonia shook her head.

"I appreciate the offer, but I think that would just be awkward for both of us."

She was right, of course. And he should have left it at that. Instead, he heard himself saying, "I just didn't want you to have to go on your own."

"I am on my own," she reminded him.

Which again was true—and reminded him of his brother's comment about transference. Maybe he was trying to do for Antonia everything that he'd never had a chance to do for Delia, but toward what end? He and Antonia both knew that he wasn't planning on staying in Thunder Canyon long-term. In fact, he'd already been away from Rust Creek Falls longer than he'd intended. And yet, he still hadn't made any plans to return.

"Then I guess we'll see you when we get back," he said.

"I hope so," she told him.

The sparkle in her eyes and the promise in her voice made him forget that, for just a minute, he'd wanted more. Because later that night, he would get to have fabulous sex with an incredible woman, and that was enough.

After her weight and blood pressure were checked and recorded and Doctor Aberline went through her usual checklist of questions regarding Antonia's activities and monitoring of fetal movements, the doctor asked a question she'd never asked before.

"Is that glow in your cheeks from the baby or the sexy cowboy staying out at your ranch?"

Antonia rolled her eyes. "Are there no secrets in this town?"

"Not that you should be keeping from your doctor."

Of course, over the years that Louise Aberline had been Antonia's doctor, they'd also become friends. And Antonia knew that Louise was also a friend of Catherine's, who was no doubt the source of her information.

"I was going to tell you," she said. "I just didn't expect that you would have heard about it from someone else already."

"I wasn't given any intimate details," Louise said. "If there are any intimate details to give."

"Yes, we've had sex," she admitted.

"Was everything okay?"

Antonia couldn't hold back the smile that curved her lips. "Better than okay."

The doctor laughed. "Glad to hear that. But what I really wanted to know was if you experienced any discomfort during intercourse?"

"None."

"Any cramping or spotting afterward?"

"No."

"Is this an ongoing relationship?"

"It's ongoing," Antonia admitted, reluctant to call it a relationship.

And the doctor somehow picked up on what her patient didn't say as much as her words. "I'm as concerned about your emotional state as much as your physical condition," she said.

Of course, she was one of only a very few people who knew the true story behind Antonia's pregnancy, and she knew how devastated the expectant mother had been when her baby's father took off.

"I'm fine," Antonia said, because she really was fine now. Because she wasn't in love with Clay, she was just having a good time with him.

Though Louise didn't look entirely convinced, she nodded. "Okay then. I'll see you in two weeks."

It was lunchtime when Antonia left the Lone Pine Medical Building and, since she was close to the downtown core, she decided to see if Catherine was free to grab a bite at The Tottering Teapot.

"I was just thinking about you," her newlywed friend said when she answered Antonia's call. "You have to come in to the store."

"What's up?"

"I just unpacked a crate of furniture from an estate sale and found an incredibly gorgeous antique cradle inside."

"You have got to stop doing this to me," Antonia told her.

"What am I doing?"

"Encouraging me to spend money that isn't in my budget."

"Just come and see it," Catherine said. "If you like it, it will be a baby gift from me."

"You wouldn't even have mentioned it if you didn't know I would love it."

"So how soon can you be here?"

Antonia sighed. "I'll see you in ten minutes."

And when she did, she couldn't deny that Catherine's assessment was bang-on. The cradle was not only incredibly gorgeous but made of cherry wood in a style similar to the rocking chair that Antonia had purchased from Real Vintage Cowboy only a few weeks earlier.

She stroked a hand over the glossy wood but shook her head regretfully.

Catherine frowned. "You don't like it?"

"I love it," she admitted. "But I don't need it. I have a crib—"

"I didn't ask if you needed it. I asked if you liked it."

"I can't afford it."

"I told you it would be a baby gift."

"You already sold me the rocking chair for about half of what you could have got if you'd put a price tag on it and displayed it in the front window."

"Or it could have sat there collecting dust for years," her friend countered. "Most new moms want the glider-style rockers, not the old-fashioned ones."

"Speaking of rockers," Antonia said. "How about lunch at The Tottering Teapot?"

"Yeah, because that was a smooth segue," Catherine said dryly.

"Seriously, I'm starving."

Catherine picked up the cradle and carried it into the back room. "I'm holding it for a week," she said, when she came back out front. "All you have to do is tell me that you want it."

"Right now, I'm only thinking about whether I want a hamburger or chicken sandwich."

The Tottering Teapot was located on Main Street near Pine in Old Town, just a short walk from Real Vintage Cowboy. The tables were covered with lace cloths and the food was served on mismatched china to an almost exclusively female clientele. It was famous for its endless variety of teas and vegetarian sandwiches, but there were free-range chicken and grass-fed beef options on the menu, as well.

Antonia ordered the grilled chicken and roasted pepper flatbread sandwich with spring mix salad and a lemon ginger tea; Catherine opted for the portobello mushroom burger with macaroni salad.

"What's new with you?" Catherine asked after the waitress had delivered their cups and saucers and miniature pots of tea.

Antonia blew on her cup to cool the steaming liquid, then sipped carefully. "Not much," she said. "Aside from the fact that I recently discovered I'm capable of multiple orgasms."

Catherine choked on her tea.

"Well, um, I'm not sure I know what to say," she admitted once she'd finally stopped coughing. "Congratulations?"

Antonia laughed. "Thanks."

"So how long have you been doing the deed with the cowboy daddy?"

"Every night since Saturday."

Her friend's brows lifted. "*Every* night?"

And several times a night, Antonia was tempted to say, but she bit her tongue because that would just be bragging.

"Where do you find the energy?" Catherine asked, sounding genuinely baffled.

"You can't be more surprised than I am," Antonia said. "Not only that I have the energy and the desire, but that *he* could desire *me* in this condition."

"Not everyone does pregnancy well," her friend said. "But you do—and obviously Clayton Traub agrees."

But Antonia could tell that she was still worried about something, and she was pretty sure she understood the origin of her friend's concern. "I went into this with my eyes open," she assured her. "I'm not expecting anything long-term. I'm just going to enjoy it while it lasts."

"Are you in love with him?"

"No," Antonia responded immediately. Vehemently.

Catherine lifted a brow.

"Do you really think I would make the same mistake twice?"

"I think that we can't always control who we fall in love with," her friend said gently.

"I'm *not* in love with him," she insisted.

Catherine held her hands up in a gesture of surrender. "Okay, you've convinced me."

Antonia sipped her tea, relieved that her friend wasn't making an issue out of something that wasn't.

She just had to make sure that she did the same.

Since Antonia had declined Clay's invitation to take a trip into Bozeman, he decided to check out the New Town Mall instead. While it didn't have anything on the scale of Toddlers & Tots, it did have a department store with a decent baby department where he was able to pick up a few things. And then, after their shopping was done, he and Bennett decided to meet Forrest for lunch.

Clay wasn't sure if his brother's disposition had improved simply by being in Thunder Canyon or because he was under Dr. North's care or participating in the veteran's pet therapy group—or maybe it was a combination of the three factors—he only knew that he genuinely enjoyed hanging out with Forrest again.

At least, he was thinking that he did before his brother commented that Clay and Antonia had been spending a lot of time together.

"We're just hanging out," Clay said.

"But only in your bedroom after dark, where you don't have to worry that anyone will see you together."

"The rumor mill in Thunder Canyon is just as productive as the one in Rust Creek Falls."

"So who are you trying to protect?" Forrest wanted to know. "Antonia or yourself?"

"Neither one of us wants to be the subject of any more speculation or gossip."

Forrest bit into his burger. "What are you really afraid of?"

Clay stabbed a potato wedge. "I'm afraid that Antonia is going to start expecting more than I can give her."

"It doesn't seem—at least to me—that she expects anything of you."

His brother was right. Antonia had never really asked him for anything. Certainly she'd never asked for any promises or guarantees with respect to their relationship. In fact, she seemed to take it for granted that their relationship was only temporary, that eventually he would go back to Rust Creek Falls and she would stay in Thunder Canyon and they would each go on with their lives as if the past week—the most incredible week of his life—had never happened.

"So maybe what you're really afraid of," Forrest suggested, "is that you want to give her more than she expects."

Clay scowled. "I'm not even sure I understand what that's supposed to mean."

"And people think *I'm* the emotionally stunted one," his brother mused.

Clay sipped his soda.

"It means that Antonia is a strong, independent woman," Forrest explained, "and you're not accustomed to being with someone who doesn't rely on you for every little thing. You want to be needed, and she doesn't need you. But—for some inexplicable reason that I couldn't possibly begin to comprehend—she wants you. So the only question left is—are you ready to admit that you want her, not just for a few nights but forever?"

Clay picked up his brother's glass, sniffed the contents. "Are you sure this is straight cola? Because you must be drunk if you just said 'forever.'"

Forrest shrugged. "So maybe you don't care about her as much as I thought you did."

"I do care about her," he admitted. "But I've only just started to figure things out with Bennett. The last thing I need is to add another baby to the equation."

Forrest shook his head. "And I always thought you were pretty good at math."

"As you once said, double the kids, double the diapers."

"I think what I actually said was 'double your diapers, double your fun,'" his brother teased.

"It's the 'double' part that matters."

"Except that hooking up with Antonia doesn't just add a second baby to the equation, it adds a mother for both of those babies. And a mother and a father with two babies equals a family."

The possibility of giving Bennett a family was incredibly tempting. Clay had been doing the best that he could as a single father, but he'd always believed that a child deserved to be raised by two parents in a stable and loving home.

In fact, when Delia had first shown up on his doorstep and Clay had been trying to get his head around the fact that he was a daddy, he'd immediately thought that they should get married. Thankfully, his rational mind had kicked that irrational thought right out of his head before it moved to his lips, because as much as he did believe in taking responsibility for his actions and that a child should have two parents, he knew that settling down with Delia was *not* a good idea.

Even when they'd been dating, they'd never been able to spend too much time together without driving one another crazy, and he knew that "till death do us part" with Delia would undoubtedly have driven him to an early grave.

But the thought of spending his life with Antonia didn't fill him with panic. In fact, the idea of building a life and a family with her was incredibly tempting. And the prospect of spending every night in her bed was even more tempting.

But how much of what he was feeling was about his own emotions and how much was based on his son's attachment to their landlady?

He certainly enjoyed making love with her. And he liked spending time with her, even when they were just hanging out and talking. He also enjoyed watching her with Bennett, the easy way she had with his son, and the baby was clearly head-over-heels for Antonia, smiling and giggling whenever he was with her.

Thinking about her now, he realized it was entirely possible that he was falling for her. But even if what he felt wasn't love, there was no denying that they shared genuine affection and sizzling chemistry, and he figured a marriage based on those factors was a win-win for everyone.

Except that Antonia had given him absolutely no indication about her feelings for him. Not that he'd asked. A guy didn't ask those kinds of questions. Although, in his experience, he usually didn't have to. Women liked to talk about their feelings; they liked to ask questions about where a relationship was headed. But not Antonia.

As his brother had noted, she didn't seem to want or expect anything more than what they had. Which made him wonder if she had any feelings for him at all.

Chapter Eleven

When Antonia went down to the stables that night, Clay was already there—and he had Bennett with him.

"He fell asleep after dinner," Clay said, explaining why his son was still awake at 10:00 p.m.

"And now he's full of energy," she guessed.

Bennett confirmed her suspicion by grinning and holding out his arms to her. Clay just sighed and relinquished the baby.

"You obviously spoil him rotten."

"Maybe he just thinks I'm prettier than you are," she teased.

"Well, I'd have to agree with him on that."

"Spending time with Bennett makes me all the more anxious to hold my own baby in my arms."

"Newborns aren't as easy to win over," Clay warned. "Their only form of communication is crying and it's your job to figure out if they're crying because they're hungry or wet or just because."

"If you're trying to talk me out of having this baby, you're a little late," she said dryly.

"I just want to give you an idea what you're getting into. And what you won't be getting, which is sleep."

"I haven't been getting much sleep for a while now," she pointed out with a smile. "Not that I'm complaining."

"You will be when you're getting up to feed a baby at midnight and then at two and again at four and six." He shook his head. "Believe me, I do *not* miss that."

Antonia didn't have any trouble reading between the lines. Clay had been there and done that when it came to caring for his newborn son and he had no interest in another baby. And if she'd been foolish enough to let herself hope that their midnight liaisons might lead to a relationship, his comments quickly put that notion to rest. He was a single dad, she was a soon-to-be single mom, but they were never going to be a family.

It was an important reminder to Antonia, and it made her appreciate this precious time with Clay all the more because it was limited. As soon as her baby was born, their relationship would be over—if, in fact, it even lasted that long. And because she knew that every night she spent with Clay brought her one night closer to the end of their relationship, she didn't want to waste this night debating issues of childcare.

So they walked around the property for a while, until Bennett finally grew tired. And when his head dropped onto Antonia's shoulder, they made their way to Clay's room. After settling the baby in his crib, Antonia took the extra blanket from the end of Clay's bed and draped it over the slats.

He shook his head, because he knew what she was

doing—making sure that if Bennett woke up he wouldn't be able to see what they were doing in the bed—but smiled indulgently.

"You think I'm silly, don't you?"

"I think you're beautiful." He drew her closer and touched his lips to hers. "And sexy." He eased her back onto the bed. "And absolutely certifiably crazy."

About you, she thought, although she didn't dare speak the words aloud. But she didn't think there was anything wrong with being crazy about a man so long as she didn't fall in love with him. Allowing oneself to be overcome with lust was fine—and perfectly understandable when a woman was lucky enough to have a spectacular male specimen like Clay hanging around. Feeling a certain amount of genuine affection for a man was okay, too. Falling in love, on the other hand, was not acceptable in any way, shape or form.

But she wasn't going to worry about such things now, because Clay had stripped away all of her clothes and his, too. He was spooned against her, his front to her back, his arms around her. He was touching her breasts and kissing her neck, and the subtle friction of his naked skin against hers was just too glorious a sensation to resist. Then he slipped a hand between her thighs, and groaned his satisfaction when he found that she was already wet and ready for him.

When he eased into her, she wasn't worrying about anything at all. In fact, she couldn't even think. Her mind had gone completely, blissfully blank, emptied of all thought except for the pleasure he was giving her.

"I have to go back to Rust Creek Falls tomorrow."

It wasn't just Clay's words but the casual tone that stabbed like a knife through Antonia's heart. Their bodies were still warm and tangled together from their lovemaking, but he was already on his way out the door.

She'd known from the beginning that he would leave, but she hadn't expected it to happen like this. Not so abruptly, and not when she was halfway toward falling in love with him. She could deny it all she wanted—and she'd been doing a pretty good job of just that—but the truth was now undeniably and painfully clear. Because nothing a man said or did could make a woman feel as if her heart was being torn apart inside of her chest unless she'd already given it to him.

It didn't matter that she hadn't intended to do so, that she'd been determined to keep her emotions in check. Because it was apparent now that all of her internal pep talks and reassurances had been nothing more than false bravado. Despite all of her efforts to the contrary, Clay Traub had somehow taken hold of her heart.

But she still had her pride, and it demanded that she at least attempt to match his nonchalant attitude.

"You've been gone a long time," she said lightly. "I imagine you're anxious to get back."

"I am a little anxious, but only because my lawyer warned me there are no guarantees."

She frowned. "Lawyer?"

"The custody hearing is tomorrow."

"Custody?"

Now it was his turn to frown. "Didn't I tell you about this?"

She shook her head.

"I went to see a lawyer before I left Rust Creek Falls in order to file a petition for full legal custody of Bennett. Delia received notice of the hearing and sent a letter saying that she had no intention of contesting, but my lawyer insisted that I should be there, with Bennett, in case she changes her mind or the judge has any questions."

"Of course," Antonia agreed, still not entirely sure what he was telling her. He was going to Rust Creek Falls for a custody hearing, but she had no idea what his plans were after that. Would he stay there and return to his work on the family ranch? Or would he come back to Thunder Canyon?

"I'm not sure how long the hearing will go or how late I'll be getting back here—"

Back here.

She exhaled slowly, the echo of the words in her mind finally allowing her heart to settle back in her chest.

"—so I'm not sure it's a good idea to make plans for tomorrow night, but I thought maybe we could go out for dinner on Saturday."

Surprise followed quickly on the heels of relief. "Clayton Traub, are you asking me on a date?"

"Yes, Antonia Wright, I am."

He sounded so earnest, and she was eager to accept, but she was also wary. "I'm not sure that's a good idea."

"Are you ashamed to be seen in public with me?"

"I wouldn't have put it quite so bluntly, but okay, we'll go with that."

He only grinned, not fooled for a second by her flippant reply. "Or are you afraid of the rumor mill?"

"Well, it has chewed me up and spit me out before," she admitted.

Most recently, it had been the news of her pregnancy—and speculation about the baby's father—that had set tongues wagging. But the majority of the local gossipmongers had accepted the Bozeman clinic story and turned their attention to juicier matters. Unfortunately, she doubted they would think anything was juicier than pregnant and unwed Antonia Wright out on a date ("Can you imagine? In her condition?") with the sexy cowboy who was staying out at her ranch ("What could he possibly see in her? And is he really sleeping in the boarding house—or in her bed?").

Of course, the story would get even juicier when Clay finally went back to Rust Creek Falls ("Poor Antonia, pregnant and alone and dumped by that rancher. Well, what did she expect? Did she really think he was interested in her? The man was probably only using her for babysitting—and whatever other services she was willing to provide—while he was in town.").

"You don't strike me as the type of woman who would let one punch take her down." He tucked a strand of hair behind her ear, then traced the outer shell with his fingertip.

The gentle caress made her blood pulse and her tummy quiver. "I'm also not the type of woman who would let a man goad—or seduce—me into going out with him," she informed him.

"Are you saying no to my invitation?"

"No, I'm saying yes—but because I want to go, not because I was coerced or challenged."

"I only care about the yes," he said, and brushed his lips against hers.

Then he kissed her again, a little longer, a little deeper. And when he kissed her like that, Antonia couldn't imagine saying no to anything…

The clerk stood at the front of the elegant wood-paneled courtroom and faced the gallery. "All rise," he commanded in an authoritative voice.

There were a total of six spectators, including Ellie and Bob Traub, and they got to their feet as instructed.

"The Family Court of Rust Creek Falls County, State of Montana, is now in session, the Honorable William T. Vaughn presiding."

After the judge settled into his chair behind the bench, everyone else resumed their seats, too.

Ellie wiped damp palms down the front of her skirt. Bob, sensing her distress, reached for her hand and squeezed it gently, reassuringly.

Clay's lawyer was talking to the judge, but Ellie could barely focus on his words. She kept casting furtive glances toward the doors at the back of the courtroom, half expecting Delia to barge in and interrupt the proceedings. For Bennett's sake, she almost wished she would.

But Delia had made it clear, through a combination of both her actions and inactions, that she had less than zero interest in being a mother. Aside from giving birth, she'd exhibited no maternal instincts with respect to her child. And while Ellie was confident that Bennett would receive all the attention and affection from his father that any child could need, she also firmly believed that a child—particularly one as young as her youngest grandson—needed a mother.

Not *his* mother, obviously, but someone who would love and nurture him the way a mother was supposed to love and nurture her child. More than once, Ellie had tried to make this point to Clay, because she knew that he wanted what was best for his son. And Ellie was adamant that the best thing was two parents.

Clay had countered with the argument that a grandmother could fulfill the same role just as well—or maybe even better—than a mother. Ellie had admittedly been distracted by his flattery, at least for a moment. But the moment was enough for Clay to pack up his son and head to Thunder Canyon, where she couldn't know who he was seeing or what he was doing.

For the first few weeks, she'd wanted nothing more than for Clay to come home—and to bring Bennett with him, of course. Then she'd met Antonia Wright and she'd begun to think that Clay's decision to move to Thunder Canyon might end up being the best thing for both him and his son.

Antonia's pregnancy had given her some moments of uncertainty. She didn't have any concerns about the young woman's maternal instincts—or if she did, they'd been alleviated as soon as she'd seen Antonia interact with Bennett. Because it had been immediately obvious to Ellie that Antonia was as enamored with the little boy as he was with her.

But Ellie had worried that Clay might not be willing to be a father to another man's child—because she knew that not every man was. She'd wanted to believe that she'd raised her son to be smarter than that, but she hadn't been certain—not until she'd seen him with Antonia.

"On the basis of the material presented as evidence in this hearing—"

The judge's voice penetrated Ellie's thoughts and drew her attention back to the present.

"—I hereby grant the request of the petitioner/father for full legal custody of the minor child, Bennett Alexander Traub."

Even as Ellie's eyes filled, Bob was pressing a clean handkerchief into her hand. She managed to smile at him through her tears, trusting that he understood how much she appreciated having a partner who knew her so well, who had stood by her through thick and thin, for better and for worse, through forty years of marriage.

It was all she'd ever wanted for her own children, that

each of her sons would find the right partner and know at least a fraction of the joy that she'd experienced in her marriage. She didn't think that any of them was quite there yet, but she was confident that, after today, Clay was at least one step closer.

Clay and Bennett didn't return to Thunder Canyon until late Friday night.

Antonia knew they'd returned because she saw Clay's truck parked outside the boarding house when she got up in the night to use the bathroom. Not that she'd been checking—she'd just peeked out the window to see if the rain that had been forecast seemed imminent, or so she convinced herself.

But when they didn't come to the main house for breakfast Saturday morning, she began to worry that the hearing had not gone as well as Clay had hoped. Or maybe returning to Rust Creek Falls, even for a short while, had caused Clay to rethink his reasons for coming to Thunder Canyon—and being with her.

It wasn't until two o'clock that her phone signaled an incoming text message from him. Dinner reservations for 7 ok?

She replied, Ok.

Not wanting a repeat of the scene she'd had with Jonah when she told him about her plans to go to The Hitching Post with Clay and Forrest, Antonia slipped out of the house early, while her brothers were still having their dinner. Clay met her halfway between the main house and the boarding house, and the evident pleasure in his eyes when he saw her helped alleviate some of her concerns—at least for the moment.

"Are we celebrating?" she asked cautiously.

"We are definitely celebrating," he told her. "But that's

all I'm going to say about it right now, because tonight isn't about Bennett—it's about you and me."

The words caused a flutter in her belly. She hadn't been certain there was a "you and me"—not until he'd invited her on an actual date.

"Just one more question," she said. "Where is Bennett going to be tonight?"

"With my brother." He touched his lips briefly to hers. "I even moved his crib into Forrest's room for the night."

Tingles of anticipation danced over her skin, but she tried to keep her focus on their conversation and out of the bedroom.

"He's really good with Bennett, isn't he?"

"Why do you sound so surprised?"

"Because, in so many ways, he's a stereotypical military man. He's got the broad shoulders and the steely gaze, and he doesn't say a lot if he doesn't have to. But when he's with his nephew, it's like he undergoes a complete transformation."

"Bennett does bring out the best in him," Clay said. "He's a great kid."

"Forrest isn't really a bad guy, either."

"I know," she said. "In fact, he can be quite charming when he wants to be."

"Don't let him hear you say that," he warned.

She smiled. "He was very charming the night we went to The Hitching Post."

"I was tempted to hit him for hitting on you."

"He wasn't hitting on me."

"He was headed in that direction, until I warned him off," Clay assured her. "But seriously, I think coming to Thunder Canyon has been good for him. In fact, I'd say that it's been good for both of us."

It was the perfect opening to ask how long he was

planning to stay. She remembered the day he'd shown up, when he'd said that they would be in town a few weeks. Almost two months had passed since then, and neither of the brothers showed any indication that he was getting ready to move on.

She knew that Forrest's therapy was ongoing, so it made sense that he would stay, but she still didn't know much at all about Clay's reasons for coming to Thunder Canyon or his plans for the future. She didn't even know about their plans for tonight.

"One more question," she said. "Where are we going?"

"The Gallatin Room."

His response made her wish that she'd asked the question earlier. A lot earlier. Because her wardrobe options hadn't expanded at the same rate as her waistline, and the only recent addition to her closet was the burgundy chiffon dress she'd bought at Second Chances the day of the grand reopening.

Since Clay had given every indication that he'd liked how she looked that night—and since he'd had absolutely no trouble getting her out of that dress—she'd opted to go with it again. This time, she'd put her hair up and added a pair of chandelier style earrings she'd picked up at Real Vintage Cowboy when Catherine's store first opened, but the overall effect still wasn't worthy of The Gallatin Room.

Clay, to his credit, immediately sensed her distress. "What's wrong?"

Antonia could only shake her head.

"You hate the food there? You dated the chef? You lost your virginity in the kitchen?"

She wished it was something so simple. But the truth was that The Gallatin Room was the fanciest restaurant in Thunder Canyon, and even if she had time to go back inside and change, there was nothing in her closet that was remotely appropriate for such a venue. "I can't go there looking like this."

His eyes skimmed over her, from the loose pile of curls on the top of her head to the simple black pumps on her feet, so slowly and deliberately that the heat from his gaze honestly made her skin burn.

"You look gorgeous," he finally said.

He sounded so sincere that she couldn't help but smile. "Maybe if we were going to New Town Cinema or The Hitching Post—" the two places they'd been out together before "—But The Gallatin Room is in a whole other dimension."

"Actually it's not that far," he said teasingly. "In fact, it's part of the Thunder Canyon Resort."

She huffed out a breath. "You know what I mean."

"I don't think I do."

"It's the type of place where people—usually couples—go to celebrate relationships and special occasions."

"I don't think even *you* know what you mean," he decided, apparently baffled by her explanation. "Because we are here to celebrate a special occasion."

"Bennett's custody hearing?"

"Our first date."

Of course, "first" implied a second or even more subsequent dates, and Antonia wasn't going to count on anything beyond this night.

The interior of The Gallatin Room was a breathtaking display of white linen, gleaming silver and sparkling crystal with fresh flowers on every table. In combination with the twinkling lights and soft music, the overall atmosphere was pure romance.

"Wow." She didn't gawk, not exactly, but Antonia

couldn't prevent herself from making a full turn around. "It's…breathtaking."

"You've never been here before?" Clay asked her.

"No."

"Then why were you so convinced that you weren't properly attired?"

"*Because* I've never been here before," she explained.

Gene had certainly never taken her anywhere like this. In fact, he'd never taken her anywhere at all—and how pathetic was that? She hadn't thought too much about it at the time because she'd had her own reasons for not wanting to go public with their relationship. It had never occurred to her that he wanted to keep things on the QT because he didn't want a girlfriend, just a warm and willing body.

And as angry as she was that he'd used her, she was even angrier with herself that she'd let him. He hadn't even made much of an effort to seduce her; he'd simply given her some attention, a few kisses, and led her off to his bed.

She realized that Clay had no reason to make such an effort, either. If all he wanted was sex, she'd already been more than cooperative in that regard. But he'd made dinner reservations at the fanciest restaurant in town anyway, because that's the kind of man he was.

And she found herself wishing, not for the first time, that her baby could have a father like Clay. But that was a futile wish, for so many reasons, and she wasn't going to ruin tonight by wanting things that could never be.

The hostess seated them at a table for two by the window and immediately disappeared again. Glancing around, Antonia saw that some diners were already enjoying their meals, others were munching on appetizers, and a few were still perusing menus. Which prompted her to ask, "Why didn't the hostess give us menus?"

"Because I preordered our dinner."

Antonia lifted a crystal goblet that probably cost more than the entire collection of dishes in her kitchen cupboards and tried not to let her hand shake. She was self-conscious and nervous and completely out of her element, but if there was one thing Antonia knew how to do, it was fake it. She'd been doing it since she was a kid, pretending to be as strong and brave as her brothers. So she sipped her water, and casually asked, "Don't you think that was a little presumptuous?"

"More than a little," he admitted, smiling at her across the table. "But I think you'll be pleased with my choices."

"What did you order?"

"Everything on the menu."

"Which doesn't tell me anything at all since I haven't seen the menu," she reminded him.

When their waiter—Marcos, according to the elegant brass nameplate pinned to his white shirt—brought a basket of warm artisan breads to the table, Clay said, "Miss Wright was wondering what's on the menu tonight."

Marcos turned to her and gave a slight bow. "Tonight's dinner features are pork tenderloin medallions in a port wine sauce with red-skinned mashed potatoes, prime rib of roast with root vegetables and Yorkshire pudding, Tuscan roasted chicken with sautéed spinach and buttered baby carrots, maple-glazed Pacific salmon with wild rice and pan-seared scallops on linguine with a tomato-cream sauce."

"Everything sounds…wonderful," she said.

Marcos bowed again and retreated.

Antonia looked at Clay. "You didn't really order everything."

"There were too many delicious options to narrow it down."

"I hope you're joking."

"I've seen the way you eat," he reminded her.

"Then you should have ordered ice cream."

He grinned. "That's for dessert."

As it turned out, he wasn't joking. And when Marcos, with the assistance of two other waiters, delivered the selections to their table, Antonia was amazed by the amount of food.

"If people weren't looking at us before, they are now," she noted.

"No one is looking at us," Clay denied. "They're all too busy staring into the besotted gazes of their dates across the table."

She lifted her brows. "Do I look besotted?"

"Completely infatuated—at least with that Tuscan chicken."

"It does look delicious," she admitted.

Marcos, who had been standing discreetly nearby, immediately came to her assistance, transferring a piece of the chicken and a spoonful of vegetables onto her plate. Clay opted to start with the prime rib, and Marcos fixed his plate, as well.

"I hope you don't expect this kind of service at Wright's Way in the morning," Antonia said.

"As long as I get a smile with my coffee, I won't complain," he assured her.

"That can probably be arranged." She popped a piece of chicken into her mouth. "Oh, this is good. Really good."

"You should try the beef," Clay said.

Of course, she did. And the pork and the fish and the pasta. Despite her frequent jokes about eating for two, she had never actually eaten so much, but she couldn't resist sampling at least a bite of everything.

"I can understand why Shane Roarke, the new chef, is the toast of the town," she said, when she finally folded her napkin and set it aside.

"Do you know where he came from?" Clay asked.

"Seattle, I believe. Apparently Grant Clifton found him when he was out there for some business meetings. The story is that Grant was so impressed by the chef's culinary genius, he made it his personal mission to bring him to the resort."

"Seattle's loss is definitely Thunder Canyon's gain," he agreed. "Although we have yet to see what he can do with dessert."

Antonia shook her head as she rubbed a hand over her belly. "I couldn't possibly eat another bite of anything."

"Not even deep-fried ice cream?"

"You are Satan."

He chuckled. "We'll work off the calories later."

"I might not be able to move," she warned.

"I can be creative."

Her cheeks flushed. She knew he could—and she'd been extremely grateful for his creativity. She was also grateful that his interest had not yet waned. Of course, she knew their relationship couldn't last forever. As soon as her baby was born, everything would change.

And that was why she was going to make the most of every minute they had together before then.

Chapter Twelve

Antonia was in the office after lunch on Thursday when Clay sent her a message asking her to meet him in his room. She didn't think he was expecting to tangle the sheets with her in the middle of the afternoon, but she ran a brush through her hair and dabbed on some lip gloss before heading to the boarding house, anyway.

Bennett was napping in his crib when she arrived, which made her wonder if she'd been wrong about Clay's intentions. Especially when he kissed her, deeply and thoroughly. Antonia realized that she'd become addicted to those kisses in a very short period of time. It was a realization that might have worried her if she thought too much about it, but right now she was more curious about the mysterious lump that was covered by a blanket on the middle of his bed.

"I had some errands to run in town today and picked up something for you."

"You bought me a gift?"

"Well, it's actually more for the baby," he admitted. "But I hope you'll like it, too."

With great flourish, he pulled the blanket away, revealing a gorgeous cherry wood antique cradle.

A very familiar gorgeous cherry wood antique cradle.

"You went to Real Vintage Cowboy," she guessed.

"I was only walking past, until I saw this in the window. Do you like it?"

She could only nod, afraid that if she tried to speak, he would hear the tears that clogged her throat.

"Your friend, Catherine, didn't want to sell it to me at first. She claimed it was on hold for another customer."

"What—" She cleared her throat. "What changed her mind?"

"I told her that no other customer would cherish it as much as you would, and she finally agreed."

"I would cherish it," she said, "but I can't accept it."

"Why not?"

"Because I know how much this is worth."

"I got ten percent off," he told her. "She called it the friends-of-friends discount."

Antonia could just imagine how Catherine's mind had started spinning when she realized that Clay intended to buy the cradle for her baby. And she knew that she had to be careful or her mind might start spinning the same way.

"It's still far too extravagant a gift," she insisted.

He took her hand. "I'd really like you to have it."

And she didn't have the willpower to say no to something that she really wanted. It was the same dilemma she faced every night when she came to Clay's room. She knew she was getting in too deep, that she was already more than halfway in love with him and dangerously close to tumbling the rest of the way. As if a romantic dinner at

The Gallatin Room wasn't enough, now he was buying presents for her baby. How was any woman supposed to hold out against a man who was so kind and thoughtful? Why would any woman want to?

Because the last time she'd given a man her heart, it had been handed back to her in pieces—and she wasn't going to risk that happening again. She knew that Clay wasn't like Gene. He'd made that clear in so many ways. She also knew that he wasn't going to stay in Thunder Canyon forever, and that meant that there was no future for them together.

Thinking of Clay's inevitable return to Rust Creek Falls reminded her of his recent trip back to his hometown.

"You never did tell me what happened in court last week," she told him. "Aside from the fact that you got the custody order."

He nodded. "My petition was uncontested."

"I'm not sure whether to offer congratulations or condolences," she admitted.

"I was torn, too. On the one hand, it's a relief to know that Delia has no intention of coming back to try and take Bennett away from me, and that she wouldn't succeed now even if she did try. On the other hand, it's sad to accept that she has absolutely no interest in the child that she gave birth to."

She touched a hand to his arm. "And you're already wondering how you're ever going to explain that to Bennett when he asks about his mom."

He nodded.

"The best thing you can do—and that you're already doing—is to ensure that he knows how much you love him," she told Clay. "His relationship with his mother isn't for you to figure out. You can't, and shouldn't, make excuses for her behavior."

"I know you're right," he agreed. "I guess I just can't understand how she could just hand him over to me and walk away."

"My baby isn't even born yet, and I can't imagine handing him or her over to anyone else."

"Not even the father?"

He'd asked the question without even thinking, and Antonia answered it the same way.

"*Especially* not the father."

It was the flash of fire in her eyes and the steel in her voice that made Clay realize there was far more to the story of Antonia's pregnancy than she'd ever told him.

"I know that I have no right to pry—"

"Then don't," she said, but she sounded more wary than annoyed.

He knew he should let it go, but he couldn't. Because he couldn't help wondering if the baby's father was as oblivious to the impending arrival of his child as Clay had been.

"You told me you went to a clinic."

She shook her head. "No, *you* said that you'd heard I went to a clinic, and I didn't deny it."

"So it's not true."

"It doesn't matter if it's true or not," she said. "It's nobody's business but my own."

"And the baby's father's," he pointed out.

"Maybe I didn't go to a clinic, but that doesn't make the father of my child anything more than a sperm donor."

It was the hurt he could hear in her voice, beneath the anger and determination, that told him more than her words.

"He didn't want the baby," he guessed.

"When he found out I was pregnant, he didn't want anything but to get as far away as possible," she admitted.

"I'm sorry, Antonia."

She shrugged. "That was his choice. Having this baby was mine."

"Have you heard from him since?"

She shook her head. "I called him a couple of times, trying to keep the lines of communication open, but Gene made it very clear that he wasn't interested."

"It doesn't matter whether or not he's interested," Clay insisted. "You didn't get pregnant by yourself and he has a legal obligation—"

"I don't want anything from him."

"You're just going to let him off the hook?"

She bristled at that. "I didn't get pregnant to hook him."

"That's not what I meant," he denied. "I only meant that he should be forced to take responsibility."

"My baby deserves better than a father who doesn't want to be one."

Clay couldn't argue with that. It was, in fact, almost a mirror of his own reasons for not following Delia to California. If she didn't care enough about her own child to want to be a part of his life, then Bennett was better off without her.

"You're right," he finally said. "If he wasn't man enough to stick around and do the right thing, it's his loss."

"This isn't what I planned," she confided. "Sure, I always dreamed of getting married and having children someday, but I never wanted to raise a child on my own. I thought that when I had a baby, I would also have a husband to share the worry and the decision-making, the joys and the responsibilities."

She dropped her head against his shoulder. "I really want my baby to have a daddy." And then immediately pulled away again, her eyes wide. "Oh. No. I didn't mean—not you."

Clay didn't even have a chance to panic. In fact, Antonia backtracked so quickly and so adamantly, he couldn't help but feel a little slighted. Not that he wanted to take on the responsibility of anyone else's child—he had his hands full enough just taking care of Bennett. But she didn't have to write him off so readily.

"I mean, you're a great dad to Bennett. But he's your son. And my baby is my responsibility, and I will do everything I can to be a good parent. A good *single* parent. Because I've never needed a man in my life before and I'm not going to start looking for one now."

He frowned at that. "So you're sharing my bed but I'm not in your life?"

"I'm going to go before I put my other foot in my mouth." She picked up the cradle, awkwardly tucking the bulky piece of furniture under one arm. "Thank you—for this. I will cherish it."

"Don't go," he said. "Not until we talk about this."

"There's nothing to talk about, really." Then she brushed a quick kiss on his lips. "But I'll see you tonight, if you want."

He slipped an arm around her waist and kissed her again, longer and deeper.

"Yeah, I want," he admitted.

And that, he knew, was *his* problem. No matter how hard he tried, he couldn't seem to stop wanting her.

He had no reason to feel any sense of responsibility toward her or her baby. But the idea of Antonia being on her own—not by choice but because the bastard who got her pregnant had no honor or decency—stirred protective instincts he hadn't realized he possessed.

He hadn't thought he was ready for one baby—at least not at this point in his life. But six months with Bennett had changed his opinion in that regard. Now he knew that there wasn't anything he wouldn't do for his son. He also knew that if he stuck around after Antonia had her baby, it would be far too easy to fall in love with another child—and to fall in love with that child's mother. That wasn't a path he'd ever wanted to walk down before. For a man who had never taken life too seriously, the prospect of committing to one woman and settling down with a family was very serious business.

But maybe it was time for Clay to give it some serious consideration.

Every night when Antonia went to Clay's room, as she did that night, she wondered if it would be their last night together. And every night, he made her feel as if she was not just desired but cherished. And every morning when she left his bed, she left a little bit more of her heart behind.

She should have known better than to get involved with him—to repeat the mistakes she'd made with Gene. But she'd been so certain that she knew what she was doing this time, that she could have a sexual relationship with a man without wanting or expecting anything more. And her brain was still on board with that plan—it was her heart that had betrayed her.

Her heart—and her best friend. Since she couldn't do anything about the weakness of the organ that pumped her blood, she took a drive into town to confront the traitorous Catherine instead.

"I can't believe you let him buy the cradle," Antonia grumbled.

"You told me to sell it," Catherine noted, setting a

cup of herbal tea on the oak farmhouse table in front of her friend.

"But not to him," she protested. "Not for my baby."

"Why not?"

"Because that did it."

The proprietor of Real Vintage Cowboy sat down on the other side of the table with her own cup. "Did what?"

Antonia narrowed her gaze on her friend. "Made me fall in love with him."

At that, Catherine actually smiled. "Honey, you were a goner long before he ever handed me his credit card."

"I was not," she denied.

Although, if she was being perfectly honest, she would admit that she couldn't be completely sure when or where it had happened. She only knew that, somewhere along the line, she had fallen in love with Clayton Traub.

In retrospect, she realized that it had probably been inevitable. Because what woman's heart could remain immune to a man who so obviously adored his son? What woman could remain unmoved by a man who wasn't just thoughtful and considerate but who willingly helped out around the kitchen? What woman wouldn't melt for a man who would sit through an undisputed chick flick in a public movie theater? What woman wouldn't feel at least a flutter in her chest for a man who stood vigil in a stable so that a maiden mare didn't have to bring her foal into the world all by herself? And what woman could remain indifferent to a man who bought a cradle for her unborn child?

"In fact, I'll bet you were halfway there before the box of Milk Duds was empty."

"I never should have told you about the Milk Duds," Antonia grumbled.

"But what I don't understand," Catherine admitted, "is why you're so unhappy about this."

"Because I don't want to have my heart broken again."

"The man who picked out that cradle is not planning to break your heart," her friend assured her.

"Of course he's not planning it," Antonia agreed. "He probably doesn't even realize he could because I told him from the beginning that I wasn't looking for any kind of commitment."

Catherine scowled. "You actually said that?"

"At the time, I meant it."

"Obviously the situation has changed."

"Not for him," Antonia said firmly.

"How can you be so sure?"

"Because he made it very clear that, as far as babies go, he's been there and done that."

"But—" Catherine looked genuinely baffled "—he bought you a cradle."

And how ironic was it that he could have chosen such a perfect gift for her baby when he had no interest in sticking around after she'd had that baby?

Not that Antonia could blame him, especially when he had his own child to take care of. She just wished her baby's father had demonstrated half as much interest in his own child as Clay had done.

But truthfully, she knew that both she and her baby were better off without Gene. She certainly didn't want to be with a man who didn't want to be with her, and she'd rather her baby never knew his or her father than to know that he didn't want him or her.

"I think you're wrong," Catherine said now. "I think his feelings have probably changed, too, and in a few weeks—"

"I can't do this for another few weeks. I can't do it for

another few days," Antonia told her. "I need to be realistic about my future—and it's not with Clay."

Catherine just sighed. "Are you going to be okay?"

"I'm going to be fine," she said, and she would be. She'd been fine before Clay came along and she'd be just as fine when he was gone. Maybe her heart would ache a little, but she had some experience in that regard.

Gene had wounded her pride as much as—or maybe even more than—her heart, but Antonia truly believed that time healed all wounds. It would take more time to heal when Clay was gone, because her feelings for him were so much stronger and deeper than anything she'd ever felt for Gene, but she was confident that she would heal.

She didn't blame Clay for any of this. Neither of them had made any promises, neither of them had wanted any. Or so she'd thought in the beginning. But being with Clay had made her want more—a husband, a father for her baby, a family—and she knew that he couldn't give her what she wanted. And she wasn't willing to settle for less—not anymore.

She would rather be on her own than with someone who didn't want the same things she wanted. And she would be just fine on her own, as she'd always been.

The baby wriggled and squirmed, and she touched a hand to her belly and whispered a silent apology to her unborn child.

She would be fine, but she wouldn't be on her own. She and her baby would have each other, and that was all they needed.

Clay was relieved to see Antonia looking as bright and cheerful as usual at breakfast the next morning.

When she hadn't shown up at the stables the night before, he'd worried that something was wrong. And when she finally did reply to the text he sent to her, the response was brief. Something came up, c u 2morrow.

The vagueness of the message was his first warning that something was wrong; the fact that she didn't hover around the table, even to fuss over Bennett, was his second. But he could hardly question her in the middle of a dining room full of other people. So he lingered until those other people were gone, and then he said, "I missed you last night."

It wasn't what he'd planned to say, but it was the truth. He had missed her. Not just making love with Antonia, but just being with her.

"I had some errands to run in town yesterday, and by the time I got back, I was exhausted."

It was a perfectly reasonable explanation, but the fact that she didn't look at him when she spoke made him think that while it might be true, it wasn't the whole truth.

"Will you be there tonight?" he asked her.

She kept her gaze focused on the plates that she was stacking. "I don't think that's a good idea."

"Why not?"

"Because I never expected that this…" She paused, as if uncertain how to describe their relationship and, in the end, only gestured between the two of them "…would go on as long as it has already."

He frowned. "Are you suggesting that you're usually more of a one-night stand kind of girl?"

She flushed. "Of course not. But neither one of us is in a position to want a relationship right now."

"And yet, we've got one anyway."

"No." She shook her head. "We don't."

"You're dumping me?"

She drew in a deep breath and, finally, looked at him. “I’m ending our relationship before I get in too deep.”

He frowned. She really *was* dumping him. Whatever answer he’d expected when he asked the question, it was not confirmation that she was ending things.

“What about me?” he demanded. “How do you know I’m not in deep?”

“You don’t do deep,” she reminded him. “You made that point very clear from the beginning, and I appreciate that you were honest with me. And the only reason I got involved with you was because I thought I could do casual.

“It turns out, I was wrong. And the more time I spend with you and Bennett, the more I want to be with you and Bennett.”

His brows lifted. “You’re dumping me because you want to be with me?”

“If you could overlook your wounded pride for a minute, you’d realize that this is the best thing for both of us, to end things before I start having expectations or making demands.”

“What if I don’t agree?”

She wiped her fingers on a napkin. “Don’t you remember telling me how much you hated those first weeks when Bennett was a baby? How he cried all the time until you were ready to pull your hair out?”

Even now, he couldn’t help but cringe at the memory—and his reaction did not go unnoticed.

“In about a month, I’m going to have one of those screaming babies,” she reminded him gently.

“You don’t think I could handle it?” he challenged.

“I don’t think you want to handle it.”

“I don’t want to lose you,” he said.

Her eyes filled with tears. “Neither one of us ever intended for this to be anything more than a temporary fling."

He wanted to deny her claim, but he couldn't. She was right. In the beginning, he hadn't been thinking beyond the short term. Somewhere along the line, though, their relationship had become something more. But maybe only to him.

"Maybe I changed my mind."

"Did you?" she challenged. "Do you want to get married and have a family?"

It was instinct, pure and simple, that had him taking a step back.

Antonia's smile was wry. "Don't worry—that wasn't a proposal, just a hypothetical."

"Just because I haven't thought in those terms doesn't mean I couldn't get to the point where I want the same things."

"But you're not at that point, and I am. I want a husband and a father for my baby, someone who will love both of us and who wants to be with us forever."

"You're not even giving me a chance," he protested.

Her smile was sad. "I just did."

When she carried the dishes into the kitchen, he didn't follow. He didn't know what to say to her right now—or even if there was anything he could say to change her mind.

And maybe she was right. They were at different stages in their lives; they wanted different things. He certainly hadn't been looking for a relationship when he came to Thunder Canyon, and even when he'd decided to take Antonia to his bed, he'd never expected that he would grow to care so much for her in such a short period of time.

Even if his feelings were deeper than he'd anticipated,

he still wasn't looking to fall in love. So maybe ending their relationship now really was the best thing.

But if this was the best thing, why did he feel so completely miserable?

Chapter Thirteen

Clay had learned a long time ago not to ignore his instincts. So when Antonia didn't answer her cell and his gut warned him that there was something wrong, his concern immediately kicked into high gear.

It was possible that she was just screening her calls and didn't want to talk to him, but he didn't think it was likely. Antonia had never played those kinds of games. Even in the four days that had passed since she'd given him the brush-off in her dining room, she'd continued to be pleasant and polite, albeit a little distant. But she hadn't ignored him. If something was on her mind, she said it, and if she didn't want to talk to him, she would have answered her phone to tell him that, too.

So why wasn't she answering her phone? And where was she? He didn't think she would have ventured too far. Then again, what did he know about the workings of a woman's mind? If there was an issue on the far side of the ranch that needed her attention, she wouldn't have hesitated to head out in that direction. Because Little Miss Independent—as he'd heard each one of her brothers refer to her on occasion—never asked for help from anyone. She never asked for anything.

He pushed open the door of the stable and immediately sensed the unrest of the few horses in their stalls. He heard a nervous whinny coming from the far end and hurried in that direction, panic clawing at his belly and his heart in his throat.

"Antonia?"

"I'm…here."

He raced toward the sound of her voice, but the relief he wanted to feel didn't come because when he reached her, she was collapsed against the door of Daisy Mae's stall.

He dropped to his knees beside her. Her breath was coming in fast and shallow pants, her eyes were glassy with pain.

"What happened? Where are you hurt?"

She shook her head. "I think…I'm in…labor."

He laid his hand on her belly, found it taut as a drum. And while he'd never been around a woman in labor, he had enough experience delivering calves and foals to recognize the basic signs of impending birth, and Antonia was definitely having a contraction.

"When did the contractions start?" he asked.

"I'm not sure. I came to check on…Maisy Rae…after lunch."

"Why didn't you call someone?" he asked, already dialing 9-1-1 on his cell.

"I didn't have my cell." She gestured to the far end of the barn. "I was trying to get to the phone in the office."

She looked at him, her beautiful green eyes filled with more fear than pain now. "It's too soon."

"My mother had six children," he reminded her. "And she was always fond of saying that babies come when they're ready, and apparently Antonia Junior is ready."

She managed to smile at that. "I am *not* naming my daughter Antonia."

"Why not? It's a beautiful name."

"If it's a girl, she'll be Lucinda," she said decisively. "For my mom."

"Lucinda's a beautiful name, too." He imagined it was common for a woman about to give birth for the first time to think about her own mother. And because he knew that Antonia had to be missing the parent she'd lost two years earlier, there was no way he was going to let her lose her baby, too.

"I'm scared."

"You're going to be okay," he promised her again. "Just try to relax."

"Relax?" She stared at him incredulously.

"Sorry. I'm not sure what I'm supposed to say or do. Breathe?"

She managed another smile. "I can try to do that."

He took her hand in his, and she gripped his fingers so tightly he could barely speak when his call connected.

"9-1-1. What is the nature of your emergency?"

He focused on speaking clearly and calmly, because he knew that giving in to his own rising panic wouldn't help Antonia at all. "I'm with an expectant mother in premature labor."

"Is this her first pregnancy?"

"Yes."

"How far along is she?"

He repeated the question to Antonia, then relayed her answer. "Thirty-six and a half weeks."

"Is she having contractions?"

He didn't need to consult with the expectant mother to answer that one. "Yes."

"When did the contractions start?"

"Less than an hour ago."

"How far apart are they?"

He glanced at his watch as Antonia's grip tightened on his hand again. "About three minutes."

"Has her water broke?"

Antonia started to shake her head in response to the question, but before he could convey her response, she let out a soft cry—and a gush of fluid.

"Just now," he said instead.

"An ambulance has been dispatched," the operator assured him. "The EMTs should be there in less than ten minutes."

He repeated the timeline to Antonia; she nodded.

"It doesn't seem as if birth is imminent," the operator said, and Clay exhaled a shaky sigh of relief, "but I'll stay on the line until the EMTs arrive and you can let me know if the situation changes."

"Okay," he said gratefully. And then, to Antonia, "You're going to be okay."

She nodded, and though he knew she was desperate to believe his reassurance, he could see the fear in her eyes.

The ambulance arrived right on schedule, and the EMTs quickly and efficiently strapped Antonia to the gurney and settled her in the back of the vehicle.

Clay realized that the paramedics probably assumed he was the baby's father, and he had no intention of informing them otherwise and risk being banished from their ride. No way was he going to leave Antonia's side. Not that she was likely to let him, if the grip she maintained on his hand was any indication.

He thanked the emergency operator for her assistance and, after he disconnected that call, placed another to his brother. When Forrest answered, Clay quickly explained the situation. After a minor bit of griping and grumbling to ensure that Clay truly understood the magnitude of the favor he was asking, Forrest assured his brother that he would take good care of Bennett while Clay was at the hospital.

And then, just as Clay was about to disconnect the call, Forrest said, "You take good care of her, too."

Beneath the gruff tone were hints of genuine affection and concern, confirming that—in the time they'd been at Wright's Way—Forrest had grown to care for Antonia, too.

"I will," Clay promised his brother.

Then he tucked his phone away and turned his full attention back to the laboring mother.

"Did you have a birthing coach?" he asked her now. "Anyone I should call to meet us at the hospital?"

She shook her head. "I took the classes online. By myself."

He almost smiled at that. Of course she did, because there wasn't anything Little Miss Independent didn't think she could do on her own.

The EMT, whose badge identified him as Wayne, set aside the stethoscope. "Your baby's heartbeat is strong and steady," he told Antonia. "And your contractions are coming hard and fast."

She just nodded.

"The dispatcher said this is your first pregnancy?"

She nodded again.

"When was your last check-up?"

"Four—" she sucked in a breath and squeezed her eyes shut as another contraction hit "—days ago."

"And your doctor didn't give any indication that you might go into labor early?"

She opened her eyes again, and Clay saw that they were filled with tears. "Is my baby…going to be…okay?"

"There's absolutely no reason to think otherwise," Wayne assured her. "I've just never known a first baby to be in such a hurry."

"Gotta be a girl," Clay teased Antonia. "Women never have any patience."

"I'd say it's gotta be a boy," the EMT countered. "Because I've never known a woman to be on time for anything, never mind early."

"How far are we…from the hospital?" Antonia interrupted their argument to ask.

"We're about four minutes out now."

"Just hold on for a little bit longer," Clay pleaded.

"I don't think I can," she admitted.

"You're doing great," Wayne assured her.

"I really want to push."

"Let me take another peek." He moved down to the end of the gurney, lifted the sheet. "Looks like you're fully dilated."

"Does that mean I can push?"

No. Please no, he thought.

"On your next contraction," the EMT agreed.

"But we're not at the hospital yet," Clay protested.

"We'll be there soon." And then, when Antonia started pushing, the EMT said, "You're doing great, Mom. Push with the contraction and pant when the pressure eases."

She drew a deep breath. "The pressure's going to ease?"

Wayne grinned. "Hard to believe right now, I know," he acknowledged. "Oh, there you go—he's crowning."

"He?"

"Or she," the paramedic amended. "I can't actually tell from the top of the head. Or even the whole head," he amended, when she'd successfully delivered that part.

"Okay, pant now for a minute—" he said, and demonstrated the correct technique for Antonia to copy.

"And push," he said again.

He repeated the push and pant routine a few more times until the driver pulled into the ambulance bay just as Antonia gave a final push and brought her baby girl into the world.

"I'll be damned," Wayne said, and chuckled. "She *is* a girl."

Antonia let out a shaky breath, tears on her cheeks. "Is she okay?"

As if in response, the newborn let out an indignant cry.

"She's okay," Wayne confirmed.

"Ten fingers and ten toes and absolutely beautiful," Clay said.

A neonatal team was waiting for the new mother and her baby as soon as they were wheeled into the hospital. Although Clay was still reluctant to leave Antonia's side, he couldn't help but feel that he was in the way in the midst of all the chaos and activity so he stepped outside to call his brother again.

After recounting the details of the baby's birth and confirming that Forrest wasn't having any trouble with Bennett, he saw Antonia's father step off the elevator.

John Wright looked as if he'd literally run to the hospital. His hair was disheveled, his face was red and—as his gaze swung from side to side—Clay saw that there was more than a hint of panic in his eyes.

But he finally spotted Clay, and he hurried down the corridor towards him. "I saw the ambulance at the barn," he said by way of explanation. "Antonia?"

In that moment, Clay remembered Antonia telling him about her mother's stroke, about her father calling the ambulance and the paramedics desperate—and unsuccessful—attempts to revive the patient. About how the sirens weren't blaring when the ambulance pulled away, because there was no reason to hurry, and he thought he understood the origin of some of the older man's panic.

"Antonia is fine," Clay assured him.

The older man's Adam's apple bobbed as he swallowed. "She's…okay?"

"She's better than okay. In fact, she's right across the hall—" he gestured to the doorway "—with your granddaughter."

"A granddaughter." John's lips curved, just a little. "Can I go in?"

"I'm sure they'd love to see you."

"Thank you." He offered his hand, and Clay shook it. "Thank you for being there—for both of them."

And Clay knew now that there wasn't anywhere else in the world he wanted to be but with Antonia and her baby.

So the only question left is, are you ready to admit that you want her, not just for a few nights but forever?

Clay had scoffed at the question when his brother had asked it, but now he didn't have any problem answering with an emphatic yes. He did want Antonia, not just for a few nights but forever.

But he sensed that the lady in question was going to need some convincing.

When Antonia heard footsteps approaching, she straightened her spine and stiffened her resolve. Clay had been absolutely wonderful through the whole birth process, but she couldn't let herself think that anything had changed. They'd had a wonderful few weeks together, but those weeks were over.

She was going to focus on her baby and her future now, and he should do the same. Hopefully back in Rust Creek Falls, because despite her resolve, it was hard for Antonia to be near Clay and Bennett every day and not be with them. So when he came back, she was going to tell him—

The rest of the thought slipped from her mind when she looked up and she saw that it was her father who had entered the room.

"There's my girl." The relief was evident in his voice. "And her baby girl, too," he said, smiling down at the infant tucked against Antonia's chest.

"Hi, Daddy."

He touched his lips to her forehead. "How are you doing?"

"Much better now," she said. "Though I was in a full-scale panic at the beginning."

"You did a great job," he said proudly. "She's absolutely beautiful—looks just like you did when you were a baby."

"Really?" She was pleased by the comment, happy to receive this confirmation that her daughter took after her side of the family. Maybe it was petty, but she didn't want any of Gene's features evident in her baby girl.

"And you looked just like your mama's baby pictures."

Antonia felt the sting of tears in her eyes. "I guess it's appropriate, then, that I named her after mama."

"You did?"

She nodded. "Lucinda Margaret."

When her father looked up at her again, she saw that his eyes were damp, too.

"I was worried about you a few months back," John admitted. "But now you've got a beautiful daughter and a man who will stand by you and be a good daddy to your baby."

"If you're talking about Clay—"

"Of course, I'm talking about Clayton Traub."

"I've only known him a couple of months," she reminded him. "He's not the father of my baby."

"Being a good daddy is about more than biology," he told her. "And sharing a biological connection doesn't automatically make a man a good daddy—I'm proof enough of that."

"What are you talking about?"

"I'm talking about the fact that I've been a lousy father since your mother passed away."

"You've been grieving," Antonia said gently.

"That's no excuse," he said now. "I might have lost my wife, but you and your brothers lost your mother, and I was too caught up in my own pain to help any of you through that."

"We all know how much you loved her."

"I still love her," John said. "And I still miss her. Every day."

"I miss her, too," Antonia admitted.

"I'm going to try to do better by you—and I'm going to be a good grandfather to your baby girl," her father vowed.

"I know you will," she said, as her eyes filled with tears again.

Apparently post-birth hormones were even more volatile than pregnancy hormones, because every little thing seemed to trigger the waterworks. She just felt so overwhelmed by emotion. First and foremost was joy that she could finally hold her daughter in her arms. Despite her fears that the baby was coming too early, she was healthy and strong and absolutely perfect. And while Antonia knew she was probably biased, she didn't think she'd ever seen a more beautiful baby, either.

But mixed in with the joy was more than a hint of sorrow, because while the birth of the baby signaled the beginning of a new chapter in her life, it also confirmed the end of another—her time with Clay. And that was a chapter that had been far too short.

Yes, she'd been the one to end their relationship—because she'd known that an end was inevitable and she'd believed that by choosing the time and place, she'd maintain some degree of control. She knew now that had only been an illusion. Because whether she'd spent the nights snuggled close in his bed or alone in her own, her heart had been with him.

If she'd had any doubts about the depth of her feelings for Clay, sharing the experience of childbirth with him had completely eliminated them. She didn't know if he'd been hurt or just annoyed that she'd made the decision to end their relationship, but he'd still been there for her. When she'd needed someone, he'd been there, and she would always be grateful to him for that and for the time they'd had together.

Her experience with Gene had left her with too many unhappy memories—a beautiful baby, but unhappy memories. When he'd walked out on her, she'd felt as if it was somehow her fault, that she'd done something wrong. She'd even wondered if there was something wrong with her that he'd never truly cared about her.

Clay had been kind and thoughtful, attentive and affectionate. Most importantly, he'd never been anything but completely honest with her about what he wanted. She'd known from the beginning that their time together would be limited, but she'd enjoyed every minute of that time and she would cherish the memories forever.

Clay was happy to give John a few minutes alone with his daughter and granddaughter because he knew it was an emotional day for everyone, but he was anxious to get back to Antonia's side. Now that he'd realized and accepted the true depth of his feelings for her, he wanted to tell her. And hopefully, if she felt the same way, they could start making plans for their future together.

But before Clay could say anything to her, Antonia's brothers arrived. Of course, the three men didn't seem to have a clue about what to do with the baby, and when Antonia offered the pink-blanket wrapped bundle, they all backed away as if she were a steaming cow patty.

Clay felt a twinge of sympathy. He'd known the same fear and panic when Delia first thrust Bennett's baby carrier into his hands. But the fear had quickly subsided—pushed aside at first by awe and affection, and eventually a love so huge it had filled his whole heart.

He'd never thought he could love anyone as he loved his son, but he'd recently discovered something about the human heart—the more it felt, the more it was capable of feeling. Because his love for Bennett hadn't lessened in the slightest, but somehow Clay had fallen in love with Antonia, too, and now with her brand-new baby.

"Since I guess you guys won't be babysitting for me anytime soon, can one of you at least call Peggy and ask her to take over the breakfast shift for the next little while?"

"Already done," Hudson told her.

"And Nora promised to be at the ranch by 6:00 a.m. to serve," Jonah added. "Although she said something about expecting a big, fat bonus for that."

Antonia smiled. "I'll make sure she gets one."

"How long are they planning to keep you in here?" John asked.

"The doctor said he wants us to stay a few days, just to make sure there are no unforeseen complications from the early delivery."

"That's good," her father said. "Because the most important thing is making sure that you and Lucinda are okay."

Her brothers were pleased that Antonia had named her baby girl after their mother—and only Ace was tactless enough to demand to know what surname she intended to put on the birth certificate.

"Wright," Antonia told him, without batting an eye.

Ace just scowled.

"Lucinda Wright has a nice ring to it," John said in a tone that warned his son the topic was closed. "It certainly suited your mother well enough."

Clay didn't disagree that Lucinda Wright sounded good, but he thought Lucinda Traub sounded even better. Almost as good as Antonia Traub. Of course, he would have to ask Antonia what she thought of those options, and that wasn't a conversation he intended to have with her father and her brothers in the room.

When the nurse came in to check on Antonia and suggested that she try feeding the baby again, the Wright men cleared out fast but Clay lingered. "Are you uncomfortable with me being here?"

She smiled as she settled the baby at her breast. "You were there when I gave birth, so it would be pointless for me to play the modesty card now. On the other hand, Bennett is probably wondering where you are."

"Bennett's hanging out with his favorite uncle," Clay told her. "I'm sure he's not missing me."

"Still, there's no reason for you to stick around here any longer."

"What if I want to stay?"

She dropped her gaze. "I appreciate everything you did today, but I'm okay now."

"Still determined to do everything on your own, aren't you?"

She frowned at that. "I figured you'd be relieved that I finally let go of your hand."

"Maybe I liked being there for you, knowing that you needed me."

"I did need you," she admitted. "I don't know that I would have got through today without you."

"So why are you pushing me away now?"

"I'm not pushing you away, I'm letting you go."

"Yeah, you gave me that same spiel a few days ago," he reminded her. "But what if I've decided I don't want to go?"

She rubbed a hand to her forehead. "You have a child of your own who needs you and a life in Rust Creek Falls. My baby and I are not your responsibility."

"Shouldn't we talk about this?"

"Not right now."

"Then can you at least tell me why you don't want me to stay?"

She shook her head.

With a sigh that was equal parts anger and frustration, he moved toward the door. But just before his fingers closed around the handle, he heard her whisper, "Because you won't stay forever, and then it will hurt even more when you go."

Chapter Fourteen

Antonia managed to hold back her tears until Clay had gone, and even then, she wasn't sure why she was crying. She couldn't be upset that he'd left—not when she'd told him to go.

"We're going to be just fine," she promised Lucy, repeating the mantra that she'd begun during her conversation with Catherine a few days earlier.

This time, however, the words didn't soothe her. Because "just fine" didn't seem like enough anymore. She wanted more. She wanted Clay.

But he'd walked away, just like Gene had walked away.

Okay, she knew that wasn't a fair comparison. Gene hadn't just walked, he'd practically sprinted out the door, and Clay hadn't walked until she'd told him—firmly and repeatedly—that she wanted him to go.

Catherine would say that he deserved credit for respecting her wishes, but Antonia would have preferred if he cared as much for her as she did for him—or at least enough to fight for her. She knew it wasn't rational, but as she tried to justify the inconsistency in her mind, she realized it wasn't even true.

Because if she loved Clay enough to fight for him, why had she sent him away? Why hadn't she told him the truth of the feelings in her heart and asked him to stay?

"If he comes back tomorrow, I'm going to tell him," she promised Lucy, as she wiped the tears from her cheeks.

She knew that she would be taking a risk, that saying "I love you" to Clay might send him running for the hills. If they did, she'd be no worse off than she was right now. But if those three little words didn't scare him off, her future might turn out a whole lot better than "just fine."

Clay didn't leave.

After Antonia banished him from her room, he paced the hall for a long time, trying to figure out what he was going to do. Should he respect her request and go back to the ranch? Or should he follow his heart and stay close to her side?

Still undecided, he went to the cafeteria to grab a cup of coffee he had no interest in drinking. When he returned to the maternity wing, he saw that Lucy was in the nursery—most likely so that her mother could rest—and Catherine was admiring her through the glass.

"She is gorgeous, isn't she?" Catherine said to him.

"Almost as pretty as her mama," Clay agreed.

As if aware that she was the subject of their conversation, Lucy's eyes opened. And for a moment, Clay could have sworn that she looked right at him with huge blue eyes filled with innocence and wonder. And he silently vowed that he would do anything he could to protect this baby girl and her mother—because he was head over heels in love with both of them.

"You really are smitten, aren't you, cowboy?" Catherine noted, amusement evident in her tone.

"I am."

Her brows lifted, as if she was surprised by his ready agreement. "Does that mean you plan on hanging around Thunder Canyon a little bit longer?"

"It means that I'm going to stay as long as Antonia wants me to stay." His smile was wry. "And maybe even longer."

"Are you going to put a ring on her finger?" she pressed.

"I don't think I should discuss that with you until I talk to Antonia."

"Fair enough," she agreed. "But just so you know, I have a fabulous selection of vintage rings at the store. In fact, there's one in particular that caught Antonia's eye, and it happens to be her size."

"I'll keep that in mind," he promised.

While Catherine went in to visit her friend, Clay kept watch over Lucy. Not that an infant who was sleeping without a care in the world needed much watching, but he felt better staying close to her. And he couldn't help thinking that she wasn't just a beautiful baby, she was a very lucky little girl because she had a mother who loved her more than anything else in the world.

Of course, that thought led him to contrast Antonia's obvious affection for her child with Delia's apparent indifference to her own. Even so many months later, he still couldn't understand how she could walk away from Bennett. Of course, he hadn't been around during her pregnancy or labor, so he had no idea if she'd had a particularly difficult time with either part. And he didn't have enough experience with babies to know whether Bennett was a particularly fussy child, but even through the worst of the baby's colic and the endless, sleepless nights, Clay could never imagine abandoning his son.

And suddenly, as he stood at the glass outside of the nursery, his memory of the long-ago conversation that had been niggling at the back of his mind since the grand reopening at The Hitching Post came clearer.

"I just don't understand how Grace could give away her own child and then go on with her life as if he'd never existed," Ellie said.

"I don't think she had much choice," Bob told her. "There's no way Doug would have been willing to raise another man's child."

Clay had been a young boy at the time, certainly not old enough to understand exactly what his parents were saying or to appreciate the implications of these revelations. But now, everything made a little bit more sense. And if his memory of that long-ago conversation was correct, then his aunt had given birth to another child that wasn't her husband's—which meant that D.J. and Dax had a half sibling somewhere.

He wondered how his cousins might react to the news, whether they would even believe it was possible or disregard the claim outright. Obviously Clay would need to confirm the details of the conversation with his parents before he shared any of his suspicions with them, but that wasn't something he was going to worry about today.

Today, his focus was on Antonia—and how he was going to convince the new mother that he wasn't just willing but eager to be a father to her baby girl.

* * *

As usual, Antonia was up before the sun.

But even as her eyes adjusted to the dimness of the room, she realized that was the only part of this morning that was usual. Yesterday when she woke up, she was pregnant. Today, she was a mother.

Lucy had been brought back into her room in the night so that Antonia could feed her and, at Antonia's request, she'd been allowed to remain in her bassinet in her mother's room. Antonia leaned toward the baby bed now and touched a fingertip gently to her baby's soft cheek. Lucy, swaddled in a hospital blanket with a tiny pink cap on her head, didn't stir.

A glance toward the window warned Antonia that her baby girl wasn't the only one in the room still sleeping. Clay was sprawled in the chair in the corner, and her heart gave a funny little skip when she realized that he was there. And, judging by the stubble on his jaw and the wrinkles in his clothes, he'd been there all night.

For just a moment, she let herself imagine what it might be like to wake up every morning with this man by her side. But despite the closeness they'd shared over the past several weeks, she had no reason to believe that he would want to stay in Thunder Canyon to be part of hers and Lucy's lives—and every reason to suspect that he would be anxious to go. But she'd resolved to tell him the truth of her feelings, and she would, and whatever happened after that would be up to him.

Clay was a wonderful father to Bennett, but she understood that a key part of that relationship was forged by the genetic link between them. He loved the little boy because he was his son, and she had no reason to assume that Clay would want to stay and be a father to a child that wasn't his own.

Yeah, she understood all of the reasons that Clay would leave. What she didn't understand was why he'd stayed with her as long as he had—and why he'd spent the night in a chair in her hospital room. But the simple fact that he had gave her hope.

Lucy started to fuss, drawing Antonia's attention back to her baby. The little girl's eyes were now wide and bright, and Antonia smiled at her.

"Look who's awake," she murmured, as she found the necessary supplies to change the baby's diaper. "And hungry, too, I'll bet."

Once Lucy was dry and swaddled in a clean blanket, Antonia settled back in her bed and put the baby to her breast. The infant immediately latched on and began suckling, confirming her mother's supposition.

When she looked up again, she saw that Clay's eyes were open now, too, and watching her.

"Good morning," he said, speaking softly so as not to startle the baby.

"Good morning," she said, feeling unaccountably shy. "Did you sleep well?"

"Better than you did, I'm sure."

He shrugged—or maybe he was trying to roll some of the kinks out of his shoulders. "I've slept in worse places," he assured her.

"Why didn't you go back to the ranch last night?"

"I didn't want to leave you, not even for a few hours."

"I can take care of myself," she told him. "I don't need anyone watching over me."

"I know," he agreed, and smiled a little. "Believe me, I know how much you value your independence, and I know you're committed to being a good mother and fully prepared to raise your baby on your own."

She nodded tentatively, not sure where he was going with any of this.

"Over the past several weeks, I've realized that the last thing you probably need is a man hanging around—especially one with his own child. But in that same time, I've also realized how much *I* need *you*."

Her heart started pounding so hard it was a wonder he couldn't hear it. But still, she was afraid to let herself hope for too much, afraid to let herself believe in the future she wanted so desperately.

"Yesterday, when you were in labor, I felt so completely helpless. I would have done anything I could to soothe your fears and ease your pain, but there was nothing I could do."

"You did help," she told him now. "Just by being there."

"I couldn't have been anywhere else," he said. "Because the other thing I finally realized—or finally accepted—is that I'm in love with you."

Clay didn't look at Antonia as he said the words. Instead, he kept his gaze focused on the window and poured out his heart to her. Maybe it was cowardly, but he was afraid to look at her, afraid to consider the possibility that she might not feel the same way, might not want the same things.

"I came to Thunder Canyon because I needed to get away from Rust Creek Falls for a while and figure out my future. I wasn't looking for a relationship—I certainly didn't expect to fall in love. But the more I thought about what I wanted, the more I realized that what I really want is a life with you and Lucy and Bennett and any other babies we might want to have in the future.

"I know I'm going out on a limb here, and probably moving way too fast. I know you might not want the same things, but I can't keep these feelings inside any longer. And I don't want to imagine a life without you anymore."

When he finally ran out of words, he drew in a deep breath and looked over at Antonia. He saw the tears streaming down her cheeks, and his heart began to crack. But then he noticed that through the tears she was smiling.

"Are you going to say anything?" he asked her.

She nodded as she brushed the back of her hand over her cheeks, wiping away the moisture. "I'm not sure I can match the speech you just gave, so I'll just say that I want exactly the same thing—a future with you and our babies. But—"

"But what?" He lowered himself onto the edge of the mattress and reached for her hand.

"What about your ranch in Rust Creek Falls? And your family? I know how much you've missed being there and working with your dad and your brothers."

"I've talked to my dad, and not only does he understand, he wasn't at all surprised by my decision. Apparently my mother figured out that I was in love with you even before I did."

"Your mother did?"

"She's not thrilled that I want to stay in Thunder Canyon," he admitted. "And she already warned that they'll be visiting *a lot,* but she is thrilled that I finally found the right woman for me. R-I-G-H-T *and* W-R-I-G-H-T."

She smiled at that.

"I talked to your dad, too," he continued. "To ask him what he thought about taking me on permanently at the Wright Ranch and as a son-in-law. He said he wouldn't accept one without the other."

She was touched that he'd asked for her father's blessing, and that John had given it. But she still had to ask, "Are you sure this is what you want?"

"I'm sure. Because there's nothing I want as much as I want you." He leaned over and touched his lips to hers. "I love you, Antonia Wright."

"And I love you, Clayton Traub."

"I want to get married as soon as we can make the arrangements."

"What's the rush?"

"I don't want you sneaking out of my room at the crack of dawn anymore—and I don't want your father coming after me with a shotgun if I spend the night in yours."

She laughed. "How about a Thanksgiving wedding?"

"That sounds perfect," he agreed. "Because this year I have more reasons to be thankful than ever before."

The baby was three days old when Antonia and Lucy were released from the hospital on October thirty-first. The new mother had spent most of those three days establishing some basic feeding and sleeping routines with her daughter and hadn't given any thought to the holiday. At least not until her fiancé and his son showed up at the hospital and she saw that Bennett was dressed up in a plaid shirt and jeans with little boots on his feet and a miniature Stetson on his head.

"Well, look at the handsome cowboys in my room," she remarked.

The little boy's eyes lit up when he saw her, and he automatically thrust his arms out toward her. Then he saw that she was already holding a baby, and his brow furrowed.

Antonia put Lucy down in the bassinet so she could cuddle Bennett, and the furrow in his brow eased.

"I think it's going to take my son some time to accept that he won't always be the center of attention anymore."

"The attention he'll have to share," she agreed. "But I think we have more than enough love to go around."

"And I have a costume for you, too," Clay said to Lucy, pulling an orange jumpsuit and hat out of the backpack-style diaper bag he carried.

Bennett watched his daddy with Lucy, his little brow furrowing again. Clearly he wasn't too happy that there was a new baby in town.

"Look at that," Antonia said to him. "You're a cowboy and Lucy's a pumpkin."

Bennett smiled, showing off not just the two tiny teeth on the bottom but a matching set just starting to emerge on the top. Antonia didn't think he understood "cowboy" or "pumpkin," but he seemed happy enough that she was talking to him.

"Should I have brought an outfit for you, too?" Clay asked Antonia.

She shook her head. "I'm happy to be out of a nursing gown and into real clothes again, but I really appreciate the suit for Lucy. I hadn't expected to celebrate her first Halloween until next October."

"Because it is her first Halloween—and Bennett's, too—what do you think about taking a walk through town before we head back to the ranch?" Clay asked. "The stores are all decked out for the holidays and I thought it would be fun for the kids to see."

"I think that sounds like a wonderful idea," Antonia said, not bothering to point out that Lucy wasn't likely to notice much of anything. Because after three days in hospital, there was nothing she wanted more than to stretch her legs and breathe in the fresh, crisp, autumn air—except maybe to walk hand in hand with the man she loved.

Clay parked on Main Street and helped Antonia out of the truck. She realized that family outings were going to be an challenge—buckling two babies into car seats, securing the car seats into the back of the truck, then transferring the car seats to the stroller assembly when they arrived at their destination, then repeating the whole process in reverse to go home again. But it was a challenge Antonia was more than willing to undertake—especially with Clay by her side.

They strolled leisurely along the sidewalk and saw scarecrows sitting on bales of hay outside of Second Chances, bundles of cornstalks tied to the upright posts outside the Super Save Mart, ghosts hanging from the covered porch of The Hitching Post, baskets filled with colorful gourds flanking the entrance to the Wander-On Inn, and a trio of grinning jack-o'-lanterns in the front window of Real Vintage Cowboy.

"That reminds me," Clay said, pausing outside of the store. "I wanted to check with Catherine on something. Do you mind waiting out here with the babies while I pop in for a second?"

Since Antonia knew it wouldn't be easy to maneuver the double stroller through the store, she agreed.

She pointed out the jack-o'-lanterns to Bennett, showing him that one had two teeth on the top and the bottom, just like he did. He grinned to show off his pearly whites.

Mrs. Haverly stopped to oooh and ahhh over the babies. Then Haley Cates, the founder of ROOTS, and her sister, Angie Anderson, crossed the street to say hi. Before Antonia knew what was happening, quite a number of Thunder Canyon residents had gathered to get their first glimpse of baby Lucy and admire Bennett's costume—and ask not-so-subtle questions about Lucy's mother's relationship with Bennett's daddy.

By the time Clay came out of Real Vintage Cowboy,

not five minutes after he'd entered, there was a small crowd around Antonia and the babies.

"Did Catherine have what you were looking for?" she asked.

He nodded. "Yes, she did."

And right there, in front of everyone, he dropped down to one knee and opened a small velvet box. Antonia gasped even before she saw the stunning diamond solitaire in a delicate antique setting. Was he really proposing to her now? In the middle of downtown in front of half of a crowd of people?

"Antonia Wright, will you do me the honor of marrying me so that we can be together forever and always?"

Apparently he was, and though her eyes filled with tears, her smile was wide as she nodded. "Yes, Clayton Traub, I will absolutely marry you."

Her hands were a little chilled but she felt only warmth and happiness when Clay slid the ring onto the third finger of her left hand.

"It fits perfectly," she murmured.

He wrapped his arms around her. "And so do we."

And then he kissed her.

It was the smattering of applause that reminded both of them that they were standing in the middle of the sidewalk on Main Street.

"Are you ready to go home?" Antonia asked him.

"Before we do, I should probably warn you that you've got company at the ranch. I tried to hold them off a few more days, but my parents are very eager to meet their soon-to-be newest grandchild and first granddaughter, and my mother is more than eager to make wedding plans with her future daughter-in-law."

"She didn't think it would ever happen, did she?"

"And I think she's afraid that if we don't move things along quickly, it still won't."

"Should I be worried?"

Clay shook his head. "The only reason I never wanted to get married before is that I hadn't met you."

She smiled. "Then let's take our babies home and start planning the rest of our lives together."

And that's what they did.

* * * * *